The UnION

The UNION

An inside look how "The Union" uses their computer to attain power, establish unholy relationships with politicians and the Mafia as millions of dollars and people disappear

PETER DAVID PERRY

ARCHWAY
PUBLISHING

Archway Publishing books may be ordered through booksellers or by contacting:

Archway Publishing
1663 Liberty Drive
Bloomington, IN 47403
www.archwaypublishing.com
844-669-3957

ISBN: 978-1-6657-1089-3 (sc)
ISBN: 978-1-6657-1090-9 (hc)
ISBN: 978-1-6657-1088-6 (e)

Library of Congress Control Number: 2021916447

Print information available on the last page.

Archway Publishing rev. date: 03/30/2022

DEDICATION

For my mother, Carmella Scuderi, who introduced me to the family kitchen and the many ways the kitchen served the family.

She was also responsible for my love of Italian cooking.

For my father, Joseph Anthony Perri, who taught me many lessons that could not be learned in the classroom.

I am grateful to both of them for such a wonderful beginning of my life's journey.

–Your youngest son

CONTENTS

CHAPTER ONE

THE TRAIN

MAY 26, 1992

C HRIS VINCENT FELT A SLIGHT tug as the train pulled out of the Rensselaer Station and began its southward journey toward New York City. The power and grace of several hundred tons of steel as it began to accelerate would be coupled with moments of boredom. The sudden forward movement pushed his head back against the seat ever so slightly. The increasing cadence of the rhythmic clicks of the wheels rolling along the tracks was almost hypnotic. It was a Tuesday, May 26, and the eighth week from the start of the implementation of new computer software at the union. Although the distance was only 145 miles from Albany to New York City, it would take the train just two and a half hours, with five stops along the way.

1

The train ran along the eastern shoreline of the Hudson River. Hundreds of years earlier, the American Indians knew the Hudson as the river that flowed both ways. That highlights the fact that this waterway is more than a river; it is a tidal estuary, an arm of the Atlantic Ocean where the salty ocean water meets the fresh water running off the land. The Hudson estuary stretches 153 miles from Troy New York Harbor, nearly half the river's 315-mile length with its flow influenced by the ocean tides.

The first stop would be Hudson, just about twenty-two minutes from the Rensselaer Station, followed by Rhine Cliff, Poughkeepsie, Croton Harmon, and then Yonkers before arriving at Penn Station at 9:45. Chris felt some comfort knowing that he would have a couple of hours to find courage and calm his emotions, which would enable him to deal with what lay ahead. He was tense, nervous, and scared. He was unsure of himself and did not have any answers to the dangers he knew he would be faced with. He feared the possible outcome. The train was heading on straight and level tracks to a known destination—not like his path, which would have many turns toward the unknown. Chris's uneasiness was not from the stress of the new software implementation he'd been managing at Local 4 since early April. His feelings of uncertainty and discomfort were from the people he had been working with and the unsavory acts they were committing.

The computer implementation was going smoothly, but he was unsure of how it would end. Dealing with the union's leaders and the political environment were things he had never experienced, and he had an uneasy feeling that he would be put in the crosshairs of the FBI. He realized that he had been drawn into a business arrangement that was illegal and fraught with danger. He had made some bad choices and knew that he would be faced with difficult decisions in the following days, which would determine his future well-being. If he continued to follow the same path, he feared that it might lead to a fast track into a padded cell. Maybe even to a small cell with iron bars. He would need courage to follow through, with the hope that he would find the answers.

The recorder taped to his chest was not very big, nor was it uncomfortable, but it was hanging heavy on his body. He could feel his heart beating against the tape that secured it to him as it pulled tightly across his torso. It weighed only three or four ounces but felt more like a boat anchor. It contained a small recorder, a battery, and a radio transmitter. There was a small wire that ran from the small box that contained the electronics to a miniature microphone taped just below his left collar bone. He could not stop thinking about the possibility of discovery. If it were discovered, he imagined that the small electronic package would somehow, without warning, blare out and announce its concealment. "Here I am, a traitor. I am wearing a wire. Hello, can you hear me? I have betrayed you. I am a rat, a snitch, a traitor to the union, and you can no longer trust me." The more he thought about it, the more uncertainty and bad possibilities ran through his mind.

Chris Vincent was the president of Advanced Computer Systems and was normally self-assured and in control. But not today. He thought about the events of the past two months, the decisions he had made, and how he had been drawn into the union's circle of corruption. He understood that his situation had little to do with what or who he was, but rather about the person he might become. Chris realized that his standing in life was the result of an accumulation of many small decisions he had made over many years. Choices established the path of life, and what one attained was a result of those choices. He finally realized that the kind of person one might become was more important than what he or she attained in life. He did not have any idea how it would all work out, but he knew it was too late to go back. He was always chasing the American dollar. He focused on his career and how to earn more money, but seldom did he consider the costs. He was on a collision course that could not be altered, since his life's mission to be successful and attain his narrow definition of success, which had been formed at a young age many years before. He realized that he would be face to face with danger once the train arrived in the city, and all he had accomplished would be lost.

Chris had a kind face and was pleasing to look at, physically handsome, but not in the sense of a film star or athlete. He did not stand out in a crowd but was outgoing and engaging. Short by most standards, he was slim with powerful shoulders. He had a tanned face and what many thought to be a perfect Roman nose that perfectly blended with his manicured chestnut hair and dark-brown eyes. The combination was a clear indication of his Italian descent. Chris knew that being Italian was a positive attribute to some women, and it was also helpful when dealing with the trade unions and the labor leaders, the vast majority of whom were of Italian descent. Many old-timers who came off the boat from the old country started with nothing and only possessed a dream of achieving a better life for their children. Even though his father had Americanized the family name from Vincenti to Vincent, there was no doubt about his Italian heritage. Hell, he was a *paesani*. He was one of them, and this meant that he could join their special fraternity of kinship.

He could feel his shirt collar tighten around his neck. He reached up and felt the inside of his collar. His neck was moist, but it was not warm in the train compartment. It was actually cooler than normal, with the outside temperature barely sixty. He reached up and loosened his tie. It made little difference to his comfort. He thought about the many hours of hard work, the business trips, the late hours, and the sacrifices he had made to establish a successful software business. It was costing him his marriage. His wife was ready to split and take the two young boys he never really got to know. They were growing up, and he now realized that he was missing an important part of family life: being a father. He worked many long hours and gave to his clients much more than they would ever return. He wondered if it was all worth it. He leaned back in his seat and peered out the window toward the gray sky as it slowly rolled in a curtain of cold, dark clouds. Another cold day was about to begin, even though it was the middle of May.

Chris realized that he should have never gotten involved with the New York City unions and never should have agreed to the deal he made with the accountant. It may have been the way business was conducted in the Big Apple, and he knew it was not legal. The FBI knew how the unions operated and had more than a strong suspicion about what had occurred. They had a tail on the accountant, and they knew about the criminal behavior of those who ran the unions and their associations with the Mafia. Chris had to agree to buy into their conspiracies with an up-front payment of $10,000. The FBI agent who interviewed him in his office a week earlier had laid the pictures on the conference table. Maybe it was innocent and proved nothing. But it was a picture of Chris, Goldin, and Greco on Seventeenth Street as they walked to Da Umberto's for lunch the first day at the union in early April. It may not have proved any wrongdoing, but it clearly showed that Chris was on the inside, and anyone on the inside played the dirty game of kickbacks. He remembered what the agent had told him: "If you sleep with dogs, you are sure to get fleas."

The agent told Chris that they were not interested in how he made a living or who he did business with. Chris had been told that there was an investigation underway for a person of interest. They said they were searching for a computer programmer who had been supplying the software to Local 4 and wanted to know if Chris had ever met him or talked to him. They needed his help and told him that they knew he had a good reputation and was a well-respected businessman. But they also told Chris that they knew he was involved and the only way to get out without any criminal prosecution was to cooperate and make a deal. They tried to scare him and kept circling back to the missing-person investigation by suggesting that he could be the next missing person.

Chris remembered what they said in Albany: "What kind of business is this union business? People keep disappearing." If they were trying to scare him, they had succeeded. That was the moment when it occurred to him that he was in over his head and perhaps he should not have made any deal with either side. But betrayal to the union could mean an even worse outcome than what the FBI called "cooperation." He knew that the FBI tail had little to do with protection. They now had Chris conspiring with the union and implied that they had the leverage to squeeze information out of him and force him to betray his friends.

The train was gaining some speed as it rolled past the rundown brick buildings in the train yard just over a mile south of the station. Most of them were now vacant. Their windows were shattered, and he could see that the years had not been kind to the old warehouses and storage sheds. Their roofs had opened to the unfriendly northeastern skies, and in their present states, they represented little hope of ever returning to a condition of usefulness. Mother Nature and the surrounding vegetation of trees and weeds were slowly invading the building openings, never allowing them to return to their past glory. He was saddened when he thought of how something so strong and functional would one day turn into a rundown, worthless pile of rubble with little hope of ever again returning to a productive and functional state. Mother Nature was winning the battle against humankind. It was the life cycle of both person and machine. Chris was a car guy and related it to the shiny new cars rolling off the Detroit assembly line, only to end up dropped off in rusty heaps at the junkyard twenty years later. He now wondered if he would experience the same fate once the union and the FBI got what they needed.

He glanced out the window and could just make out the Albany skyline across the river. He'd loved train rides ever since that first trip to New York City, when he took his two boys, Peter and Robert, on the train to see the Christmas show at Rockefeller Center. They were eight and ten years old. He thought about an earlier time when he had lost his balance and fell from the tree house that he was building in the backyard for the boys. He liked fast cars and trains but avoided air travel when other options were available. He'd had a fear of heights from the time he was a young boy and was deathly afraid of ladders and anything higher than just a few feet.

The more he tried to mentally trace the events leading up to his present situation, the more he began to question his choices. He wondered how he could avoid falling deeper into the trap. He could have simply refused to play ball with the FBI but then thought he might find a way to free himself from their grip without betraying the union. He'd always thought things through but was now facing real danger. Chris's success was due to his ability to solve problems, big or small, from the very trivial to the more complex. And so, computers and his computer skills were perfectly suited to the business of creating computer software. But as he traveled toward the city, he felt lost and defeated. He recognized that he was drawn into the trap because he had let his guard down and failed to anticipate the many bad outcomes that were possible. He believed his friends at the unions would never betray their trust. However, deep down, he was not certain since he did not know what the true meaning of trust was.

Chris was a first-generation Italian American who had a powerful presence when he talked about his work. He spoke with great sincerity, and his clients trusted his judgment. When he said he would do something, he always delivered on his promises. He could handle any type of problem without getting emotional. He handled stress extremely well and was especially good at running and managing several union clients. But not this time. He was troubled, and his dark skin was pale. Small depressions appeared under his dark-brown eyes. One could see that his blank stare reflected his troubled state. His eyes seemed distant from the bright expressions that would normally radiate from his face. His shoulders normally were square and rigid behind his upright posture. But now they were rounded and slumped forward and downward. Chris was afraid of what he would face in New York City. It was now clear to him that he never should have agreed to buy into the union's payback schemes. Agreeing with their arrangements was risky and contained great danger. How would he find a way out without betrayal to his unifying principles?

Sonny Russo and Chris had been friends since high school. When Sonny graduated, he joined the local union as a laborer. He was not a good student in high school, so college was not an option for him. But his father was in the building trades and had family connections with the laborers' union in Albany. Sonny possessed a very natural and persuasive demeanor. As a laborer, he knew what to say and how to say it to gain the trust and support of the union's rank and file. He was tough, outspoken, and Italian and perfect for a leadership position in a trade union. After only fifteen years as a laborer, he was elected as the business agent for Laborers Local 290. He was respected by all the members and quickly established a reputation as an expert negotiator and an outstanding figurehead within the organized-labor movement across the state. Chris and Sonny were more than friends; they were trusted friends who could depend on one another.

Chris turned his head to the right and peered out the train window at the Hudson River as the sun struggled to push rays through small openings in the clouds. He loved the Hudson River. He noticed a large cement barge heading south that was low in the water as it bore the weight of its heavy cargo. He guessed it to be a barge from the cement plant just south of Albany. His thoughts turned to the cement contractors and the Mafia who cleverly stole hundreds of millions of dollars through their illegal bid-fixing schemes. It was an ingenious scam that involved fixing the bids for construction projects by a select number of contractors who were referred to as members of The Concrete Club. Because of the complexity of the construction projects, the specialized workers for each of the trades were hired separately through different subcontractors who submitted their bids for the project through a third-party negotiating organization or association, which was controlled by the Mafia Commission. The commission consisted of the five major New York crime families: Gambino, Genovese, Columbo, Lucchese, and Bonanno. They could then fix the bid amounts among each of the contractors. The contract would be awarded to the low bidder, whose bid amount was well above any reasonable bid in a fair and competitive bidding environment. This produced an extremely high profit for the winning bidder, and the excess profits would be distributed to the other contractors who were involved in the fix.

The Mafia Commission was behind the scheme and raked in 2 percent from the top of every cement contract awarded over $2 million. While the scheme was dismantled by Rudy Giuliani, RICO, and the FBI in 1987 with several members of the commission spending their remaining days in a prison cell, there were still some remnants of the illicit activities that remained. The Mafia-owned concrete businesses controlled the material and the unions controlled the labor, so they could easily shut down the construction projects if they did not get their way. Together, they could eliminate access to workers and concrete and stop construction to New York skyscrapers, housing, highways, hospitals, and government buildings. For the Mafia, it was a great money-making scheme in the '80s, since the building boom in the city amounted to over $10 billion annually.

Chris suspected that the union played a role, and some form of the price fixing was still taking place. He also suspected that Goldin's accountants on the seventh floor of the union's office building played a part in laundering money back to the contractors and the leftover bosses from the Gambino crime family. He knew the computer played a part in the process, but he was unsure as to exactly how it was accomplished. The old crimes of gambling, loan sharking, and prostitution were slowly being replaced by bigger and more lucrative crimes using legitimate business enterprises. Every new building in New York City used cement, and the cement contracts over the last thirty years in New York amounted to billions of dollars. If syndicates could organize the other trade groups and other contractors together to rig the bids, there would be hundreds of millions of dollars to be shared through this collaboration. Chris did not know how it was accomplished or to what extent the union played in the scheme, but he had a hunch that it took place on the seventh floor. Goldin's auditors reconciled and entered the contractors' reports in great secrecy, and Chris was curious to know how it all worked.

The auditors entered the reports, and the old software programs were locked in a secure library in the mainframe computer. Marty Bloom had written the software, and if there was a cleansing operation going on, Bloom had to be involved as well. Bloom was missing, and perhaps the reason was that he knew too much. Chris was next in line and began to understand how dangerous the union software business had become when you had clients like those at Local 4. It frightened him when he thought about the crimes that were being perpetuated and how his business could possibly be destroyed. Chris could be the next missing person if he did not go along with their scheme. The accountant told Chris that Bloom was on vacation in Florida, yet no one had heard from him in over two months.

The train's speed was at least five to six times the speed of the barge traveling southward in the river. It disappeared to the rear in less than a minute—more cement heading to New York and more money that would flow to the members of the club and the organization. The train car slowly rocked sideways as it sped over the slight changes in contours of the tracks. Chris tried to imagine how comfortable it would feel to be the captain of the barge they had just passed. Its course was slow and steady, and the captain knew where it had been and where they were heading. No surprises and no big decisions required. Just gently steer and follow the river to the south.

Chris was told that his FBI handler would meet him on the train and provide last-minute instructions. The handler would be wearing red or carrying something red. What did that mean: a red baseball hat, red tie, red handbag, red scarf?

He thought about how it all had started. The beginning was that first meeting with the accountant at the golf club eight weeks earlier. At the time, he felt good about the possibilities of business in New York City. No more banks needed to borrow money from. No more doing without a paycheck. He had seen it as the big opportunity to break out into big business, and Local 4 would be the first of many big union clients.

Chris's company supplied all the computer software for Local 290 and several other upstate trade unions. Sonny had set up the golf match with the accountant from New York City, and Chris, despite not knowing what to expect, knew that the meeting would be critically important.

It had taken Chris more than eight years to design and create the new software that would revolutionize the accounting systems for unions. Laborers Local 290 was where it all began, and Chris owed a lot to his good friend Sonny for the opportunity. And Sonny was grateful for what Chris had accomplished for his union. The union was not big but had over $75 million in their trust funds, and the computer processes were critical to their operations. Sonny had been involved with the regional and international councils and had connections throughout the state with all the trade unions. He had told Chris that when the time was right, he would introduce him to the big unions in New York City and that those introductions would help him get into the big time, which meant Laborers Local 4. This union had more than ten thousand members, and more significantly, the union had close to $500 million in their trust funds. That meant that they could spend hundreds of thousands of dollars on their computer systems. Chris was not selling computer hardware for IBM; he was now in the software business and would be selling his software—expensive software—for a company he controlled and owned. He looked down at the stainless-steel Rolex watch on his wrist and knew he would earn much more money. The Rolex was a sign of success that he attributed to the software business. Local 4 was only 150 miles away, and bigger fees were well within his grasp. He thought about the unions in New York City and all that money that he would charge for his software. Fees would be well above the amounts he had been charging the smaller upstate unions. The next Rolex would be solid gold.

He relaxed and rested his head against the seat cushion. He closed his eyes and thought about that first meeting at the country club with the accountant, Paul Goldin. The train now began to again pick up speed as it moved forward toward the city, and his thoughts drifted back to early April. He wanted to think about the events of the last several weeks by retracing his steps in the hope that he might find the answers.

CHAPTER TWO

THE ASSIGNMENT
MAY 7, 1992

A FEW MINUTES PAST SEVEN P.M. on a Thursday, the twin-engine Gulfstream 14 passenger plane broke through the low overcast blanketing Washington, DC, then sharply banked left over the Potomac River for its final approach to Joint Base Andrews. The Lincoln Memorial came into view on the right side of the plane, and Special Agent Marco Richards looked out the window and eyed the Washington skyline. He would soon be on the ground and soon be a real field agent. Traveling was one of the necessary parts of the job that an FBI field agent had to endure. He just was not quite used to it, since he had been an FBI analyst working in an office for most of his career. Since he would now be placed in the role of field agent, he would have to adjust.

This was the first time Marco had been called to Washington in this manner. He was a senior computer analyst working out of the Chicago District Information Center. It was only nine hours earlier when he had gotten the call and told that he would need to be in Washington by eight o'clock that evening for an urgent meeting authorized by an assistant director to meet with the special agent in charge assigned by the Washington bureau chief. They had developed an organized task force of FBI agents along with an assistant director in charge of the Organized-Crime Task Force, working out of the New York City field office. He normally would have flown commercial, but there was no availability on the last remaining commercial flight to Washington. He knew it was an important assignment since he was offered a charter flight on the assistant director's personal jet with the specific purpose of ferrying him to the meeting. His current caseload was important, but he was told that there was a special assignment needing his special talent. He was flattered, since he had never been elevated to this level of importance. Use of the director's $15 million Gulfstream just to get him to a meeting in Washington was gnawing at his curiosity and common sense. Richards was usually very calm but now was overcome with anxiety. When the call came from the New York assistant director's office, he was told that he was to drop everything, pack an overnight bag, and abandon his present assignment for a matter of grave importance. He was ordered to immediately report to gate 36F of O'Hare's private terminal. What could be so important that he would be allowed to abandon six months of research work? That was the specific term used— *abandon*—not put aside, not stop, not put on hold, not transfer. "Abandon!"

Richards had just turned thirty-eight and was an unlikely candidate for a career FBI man. He had originally taken the job because of a college internship with Aetna's health insurance division. His corporate sponsor had involved him in a special government project that turned out to be funded through a covert FBI slush fund, which led to a permanent position.

He was dark-skinned and handsome with jet-black curls, and one knew immediately of his Italian descent. A native of Pittsburgh, Richards was the son of a machinist and the grandson of an Italian immigrant who, at the age of twenty-three, came to America in 1894. Richards was a formidable FBI man and had always been graded as "consistently exceeded" in all categories in his performance evaluations except the obstacle course. Marco's specialty was computer software engineering and forensic accounting. He was an expert at tracing the sources and paths taken by money laundering and white-collar crime. His claim to fame occurred as an analyst on a case with less than one year on the job. His analytical skills and experience in computer programming proved to be the critical factor in uncovering crucial evidence in the conviction of a group of Russian hackers who were stealing millions of dollars from Medicare. The operation spanned from Chicago to South Florida. The Russian Mafia was involved in the scheme, stealing close to $5 million a month. Everyone thought he was a genius since he had been able to hack into the criminal's computer network and track the flow of money. No one knew that it was not due to the genius of the law-enforcement hacker, but rather the stupidity of the criminals. It took him less than one hour to figure out the password. For God's sake, this was Chicago, and who would have ever thought that the password could be so simple: *BULLS.*

He laughed every time he thought about it. This was his secret, and now he would have to live up to his genius reputation, which was gained only through the ignorance of criminals. No one but him knew, or would ever know, that the computer administrator was a basketball fan and loved the Chicago Bulls. At that time, over six thousand Chicago basketball fans used *BULLS* as their password. And the criminal mastermind had used the same one.

Through a tiny window over the left wing, Richards could see the Capitol dome glinting in the splinters of sunlight that had escaped through the pillows of white low-hanging clouds. It was early May, and Washington was basking in its early-spring glory. He looked toward the ground and could just make out the landscape with varying shades of green and flashes of blue and gray from the sky reflecting up from the Potomac. On his left during the plane's final approach to the runway stood the Washington Monument. Its height at 550 feet appeared slightly above the plane's altitude. He saw the splendor of spring, with smears of mixed colors—yellows, oranges, and bright greens. Marco knew immediately that the assignment was going to be somehow related to electronic fraud, and it was a real lift to his ego. After all, the Washington FBI lab had hundreds of computer experts, and the fact that the wheels of justice had selected a computer analyst from the Chicago lab for a special assignment was now beginning to sink in and boost his ego. Marco hoped he would be up to the task.

The plane continued heading straight for a few minutes and then, in an instant, smoothly dropped the last three hundred feet to the runway on Joint Base Andrews. Marco felt the sudden loss of altitude and tightly gripped the sides of his seat. The plane slowed quickly as the noise of the thrust reversers overtook the sounds in the cabin and thrust his body forward. The plane then suddenly turned onto the taxiway to the left. As they taxied along the side of the runway, Marco noticed that they were passing alongside a large, gray hanger. He looked out the window and saw three F-116 interceptors with guards patrolling just to their rear. M16s were slung over their shoulders. As the plane rolled to an abrupt stop, a tall, thin officer and a bearded man in a dark-gray suit approached. The door opened and with his first step out of the cabin, he was greeted by the marine captain.

"Welcome to Joint Base Andrews; you must be Agent Richards. My name is Captain Blake. How was the flight?"

"It was just fine, sir," replied Marco.

The bearded man in the gray suit was expressionless and did not say one word.

The captain spoke again. "We have been instructed to take you directly to the FBI welcome center on the south side of the base for a briefing. It was converted about three years ago from a marine barracks. Afterward, I am going to handle the logistics of your stay here at the base."

"I assumed that I would be working at the computer center downtown and that this was going to be a very short assignment," Marco replied.

"Can't say. I can only tell you that my orders are to bring you to the welcome center for your briefing and to get you anything you may need during your stay. Here in Washington, things are done differently. Especially when we get our orders from Colonel Macey."

Macey was the special agent in charge that specialized in organized crime, and Marco concluded that Macey would be the team leader making all the key decisions. Richards had met him at the academy years earlier and recalled that Macey was a chain-smoker. He smoked Camels and had a sharp, piercing voice that was at the point of being annoying. Marco thought, "Camels? Who the hell in their right mind still smokes Camels after all the cancer-scare news?" He thought about his uncle Mario, who had smoked Camels and died of lung cancer years before they ever confirmed the link between cigarettes and lung cancer.

Marco was nine years old when he stole a Camel from Uncle Mario and hid under the front steps of his grandmother's back porch to light up. After just one drag and a few muffled coughs, he decided that smoking was not for him. He never touched another cigarette. He often wondered if it had been something a bit milder, perhaps a Kool or even a Marlboro, it could have changed his thinking on smoking perhaps for the rest of his life. If it were not for Camels, perhaps his uncle Mario might have survived past beyond the ripe old age of ninety-six.

Macey was the special agent in charge, and Marco remembered him from the academy. His opinion was not entirely positive. What was most annoying to Marco was Macey's arrogance. There was no question of his intelligence; he was one smart FBI agent. In fact, he was brilliant and had an almost God-like following among the junior agents he had trained. He was a marine colonel who had served in the Vietnam War and had been awarded a Silver Star and a Distinguished Service Medal. No one knew the exact details of the matter, other than that he had infiltrated a North Vietnamese supply depot and was personally responsible for the capture of over forty tons of munitions. Marco was curious as to why the story was never officially verified or made public. Macey was a super sleuth with an uncanny ability to remember details. He was more than smart. He was brilliant and always presented a winning position in any debate. You would seldom win an argument unless he wanted you to win. Macey's words were carefully choreographed, and if you confronted him, his back had no bend in it. He came at you with both guns blazing.

Although Marco's known expertise was in computer programming and analysis, he had developed exceptional skills in mathematics and statistics. He was especially drawn to the study of statistics and was a follower of the late W. Edward Deming, the genius who revitalized Japanese industry after the war. It was Deming's unorthodox system that essentially turned the modern management system upside down and brought to light new approaches to quality improvement in manufacturing. It was Deming who dispelled the notion that defective products and rejects were normal and acceptable by-products in any manufacturing process. The Japanese were the first disciples to grasp his theory that if you improve quality, you will not only reduce rejects, but at the same time reduce costs. If there was a credo for statisticians and one that Marco would remember from his studies of Deming, it was, "In God we trust; all others must bring data."

And so it was with Marco, that he would build his professional reputation within the bureau on performing data analysis and authoring research papers. So much so that he would spend all his time collecting and analyzing statistical data, often neglecting his field-duty skills. He would rather be sitting at a desk in front of a computer terminal than out performing James Bond-like assignments. He was comfortable sitting in front of the keyboard and approached his job as if it were a treasure hunt.

The bearded man in the dark-gray suit pointed to the jeep alongside the plane, and without instruction, Marco climbed into the open back seat. The gray suit placed Marco's luggage in the empty seat in the back and climbed into the front passenger's seat, while the marine captain jumped behind the wheel. Nothing was said, and Marco jumped into the back. The security center was a two-story brick building surrounded by a tall, iron-link fence running along the rear of the building and connecting to the outer perimeter about a half mile from the north-south runway. It reminded him of an old World War II army barracks, with the aging yellow bricks and the uniformity of the windows neatly running down both sides of the building. As the jeep pulled up to the front, he noticed the iron bars bolted to the outside of the blacked-out windows. He thought it did not resemble a welcome center and looked more like a jail. The bearded gray suit, who up until this point had not spoken a word, asked, "Do you have any weapons on you?"

"Well, not on my person. It's in my suitcase," Marco replied, somewhat surprised by the question. "My laptop is my weapon, and that is my bag in the back."

"I am with the Department of Labor. I will be working with you on this assignment." After a brief pause, the man added, "I am the liaison officer for the department. My name is Charles Crowley."

"Pleased to meet you," Marco replied hesitantly. The three of them jumped out of the jeep and walked up to the front entrance. There was no reply as the driver picked up his bag and brought it to the entrance.

Marco thought, "*What a joke.*" The Labor Department was the worst entanglement of government bureaucracy that he had ever encountered. He had worked with the department in the past and did not have much confidence in their ability to get anything useful accomplished. He learned very quickly that the Labor Department agents' purpose was strictly to protect their turf—to protect their jobs and, of course, protect their pensions.

There was a set of glass doors and they entered a small lobby, where they were greeted by two clean-shaven marines from behind what appeared to be a bulletproof glass window. There was a sign at the bottom of the window that read in large black letters: "Place government IDs in drawer." A small stainless-steel drawer slid out from under the window, and the three of them deposited their government-issued IDs. Inside, the marine on the left slid each of the cards over an electronic scanner as he peered at a computer screen. He then returned them, along with three numbered yellow tags. Marco's number was 236. Under the number in bold red letters was the date, "May 7 – May 8 1992 – All Day."

"Okay, gentlemen. You are clear; please place the visitor badge on your person so that it is clearly visible, and then please proceed to the waiting area just down the hall to your left, first door on your left."

Marco clipped the badge to the lapel on his dark-blue suit jacket as the buzzer sounded and the second glass door opened.

As they began to walk through the door, a tall, trim man appeared from a door on the right. He wore light-brown pants and a white shirt with his sleeves rolled halfway up, with his red tie hanging loosely around his buttoned-down collar. He was slightly balding. "Hello. Marco Richards, I presume. Glad that you were able to meet with us on such short notice."

"Hello, sir."

There was a cigarette loosely hanging from the right side of Macey's mouth. "I have heard some very good reports from the Chicago lab, and I am really glad that you have been selected for this assignment."

Macey reached up with his right hand and placed the cigarette in between his right thumb and forefinger. He exhaled a large plume of gray smoke as he took the cigarette from his mouth. Marco noticed that it was a Camel.

"Thank you, Colonel," replied Marco as he reached for Colonel Macey's outstretched hand.

Macey ignored the outstretched hand, since the cigarette held his attention. "Well, welcome to Washington. We are all looking forward to your assistance on a very important assignment. You have gotten noticed by some very important people in the bureau and come to us with a very good resume."

Macey went on. "Look, I know you have been pulled from some other important assignments and I know this has been a long day for you, but we need to get right to the project objectives. I would like to start immediately, if you do not mind, by providing you with some background on the case. If you will follow me, we have reserved a conference room. I also have sent out for some pizza. You like pizza, don't you?"

"Yes, sir," Marco replied as he followed them into a small room to their left. Marco thought, *"What the hell does that mean? Is it a slam just to put my Italian heritage in place? If I were Chinese, I suppose we would be eating chop suey."*

Sitting at the far end behind a small reception desk, another marine sat staring straight forward, almost zombie-like. There were several stripes on his left shoulder and four horizontal stripes on his lower sleeve. Marco thought, *"A lifer."* The marine jumped up and gave Macey a very loose salute.

The four of them walked to the far end of the room and up to a gray metal door. Marco noticed that there was no handle or doorknob on the door. Macey pulled his magnetic ID card that had been clipped to his shirt pocket and inserted it into the magnetic card reader along the right side of the door. With a low-sounding click, the door opened by slipping into the wall to the left. Macey, the gray suit, and Marco entered. The marine captain and the sergeant remained outside the room. Macey pulled a pack of Camels from his left breast pocket. He flipped a cigarette out, placed it in his mouth, and brought the tip of the old butt to the tip of the fresh Camel. He puffed two or three times and brought the new cigarette to life. He extinguished the old Camel in the ashtray sitting on the table.

As they entered, Marco noticed a pizza box and an ice bucket filled with several cans of Pepsi sitting in the middle of a long, wooden conference table. Most of the ice had melted. There was a pitcher of water in the center and several empty glasses. There were about a dozen high-backed chairs surrounding the table. A laptop computer with a small projector and two large computer screens sat at the far end to the left, with the projector pointing to a projection screen pulled down on the far wall. It was dead silent, and Marco could hear the air blowing in from the air conditioner vent directly over the table. The room was smoky, and he could see the smoke from Macey's cigarette being pushed down closer to the table. Marco thought, "Not very extravagant or upscale when you consider all the money that is thrown at the FBI from Washington."

He could not help but wonder about the lack of common-sense priorities. "A $15 million private jet to bring me to a meeting in a dark, smoke-filled conference room in an old, converted army barracks at the end of an airport runway. And some dried-up pizza for dinner."

A female voice broke the silence. "You're Italian, right? I figured you would rather have pizza than a turkey sandwich—right?"

Marco thought to himself again, "I was right; the son of a bitch is trying to put me in my place right off the get-go. It is obvious that they did their research on my background. They are anti-Italian."

He responded, "Yes, sir—ah, I mean ma'am." He gazed across the table and noticed the pretty brunette sitting in the dark at the far corner of the room to the right of the projector.

"Hello, Mr. Richards. My name is Connie Samples, and I work out of the New York City FBI field office. I am assigned to a special organized-crime task force." She rose from her chair to approach Marco with an outstretched hand. "I am the lead case agent on the ground."

Marco reached out with his right hand to greet her and noticed her perfectly manicured nails. He caught a wisp of her sweet perfume in the air. "Hello; it certainly is nice to meet you," he said and thought, "Wow, very pretty."

Macey continued, "Well, let us get started. I have asked Miss Samples to assist me as we introduce you to the case."

The thin brunette moved over next to the computer terminal and the projector. "Okay, let me brief you on the targets of our investigation." She clicked the PowerPoint icon on the projector.

Marco looked up and peered at the title page as the screen lit up. Emblazoned in deep-blue letters were the words: "Laborers Local 4 Union, New York City."

Samples went through the slide presentations with pictures of the Laborers Local 4 principal subjects, including Paul Goldin, the accountant; Greco, the fund administrator; and Ernesto LaCola, the business agent. She spent a few minutes on each and had slides of Senator Vic Sano and Sonny Russo, the business agent from the Albany Laborers Union Local 290. She also had pictures of Marty Bloom but did not provide any detail beyond acknowledging that he was their software consultant but had not been seen for the last several weeks. She did not cover the specific plans and the investigation strategy or Marco's purpose, since that was left to Macey. Samples' presentation took less than thirty minutes before it was turned over to Colonel Macey.

Macey looked around the table and then stopped when he came to Marco. "We have a lot of work and little time to do it. We have a critical timetable to meet, which has been approved by the assistant director. I expect to meet with him first thing in the morning. He wants to meet you, Richards, so he will be joining us for breakfast."

He went on. "Connie, thank you. Connie will be the lead case agent on the ground in New York and will be assisted by Charles Crowley from the Labor Department and a few others from the Southern District of New York. We also have some agents from the FBI's Organized-Crime Task Force from New York working with us, but this team will be independent from the other FBI investigations." He continued. "This is a small team with very specific priorities. But I would like to tell you about the scope of the assignment, which is all included in the package sitting before you on the table.

"Well, first, let me welcome Marco Richards, and thanks to our friends in the Chicago-area office for loaning us Marco. He is going to be working on the computer forensic data and, so I have been told, is an expert and is going to hack into the union computers. Please stand up, Marco, and welcome to the task force."

Marco stood for a moment. "Thank you, sir. I am happy to be here and feel privileged to be working with this team on such an important assignment." He then quickly sat down and nodded as he looked around the table.

Macey sat down directly across from Marco and opened a manila folder in front of him. He briefly looked down and then back up as he stared at Marco. No one said a word for a few seconds, but Marco knew he was onstage.

"Welcome to Washington; glad you were able to come on such short notice. First, let me tell you why you are here. As you may know, the bureau is required to develop a thorough scope for any investigation. This starts with a written plan and must include the targets, the criminal activities that we suspect, the reasons, the legal basis, the team members, the resources, and an estimated timetable. This investigation is about organized labor—specifically, corruption within organized labor—and illegal activities involving the construction industry. We have reason to believe that there are millions of dollars being siphoned from these unions.

"As Connie has addressed, the union target is Laborers Local 4 in New York City. They are one of the biggest trade unions in the country. We know a lot about the various forms of union corruption. There is loan-sharking, gambling, protection and kick-back schemes, and, yes, they are involved in drugs. While we were successful a few years ago with the dismantling of the commission through surveillance and wiretapping, they have elevated their game using legitimate businesses and technology. We did this through surveillance and wiretapping, but today, the tools they use are much more sophisticated. They are smarter and are very careful when they discuss business on the phone, so wiretapping is not as useful as it once was. But the union needs computers to manage all that money flowing in and out."

He looked at Marco and continued. "Marco, that is why you are here. This union has close to half a billion dollars in their trust funds, and the computer is how they manage all that money. We have tested their financial reports from the annual audits and have discovered that there is serious money missing. Millions. We know the metrics of the benefit fund expenditures and know that the numbers are well above the statistical standards by at least 8 percent. We also know that the hours reported by the contractors are well below the norms when compared to construction projects in the city. This is the conclusion reached by our actuarial studies.

"By the way, thank you; we used some of your data metrics from the white papers that you prepared from the Chicago Medicare fraud case. Those algorithms you developed were very helpful and are the reason that I wanted you on this assignment. The algorithms have confirmed that they are skimming close to $20 million annually, but—" He paused and placed his hands on the table as he leaned toward Marco. "We have our suspicions, but we cannot prove it. Where is the money going? While we have had some early success that has confirmed our assumptions, we still need proof. Just when we think we are getting somewhere, our assets refuse to testify or come up missing. So we need to start all over and hack into the bowels of their computer programs. We need evidence, proof of what you refer to in your research papers, data. We need people who can testify, and we need to find the money trail that we can be prove in a court of law. Hard evidence is what we need, and Marco, a lot is riding on your skills.

"The mafia still exists and is involved because we have an asset who has given us some helpful information. They rig bids; they skim off the top; they process phony health claims; and they steal millions of dollars. This money is then used to fund drug-distribution and real-estate schemes. We have a few judges who have given us the necessary court orders but cannot get access to the union computer because much of the data is protected. We need to get more aggressive and push and squeeze. The clock is ticking, and we are running out of time. There are some political changes in the wind, and we need to close in by the end of the year. Otherwise, they may disband our team."

Macey reached down and brought the Camel up from the ashtray. "We have developed a detailed work scope, which has been approved and signed off by the assistant director. Connie Samples has provided an introduction of the principal targets we are surveilling. A copy of the work scope of the investigation will be included in the case file, along with our assets and copies of their affidavits. All team members are expected to review and understand every detail, forward and backward. In addition, you are expected to abide by the plan and abide by the bureau's policy standards and operational guidelines."

Macey paused for a moment as he brought the Camel to his lips and took a drag. "I would like to take a few minutes and say a few words about my views and my expectations. You may not know this, but we work in cooperation with the Justice Department through the Southern District of New York. You should be aware that the Justice Department has several investigations underway, and considerable resources have been assigned to investigate organized crime and, in particular, the Gambino crime family. We have made great progress, and John Gotti is finally getting his just rewards. This investigation is an offshoot and is not directly connected to any other investigation, although there is always some overlap when it comes to labor and organized crime. We investigate but do not prosecute. I have no doubt that the team will perform to the highest standards of the bureau, and I expect results. This can only occur through performance of service, focus on our purpose, and total commitment to teamwork. I want total dedication to our mission, even though we know that we cannot get in front of their activities, let alone stay abreast of their operations."

Macey went on. "The Department of Justice has a primary mission to keep American people safe. We, the members of the FBI, play a critical role in the federal government's shared effort to combat crime, especially when it comes to organized labor. We know that the Laborers Union Local 4 in New York is siphoning millions of dollars from their trust funds. We know that the computer serves a vital role in their nefarious activities. We also know that they have recently entered into a contract to install new software."

He took another puff on his cigarette and finally placed the butt in the ashtray to allow it to slowly burn its way out. "They are hiding something. This may be an opportunity for us. Marco, your job—and I repeat, *your* job—is to get inside their computer and help us to identify how they are doing it. Sounds simple enough, but they are smart bastards, and their old computer expert, Marty Bloom, has disappeared. He was in business for himself, and he was close to cooperating with us when he disappeared. We don't know how you are going to do it, but this is your assignment."

Macey looked around the table at the others. "These are the key team members that you will be working with. You work for the team, and the team works for me, according to my directives. Connie Samples is the team leader, and you will follow her orders. Connie has complete authority regarding the investigation. I do not want any star performances and want you to concentrate on making the entire team successful. Coordination of the team effort rather than individual heroism is what I want every agent to understand."

He hesitated, then continued. "We expect to know everything, good and bad, as it happens. We have a long and arduous task before us, and I expect results. Okay, you get a few days to review the case file, and I expect you to report to me early next week before the team gets back on the ground in New York.

"We not only stop crime and put criminals in jail; we also learn from every case. We will need to gain a better understanding of the technology, so document everything and do not overlook anything. Dig, dig, dig until you establish the criminal activity that we know exists. Marco, you have a vital role in this assignment, and we are counting on you to hack into the union computer system and figure out how they are getting the money out. The new software company that they are working with must in some way be involved in the scheme. So get into the software and find the money trail. That is your assignment. I expect Connie to put pressure on the new software company to cooperate. No one is off limits, and nothing is off the table. Good luck to all."

Macey occasionally looked down at his folder, but only for a brief second or two. It was obvious that he needed no script and knew exactly what he wanted to say, since he had repeated the lecture many times in the past. No rehearsal was necessary to make his point.

Macey continued. "In addition, over the next few months, the department will build upon our findings, and we will be asked to provide recommendations to the director and the attorney general as to how the bureau can more effectively manage growing cyber-challenges and white-collar crimes involving the unions." He smiled as he directed his stare toward Marco. "When we are successful, I suspect you will be obliged to write a few white papers on cybersecurity."

Macey reached for another Camel. He paused for a moment as he took out an old silver Zippo lighter. Through the light, Marco could see the worn lettering on the side: "USMC 3rd Infantry Division." He flicked it open with his thumb and, without looking, rolled his thumb across the small wheel. He brought the flame to the Camel that hung loosely in his mouth and once again puffed in with a long, slow drag. "Are you with us, Agent Richards?"

The room fell totally quiet and there was a long silence. Marco had almost disconnected from Macey's words, but he knew it was now his time to speak. Without thinking and almost as a reflex without any forethought, unconsciously, he heard the words roll across his teeth and out of his mouth. "Yes, sir, understood."

It was reflex and there would be no other possible answer. It was his duty to obey and follow his superior; there could be no argument or reply that would possibly be expected. He was in, regardless of whether he agreed or not.

Macey nodded a few times and, with a tight-lipped smile, finally sat down. "Great, that is about it." He placed the cigarette in the ashtray to allow it to burn out. Apparently, he was consumed by the importance of what he was saying. Directing all his attention to Marco, Macey was feeling good and knew the new field agent, Richards, had gotten the message.

Macey now closed the folder in front of him and reached out to the pack of Camels sitting on the table. He put the half-empty pack into his shirt pocket and once again sat down. The room was now smoke filled, even though Macey was the only smoker.

Marco was finally relieved, thinking the lecture finally over.

Macey then went on. "Okay, okay, but understand this: we are the law, and no one is going to question how we get the job done, just as long as we get the fucking job done."

The bearded gentleman in the dark-gray suit, who was now finally known by his first name, Charles, was still standing in the corner and finally approached the left side of the table He sat down just to the left of the overhead projector and finally spoke.

"Agent Richards, my name is Charles Crowley, and I am with the Department of Labor. I am a special agent working with this team. I conduct the annual audits at Local 4 for the Labor Department, so I will need your help once we are able to hack into their computer. They usually cooperate, but we do not know what to expect with this new software."

Macey waved his hand in front of Crowley to cut him off. "Hold on, Charles." He lifted his right index finger and pointed directly at Marco's nose. "We can talk about the logistics next week, but before this meeting is adjourned, I would like to have a few words with Marco privately." He stood and turned to Marco. "Can you please step out in the hall with me for just a minute?"

Marco nodded. "Yes, sir." He then stood up and followed Macey into the hall.

Macey continued. "Richards, we will bring you to your quarters tonight and send a car for you at seven o'clock tomorrow morning. We are all having breakfast in the officers' dining room. We will then give you a copy of the complete case file. You will then travel back to Chicago to get your things together and return here next week for a briefing by the team next Thursday. Study the file. The team will then travel back to New York and get this investigation moving. But I need you to understand how this investigation will proceed.

I have kept this special unit down to just a few people, and you report directly to Connie. She reports directly to me. I do not want you to question how or what she does regarding the court orders authorizing the computer hacking. This is a relatively new environment for the bureau, and I do not want you to concern yourself with the court orders. The judges have no idea as to what we need. I personally will take care of that end, and I just want you to use all your skills to get them in front of a judge. Understand? You are on your own and can do whatever you think is necessary to hack into their computer."

Marco was not sure what to say but then caught the words about to come out of his mouth. He muttered, "But ..." and then stopped, as he knew there could be no other reply. "Yes, sir, you are the boss and I understand."

Macey smiled. "And one other thing: I only want you to share your findings with Connie. I do not want you to share anything with Crowley, understand?" He then turned and went back into the conference room, with Marco following closely behind. Macey then stood before them all and spoke. "Okay, that's about it. See you all in the morning. School is out, and welcome to the real world."

The next morning, the team had breakfast in the marine officers' mess. They then conducted a final review of the scheduling and logistics of the plan. Macey gave Marco a letter signed by an assistant director that provided the necessary change of assignment for Marco. After two days in his Chicago office, he had organized his case files and research papers and passed them off to his supervisor. There were no questions asked, and he was now focused on his travel plans back to Washington. This time, it would be flying coach on a commercial flight. In Washington, the plan was to meet with Macey and review each team member's role once again. They had two days before meeting with Macey, and if everything was approved, they would be given the green light to proceed. The plan sounded simple. Surveillance, computer cyber-hacking combined with wiretaps and bugs to find the crime and who and how it was being accomplished.

The New York Organized-Crime Task Force members of the FBI had over 100 agents assigned to the case. The majority would focus on the Gambino side of the investigation and attempt to turn witnesses over to the special unit. They would exchange information with Macey's unit when they arrived in New York but most of the information shared would be for the benefit of Macey's unit. Marco's job would be to find the evidence that would allow them to trace the flow of money and prove criminal activity. They needed evidence, and they knew that the computer was the tool that made it possible. No hard evidence of a crime and only suspicions. They suspected that millions of dollars were being siphoned out, and the team would be relying on Marco to unlock the door and figure out how it was being accomplished.

CHAPTER THREE

THE ACCOUNTANT

APRIL 2, 1992—ALBANY

T WAS EARLY APRIL, IT was sunny, and the sun's rays were warming the green landscape below. The sky was an intense blue, and the soft springtime breeze carried the scent of freshly cut grass from the golf course. They had just finished the quarterly trustee meeting for Local 290 at the country club, and it was a perfect spring day for the golf match, which was the usual program following Local 290's union quarterly trustees' meeting. It had been a positive quarter, and the union trust funds were earning money from their investments, the bank accounts were all in order according to the CPA, and the computer system was doing what Chris had promised. Chris and his team of programmers and trainers had done a great job, and the health fund's claims system was now paying checks accurately and on time. They were running just like a little insurance company from Hartford. The fund accounting system was working well, and all the other funds, including the pension and annuity systems, were perfect. There was close to $100 million in the funds, and they were operating efficiently and in an organized fashion. The union was in great shape financially.

Along with spring, golf season had arrived early in upstate New York. Sonny and Chris were good friend and there was considerable trust established. Sonny Russo ran everything at Local 290 and made all the business decisions. He was the big boss at the union, and whenever a vote was required, Sonny cast the first vote and all the other union trustees followed his lead. As the business agent, he controlled all the union's business activities and was responsible for all the funds. When Sonny needed help to improve the union computers, he turned to his trusted friend Chris to install the software. It was Chris's turn to host the golf game after the Local 290 luncheon meeting. Chris was looking forward to it, since this was the day that he would meet the accountant from Local 4 in New York City.

It was just past two o'clock and Chris was in the locker room changing into his golf clothes. He took off his shirt and tie and hung them in his locker, revealing a band of sweat just below his chin. He then took off his suit pants and carefully hung them on one of the three wooden hangers in his locker. Chris then removed the green golf shirt with the Pebble Beach logo from the carry bag and pulled it over his head, along with a matching green golf hat. The logo on the front of the hat depicted an owl and the letters "WRCC," which stood for Wolfert's Roost Country Club. The creases in his golf shirt were almost perfect.

The locker room had the typical country-club locker room smell of cheap aftershave lotions and hair tonics loaded with alcohol mixed with the background smell of cooked body odors from the steam room. He loved everything about the club: the men's bar, the card room, the red-hot showers, and especially the steam room. It was the perfect place to get away from it all, have a beer, take a steam and a hot shower, and just forget about every problem that one could ever encounter in the outside world. When you were at the club, it was as if you wore a suit of body armor that deflected all the ugly influences of the outside world.

It was an unusually warm day for early April and, he thought, perfect for golf. They'd had a cold winter in Albany, but the club was able to open for play a week earlier. Sonny Russo was already on the practice range with a fresh new driver borrowed from the pro shop. It was one of those clubs that would permanently end up in Sonny's golf bag.

To Chris, it was not about how good you were at the game, but rather about how the game was played. It was about the rules, and you must abide by the rules. Golf had rules, and the unions had rules as well. In both cases, winners and losers were determined. But for Chris, it was how you followed the rules that was more important than winning. It was how you played the game according to which set of rules. Sometimes, business got in the way. When you played with the union boys, you never argued over the money. You showed your respect by acting like money didn't matter.

Today, he figured it would cost at least a thousand for the golf, dinner, and any equipment in the pro shop that struck Sonny's fancy. That was strictly the way it was. That was how the game was played when you played with the people that ran the unions—it wasn't necessarily bribery but rather, a cost of doing business. If you wanted to do business with the labor unions, then you had to learn the first lesson: you paid when you played with these guys. They never paid for anything, and they never reached in their pockets, regardless of whether it was a dinner, a beer, or a round of golf. None of it mattered. It was simply friendship mixed with a little bit of business, and if you couldn't buy a little business with a little gift or two, then you were not going to play in their circles and you were not considered a friend. The Internal Revenue Service called it "entertainment expenses." Hell, it didn't hurt anyone, and besides, you could always charge them a little more to make up for the extra cost of doing business. They expected it. In the long run, it wasn't really their money; it was the union's money that was feeding the whole system. One big, happy circle of money laundering among a circle of friends. Just a cost of doing business with the unions.

Chris had finished dressing and was heading down to the pro shop to meet the others when suddenly, a tall man with piercing blue eyes with a dark-green golf hat appeared from around the row of tall lockers. Chris guessed that he was about sixty years old. His black hair with silver streaks was well groomed and contrasted well with his slightly tanned skin and neatly trimmed eyebrows. He reminded Chris of an older Cary Grant, but not quite as good looking. He was neatly dressed in a yellow golf shirt and tan trousers, and there was a broad smile across his face. He had a gold chain around his neck with a gold mezuzah hanging from it. Chris noticed the logo embroidered on his shirt, which read, "Shinnecock Hills CC."

"Hello, you must be Chris," the man said. "I have been looking forward to meeting you. I'm going to be playing with you and Sonny." He approached Chris with his right hand outstretched and his forefinger pointing to Chris.

Startled and a bit surprised, Chris turned and looked up. "Hey, ah, hello, you must be Paul. I'm pleased to finally meet you."

"Yes, Paul Goldin, and the pleasure is all mine. I just drove up from Columbia County." His smile showed off a full set of beautifully capped teeth.

"Sonny tells me that you have never played here at the club before."

"Well, not exactly. Last fall, Sonny had an outing here for the international union people from New York, I came up from the city to play, but unfortunately, we got rained out after six holes."

Paul placed his left foot up on the bench and looked directly in Chris's eyes. He was wearing brown and white golf shoes, and the steel spikes dug into the wooden bench with a crunch. "Well, it looks like we picked a great day. Did you order sunshine especially for the occasion?"

Chris chuckled. "Finally, it's a good day. Spring has arrived a little early; even though winter was not very kind to us this year, but this is Albany." He was annoyed with Paul's shoes on the bench. "The course is in great shape and yes, the greens are quick but fair, but the weather is perfect."

Paul grinned. "Well, I am looking forward to the golf. I am a little rusty, but I did get to play in Florida. I have a place in Boca and spend January and February there. It's different up here." He took his foot off the bench and sat down.

"Well, I have been looking forward to meeting you. I have been thinking about joining the Roost. You know I have a farm in Columbia County and play at Columbia County Country Club. I hope to spend more time upstate, play a little golf, and get involved in some of the union business up here in Albany. New York City is just too crazy lately, and I need some quiet time to get away from the rush of the big city. I understand that this is the club to belong to in the area and that the food is great."

"Food is good, but not like Café Italia," Chris replied. "Our claim to fame is the golf course. I know you will like it. The putting greens are small but distance-wise, it is not a long course. The length plays shorter on some holes especially on a few of the downhill holes. We will be playing from the white tees, since I know that Sonny will want to play from the front tees."

Chris now realized that Sonny was an exceptional friend, since he had set up the golf to include the accountant.

"I understand that Mike White is playing with us." Chris went on. "I think Sonny may have introduced you to him. He is with the upstate contractor's association."

"Mike White? Oh, you mean Mike Biance. Is that what you call him?" Paul asked.

"Well, that is his American name. He goes by both, but White when he does not want anyone to know that he is Italian. It is an old mob thing, and he likes to play the role. Who knows; maybe he is connected?"

Paul Goldin was typical of many New York City accountants. He was smart, quick-witted and loved to work with money. He did, however, have one very special and unique talent. He was connected with what many called "The Organization," and it was rumored that all the trade unions in the city had connections or did business with the Gambino crime family—and they were the crime family that controlled all the union business. Goldin was a CPA and a lawyer but had chosen public accounting as his principal profession because he loved money more than he cared about the law. It was his understanding of the unions and his intimate knowledge of the laws that governed the unions and union accounting systems that made him especially effective at his job. The job of finding money and using money to make more money overpowered everything else. Fortunately for him, but not always so fortunate for his clients, it was always other people's money that he worked with. He knew how to separate people from their money quickly and efficiently. And during any exchange, there was always some that stuck to Paul's hand and ended up in his pocket.

Goldin was everyone's picture of success. He was tall, still had a full head of hair, and was pleasant to hang around with. He earned his law degree from Columbia and his accounting degree from Rutgers. Funny, yet serious; clever, yet down to earth; he was always the center of the conversation when he walked into the room. And it didn't matter what the conversation was centered around; Paul always seemed to know something about what you were talking about and always seemed to move the conversation to the subject of money. He was intelligent, quick-witted, and funny. But perhaps his greatest asset was that he had all the connections, especially the connections with the union business in New York City. He knew all the right people and used it to his advantage to get what he wanted: more money. He also had money—lots of money.

Chris thought it was interesting that most people who did not have money wanted to hang out with people who had money. Paul was looked upon as being very successful without having to work at it. He belonged to two country clubs, ate at fancy restaurants, vacationed in Europe, and owned a high-rise apartment in Manhattan. He also owned a condominium in Florida and a farm in Columbia County. His accounting practice dealt strictly with unions and labor organizations. Most of his clients included the large New York City unions. He was now making a move into some of the smaller upstate unions. He was a money guy and showed it by driving a big Mercedes-Benz S550, while his wife drove a sporty two-door Lexus.

Chris knew that Goldin had the right connections and could help to arrange business meetings for companies that wanted to do business with the New York unions. Gaining favor with the unions required connections. You were either a friend or, at a minimum, a friend of a friend. And when the connection was made, you had to know how to leverage the relationship. That was easy; you just had to be sure to treat them to lunch, treat them to dinner, treat them to golf, and treat them to whatever they wanted. They thought they were special, and you had to specialize in treating them like they were special. You didn't expect them to reciprocate, because it would never happen. The only chances of getting a free lunch were the annual union Christmas party and the annual union clam bake.

Local 4 was one of the oldest unions in the city and had a membership of over ten thousand. The pension fund alone had investments of close to half a billion dollars. Their computer operation was big time; however, despite its size, from a technology point of view, its software was not terribly sophisticated. They liked it that way because they did not want the computer to make it easy for someone on the outside to count all their money.

"Sonny told me that you straightened their computer system out and it is running like a Swiss watch." Paul went on. "And he also tells me that you're a pretty good golfer, so I am going to need a few strokes off your ball. Regardless of the partners, I will ride with you. I would really like to get to know you."

Chris was excited about the golf meeting and knew that Goldin would be the person to introduce him to Ernesto LaCola, the business agent of Local 4. The title of "business agent" did not mean much to the world outside of organized labor, but for those on the inside and in the know, it was the business agent, the BA, who held the position of power in the union. The BA was the man. He ran the union. He decided who got in and who stayed out. He also decided who got the jobs and who got a steady paycheck. More importantly, he also made the decision as to who got to do business with them.

Ernesto LaCola, just like Sonny Russo, gave out the jobs to the members and controlled all the business affairs of the union. He negotiated deals with the contractors and kept the union focused on making money and protecting the benefits for their membership. He was the big boss, and everyone else obeyed his directives. He also was the chairman on all the employee benefit funds. The funds were where all the power was, because that was where all the money was. If you controlled the funds, then you had the opportunity, if you were smart, to get at the money. The BA decided who the money managers were that would manage the fund and how the money was invested.

LaCola was the man on the inside and the outside. Everyone kissed his hand—literally—and figuratively kissed his ass. He told you where you were going to eat lunch, who would eat with him, and what you were going to eat. And guess who would pick up the check? For sure, not the BA. It was no different with the other labor union leaders. Big or small, it was the BA that was calling all the shots and choosing the vendors, the investment managers, the bankers, the hired accountants, and the computer-software suppliers.

Chris and Goldin were playing along, and very little was discussed with regard to the software. Local 4 needed somebody to do their advanced scouting work to hire professionals, and it was Goldin whom they relied upon. They paid the accountant's firm lots of money, and Goldin had demonstrated that he was an expert on any matter involving union operations. Union organizers consisted primarily of elected field guys, and there had always been a heavy reliance on retaining professionals to assist them in running the union operations.

The labor leaders in the trade unions had started as tradesmen. The labor leaders in the carpenters' union started out as carpenters. Those who ran the bricklayers' union were bricklayers. Those that ran the labor union started out as laborers, many pushing wheelbarrows or mixing cement. Within the unions, those with political skills and connections worked their way to power within the union—some by their brains, some by their muscles, and some by their fathers. Few, if any, were college graduates. In most cases, they worked their way up in the organizations from the very bottom. They were labor organizers, and it was their relationships with the members and the promises that they made that got them to their positions. They made promises to get elected just like any other politician running for public office.

The management and administrative functions of a union were not simple. There were many diverse business disciplines, and each required skilled employees using sophisticated computer systems. They operated as an insurance company, a contractor, a financial institution, an investment company, a bank, a real-estate developer, and an employment agency. Each department required a high degree of business knowledge, and there was a need for specialized software for each. Hiring experts and professionals was a common practice, since most of the leaders who ran the trade unions lacked the formal education or business experience to manage the many facets of the operations. They were good in a leadership role but usually poor administrators. Many never even graduated high school. It was especially vital to the union when it came to the engagement of the lawyers, the investment managers, the accountants, and the computer software vendors that they needed to be competent and trusted professionals, since they had access to the money.

Trust and loyalty were essential, since there were millions of dollars that needed to be managed. The computer and accounting systems served critical roles, and hired professionals legitimatized the organization. The reality was that most of the union organizers and labor leaders lacked the skills necessary for sound business management. Sure, they could certainly talk a good game when they were out in the field negotiating a contract with a contractor, but when it came to office matters and the financial-management side of the business, they depended on the hired professionals. That was not exactly the case with Local 4, and Goldin made that clear when he spoke about LaCola.

"Chris, when I introduce you to Ernesto LaCola, you will be impressed with his knowledge of union operations. He is highly intelligent and is a college graduate, not like many of the labor leaders you have dealt with."

Chris knew he was being interviewed for the job in New York and that he would be tested not on his golf score but rather on how he played the game. The software was secondary; Goldin would only be focused on what kind of a person Chris was. Chris understood that this was not a game of golf but rather a test of character. Today, his character would be judged, and he would be tested for his trust and loyalty to his union clients.

Goldin began to probe. "So, I understand that you and Sonny are good friends. How long have you known Sonny?"

"We met in high school when we were in the same gym class. We were friends but not very close back then."

"I know they have a PAC fund; how much does Sonny have to pay his buddy, Senator Sano?"

Chris saw this one coming and was not about to disclose anything, even to a trusted associate or friend. "I don't know and do not get close to any of Sonny's business affairs."

Chris stopped the cart and walked over to his ball. He hit his second shot toward the green; it took a few bounces forward and then rolled to the back edge of the green before stopping.

Goldin watched. "Nice shot."

Chris went on. "Look, I know unions and know what unions need, but I do not know or get involved in their business affairs. Nor do I care to know what or why. They hire me to do a job, and I do what they want me to do. I especially do not get involved in the politics."

Goldin responded, "You're right, and I agree wholeheartedly. It is all about getting the job done, but it must be done the union way. I should not have asked you something so confidential."

Chris replied, "I know that, and I understand."

Goldin continued to quiz Chris. "Well, I hope you do not mind my asking, but why are you interested in the New York City unions?"

"That is simple. I am interested in the money and would like to bring my business to the next level. I have over a dozen union clients in upstate New York, and unless I can expand my markets beyond the upstate region, my growth will be limited. We have invested millions of dollars in the software, and I think we may be at a point where we can capitalize on that investment."

"Well, makes a lot of sense, and I can appreciate that. Maybe I can help you with some introductions," said Goldin.

There was a loud *thump* as the accountant swung at the ball that was lying in the bunker. The ball popped up and rolled about seven or eight feet past the hole before it stopped. The accountant then walked over and picked up the ball. "Four—that's good for a par." Chris knew it was his fifth shot on the hole, but he remained silent.

"Look, Chris, I am, as you know, a trusted associate for Local 4 in the city. I am a CPA and manage all their accounting systems. They have asked me to find a new software company for their new computer. I have already had a talk with a few of your union clients in Albany. I am confident in your ability and knowledge of union accounting. Sonny is very satisfied with your performance, and I have had a good look at the software. Sonny told me you guys go way back. Local 4 has an old system; it continually goes down, and even when it is running, they cannot balance out the money in the funds. The software is a mess."

He continued. "We need someone who knows how union accounting systems work, has good software, and knows how to solve problems. Local 4 has invested over half a million dollars in their new IBM hardware, and the company they hired to write the software is not getting the job done. They can't find the guy who owns the company, and to make matters worse, he wrote all the special programs. He is the only one who knows how the system works, and they believe he is now living in Florida. We need someone who is not going to disappear. We need someone we can trust. Are you interested?"

"Paul," Chris replied, "as I said, I would love to meet with your union clients, and you need to know that we will do whatever is necessary to straighten out their computer problems."

"Well, it is a little more than that; they need to get some of these old records cleaned up first. They have data records that still need to be converted from the old system, and the old data files don't match with the computer numbers. Everything is, well, pretty fucked up. You need to understand that these records go back close to fifty years, and it is really a mess. You are not going to get any cooperation or help from their current software vendor. We are going to need you to personally get involved in the process.

"We know you have good people, but as you know, this process can be extremely sensitive if gotten into the wrong hands. These guys will be running for election next year, and the politics are very dirty in this business. Everything needs to be kept very confidential. We need you to maintain an extremely low profile until we get the data all straightened out. Sometimes, we may need to plug in data that is not necessarily reflected in the old cards. Their old equipment is no longer used; it's crap, and there will be quite a bit of manual effort involved. We get audited every year by the Labor Department, and we need a clean system. We often have to make adjustments to clean the data. You might say that sometimes there are two sets of books. Data conversion is the challenge, and we need to sometimes fill in the missing pieces."

Paul Goldin continued. "Chris, we also need you to buy into the deal. It is the way business is done in New York. This is the way it is, and you should think of it as a matter of mutual trust. Think of it as an investment."

"Paul, New York is just a couple of hours away, and I can handle it," Chris responded, holding back his enthusiasm. This was one of those business opportunities he had been waiting for. However, it was also the first time that they mentioned it would cost him. If you wanted to do business in the big city, then there was a cost associated with making the contacts and making the deal. It wasn't just the cost of a golf round, but much more. He now realized it was a new beginning to the same old story. It would be at a cost.

As Chris thought back and remembered Goldin's words, he now realized that there would be a catch. "What do you mean, buy into the deal?" he asked.

"Chris, you are going to pay some fees that you may not be familiar with, but don't worry; it will not come out of your pocket. You know how the unions do business. We all work according to the systems that they have set up. There are lots of costs associated with rent and subcontractors. When we get together in New York, I will fill you in on the details."

Paul went on to say, "If you are as good as Sonny says you are, then you can make lots of money. If you are going to be a friend or at least a friend of a friend, then you will get the Local 4 account, and it is only the first of many—if you do the right thing and work with us as a partner and not as a vendor." Goldin pointed his finger almost directly at Chris's heart. "Then you can become a trusted friend, a trusted business partner."

"Sure, but as long as I can spend some time to check out the hardware and the data. It will take me at least two or three days to review the system and get up to speed on their benefit plans before I can provide an estimate for the conversion," Chris replied.

"That's not what I am concerned with. Forget that crap. I know you have the software and the staff. We have already checked you and your people out. Especially your software. I know you have the software and the experience, but we need to be certain you have the guts. You must realize that we are always under the government's microscope, and we are careful in all aspects of our business relationships. Why do you think most unions have so many attorneys working for them? The laws and the regulations are very complex and egregious. We all must be extremely careful when the fucking government is sticking their nose into everything we do. We have political connections, and they help us out on occasion. The State of New York, the Labor Department, the FBI, the NYPD, Washington, you name it—they all want a piece of us. They are always trying to pick our pockets.

"The problem that faces today's labor movement is the government. Even the politicians and the blood-sucking bureaucrats who pretend to be on our side are always looking for something. The Democrats want our votes and want our money. The Republicans want our votes but still haven't figured out how to get them. The unions are under the scrutiny of the government, and their power gives them ability to do anything they want to us. The only weapon we have to fight them with is our money. That's why we have established PAC funds. The Political Action Committee money gives us some leverage, but we still have to pay for everything we get from the politicians. They always have their hands out when we need a favor."

Goldin continued. "Unions have money—lots of money—and that is the currency they use to conduct business. Get it? We trade favors with people who know how the game is played. Trouble is, the son of a bitch politicians and bureaucrats who pretend to be squeaky clean are always there with their hand out. There are a few, for the most part, who understand our business model; however, they have their hands deep in our pockets. Don't you ever kid yourself; the government side is dirty. They have an advantage: they have the system on their side. They are above the law because they make the rules."

Chis nodded in agreement even though he had a tense and uneasy feeling which he could not shake. "Paul, I understand. I know something about unions. I have a dozen union clients, and I have a great deal of respect for their work on behalf of their members." He deliberatively gazed directly into Goldin's eyes. There was a meaningful pause. "I get it. I know what is expected of me. I am a friend to the labor unions."

Paul pursed his lips and stared directly back into Chris's eyes without hesitation. "Chris, that is all bullshit. The reality is that when you step over to our side, it is with both feet. There will be no turning back; you are either in or out. It is that simple."

Chris was astonished that Goldin would speak so candidly about the dark side of union operations at their first meeting. "What are you trying to say?"

Goldin continued. "There may be some things you will be asked to do that you may not like or understand. You must accept them and, at all costs, remember that if you want to be successful in this business, you had better trust us—but more important, we need to know that we can trust you. Can we trust you?" He paused for a brief moment. "First rule: don't ever discuss union business with anyone on the outside. With no one. And especially do not discuss with your family and your employees. Second rule: when you have a problem or question, you come to me."

Chris lowered his head slightly, then looked back up to the sky. "Paul, I understand and am with you; I have been working with unions for over eight years."

"Do you?" Goldin removed his hat with his left hand and pushed back his hair with his fingers on his right hand. The look on Goldin's face took on a note of seriousness. "Look, I told you that there is lots of money, as long as you are on our side. We don't give a fuck what the software costs, but we do need to know that aside from getting the job done, you do it our way. So that means you must trust us. Third and final rule is that the family comes first. That means all of us who are working for the union. The union is the family; get it? This makes it very simple. No one ever does anything that can hurt the family."

Goldin then sat back in the golf cart next to Chris. "Okay, here is the deal: when you come down next week, I need you to bring a check made out to 'CK Consulting' for $10,000. Consider this an investment, and you will get a return many times over. There are some consultants that will need to be paid under your contract. Next week, we will have a short meeting with Greco and then go to lunch. At lunch, you will discreetly pass the check to Greco. I will explain everything next week and tell you how we are going to work together. You need to bring a check, since we do not try to hide anything.

"Chris, I understand that your software licensing fees are $300,000. That is low for us, so you need to change the price. You need to change your invoice, and there is extra work that we have yet to define. We will discuss the extra work next week when you come to the city. Anytime someone is not making money, they tend to take shortcuts, and that is when mistakes are made. We want this job to be profitable for you, and Albany prices are not the same as New York City prices. And we do not like mistakes. So, bring along a new invoice with the software licensing fee at $450,000. How does that sound?"

"Well, sounds pretty good, but—" He was not sure he'd heard Paul correctly. "Did you say $450,000?" Chris stuttered his response slightly as he began to realize what he was agreeing to. But it was done, and he realized he had just taken that first step—and $10,000 was a big step. But then, the $150,000 was a much bigger step.

Goldin continued. "Chris, it is a budget thing, and we have shifted some extra cleanup work during the conversion to your contract, so don't worry about this shift."

Chris began to realize how different these people were when it came to union business. It was more than trust; it was about money and had little to do with one's product or service.

Money was counted in a different denomination in the city. Local 4 was the big prize, and Chris wanted a piece of it. Those trust funds needed computers and software to help manage all that money. And for Chris, he knew that the New York City unions would bring his business to the next level. The higher fees were the part of the deal that was easily acceptable.

Chris's computer business was well matched to his problem-solving skills, and the best part of it was that he could make money doing something he enjoyed. At the time, he did not realize it, but he would soon learn that money would not be the most important thing in life. He would soon discover that money would become secondary to many more important matters such as family, friendship, honesty, and character. He would also learn that the business of problem-solving would no longer be enjoyable and would soon become a burden. His freedom would be threatened.

The jump from small-town Albany to New York City would mean a big jump into the big unions and the world of big money, and the stakes had just been elevated to heights he never could have imagined.

That evening at dinner with Goldin and Sonny, Chris thought about what his mother had preached to him on many occasions: "Chris, something for nothing is worth nothing." Sure, this was an easy deal to make—maybe too easy and, in fact, he should have thought it through very carefully. If he had, he would have realized that there had to be a catch. It sounded too good to be true, and although parts were true, it was going to turn out not to be that good after all. It really would turn out to be too good to be true. He would soon figure out that his mother may have been right.

Sonny was sipping a glass of white wine and looked over to Goldin. "So, Paul, too bad you have to drive back to the city this weekend. Saturday is our big day here in Albany. This groundbreaking event for the waterfront tech center in Albany is going to be a big deal. We are having a special celebration at Café Italia afterward, and the dinner party is going to be very special. Chris, you are going to make it for sure."

Chris replied, "Thanks for the invite, Sonny. I would not miss it for the world."

"Well, we have a trustees' meeting in New York at nine o'clock on Monday, so I have to be at Local 4 early. I have to prepare this weekend. Sorry to miss it, especially the party at Café Italia," Goldin answered.

Chris signaled the waiter to bring them another round of drinks.

Goldin stood. "Not for me, thank you. I do not want to get a DWI up here. I have to drive back to the farm tonight and besides, I will need to leave early in the morning to drive back to the city. If I get stopped, I don't have the connections."

He turned to Chris and offered his right hand. "Chris, thank you for the golf and the great dinner. The steak was perfect, but the clam chowder was just great. Remember what we discussed. I will see you Tuesday morning at 230 Park Avenue South."

Sonny looked up at Goldin. "It would not have been a problem, Paul. I do have the connections up here. This is my town."

Goldin turned and walked out as Sonny turned his attention to Chris. He felt safe to talk openly since they were the only ones left sitting in the club's dining room. "Well, how did it go? I know he asked you to bring something for Greco. Do not worry about it; it is safe, and you will get many times that amount in return. It is just a test and the way things are done in the city."

Chris nodded his head in agreement. "Yes, I understand, and I am not worried about it. Just another cost of doing business."

"Did Paul mention the importance of the waterfront project here in Albany?"

"Well, we spoke briefly about it but did not get into it in any depth."

Sonny went on. "Chris, this project is one of those jobs that comes along maybe once every fifty years. This is life changing, not just for my members, but for the unions in New York. It's bigger than the Rockefeller South Mall project, and no one will allow anyone or anything to jeopardize it. Local 4 is leading the way, and your work will be crucial, so remember how important it is to all of us. I have gone out on a limb for you, so don't disappoint me, Paul, or the boys in New York. They play hardball. We are all counting on you. Just do what they ask you to do, and you will be fine. Everyone is protected."

Chris now knew that he was in and there would be no turning back. Regardless of the cost, he recognized that this was a high-stakes game. "Sonny, I am with you guys all the way."

CHAPTER FOUR

THE VILLAGE VANGUARD
MAY 17, 1992 – NEW YORK CITY

T HE GREENWICH VILLAGE BASEMENT HAD recently celebrated its fifty-eighth year just one week earlier. The club's seating only provided for 123 customers and was always crowded. There were no empty seats, and this evening was no exception. It was at full capacity. The Vanguard, known as the Village Vanguard, was perhaps the most famous venue in the history of music. It was the place that has hosted the most live recordings, booked the greatest musicians, and, more than any other room, embodied the creative genius between music and innovation that sparked the best jazz.

In New York City in 1960, it was the place that nineteen-year-old Barbra Streisand sang a Sunday matinee during the same week in which Miles Davis headlined. History records that the trumpeter objected to the headlines and refused to perform. He said, "I don't play behind no girl singers."

The place was small and uncomfortable, and no cameras were allowed. The quartet on the stage was playing a tribute to Cole Porter. There was no talking during the show, and afterward, you were presented with a check and politely asked to leave. A young man about thirty-five years old was standing at the far end of the bar closest to the entrance when two men walked up and stopped to his immediate left. The taller one was wearing a white turtleneck sweater under his jacket. He opened his jacket and flashed the badge hanging on the inside of the blue blazer. He also made certain that the man saw the Glock holstered on his belt line.

"Hello; how is the show?" The taller one asked.

"Okay." The man noticed the badge and, hesitating slightly, said, "Can I buy you guys a drink?" He was surprised and not sure what to say.

"No, thank you, but we sure would like to speak to you for just a few minutes."

"Well, what can I do for you? What's this about?" Now the young man was visibly nervous and rattled the ice cube around in his glass before he brought it to his lips and finished all that remained at the bottom of the glass.

"Look, we will not take up a lot of your time. We simply want a few minutes to ask you a couple of questions about your software business. We need your help."

"Well, we are not supposed to speak during the show, so let's wait until this set is over." The young man tried to brush them off. He turned away for no more than a few seconds. The taller man with the badge silently stared at the back of the man's head and then walked around to face him. He looked directly into his eyes. They were eye to eye and no more than a few inches apart. The young man stood his ground and was motionless as he returned the blank stare. He regained his composure and did not offer any hint of intimidation. The exchange seemed like it lasted for an eternity, even though it was no more than a few seconds. "Look. I am just enjoying the music and having a late-evening drink. If you will give me your number, I will be happy to call you tomorrow."

"Well, look, I had hoped we could take care of this tonight. Tomorrow is our day off. We will not take more than a few minutes, so please, let's not make a big deal out of this. We need your help and only have a couple of questions we want to ask you about your union business."

Just then, the bartender came over to the three of them and whispered across the bar. "Gentlemen, would you kindly refrain from talking during the show? Not allowed. Show some respect to the performers and take the conversation outside, please."

The tall one turned his head toward the door. "Sure, no problem."

The young man raised his eyebrows as a gesture of acceptance. "Okay, but I can tell you, you are wasting your time. I have no information about my union business. I doubt that I can be of any help to you."

The three of them turned and walked slowly to the door and up the stairs to street level.

Once outside, the cold air sent a chill along Seventh Avenue, which gave no indication or hint of the season. It was a chilly New York City night. You could still hear the upbeat sounds of the music from the quartet performing on the small stage inside the basement club. The song playing was, "Anything Goes."

"Lieutenant, it's freezing out here; can we sit in the car?"

The man looked puzzled and saw that the shorter man had withdrawn a handgun from his holster, yet it remained hidden from plain view of the people who were waiting under the awning for entry to see the next show. The man now realized that he may have made a big mistake and should not have agreed to leave the Vanguard. He silently cursed himself, but it was too late.

The black SUV pulled to the curb almost simultaneously as they neared the street.

The shorter one opened the back door of the big Lincoln and motioned for the young man to step inside. No lights and no special fanfare. "Please, just get in. We only have a few questions." The shorter man waited for a few seconds and began to push the young man toward the open door. He reluctantly stepped in and slid across the back seat to the left side. The shorter man followed him into the SUV, his pistol still held to the young man's side and jammed into his ribs. The hand holding the shiny .38 Special was steady.

The young man now realized that these guys may not have been detectives after all.

"What the fuck do you guys want? You are not cops. What is this all about?" His mouth tightened as he looked down at the gun jammed into his side. "Please, that thing makes me nervous. Is that necessary?"

The taller one jumped into the front passenger side of the Lincoln, turned, and pointed his 9mm automatic directly at the man's nose. The windows were blackened, and no one could see what was going on inside the SUV as it sped away.

"Relax; we just want to have a chat. Is that okay with you?"

"Well, apparently, I have no choice at this point. What the fuck do you guys want? I told you I cannot help you and know nothing about the union's business affairs. I know some people who can answer your questions, and that is about it. I cannot help you."

Now the shorter man in the back began to speak. "What can you tell us about Local 4 business?"

The young man nervously answered. "Well, I know Greco and the accountant, Goldin, and that is all I can tell you. Ask them. I only met LaCola three or four times, so I don't know anything that goes on inside." He paused for a few seconds. "But that is not what this is about, is it?"

It was the tall man in the front that replied. "Look, we will ask the questions. We know about you, and we know about your little software business at the union. We don't care about that, but we need to know who your partners are regarding the business on the seventh floor. Who else besides you and Goldin know how this works? What kind of deal do you have with your partners?"

"I don't know what you are talking about." He now was visibly shaken and knew that he was in trouble. But he could think of nothing he could say or do. "Look, I may have access to lots of money, but I have no way to get at it. I simply write code. I am just a programmer. I am willing to tell you everything I know, but trust me, no one knows what is going on, especially on the seventh floor. You got it all wrong and I don't know who sent you, but I can't tell you anything. Ask the accountant or Greco. I do not have any partners. I work for Greco and report to Goldin, and that is all I can say. I know nothing."

"Where is the source code kept at Local 4?" The driver now joined the conversation.

"The source code is in a special library on their computer. No one has access to this library. No one knows about this, and the arrangement I have is with the accountant. No one knows how it all works, not even me. I keep telling you, ask the accountant or ask Greco. Even Stanley has been kept in the dark. The seventh floor is off limits to everyone, including me. I have access to lots of things but have no idea what you are looking for. I am just a programmer and write code based on what they tell me to write. I have no idea as to how it is used."

The SUV continued its southward journey to Houston Street, where it made a left turn. It then proceeded to FDR Drive and turned south toward the Brooklyn Bridge. They were in Brooklyn in less than fifteen minutes and the SUV pulled up to an iron-gated yard. The driver flashed his high beams and pushed the button on the visor. In just a few seconds, the gate opened, along with a large overhead door about thirty feet beyond the gate. They drove into a large, open garage where there were two large delivery trucks parked next to one another just beyond the garage door. The young man could barely make out the writing on the side of the trucks: *Brooklyn Meat Processing Company.*

"Are you guys trying to scare me? Okay, you win; I am scared shitless. What do you really want?"

"The truth. Simple, we want to know what you know about the seventh floor and who else knows about what is going on. What do you know about the auditors? Who is your partner? And where you keep the source code for the special programs?"

The young man began to tremble uncontrollably. "Look, guys, I told you everything. I have access to a lot of money. But I am not involved in anything on the seventh floor. They trust me with millions of dollars, but they trust no one concerning the seventh-floor operation. That is the accountant's department. Ask Greco or the accountant."

"We just want to know what you know and who your partners are. Who are your friends?"

The man was visibly shaken as he sat in the back seat of the SUV.

The SUV pulled into the far end of the garage as the automatic door rolled to a close. The driver and the other two men slowly stepped out of the car. There was a bearded man wearing a white plastic bodysuit standing alongside a metal table. The clear plastic face shield was tilted up on top of his head. There was a metal chair next to the table. There were several butcher knives, a saw, and a large spool of wire sitting on the metal table. The chair legs were sitting in four small buckets of hardened concrete.

They opened the passenger side of the back door. The man's face was filled with terror. He was paralyzed and could not move.

"Please step out of the car. We only want to ask you a few more questions, and then we will take you back to wherever you want to go."

The man resisted, but it was of no use. The fear overtook his bodily functions, and his face had a clear expression of plain torture. They reached in and pulled him from the SUV. He could hardly stand on his own as they held him upright and dragged him over to the chair.

"Please sit down," one of the men said.

The man saw the meat-cutting tools on the table and was overcome with terror. He could feel the warmth and wetness of his urine as it slowly and uncontrollably rolled down his pant legs. His mouth was dry, and he fought to draw air into his lungs as he tried to speak. He began to cry and struggled for a few short gasps of air. He muttered a few words that were barely audible.

"No, no, no—please, no!" he begged, as he finally realized what was about to occur.

CHAPTER FIVE

THE SENATOR

APRIL 3, 1992 – ALBANY

S ENATOR VIC SANO WAS A friend of the labor movement in New York State. He was known as the big brother to labor in the New York Senate, and he was well connected to all the union labor leaders. The senator was not a large man by any standard. He stood about five feet, ten inches tall and weighed about 160 pounds. He was muscular, with a strong chest and square shoulders. He was strikingly handsome, with a perfectly squared chin masked by a neat black mustache above thin, neat lips. Even though he was nearing sixty years of age, he still had a full head of black, wavy hair. He was fond of the ladies, and although had been married for over thirty-five years, he still had a roaming eye.

As a senator and as the president of the New York State Senate, he had his hand in every piece of legislation. He also had money, lots of money. He was the unions' go-to guy in the state Senate, and he always made things happen for their benefit. Sano was also a very successful businessman and was sought after by numerous special-interest groups. The senator was able to engage in a number of special consulting arrangements that were not publicized. He had a special relationship that enabled him to legally collect up to $100,000 a year from a financial-investment company that managed trust funds for several unions. He was the door opener and never had to say one word, since the labor leaders understood the arrangement and knew which money manager they needed to hire to invest the millions of dollars held in their trust funds. The senator also owned a small private telephone company downstate, along with a number of high-end apartments in New York City. The New York newspapers often ran editorials about his business dealings and implied that he was not entirely legitimate, but they could never get any conclusive evidence to support their allegations.

The people loved him; he was the man that brought the pork to their district, and there was no way that they could ever get anyone to mount a serious campaign to vote him out of office. After all, the majority of politicians at both the state and federal level were judged by a different standard. This was common practice in Washington and went all the way up to the oval office. Everyone was on the take, and most of these career politicians and members of their families became quite wealthy either during their term in office or soon after leaving. It was actually about more than money; it was about the power. Once they got a taste of it, they wanted more. It was like a disease that had spread throughout the halls of governing bodies, at all levels. It was the norm in politics—once they got a taste of the power and the money, greed set in and they wanted more.

The process of getting money into the politicians' pockets was actually easy and worked through a series of layered relationships.

The obvious one was, of course, the fundraiser. They were always on the campaign trail and always looking for donors for their reelection campaign fund. The unions had lots of money in their PAC trust accounts, and the politicians felt entitled to that money since they could leverage their position regarding legislative matters related to the interests of the union. The PAC fund was a well, and they felt entitled to quench their thirst with the water from it. Each union had a PAC that collected money for each hour the member worked. The fund, or what was commonly referred to as the PAC fund, was set up with one purpose: to allow the union to direct political contributions to their political friends.

Senator Vic Sano and Sonny Russo were the best of friends and had been meeting at Lombardo's Restaurant in Downtown Albany on a regular basis for many years. They had a special relationship and one that enabled the union to trade money for political favors that benefited the labor movement. For the last two years, they had been collaborating with other state and federal politicians to gain approval for the Hudson Valley Life Science and Technology Center to be developed in downtown Albany along the shoreline of the Hudson River.

The newspapers were always on the Democrats' side and were enablers of the power grab. The truth did not matter. It was always the story that was more important. They were tipped off to the scandals and questionable antics, especially when it came to sex. These topics always made for good reading that sold newspapers. It was the politicians that usually tipped them off, since it worked as a diversion from the real game that they played, which was filling their pockets and their friends' pockets with money. As for their constituents, as long as you continued the flow of pork to your congressional district, then you were going to get reelected. This was the way it was in Albany and in most other state capital cities, and it was exactly the same in Washington, only on a larger scale.

Senator Sano was prohibited from entering into private arrangements with other businesses or companies unless he fully disclosed those arrangements and provided that they were not in conflict with his senatorial duties and responsibilities. Because of his good understanding of the labor movement and the business of government, it made good sense for him to establish consulting arrangements with banks and financial-investment firms that conducted business with the unions. He knew all the labor leaders, and it was common practice for him to serve as the door opener to introduce these companies to the union labor leaders and to assist them in establishing business arrangements. All he did was collect a monthly retainer of anywhere from $5,000–$10,000 from each of these firms to help them gain access to the union fund administrators and union labor leaders. He met with most of the trade unions on a regular basis, and it was simply a matter of him passing out his business card.

He actually didn't even need a business card, nor did he need to show up in the office. Everyone knew that as the president of the New York Senate, he was the man that could influence legislation in their favor. They knew who he was associated with and knew that they would be expected to do business with the companies he was affiliated with. He made the recommendations to the union bosses without ever saying a word. A friendly lunch once or twice a month was all that was necessary. The investment advisors would earn a healthy fee well above their cost for their special consulting arrangement. It was simply a cost of doing business. The scheme worked well, and no one ever got hurt.

The senator also could influence the selection process for large construction projects. Contractors were always very generous to political campaigns. It was a circle of friends that passed influence and money around, and you wanted to be part of it. Everyone in the circle benefited. Contractors could charge more for the project, union workers got jobs, and the union funds grew and could help improve benefits for their members. This was really a great system, and the best part of it was that it was legitimate. The senator was no different than any other politician. He held a position of power and influenced business enterprises. Campaign contributions were a simple and legal kickback scheme that the public accepted. In performing his senatorial duties, he would make public statements that reaffirmed the cause for his constituents. He was not just a senator; he was a respected businessman, an entrepreneur, and he believed in capitalism. More importantly, he was the man that was bringing home the bacon. This was the pork, and the unions, the union workers, the contractors, and the suppliers would all benefit from projects like The Hudson Valley Life Science and Technology Center.

The NYS Laborers' Political Action Committee (PAC) was created in 1987, and their purpose was to provide a voice in the political affairs of the state and the country. There was a six-member committee that represented the regions across the state. The members had been chosen by the international council from various unions across the state. This PAC had become one of the state's most powerful within the state and decided on contributions that would flow money to state politicians and the Laborers Political League in Washington, DC. Coupled with other PAC contributions from other states, this was the entity that controlled the flow of millions of dollars to federal candidates and influenced the election outcome.

Sonny, recognized as a rising star in the labor movement, was expected to be elected to one of the six committee positions and would have a voice in where the political donations would be directed. He would even be able to influence his associates sitting on the board of the Laborers Political League, an organization that yielded power through contributions to national candidates who supported legislative issues that would assist both the unions and their affiliated contractors. And so, the labor unions had the power and money to influence political outcomes in federal, state, county, and local issues, and Sonny was a key player with a powerful voice. Most of the efforts went to promoting construction projects to improve infrastructure, build roads and bridges, and stop anti-labor and right-to-work legislation.

Many other legislative issues were addressed, including support for wage protection, environmental issues, and workers' compensation reform. One of the more important functions was to encourage their members to make their voices heard through get-out-the-vote campaigns, voter-registration drives, and letter-writing campaigns. It was obvious that the unions had a loud voice when unified and gave them the political connections that could be translated into political protection.

The local unions, the district councils, and their relationship with national affiliates not only strengthened but concentrated their forces into many and more effective coalitions and formal programs that gave them power and allowed them to influence political outcomes and projects not just in the state, but all the way to Washington. There were too many involved and too much at stake that would benefit to oppose the Albany waterfront project, and Sonny and Senator Sano were celebrating their successes and looking forward to the groundbreaking to occur on Saturday in downtown Albany.

The senator grabbed a piece of Italian bread from the basket in the center of the table, tore a small piece from the slice, and dipped it into the dish of olive oil. There was also a small dish of anchovies alongside the breadbasket. The waitress had ground some fresh black pepper on top. Lombardo's Italian restaurant was an Albany institution and was known for the hand-painted murals painted on the walls. It had black-and-white tile floors and booths along the walls. Some of the walls and the bar were paneled in dark walnut. Softly lit, it was a warm and comfortable restaurant and served large portions of old- world Italian dishes. The sauce, which was prepared each morning, was fresh and bright red and made the pasta one of the favorite dishes for the locals. Garlic, onion, fresh basil, and some parsley for color were the only ingredients added to flavor the imported Italian tomatoes. Never compromising the quality of the ingredients, the sauce was always consistent. The restaurant had been opened in 1919 and was a favorite luncheon hangout for state workers and members of the New York State Legislature.

Senator Sano looked across the table at Sonny, waved the bread above his dish in Sonny's direction, and said, "When my grandfather got off the boat, the city was run by the Tammany Hall gang. They handed out all the jobs. My grandfather, like most Italian immigrants, could not speak one word of English. His first job was at the docks working as a stevedore in New York City for thirty-three cents an hour. Thirty for him and three for the association. And he didn't get to keep it all. He had to pay for that job, two bucks a month for payola. The Italians were on the bottom of the pecking order. The cops, the politicians were all corrupt. They gave the Irish the fucking St. Patrick's Day parade up Fifth Avenue, but today, they still have a problem with the Italians on Columbus Day. How does that work? Pretty soon, they will be ripping the statue of Columbus down. Italians owe a lot to Fiorella LaGuardia."

The senator stopped momentarily as he took another bite of bread. "You know, before he was elected mayor of New York, he put himself through law school and was the first Italian-American to be elected to Congress. Think about that; this was 1917. When he became mayor in 1933, LaGuardia took on the corruption of Tammany Hall. He campaigned on an anti-corruption platform. Italians understood his message and finally could rally around his cause. He was the underdog. The Tammany thugs intimidated the voters, and they never thought that an Italian could win. However, they learned a very hard lesson."

He paused momentarily. "Good bread. Always liked the bread here." He continued, "Too bad for the Irish back then, because over 350,000 Italian-Americans voted in that election, and those votes made the difference and secured LaGuardia's victory. It was a political revolution, and it was the Italians that began the transformation of New York City. He broke down barriers and helped to give the Italians a voice." He paused again, dipped the piece of bread into the olive oil, and took another bite.

"I love the roasted garlic." He paused momentarily as he continued to chew. "What the fuck is Irish bread?" He paused again as he swallowed. "Can't say I ever had it."

He continued. "Think about this, Sonny; this was in the middle of the Great Depression, at a time when there was no hope. LaGuardia cleaned up the city and brought honesty back to city hall and gave Italians the respect they deserved. Look, Sonny, you might think that the government takes and does not give. But we are in the same boat. The politicians and the unions are paddling—often, it seems, paddling upstream—and although we are moving slowly, we are moving in the same direction. We are one and the same, and we must stick together. It is up to you and me to deliver the jobs to your members. The laborer built the cities, and we lead the way to help the working man get a small piece of the American way."

Sonny was smiling. "Thanks, Vic, and the Italians will once again accomplish something that just a few years ago, many thought impossible."

"Sonny, you are absolutely right. We beat out many other cites, bigger and with more support, and better locations, but we did the impossible, and you were instrumental in getting the New York contractors behind Albany."

"Well, I know of one Italian that was instrumental, and you can count on all of us to help with your next election." Sonny now ripped a piece of bread from the loaf in the basket. He then pointed directly across the table at the senator.

Sonny Russo and Senator Sano had been meeting in one of the back booths at Lombardo's on Madison Avenue in downtown Albany at least once a month. Lombardo's was first opened after the Great War and remained one of the oldest surviving Italian restaurants in the city. Family run, it had had the same menu for the last fifty years. Same food, except for the prices. The chef was now in his eighties but still showed up for work every day at seven in the morning. The food and the service were beginning to slip a little, but it still had a loyal following. They were always very careful to not speak directly about their private business arrangements, even though they felt secure in knowing that the place was not bugged.

Usually, they would talk in code, but today, they seemed to be more at ease with their discussion about union business. The political action fund was the legal mechanism that enabled the union to make political contributions to their political connections, and they both felt comfortable talking about it publicly. It was basically a pass-through mechanism through which they could make contributions to those politicians in return for political favors. The right-to-work bill would come up every couple of years and was a bill that if passed, would enable nonunion contractors to bid on government contracts. It was actually a scam by the politicians to collect money from the unions. The bill would always get killed in committee, but for reasons not publicized, it would be resurrected again every couple of years when the politicians' campaign funds were getting low. It didn't matter if they were Republican or Democrat; they all milked the system in the same way.

"Vic, we are all set for the groundbreaking on Saturday. I think we have the people on our side. And I have planned for a special party at Cafe Italia. Our friend from the city, Sal Barone, is picking up the tab. As you know, the boys from New York wanted to keep a low profile. Some of them will not be coming up. They will host a big event in the city when the time is right. They are being watched, so they have agreed to remain out of the picture for a while, but they will be sending PAC money. I will be making the arrangement with the contractors, and I will send them the amounts once you finalize who we need to bring over for the votes. They know this could not have been accomplished without your efforts, but I will remind them."

Just then, the waitress walked out of the kitchen toward the booth. Marge was in her late seventies and dressed in a white uniform with a small, red apron wrapped around her waist. "Hello, Mr. Vic, Sonny. Would you like me to take your order?"

"Hold on; just a second." The senator held up his right hand to the waitress and very quietly said to Sonny, "I will have the list Saturday." He then brought his hand down and glanced back up to the waitress. "Okay, Marge."

Sonny looked up. "Yeah, Marge, I would like the chicken parm with a side of spaghetti."

Marge looking at Sonny. "Sonny, do you want the chicken or the veal?"

"Chicken please, Marge. "

She turned toward the senator. "And for you, Mr. Vic?"

"How about the cheese ravioli and meatballs. But just one meatball, not two, okay?"

"But you get two." Marge then turned towards Sonny and asked again, "Veal or chicken parm?" She was not writing anything down and would usually take the orders to the kitchen from memory.

"Chicken," snapped Sonny, appearing to be mildly irritated.

Marge turned and began to walk toward the kitchen. After taking five or six steps, she suddenly turned around and looked at Sonny. "Sonny, did you want veal or chicken parm?"

Sonny, now really annoyed, slid from the booth and jumped up on his feet. He began to jump up and down and flapped his arms to mimic a chicken. He shouted, "Bwak, bwak, bwaaak!"

The senator just about fell out of the booth and began to laugh uncontrollably. "I think she finally got the message."

Sonny slid back into the booth. "She is really losing it. How many times did I tell her chicken?"

"What the fuck do you expect? She has only been doing this for the last sixty years. I think she sleeps upstairs. And I don't think I have ever seen her write anything down. I have never been in here without seeing Marge."

Sonny smiled and slid back into the booth. He now appeared more relaxed as he smiled. "Ha, she is really a piece of work. I don't think she knows how to write, but I love her. I sometimes think that I would not know what to do if this place ever shut down. The food is not great, but it's still okay. I just love the place. The sauce is fabulous. It is just like you are going back in time. My father used to bring me here for my birthday when I was a kid. In fact, I think this was the first place I ever ate out in a restaurant. I think I had the ravioli and the meatballs."

The senator asked from across the table, "One or two meatballs?"

Sonny nodded his head but elected to stay with the serious side of the conversation. "I don't remember, but I am sure it was two. Anyway, how much do you think you need? They are pretty big balls."

"Well, how much do you think I need money? I will write it down, and you can deliver it to LaCola."

You could hear the passion in the senator's voice. "I will tell you one thing that is for sure: if the labor movement continues to bring us the vote, then we will make certain that the unions will get the jobs. The fucking right-to-work bill in the Senate will not make it through committee. I guarantee it. The money your people provide will make a difference, and this is for certain: I will continue to fight for labor and the unions. I am a Democrat, and you are a Democrat, and the Democratic Party has been there in the past, and we will be there in the future. The labor movement brought trust in the system to enable our party to make politics work."

Sonny smiled and looked directly across the table at the senator. "Vic, I can deliver the PAC money from the boys in the city. I can deliver the $50K now from my local this year and more as the project starts to gain traction. I think you should get at least $300,000, maybe $400,000 from the unions alone, and as for the contractors, when you add it all up, I think you should see the numbers go well beyond a million. Just kill that right-to-work bill before we start digging."

Sano replied, "We may need to bend the rules a little bit, and sometimes it costs a few dollars, but this is the way it works. This is the way it has always worked. By the way, I don't think we need to talk about the money managers. The boys out of Hartford are good investment advisors, and that's all I have to say about it."

Sonny smiled across the table at the senator and replied, "You're right; we do not need to discuss that. The other trades all go along with our union."

The senator broke another piece of bread and dipped it into the olive oil. It had roasted garlic, freshly ground black pepper, and a sprinkling of crushed red pepper. The senator sprinkled some Italian cheese from a little bottle on the table. He was really enjoying it.

"Besides, they are making you money, correct?" he asked.

Sonny was not about to argue and was loyal to the investment firm that the senator was associated with. "You know I would never change our relationship with the investment managers."

The senator shook the small bottle of cheese but none came out. "These fucking cheese bottles never work. The holes are too small. I wish they would just bring a small dish of cheese." He finally lost his patience and unscrewed the top and poured cheese into the bread dish.

Sonny nodded his head in agreement. "Don't worry about anything. I make all the decisions. And besides, the trustees all go along with my vote. We pay the contractors association five cents for every hour from the contractors reports, and they like the little kick we give them. The contractors are on our side as well. They know where their bread is buttered."

Sano replied, "I know, Sonny, and I am loyal to you as well. I think you know that. When you meet with our people next week, hopefully we will have the budget for our campaign all worked out for you." The senator paused momentarily. "Hey, Sonny, how is your golf game?"

Sonny was in a good mood and was happy that the new project would be started in Albany. He was still on track to talk about the project. "Vic, this is the biggest deal we have ever made and will be the biggest deal ever for Albany and for our union. Bigger than the South Mall. The other trades will all go along, and we have discussed the amount of contributions from the PAC funds. Everyone is cool. There is plenty of money in our PAC fund, even some for the mayor and the governor. I think you can count on plenty from our friends in New York."

Sonny continued. "As for my golf, pretty good. I got a new driver. It is the Big Bertha, and I am hitting the crap out of it."

The senator leaned toward Sonny and whispered, "I know this project will be great for the economy and will reach well beyond the capital district. Your friends in the city will make lots of money, and I expect will be very generous."

Sonny was listening intently to the senator. There were only two other tables with diners sitting at them, but they were near the back of the restaurant and too far away for their conversation to be overheard. Nevertheless, he leaned forward as he spoke.

"The New York City unions will go along, and they are excited about the jobs that go with it. The project promises hundreds of jobs—no, thousands of jobs—for them, so they understand what is at stake. I have already spoken to the contractors that have been selected. They are with us. Our friends in New York get it."

"Good, good." The senator nodded in agreement, leaned back, and, now that his right hand was free from the breadbasket, raised his right hand with his thumb pointing to the ceiling. He smiled from ear to ear, with his bright-white teeth on display. "We have the contracts all finalized, and as you know, they are cost-plus contracts."

"Well, I can tell you this: the boys in New York understand, and they are very happy how this is turning out. Me too." The senator nodded as Sonny continued. "We had a meeting, and the trustees in the union that vote know exactly who butters their bread. No, actually, the kind of olive oil that piece of bread in your plate is dipped in. You can count on all of us."

The senator smiled. "You are right; extra-virgin olive oil goes much better with this bread. Extra-virgin Italian olive oil."

Just then, Marge walked over with two large platters of food. She waved the dish of ravioli in front of Sonny and was about to set it down but then hesitated for a moment as she realized that she was about to make a mistake. She turned toward the senator and set the dish of ravioli in front of him. There were two meatballs sitting on top of the ravioli. The senator shook his head. She then placed the platter of parmigiana in front of Sonny. Sonny looked down at the dish before him and realized that it was not what he had ordered. It was veal, not chicken. He looked up and smiled at the senator as Marge walked back into the kitchen. Both Sonny and the senator began to laugh hysterically.

CHAPTER SIX

BREAKING GROUND

APRIL 7, 1992—ALBANY

S PRING HAD ARRIVED IN UPSTATE New York and the ground was thawing out, allowing the bulldozers and backhoes to begin digging. Although winter was not quite done, the weather was perfect for a spring picnic. Just to the rear of the tent was a big banner hanging from the Dunn Memorial Bridge; emblazoned across the front were the words: "The Hudson Valley Life Science and Technology Center, Thanks, Senator Sano." On the lower right-hand corner, it read, "Friends of the Labor Movement, Laborers Local 290 AFL-CIO."

Nestled between the Hudson River and the Empire State South Mall in downtown Albany, the project was expected to create thousands of new construction jobs over the next seven to eight years and provide a major boost to a very poor and deteriorating neighborhood in a deteriorating city. The project would create a flow of hundreds of millions of dollars through the trade unions. It would have far-reaching consequences for the contractors throughout New York and the surrounding states. The tradesmen would be drawn from many of the trade unions near and far, especially from New York City.

Sonny Russo turned to Chris, who was standing next to him. "Chris, do you understand how important this project is to our union and the unions in New York City? This project means union jobs and lots of money for not just the unions but for all the union contractors. Especially for the boys in New York. We all have invested millions of dollars to make this happen, and our future is riding on this project. My family and yours will benefit greatly and especially the families of the members in our union. I trust you, and as a friend, I want you to know how important this project is to all of us. I spoke to Paul Goldin and he tells me that he is bringing you into the city and setting you up with Local 4. Just a word to the wise—be careful and do exactly what Paul Goldin tells you to do. He put this together and will protect you as long as you remain loyal. You are good at what you do, and I know you can get the job done. I just want to tell you that we cannot put this project in jeopardy. They need new software, and it has to work for them. They do things a little differently down there. We are almost to the finish line, and Goldin will introduce you to some very influential people. Be careful and listen to him. There are some very serious people involved, and when millions of dollars are at stake, they play hardball. That is all I can tell you for now. It is not a game of checkers. It is more like chess; understand?"

Chris groped for the right words. "I know; I know, and I appreciate your friendship. I will not let you down."

Sonny continued. "The concrete and cement work alone is expected to eclipse over $2 billion, with close to $1 billion in labor flowing directly through the trade unions."

Chris's expression was one of surprise. "Wow, that is a lot of money, and I know there is a lot at stake."

Sonny went on. "You should also know that we have friends at the Capitol, and Senator Sano is very involved. New York State is not a right-to-work state, so the project would be developed using union workers. I think you get the picture. This is bigger than the South Mall project. And remember, I have vouched for you, so do not let me down. You need to do it correctly the first time, since there are no do-overs. No second chances to make up for any mistakes."

Empire State Mall was the office complex that was completed in 1976 at a cost of over $2 billion. It took eleven years to complete and was championed by then-governor of New York Nelson Rockefeller. It provided New York State government offices to over ten thousand state workers. This tech-center project was estimated to be two to three times bigger than that project had been.

The Parker Dunn Memorial Bridge, just to the south of the project, opened in 1933 and was the only toll-free bridge across the Hudson River between New York City and Troy. It was a stretch of just over 150 miles. It was named in honor of Parker F. Dunn (1890–1918), a long-forgotten by most Albany World War I hero and recipient of the Congressional Medal of Honor. The new Life Science Tech Center would be sandwiched between the Dunn Memorial Bridge and the South Mall.

Senator Vic Sano was very influential within the Democratic party and always came through for his constituents. He had been in office for over twenty years and was the epitome of the established politician, a powerful political boss in his party. He was serving as the president of the New York Senate and everyone wanted to get near him so that they could buy political favors. He did bring money back to his districts; however, it was always at a cost. The politician always received a benefit in the form of a vote or political contribution. This project was going to be a partnership with both public and private participation. All levels of government were involved in the funding, including the city and state as well as the federal government. They all played some role, and all kicked in hundreds of millions of dollars. It had received national attention since the costs were estimated to exceed $4 billion. Some thought closer to $5 billion, since work was to be performed on a cost-plus basis and the actual costs were yet to be determined.

The newspapers and the public were very favorable toward the project. The unions loved it, since it represented hundreds of millions in revenue that would flow through their operations. The senator was instrumental in the promotion of the project and played a leading role in navigating through the approval process. It had been placed on a fast track and the legislative approval and the funding was accomplished in less than eighteen months, despite numerous roadblocks and environmental obstacles it faced. The Democrats were in power, and they were calling the shots. This project was going to go into a predominantly Black neighborhood linking the Hudson River waterfront with the New York State South Mall Plaza. The project promised to restore some needed self-esteem to upstate New York through the creation of a center of excellence and research center for computer technology. There was a microchip-manufacturing component that would add thousands of needed jobs. The State University of New York at Albany was involved, as well as IBM, and microchip companies from China and India. China had sent money and many of their leading scientists to participate. This would be the senator's greatest accomplishment and was well covered by the media on both a state and national stage. He was no fool, and many believed that if this were successful and if he could deliver on his promise of establishing a center equal to Silicon Valley, he would be the next governor of New York.

The senator was all smiles and shook everyone's hand as the attendees marched past the dais, which was set up in the front of the tent. They expected over three thousand to attend the groundbreaking, many self-proclaimed dignitaries from the various unions and local political arena. The governor was not in attendance because he had been scheduled for a governors' conference in Chicago. Clearly this was no accident, since Sano was the leading state politician and was never eager to share the limelight with the governor, who was his political opponent. This was Sano's deal, and he was not about to give any credit to the governor. Everyone knew that the senator had his eye on the governor's mansion on Eagle Street.

The ribbon cutting was to be followed by an invitation-only party at Café Italia. This was the best Italian restaurant in upstate New York. It would be a very expensive affair and would be paid by Barone Construction, the largest cement contractor in the Northeast. The company, headquartered in New York City, had been selected as the general contractor for the waterfront tech-center project, and the party was going to be a no-holds barred affair. Sonny arranged the party and cost was no object since Barone's company would make well over $200 million from the project. It was a big deal if you were invited; it was confirmation that you were a special person and a friend of labor. The tech center was going to be a mixed-use development and would include a retail shopping center, government offices, convention center, high-tech manufacturing research center, theaters, retail shops, and restaurants. Word on the street was that Pauly Romeo, the owner of Café Italia, was going to open an exclusive restaurant next to the Hudson River shoreline within the heart of the retail shopping district. It would be adjacent to the planned theaters and conference center.

Pauly had the connections and had been feeding them for over twenty years. His father, Joe, had opened Café Italia years earlier, and it all began from a small card game in the basement of the building next door. The players would come in at around nine o'clock at night and at midnight, Joe would serve them Italian specialties. At first it was spaghetti and meatballs but eventually grew to include many wonderful dishes of eggplant, veal, ravioli, and seafood. With his five-dollar-per-hand winnings from the card game, Joe did very well. He was eventually able to buy the building next door, which he converted into the best little Italian restaurant in Albany, which he named *Café Italia*. The card game continued for several more years. Every six months or so, the cops would raid the game and shut it down. But, with their political connections, Joe would simply pay a small fine of fifty or sixty dollars, and the game would be back in business the following night. After all, both the mayor and the chief of police were players at the game and regulars at the café, and they needed their café fix at least two or three times a month. After a while, they were finally pressured into shutting the game down for good. They moved the card game to an upstairs apartment over an Italian bakery just across from the third precinct. Café Italia had more than a great reputation, and it was more than a fine Italian restaurant. It was an endearing institution with many loyal and devoted followers.

Pauly was just a short, skinny kid of fourteen when he first started working as a busboy clearing the tables. Twenty years later, he was pushing the needle on the scale to well over three hundred pounds as the head chef. All of the politicians went to the café, and costs did not matter since the lobbyists were the ones picking up the check. Chris had been to the union's Christmas luncheon last year at the café and the final tab was over $5,000. It was a little over the top when you considered there were only thirty-five people at the party. But the labor leaders loved their Italian food, and they loved being treated special whenever they walked into the café. They were, after all, very important people, celebrities of sorts, and they expected to be treated with respect and treated to the very best Italian food.

All the contractors, vendors, and suppliers who did business with the unions were expected to be at the ribbon cutting. However, not all were invited to the luncheon.

The tech-center project was almost totally funded through public grants and bonds amounting to over $3 billion. The state's contribution was well in excess of $1 billion. Combined with the federal contribution of another half a billion and the fact that this was only the first phase, the unions were expected to reap hundreds of millions of dollars in construction projects in the adjoining neighborhoods over the next several years. This was going to put thousands of union tradesmen on the job for many years and make millions for the contractors. It was no coincidence that before it hit the papers, there was not even a whisper of the project, when most of the run-down buildings were sold to a few fortunate investors. Timing was perfect for the lucky few, because real-estate prices would triple once the project was brought to into the public limelight. It was just a coincidence that many of the relatives of the politicians and friends of labor were lucky enough to buy some of the properties. One of the companies that purchased entire neighborhoods was CK consultants."

Sonny was careful not to upstage the senator as they approached one another. He offered a customary Sicilian embrace, a kiss to each cheek, and said, "Good afternoon, Senator, and congratulations. This is a great day for New York and a great day for labor." Sonny didn't want to let go of Senator Vic Sano's right hand.

"Thanks, Sonny. We all have worked very hard, and I, of course, appreciate your support. You are truly a great friend."

Just then, Pauly Romeo, wearing a black chef's jacket, pushed through a group of coat and ties with hard hats and rushed forward to Sonny and the senator. He worked his way to the front of the line of dignitaries and immediately embraced Sonny and the senator in a Sicilian fashion—with open arms accompanied by a warm greeting. It was the invitation for you to show a sign of respect. You would then open your arms and reach forward to embrace one another in a manly hug and then project your head forward with a slight bump of your right cheeks with a small pucker of the lips.

That pucker was meant as a kiss and the true sign of respect. This was then followed by a cheek to cheek on the other side. The Italians always performed this greeting on both cheeks. You never would see a real Italian man plant a real kiss on another man unless it was a permanent goodbye kiss.

"When do you want me to fire things up in the kitchen?" Pauly asked as he faced Sonny.

Sonny answered quickly. "Well, we should be there about two o'clock. Probably service in about an hour after the good Senator arrives."

"Okay. I will see you later, Senator. Sonny, congrats; we have a great dinner planned."

Sonny and Chris had been given special badges that allowed them entry into the VIP area. The black chef's jacket was Pauly's badge to the event, and besides, the cops standing guard around the VIP area all knew Pauly. The white picket fence surrounded a grassy area that held close to three hundred white folding chairs. For the occasion, over one hundred pallets of sod were brought in and laid over a section of Dungan Avenue between the Interstate and Green Street. At the front, there was a broad gold ribbon spread between two large faux concrete columns. Behind the ribbon were two brand-new cranes with their outstretched booms reaching upwards of 120 feet. Several other pieces of heavy equipment sat behind, all lined up like neat little tin soldiers. At the top of the outstretched cranes was a huge banner stretching at least forty feet that read, "Hudson Valley Life Science and Tech Center."

Chris felt pretty good; he was with all the contractors, the union bosses, the money guys, and the politicians. There were another two thousand on the other side of the picket fence in attendance, along with all the local and national TV crews. It was those on the outside looking in to see who was on the inside. Today, Chris was on the inside of the white fence. He had the connections, and he was going somewhere. Not just in Albany, but now New York City, and who knew, maybe national. He also was invited to the lunch at the café, and he knew this was going to be a sign that he was considered a real friend to labor.

The three of them turned as they noticed the mayor approaching them. The mayor was grinning and shaking every one's hand. "What the fuck does the mayor think he is doing? He is acting like it is his party, he is going to have a sore hand before the day is through," said Sonny.

Senator Sano replied, "Well, he is running for re-election and needs to get a little mileage out of this. The state had to cut a deal with him on taxes, and this project is going to drive some of the section-eight housing uptown. I don't think we could have pulled this off without him. He is good at what he does, but you know, they got a black council person running against him this year, and he is worried. And besides, she is a woman. He needs at least 50 percent of the black vote. The city has become a shithole these last twenty years, and we need to clean the place up. The project will provide lots of jobs for many years to come."

Sonny said, "Well, Albany needs jobs just like every other city in the country. Shit, the city was lucky to pull this off. After all, Albany is the capital of the great state of New York." He smirked and laughed softly. "The great state of New York. If they only knew."

Sonny looked back at Chris. "My laborers are going to work, and the size of our union should at least double over the next five to ten years. I can tell you that." A broad smile crossed his face. "Organized labor is very happy."

Sonny took one step forward and reached out to shake the hand of the mayor but directed his words to Chris. "Luck has nothing to do with it. Every city wants the jobs, and most cities want some of that federal infrastructure money, but most cannot figure out how to get it. We had to redefine the meaning of infrastructure, if you know what I mean." He then gave his attention to the approaching mayor. "Congratulations, Mayor. The day is finally here, thanks to you."

The mayor was now standing next to Sonny. He leaned forward and whispered into Sonny's ear, careful not to allow anyone close by to overhear his comments. "Hey, Sonny, a message for our friends. The selling price for the city-owned properties is settled. We spoke to the appraisers, and they understand. I think this should turn out to be very profitable for all the investors. Especially those involved in the parking garage."

Chis overheard what the mayor had said to Sonny and wondered what was meant by the words "profitable for all the investors." He knew a number of properties had been sold to an investor group. He suspected that the pricing had been rigged and that once the project was approved, the real-estate values would jump significantly.

The senator stood alongside Sonny and, not paying too much attention to the mayor, and turned and said, "Mayor, my committee will take up the tax-credit issue we discussed at the next session, so hang in there."

Then the senator's attention turned toward the attractive brunette walking toward them. Sonny leaned over and spoke softly to the mayor. "We all appreciate your help, and we are all behind you, but you realize that we will need your continued support for the old section-eight housing projects. We need to know that the rehab contracts will be awarded to the right people. Our friends in New York appreciate your consideration, and I know that you will appreciate their support this coming November."

Sonny continued. "Oh, Ernesto LaCola from New York sends his regards. He had some business in the city and could not attend, but he will send his appreciation."

"Thanks, Sonny, and be sure to thank Mr. LaCola. I appreciate his efforts and the investment the union is making. I hear that they will be taking a piece of the private equity loan. Also look forward to his continued support in November."

"Hey, guys, excuse me." The approaching brunette stopped in front of them. "They are about ready to begin, and they need the senator to come up to the stage since he is the first speaker."

The senator immediately turned and began to walk toward the dais. "See you guys later at the café."

Jackie was the long-time secretary to the senator and now had a cushy job as a deputy commissioner with the state labor board. She had worked for the senator for over twenty years, but everyone knew that Jackie was also the senator's longtime girlfriend. She was somewhere in her mid-forties but still had the girlish figure of a twenty-five-year-old. She had deep-brown eyes that blended perfectly with her wrinkle-free complexion. Even though she had never married, she would have been the perfect trophy wife for any member of the rich and famous. Always at the senator's side, she was smart and was the perfect assistant—the perfect "Girl Friday" and if the senator needed a pen, handkerchief, or bottle of water, she was there. Today, she wore a pleated bright-red dress that curved tightly around her midsection and buttocks. From there, it flowed loosely out to about eight inches above her knees. When she turned quickly, the dress's pleats would twirl the skirt upward, opening up like an umbrella to provide more complete exposure of her perfectly shaped thighs.

Chris was somewhat disappointed that she did not acknowledge his existence. As she walked back toward the dais with the senator at her side, he could only think of one word to describe her: "perfect."

As the senator approached the microphone, the crowd began to cheer. He smiled and took in all the acclamation, but it was less than a minute when the crowd suddenly took on an eerie calm as the senator's words began to blare out from the sound system.

"Good afternoon, ladies and gentlemen. Hello, citizens and friends of Albany. Hello, New York. My name is Vic Sano, your senator, and I am the president of the New York Senate. I am also co-chair of the Albany County Economic Development Council and the chairman of the Hudson Valley Life Science and Tech Center planning committee. I am very excited to be here today and privileged to introduce some of the people who have worked diligently these last several months to bring this project to reality. Today marks the beginning of a new era for the city. This project is the future for not just the great city of Albany; it represents the birth of a new era for the entire Hudson Valley region and upstate New York. Technology is the key to our future." He was forced to pause for a few seconds as the crowd erupted in applause. "We will all have a hand in its success for many years to come. And we owe it to the efforts of many individuals who are here with us today."

Sonny nudged Chris with his elbow to gain his attention. "He is something and never one to disappoint. When you put a microphone and two people in front of him, he is right in his comfort zone. Isn't he a devilish charmer? But as soon as he gets through the introductions, let's get the hell out of here. I have heard all the same bullshit many times before. We need to get over to the café and make sure that Pauly has gotten everything under control. Italian food is more important than listening to this crap."

Chris was still listening to the senator. "You're right; he is never one to disappoint."

The sun began to beat down on the attendees, and Chris could see that small beads of perspiration were beginning to form on Sonny's forehead. He had been told earlier that at some point, the senator would acknowledge Sonny's presence, so they would have to wait it out until the senator had mentioned Sonny and the union's involvement. "Hold on; we need to wait until he is finished speaking," Chris said.

The introductions continued for another ten minutes and then followed with a short political message about the upcoming election and the need for campaign contributions. He began to close with a big smile and a wave of his right hand, which he immediately pointed toward Sonny.

"Ladies and gentlemen, finally, I would like to take this opportunity and again thank all of the people of Albany for their support, especially a man who has dedicated himself to the working man. A man who serves the city and the state through job creation. Sonny, please stand. I would like to recognize Sonny Russo, business agent for Laborers Local 290 and who is also a soon-to-be trustee of the New York Council of the Laborers International Union. Thank you, Sonny. For those of you who do not know, Sonny has been a driving force on this project and has worked tirelessly for the last two years to make it a reality. He brings jobs to Albany and to New York, and this project will propel the Albany economy to soaring new heights. Thank you, Sonny, for your dedication to the working man." He clapped and nodded his head. "Sonny Russo, thank you."

The crowd began to clap, and quite a few cheers came from the Local 290 contingency in attendance on the other side of the picket fence. They all wore white construction hard hats with the number *290* emblazoned across the front.

Sonny stood, nodded his head to the senator, and turned toward the crowd. He waved his right hand and then quickly sat back down.

The senator continued for another few minutes before he made his closing remarks.

Sonny leaned over toward Chris and said in a low whisper, "Now we can get the hell out of here. I am hungry. I have not been to the café in a couple of days, and I am getting withdrawal symptoms."

Chris smiled in agreement. Sonny and Chris stood and walked over to the gray Lincoln Town Car, which was parked next to one of the cranes.

CHAPTER SEVEN

BREAKING BREAD
AT CAFÉ ITALIA

APRIL 7, 1992 – ALBANY

PAULY **R**OMEO **WAS THE OLDEST** brother of the Romeo clan. He was the owner and chef of Café Italia, a small family run Italian restaurant just twenty blocks west of the state capitol on Central Avenue. Café Italia was considered by many as the best Italian restaurant not only in Albany, but in upstate New York. It not only had great food and impeccable service; it was also the place to go and be seen and to make business connections. It was the most favored restaurant of many of the New York state politicians. It was also the place where lobbyists would take the politicians to trade political favors. Many dishes were named after the senators and assemblymen that came in during the legislative sessions. Senator Sano had a special dish that he always ordered, which was sautéed veal and eggplant served on a bed of escarole in a white wine, garlic, and butter sauce. It was called veal antica and was seldom found on the menu of other Italian restaurants.

The café not only served excellent Italian food; it had New York City prices to go along with it, but few complained. It was the place to entertain your clients if you wanted to impress them. It was a place not just to eat but to be seen and make deals. When you went to the café, you thought you were in an Italian restaurant in the old country. It was a small, dimly lit restaurant with only fourteen tables. White tablecloths were draped over each table with a tall, thin glass centered on each. Three fake flowers protruded from each of the glasses. Along the back wall was a raised stage area with a long table stretched in front it. The table was larger than all the others and could seat ten to twelve diners. This was the special table where all the special politicians and VIP customers dined. This is where all the deep, dark secrets of union business were conducted, and if you got to sit at the table with those guys, then you knew you had achieved a special stature. Café Italia enjoyed most of the union dining business. It hosted the special parties, the birthday parties, the Christmas parties, and, of course, the special luncheons that the unions would sponsor.

Today, it would host a special party to celebrate the Hudson Valley Tech Center's ribbon-cutting ceremony. Most of the time, the union bosses and politicians never paid for anything. It was the lobbyists and vendors who picked up the tab, so the cost was never a consideration.

It was just fifteen minutes past two and the union leaders, trustees, fund managers, and special guests were starting to arrive. Today for the party, they had arranged the six-top tables to form long table rows that each could seat sixteen to eighteen guests. There were two rows that ran front to back along each side of the dining area. It appeared that there was seating for about forty-five guests. The table on the dais, the VIP table against the rear wall, could seat ten. Sonny, the senator, and the mayor would be sitting at the special back table, along with a few of the union officials from the international organization. They also had two bank presidents and the BA from Bricklayers Union Local 24 from Long Island seated at the special table. Sal Barone was the hosting contractor and was paying for the entire affair but was unable to attend because his daughter was getting married the following weekend. He had the most to gain since his company had been awarded the biggest contract. Barone controlled all the concrete business in the greater New York area and had business in every state east of the Mississippi.

At the entrance, there was a small four-top table covered with a black linen tablecloth that greeted guests as they entered. There was a bottle of champagne in a bowl with crushed ice, and another bowl held four or five dozen cigars. A small sign read, "Welcome, friends of labor." Another smaller bowl contained dozens of matchbooks to go along with the cigars. On their covers, bright-blue printing read, "Laborers Local 290. Thank you, Sonny Russo." Sonny did not miss a trick and saw to even the smallest detail. Of course, there was another election coming up next spring. Great way to invest pennies and turn them into hundred-dollar bills.

Each of the long tables were draped with snow-white linen tablecloths with a small vase at each end that held three freshly cut flowers: one green, one white, and the third red, signifying the colors of the Italian flag. Each setting had a black linen napkin rolled up loosely that pointed upward. There were wine glasses, water glasses, plates, silverware, and dishes of varying sizes at each setting. It reminded Chris of a small, private wedding reception. Music flowed ever so softly from the tape player. Dean Martin sang "Volare" in Italian.

There were no menus or place cards, other than one small card on the back table that read, "Reserved."

Sonny and Chris walked toward the back, and Sonny pointed to the far table to the right next to the stage. He said, "Chris, why don't you sit here? This is the best table, next to the back table. Charlie and John from 290 will be sitting along this side with some of the boys from the city." Sonny took one step up, grabbed a wine glass from the back table, and poured some white wine into it.

"I will need to sit up there." He pointed to the VIP table along the back. "I am expected to say a few words before we eat, but I am waiting for Vic before we sit down."

There were two bottles of red wine and two bottles of white wine at the ends of each table. Chris noticed the label on the white wine, which read "Santa Margherita." Chris was not surprised. He knew he would not be sitting at the head table with the big shots and was overjoyed that he had been invited. His table was just in front of the VIP table, and in some ways, he thought, the farther back you sit, the higher the importance. Most of the attendees were Italian, and the more wine that flowed, the louder the conversations became. There was another dinner reception that would follow for those who did not make the Café Italia cut. This dinner was at a cost of $250 a plate, and naturally, a portion of the fee would be allocated to the re-election campaigns for the senator and the mayor. That event would be a much larger affair and would be held at the downtown Hilton to accommodate 350 invited guests. But the café was the dinner party to beat all other dinner parties.

Sonny was near the door when the senator walked in with the mayor. When Senator Sano walked into a room, people could feel the electricity. It was as if he was supercharged. They all were smiling, and Sonny politely went over and gave each of them a big hug. They all beamed with excitement as Sonny reached down and grabbed a few cigars and handed them each one. "Congratulations, and thank you for your support of labor."

It was now 2:45, and Sonny walked Senator Sano over to the back table. They stepped up and sat down next to one another.

From the small alcove where the servers would retrieve the food from the kitchen, Mikey was standing and could see that the room was nearly full, and the senator had finally arrived. He turned and went into the kitchen. Mikey was the youngest family member and had started to bus tables when he was a boy of thirteen. He had grown up and was now married with two children. Pauly was his older brother and the head chef. He was assisted in the kitchen by Marie Perri and two line cooks who did exactly what Pauly and Marie instructed them to do. Marie had come over from Italy years before and was, in her own right, an outstanding chef. No questions asked, since the quality of the food was a ritual that was always adhered to. No one in the kitchen had ever been formally trained, yet the product that came out of that kitchen was from old-world recipes handed down through many generations of Sicilian families. There were no other Italian restaurants in Albany that could come close to the quality of the food or the level of service. Every dish served had the best ingredients prepared with uncompromised fundamentals of cooking. Joe Romeo had passed away many years earlier; however, his legacy would remain untarnished.

Finally, Sonny and the senator took their seats at the VIP table, and the other attendees knew it was time for the party to begin. It was Sonny who finally stood and tapped his glass with a spoon.

"Welcome! This is supposed to be a celebration. Where is Maria, Jimmy, Mikey? So where is all this fancy food? The bread is great, but when do we start to see some real Italian food? Before we do, allow me to say a few words. I am not going to be the one between you and this wonderful meal that Pauly and Marie have prepared, so it will only be a brief announcement. We heard all the speeches at the groundbreaking, and we recognized all the dignitaries who attended. I would, however, be remiss if I did not say a special thank you to all who have been instrumental in pushing the vision of this project to a reality. There have been millions of dollars provided from both public and private organizations, and those in attendance today are true friends of labor. There are two people who deserve special thanks: Senator Vic Sano, who is the president of the New York Senate; and the Honorable Marty O'Brian, mayor of the great city of Albany. Thank you both for your hard work and commitment. Two great Italians who are true friends—" Laughter drowned out Sonny's words.

"Oh, excuse me; I didn't know that the good senator was Irish."

Again, the room erupted with even louder laughter.

"Anyway, let's all stand and please raise our glasses to two true friends of labor who know how to create jobs, strengthen our economy, and help to make this great city even greater." He paused, raised his glass, and said deliberately, "*Salud!*" Several glasses clinked together, and several in the group shouted along with Sonny. "*Salud!*"

"Before I sit down, I would like Father Anthony Sidoti, formerly with Saint Anthony's Catholic Church, to provide a blessing," He looked toward the front of the restaurant and pointed. "Father."

At the end of the table closest to the door, a gray-haired man in a worn, tattered, wide-lapeled black suit stood. "Thank you, Sonny."

He was in his nineties and rocked slightly; he appeared very frail. He had a cane in his left hand and used it to steady his footing. "Lord, we thank you for blessing this great city and ask that you bless this project and continue to provide your blessings to those of us here today to share in this wonderful occasion. We also wish to thank you for the food that is about to be served, and thank you for the hands that have lovingly prepared this food. In the name of the Father, Son, and Holy Ghost, amen."

His delivery was crisp and clear and conveyed a great strength that contrasted with his fragile and worn appearance.

The timing was perfect because just as the old priest had completed his blessing, Maria, Mikey, Jimmy, and two other waiters marched out, each carrying two large platters of appetizers. They carefully placed them on each end of the long tables. Sonny had influence in Albany, and it was obvious he was putting on a show to impress the trustees from the International Laborers Council in New York City.

The waiters returned to the kitchen, and the ritual of bringing out platters of food was repeated two more times. Chis looked down and could not believe how wonderful the food looked. There were three platters at each end of the long tables. The platter placed nearest to him had at least three to four dozen clams casino. They were roasted little neck clams on the half shell stuffed with breadcrumbs, roasted red peppers, and bacon. He could not resist and moved three clams to his plate. There were two other platters, one full of rolled eggplant stuffed with mozzarella and ricotta cheese and topped with a rich red sauce prepared with plum tomatoes, garlic, and emulsified anchovies. The third platter was a deep bowl filled with escarole and fresh cannelloni beans. There were four or five dishes of freshly ground Parmigiano-Reggiano cheese.

The senator leaned over to Sonny and whispered in his ear. "Sonny, we need to discuss the money that is needed for the committee members. We have to raise at least $400,000, maybe $500,000, just for them. You will need to talk to your boys in New York."

Sonny nodded. "Do you have the names?"

"Yes. Here is the list of the committee members on our side who will vote in our favor against the bill. This is a done deal. Deliver this list to your people at the union in New York."

The senator directed his words to Sonny as he reached into his pocket and handed over a folded piece paper. Sonny unfolded it and glanced at the list of names with the numbers beside them. He only looked at it for a few seconds before he folded it up and put it in his pocket. "Okay, that is what I need. And just so you know, I am sending Chris down with it next week to give to the boys at the union. We can count on Chris; he is an old and trusted friend."

The room, which had been full of several muffled conversations mixed with laughter, suddenly became subdued, and the chatter was replaced by the clicking of knives and forks as everyone began to pass the platters around the tables.

The senator nodded in agreement. "Good, you know how to handle it. Good."

As most guests focused on the plate sitting before them, the senator casually leaned toward Sonny again and whispered.

"Sonny, we have another problem that you will need to take care of. There are two Albany councilmen who are rocking the boat, and they are making noise about their districts. Clinton Avenue and North Pearl Street. Your people need to pay them a visit and get them back in line. They have met with the mayor and are complaining that the new neighborhood relocation program is unfair. Pay them off or whatever you need to do, because this will delay the start date. They are complaining to the mayor that the shift in the electoral count will hurt their campaign. This is in your hands."

Sonny looked back at the senator. "Vic, we already have talked to them and have made arrangements with the supervisor of elections, and they have agreed to back off. They also have been given a share of the row houses that we are buying. They will receive a handsome return on their investments, and the council is changing the redistricting boundaries."

The senator smiled. "Good, good. You are always one step ahead of me when it comes to this sort of thing. But one other thing—we are ready to pull the trigger on the properties before we announce the new location of the access roads to the pier. If you want to buy in on the buildings, then you need to send money to our connection. The purchase contracts are ready to be signed, and we need to get all the partners' shares wrapped up in the shell company. The drop is to our guy from Poughkeepsie."

Once again, the waiters came out of the kitchen, each holding a large platter of shrimp and chunks of lobster. Chris had never seen shrimp so large. The servers marched by each table and offered servings to each guest. As the platters emptied, they would go back into the kitchen and return with the platters loaded up with more shrimp and lobster.

Sonny grinned at the senator. "Okay, I will send it down next week. Where is our guy supposed to be?"

"Your buddy sitting at the next table, Chris, can he be trusted?" The senator was more serious as he questioned Sonny.

"Yes." Sonny turned slightly toward Chris. "He is an old friend, and I trust him completely."

"Good." He hesitated for a brief moment. "Remember, our drop is to the man from Poughkeepsie, and Chris does not need to know anything other than that."

It was now 3:30, and three busboys began removing empty platters. Most of the guests refused to allow any of the platters to return to the kitchen with even the tiniest of morsels or scraps of food remaining. Everything was consumed. After they were cleared, again, the wait staff came out like little soldiers, each carrying two large platters. Chris wondered how such a small kitchen and such a small staff could produce such a lineup of wonderful dishes with such precision. He looked up and smiled at Sonny, who scanned the room. He could see that it was going well, and everyone was very pleased. As before, the platters were placed at the ends of each of the long tables. The first one was fresh mozzarella caprese, comprised of slices of garden-fresh tomatoes topped with fresh mozzarella cheese, roasted red peppers, and sharp provolone cheese. Freshly sliced basil, extra virgin olive oil, and a drizzle of balsamic glaze completed the presentation. The second platter was a chopped lettuce salad with homemade balsamic vinegar and gorgonzola cheese topping; it wasn't impressive to look at until you tasted it. One would wonder how two simple ingredients, when combined, could contain such a wonderful and complex taste.

As the dinner progressed, the busboys scanned the tables and continued to replenish the tables with fresh loaves of bread from

Perreca's Bakery in Schenectady. Each table had three or four dishes of Sicilian olive oil with sprinkles of crushed red pepper, ground black pepper, and cheese. There was a large bowl of Sicilian olives and provolone cheese on each table, which kept the attention of the busboys as they ran back and forth from the kitchen to keep them replenished.

Things began to slow down as everyone consumed all the wonderful food placed before them, and the chatter once again erupted with jokes and stories. They knew that pasta would be next, and many pushed aside the half-eaten salad since this was an opportune moment to give their stomachs a rest and clear their pallets. Once again, all eyes were pointed toward the kitchen entryway as the procession of waiters entered with large platters of food. Each platter had different shapes of pasta layered with different sauces. Their eyes bulged as they witnessed the different shapes and colors. They were aware that the main feature would follow, but for most of the guests, macaroni was something they had been accustomed to from the many Sunday dinners that their Italian mothers had served. It started with two large platters of rigatoni topped with a fresh-tomato Bolognese sauce, and the second was fettuccine alfredo.

There was a third pasta dish that was called The Dugan, named after Assemblywoman Dugan, who was a frequent patron of the café. This had become a featured dish at the café and was quite popular. It was angel-hair pasta with fresh shrimp, lobster meat, and spinach in a rich white-wine and butter sauce. This was Chris's favorite and had captured all of his attention. Just when he thought it was done, another platter arrived before him. It was The Seminerio, a dish named after Assemblyman Anthony Seminerio, who had served for many years in the New York Assembly. It was broccoli, large chunks of shrimp, and fusilli pasta in a white-wine and butter sauce. The assemblyman was first elected to the assembly in 1978 and built a persona as a streetwise, tough-on-crime, conservative

Democrat, opposing abortion rights, favoring the death penalty, and making high endorsements of Republicans like Rudy Giuliani and George Pataki. He was a VIP customer and could be seen at the café two or three times a week when the assembly was in session. He sat at the end of the VIP table, occupying the last seat alongside another Democratic assemblyman.

Senator Sano reached for the dish of grated Italian cheese as he leaned over to Sonny. "See, the cheese is in a dish and not in those little pesky jars with the little holes on top." He then spooned some cheese on his pasta.

Two hours into the feast, many became aware that they were nearing the main course. It was now 4:30, and once again, the wait staff marched out with more food. This time, there were three different entrees. The first platter was veal antica, and Chris recognized it immediately: veal medallions sandwiched with eggplant, seasoned in an egg-cheese batter and finished in a lemon, butter, and white-wine sauce. This was layered over sautéed escarole and garlic. The next dish was saltimbocca ala Romana, layered prosciutto, provolone cheese, and sage leaves over a bed of spinach and topped with a creamy sherry-wine and butter sauce.

The third dish was simple, yet delicious, a sautéed grouper poached in a light mariachero sauce, which was a light red broth with plum tomatoes, fresh herbs, capers, garlic, and onion. There were also platters of flounder and shrimp francese, which was fish was coated with a light egg batter and sautéed with lemon, butter, and white wine. Platters adorned with meats and fish were at every table, and smiles adorned every face.

The clock was nearing six when all began to slow down. There was much happiness and cheer in the room. The coffee had been served, and several platters of Italian cookies and cannoli were set on each table. It was now a task to clear the dessert platters, as most had overeaten. They could not help themselves had consumed almost everything that came out of the kitchen, acting as though they had not eaten for weeks.

Sinatra now played from the speakers, and the wine never stopped flowing. Sonny went into the kitchen and walked back out with Pauly and Marie following him, now clad in fresh, clean, white chef's jackets. He walked them into the middle of the dining room. Everyone was smiling, and as they noticed Sonny, the room fell silent. Sonny grabbed a wine glass. This time it was half full of red wine. He raised it above his head.

"Please, please, ladies and gentlemen, I would like you to see the magicians who were in the kitchen and behind this wonderful meal." Maria, Mike, Jimmy, and the other two servers walked out of the kitchen and to the head of the line. "But first, please allow me to introduce the wonderful wait staff. This is Maria Romeo, Mike Romeo, Jimmy Abraham. I think they have been serving you from day one, and the two new servers, Anthony and Nicholas, are on loan from the Italian club on Washington Avenue."

They each bowed to the cheers and clapping, turned, and walked back to the kitchen.

"And now, may I present Pauly Romeo and Marie Perri. Thank you, Pauly and Marie; you certainly have created magic in that little kitchen in the back. Thank you for all that you do, and thank you for this wonderful celebration. Let's hear it for Pauly and Marie and their deceased father, Joe Romeo, the man who had a vision to create the best Italian restaurant in Albany, New York." He raised his glass and shouted, "Café Italia!"

Everyone clapped and shouted.

"Hooray!"

"Great job! Wonderful meal."

Sonny and Senator Sano smiled as they walked around and greeted some of the café regulars who were in attendance. The mayor was following close by but did not get the attention that Sonny and the senator were receiving.

Sonny continued. "Finally, I would just like to express a special thanks to Sal Barone for hosting this wonderful dinner. Sal is in New York and was unable to attend this celebration, but many of you will be seeing him in Albany since he has been selected as the general contractor for the technology center. He sends his best regards. Thank you, Sal."

Finally finished, Sonny once again began to walk around the room to greet everyone individually. Everyone was hugging, shaking hands, congratulating Sonny, and thanking him for such a great meal. Many now lit up their cigars that Sonny had handed out. He did not care about the cost, since this was paid for by Barone.

When he finally came over to Chris, he leaned over and whispered in his ear.

"Hey, I need to see you first thing in the morning. I have something I need you to do for me. Just a small favor." He turned away and then turned back to Chris. "How about the Gateway Diner on Central Avenue, say, nine o'clock tomorrow morning?"

Chris nodded. "Okay, but I won't be eating breakfast."

CHAPTER EIGHT

DELIVERY BOY

SUNDAY MORNING

IT WAS JUST TEN MINUTES to nine when Sonny walked into the Gateway Diner. Chris sat at a booth to the right and waved to Sonny, who walked over and sat down across from him.

"Hey, have you recovered from yesterday?"

"Wow, Sonny, I have to say that that was best meal I ever had. Thank you for the invite and for making me feel special. I know it had to be something like preparing a wedding invitation list. The café is a small place, and I know there were probably at least a hundred people you would have liked to invite."

"Well, Chris, you are a special friend, and I know I can trust you. That is why I am asking you for a favor."

"Sure, you know I would do anything I can for you," replied Chris. "How can I help?"

Sonny leaned slightly forward. "Okay. You are going to be going down to Local 4 this coming week? Right? I need you to deliver something for me."

"Sure, anything to help."

Sonny reached into his suit jacket and pulled out two envelopes, one white and one yellow. The yellow envelope was thick, and Chris thought it looked like it contained money. It was sealed and had a thick rubber band wrapped around it. Sonny looked around and put his hand over it as he placed it on the table. He then pushed it across to Chris.

"I need you to deliver this envelope to someone. I am going to be in Syracuse for a few days, so I thought you could deliver it since you are going to the city tomorrow." He hesitated for a moment. "I need this delivered, and no one needs to know about this. Understand?"

Chris looked across and saw the seriousness on Sonny's face. "Sure, Sonny, anything. I am going down tomorrow morning and will be meeting Goldin at the union offices."

Sonny was quiet at first, and then he smiled. "Great. I need you to deliver a couple of things. This yellow envelope is to be delivered to someone who will meet you at the Hilton. That is where you are staying, correct? Probably tomorrow night, but I am not certain as to the time. He will ask you where you are from, and then he will tell you he is from Poughkeepsie. Understood?"

He hesitated slightly as he looked down at the envelope. "No one must know what is in the envelope. It is critical that you do not lose it. Understand? In fact, forget the entire errand when you complete it."

He finally took his hand off the envelope and continued. "Here. Treat this with much respect, and do not let it out of your sight."

Chris picked up the yellow envelope. "Feels like money. Lots of money, actually."

Sonny answered. "You don't need to know how much, even if it is money. You do not want to know what is in the envelope, but it is good that you think it's money, so that might be a good way of treating it."

The waitress came over and stood waiting for Sonny to order something.

"Black coffee, please?"

Sonny then handed Chris the second envelope. "Paul Goldin likes you and told me that he is introducing you the boys at Local 4. You will meet the BA, Ernesto LaCola, at the union in the next couple of days, and when you do, just give him the white envelope. He is sharp and is expecting it from you. Remember, they run a big operation and a tight ship, but you will do just fine. Paul told me that he is impressed with your software."

Chris picked up the white envelope and placed it his inside pocket of his suit jacket. It could barely fit it into his pocket, since the yellow envelope took up most of the space. He did, however, welcome the feel of the envelopes as they pressed against his chest.

Chris was anxious to make the delivery not thinking about what was in the yellow envelope. He wasn't sure as to whether it was legal, but it did not matter. He just knew that he owed it to Sonny. This was the least he could do for him. They were friends.

"I am going down later Monday morning and expect to meet Paul first thing. I will take care of it." He continued. "If all goes well and I get the okay, I expect to be in the city every week for the next several months. But, about this yellow env—"

Sonny cut him off. "I don't know when you will meet this person or when the handoff is, but it will be at the Hilton. And remember, he is from Poughkeepsie. Oh, and by the way, we are going to have the next trustees' meeting at The Meadows in July, and Paul Goldin will be up from New York. He wants to play some golf after the meeting. He said he expects that you will be fine with Local 4, and once they are up and running, he would introduce you to another union in Long Island." Sonny hesitated slightly and smiled. "The groundbreaking was a lot of fun, especially the lunch at the café. Glad you were able to make it. We expect lots of workers from the city, as well as Syracuse and Utica. That's why I have to go to Syracuse for a few days to work out the reciprocity contracts."

Without touching the fresh cup of coffee that the waitress poured, Sonny stood up. "Look, I have to go to mass, but please understand that the delivery of the envelopes is critically important to the project up here. Don't forget the envelopes."

"Count on me, and consider it done." Chris went on. "Do you want me to call you afterward?"

Sonny leaned over. "No, that is not necessary. I will know when they are delivered. We do not need to discuss this again."

Chris saluted Sonny loosely. "Okay, Sonny. I understand. Never happened."

Sonny turned and walked out of the diner and to his car.

Chris placed a ten-dollar bill on the table and followed. He placed his hand over his breast pocket, as if to prevent the envelopes from jumping out of his pocket. He could feel that the yellow envelope in his jacket was secure. He wondered what this was all about but did not question it. He trusted Sonny, and it was obvious that Sonny trusted him.

CHAPTER NINE

THE INTRODUCTION

THE TRAIN MADE A BRIEF stop at Rhine Cliff, which startled Chris. It brought him back to reality and the gravity of his situation. It was late May and he had gotten into a dangerous situation because of the bad choices he alone had made. He had to accept the fact that he was responsible. He heard the voice from the train man, but then thought about the envelopes.

"Rhine Cliff; next stop, Poughkeepsie."

Chris was thinking about the events that had brought him to this moment. He was unsure of himself and began to think back to the first train ride that day in early April. That was a time when he was eager to meet the union labor leaders.

Yes, April and the introductions. It was a bright spring day back then and Chris was feeling comfortable. The accountant would introduce him to the business agent and the fund administrator at the union and he was certain that he would get the account. Things did not come easy for Chris, and although he was smart, he worked long hours. Nothing he had accomplished was by chance. He knew where he was headed. He finally had the business where he could break out to another level, and Paul Goldin was the link to that next level. He was well prepared to make his sales pitch. He remained excited and eager, since that was the day he would be introduced to the union bigwigs. The meeting would take place at the union's building at 230 Park Avenue South, across from Union Square. This was located just south of Seventeenth Street. Union Square intersected with the lower east side of Manhattan. It was actually a public square in lower Manhattan and was considered to be an important and historic intersection, located where Broadway and the former Bowery Road—now Fourth Avenue—came together in the early nineteenth century. Its name celebrated neither the federal union of the United States nor labor unions, but rather denoted that "here was the union of the two principal thoroughfares of the island."

Coincidentally, it was the scene of many social public demonstrations over the years. In the past, it had been the headquarters for Tammany Hall. But in the eighties and early nineties, it was the mob's playground. Lower Manhattan had a rich and storied crime history laid out from sixty-five years earlier. Yes, there was an Italian influence by mobsters like Lucky Luciano, John Torrio, Frank Costello, and Capone. Although all from Italian heritage, they were Americanized by their criminal associations with many non-Italians like Abe "Kid the Twist" Reles, Hymie "Loud Mouth" Levine, Mike de Pike Heitler, and Harry Guzik. Later, in Chicago, Guzik oversaw the whorehouses for Capone, and his chief collector was Loud Mouth Levine. And so it was that today's union labor leaders of mostly Italian heritage also had their non-Italian moneymen handling their finances. The accountant, Paul Goldin, fit in perfectly.

Chris smiled as he thought about the promises that Paul Goldin had made at the country club. Back then, it was a new experience and seemed so easy. He was confident and looking forward to the meeting and had arrived early. Chris was excited and anxious to meet the people and present his software advantages. All the unions were connected, and it was like a big board game. Selling to them was always a gamble. You rolled the dice in a game of Monopoly and hoped you would pass "Go" so you could collect another two hundred dollars or land on the "Get out of jail free" space. If you could get your hand on the dice or your foot in the door with Local 4, the other unions would all topple over just like a long line of dominoes.

In the old days, the unions watched the money with green-eye-shaded bookkeepers and handwritten ledgers. They then progressed to ledger cards, magnetic striped cards, punch cards, and magnetic tapes. Finally, along came the computer revolution in the seventies and eighties. But specialized software was needed. The computer hardware was simply an empty vessel without its software, and it was the software that would determine the effectiveness of the computer. And so, the computer industry saw the birth of a new business—software—and Chris was lucky to have gotten into it early.

At first, it was a "cottage" industry that was comprised of small mom-and-pop companies, not too different from Bill Gates or Steve Jobs launching their enterprise in a garage—although enjoying a different level of success. Many started out with one or two employees. The early union software programs were not terribly sophisticated and addressed only the accounting functions. The management and reporting within the framework of the early systems were nonexistent. There were early attempts to modify and enhance the programs to accommodate the changing landscape of their environment. But these small software companies provided limited functionality and seldom provided adequate programming and little or no documentation. As a result, modifications were problematic, and the programs became very piecemeal and difficult to maintain. Their systems were experiencing fast-paced changes to the technology.

To keep pace, the unions had undergone several changes to the hardware and software, and with each change, the data had to be reformatted and converted for compatibility with the new software and hardware platforms. The pension system alone had work records for some of the members that went back fifty to sixty years, when the members had first joined the union. The records had to be maintained because when a member retired, all those work records were used to calculate their retirement benefit amount. For many unions, the computer history records were flawed, and their accuracy came into question. This caused disruption in their computer operations and created computer downtime. The users would then need to fall back on their old manual processes and paper records. As a result, there was little or no confidence in the computer systems, and there was even less confidence in the computer programmers.

For the union, the fund accounting operation was the front door and the first step in which the money and hours worked were entered. The dollars had to pass through the process and were allocated into the appropriate bank accounts of each fund. The hours represented the hours worked for each member and were directed to the members' individual trust accounts. The rate file determined how the hours translated into dollars and benefits for each member. The seventh-floor auditors would enter the contractors' reports, which were accompanied by a check. The totals had to balance. The hours were used to calculate the members' accrued benefits earned. For pension, each hour was worth four dollars and worth one credit hour in the member's pension account. When added up, the pension hours determined the years of benefit credits earned and were used to calculate the pension benefit amount at retirement. But when you added the other benefit dollars for the health fund, dues, vacation, savings, legal and political action funds, each hour was worth over $16.25. This amounted to more than $20 million flowing into the local's bank accounts from the contractor reports each month.

The unions began to understand that the computer system was critical to efficient operation. But there was a downside. The computer, with all its positive features, also tracked money, regardless of how or where it went. Union software had to keep track of all those transactions coming in and going out, and all those little transactions had to balance when added and subtracted. In the old days, a missing dollar here or there could be corrected by a simple stroke of the pencil. Or maybe it was the other end of the pencil. The opportunity to drop a few dollars into the pockets of the labor leaders was just too tempting. And besides, who could possibly add up the hundreds of thousands of transactions to balance out with the years of manual recordkeeping? Everything revolved around the money, and more than $200 million in benefit dollars was collected from the contractors every year. The computer had become much more than an adding machine; it was the door to a safe that controlled the flow of millions of dollars from the contractors. There were also many back doors in the safe. The direction and opening and closing of those doorways were controlled by creative accounting methods and creative computer programs. The computer program held the combination of the safe, and the programmer had to know the combination of the safe to control the flow of the money.

Because Chris had been working with several unions for several years, he knew how it was supposed to work. He knew that the rate file held the combination to the lock, but he did not know exactly how it was to work at Local 4. The fund manager and the accountant were the gatekeepers. The bankers held the money, the investment managers invested the money, the accountants counted the money, and the lawyers made sure that they could keep the money. It was a neat little business because there was money flowing in and out every single day and, combined with the investment earnings and holdings in the bank, it was near impossible to tie all the fund balances to the actual money held within each of the bank accounts and the investment accounts at any given point in time. There were too many accounting obstacles and too many transactions with history going back fifty years. The rules were complicated, but Chris knew how his software needed to work.

Goldin had promised Chris that he would set up the meetings and he would introduce him to Nick Greco, who was the fund administrator. He needed to convince Greco that this small computer-software company from Albany could handle the job. Goldin had already tested him when they played golf and wanted to see how he reacted when they kicked the ball or wrote the wrong score down on the card. When they played golf at Chris's club, he was expected to treat the group to golf, as well as cocktails and dinner, which set him back another four hundred. But Chis thought, "It's worth it and just part of doing business with the unions. Next month, I will just bill them another three hours at $150 an hour. Or two hours at the New York rates." That was perfectly acceptable.

He was troubled with the envelopes in his breast pocket but knew it was too late to back out. The yellow envelope was especially troubling to him, and the check he was to give to Greco was even more disturbing. He trusted Sonny and believed that maybe he was not breaking the law. Maybe it was just a little bending. This was the way it was done with the big boys, and he was now playing ball in their ball field. He had graduated from the minor leagues to the majors and convinced himself that this was normal practice in the big city.

The plan was for a short meeting with the fund administrator, followed by lunch. He would learn that although Greco, had total responsibility for the administration of all trust funds and overall management of the computer system, he had little direct interaction with their operations. In fact, computers frightened Greco; he couldn't speak the lingo, nor did he have any ability to discuss the software problems that they were experiencing. He only knew what his staff would tell him and could only do what the staff told him he needed to do. He had a computer terminal sitting on top of his desk, but Greco seldom turned it on. On special occasions, Larry Smith, the operations manager, would light up the screen and show him the money balances in the each of the trust accounts.

Chris brought along several reference letters from his upstate union clients. He was well prepared. If time permitted and based on what they wanted to see, he was prepared to remotely connect to his computer in Albany and show them how the programs worked. He felt good about everything and left little chance for failure. He learned long ago while working for IBM that for every meeting, one must be fully prepared to expect the unexpected. Chris had planned well. Every meeting must have an objective, a purpose. And it was always the same: "Get to the next meeting."

Chris was pleased the first time he first saw the gray stone building when he stepped out of the cab. He remembered the small gold letters on the façade of the building: "230 Park Avenue South."

He walked through revolving glass doors framed in shiny brass. It looked like they had just been polished. There was a narrow lobby with highly polished granite flooring. There was a small booth directly to the left and a counter with newspapers and candy bars. An older Black man was sitting behind the stack of newspapers reading the *New York Post*. Chris noticed the two elevators down the hall to the right. A balding attendant stood guard over the elevator toward the end of the hall. The marble floors reflected the clickity-clack sounds of the men walking in and out, with an occasional squeak from sneakers.

"Floor," was the only word that the elevator operator said as Chris stepped to the side to allow a gray-haired lady of about sixty to enter before him.

"Seven, I think. Local 4 pension fund office."

"Nope. You have to check in at five first. They will come down for you."

As the door opened to the fifth floor, Chris stepped into a dimly lit hallway. A double glass door was directly across the lobby from the elevator. Across the top in bold gold letters were the words, "Local 4 Benefit Administration. International Brotherhood of Laborers AFL-CIO."

Chris attempted to open the door facing him as he walked from the elevator, but the bosomy redhead on the other side sitting behind the marble counter failed to look up to acknowledge him. He then noticed a small button to the left under a small magnetic card reader with a small sign under the button that read, "Visitors." Chris pressed the button and could hear a faint buzzing on the other side of the glass doors, but the redhead still did not look up. After a few moments, she finally looked up, acknowledged Chris with a weak smile, and released the electronic latch that secured the door. He grabbed the handle on the side marked "This Side Please" and politely allowed the gray-haired lady who had accompanied him in the elevator to step out before him and enter. He then followed her into the reception area.

"Hello, Mrs. Scuderi. How is your husband doing?" asked the redhead as she rocked her head upward and finally appeared to show some interest.

The gray-haired lady, smiled broadly and responded in a thick Italian accent. "Tank a-God, he is a-gonna be a-good."

"Where are you going today? Claims?" the receptionist asked.

The older woman replied, "You a-gotta it."

"Go ahead; you know where they are." Finally, she looked Chris squarely in the face. "Yes, how can I help you?"

"I am Chris Vincent, and I have an appointment with Mr. Greco. I believe Mr. Goldin is going to join us."

"Thank you. If you don't mind, please take a seat, and I will check with Mr. Greco's secretary." She once again turned her attention toward the computer terminal.

The lobby was not at all impressive and not what Chris had expected. There was a long U-shaped counter with a green marble top where the redhead guarded entry. It was higher than normal, and from the outside, one could not see what was on counter on the other side. He did, however, notice an IBM computer screen directly to her left side, and this appeared to be what had held her attention away from the front doors. *Click, click, click, click,* went the keyboard as she once again withdrew her attention from the lobby and the visitors and bent her head back down to the computer screen.

On the wall to her back, letters in dark blue surrounding the colorful logo and read, "International Brotherhood of Laborers – Local 4 Benefit Administration Office." Under the logo, which he guessed was about three feet across, there were two more lines of dark blue that were slightly smaller in size than those at the top. They read, "Ernesto LaCola – Business Manager," and then directly on the line beneath read, "Nicola Anthony Greco – Fund Administrator."

The receptionist must have buzzed someone or sent an instant email to Greco's office, because he did not hear her make any calls or notice any other motions. After about ten minutes, from the large mahogany door to the left of the reception counter, a well-groomed woman in a light-blue pantsuit appeared. She had dark-rimmed glasses and her long, black hair was pulled up in a bun. Chris thought she looked Greek or Italian and figured her to be about fifty.

"Hello. My name is Clara, and I am Mr. Greco's secretary. Mr. Goldin is running late, and Mr. Greco asked if you would not mind waiting in the conference room. It is right this way."

"No problem; thank you." Chris grabbed his briefcase and garment bag and stood up. He turned and asked the redhead if he could leave his overnight bag with her in the reception area. She nodded, and he followed Clara as she quickly turned and walked back through the mahogany door.

The conference room was directly to the left of the door where he had entered. There was a good-sized rectangle-shaped conference table surrounded by twelve chairs. In the left corner of the far wall were three flagpoles, with flags hanging from each. The flag in the center was the American flag, and to the left was a slightly lower flagpole with some sort of blue flag attached. He assumed it was the union's flag. The flag to the right was of similar height, and that one he recognized as a New York State flag. He was not surprised to once again see the international union logo emblazoned across the center of the back wall, slightly smaller than the seal on the wall of the reception area. Same color blue.

Chris thought, "This meeting already seems to be getting off to a bad start. It was less than twenty minutes and the first three people I met in the building were cold and unfriendly." He was hoping that this poor reception was not an early indication of how he would be treated by Greco.

After about ten minutes, the conference room door opened, and two men walked in—Paul Goldin and another, younger man. Paul flashed his beautiful white teeth toward Chris. "Hey, Chris; glad you could make it. This is Larry Smith, who you will be working with on this project. Larry is the data center manager, and he is responsible for keeping the computer operations running smoothly. That is, when it is running. He is a direct report to Nick Greco. I will go and grab Greco. Be right back."

Goldin turned, walked across the room, and went through the dark-mahogany door toward the rear.

Smith stuck out his right hand to Chris for the customary handshake. "Hello. Happy you are here. I have heard that you do quite a bit of work for the upstate unions." Smith had a small gold earring in his left ear. He was wearing jeans and an orange T-shirt with the union international logo on the left breast pocket. Underneath, in faded blue letters was, "Local 4."

Smith sat down in the chair closest to the door and immediately, a short, balding man who Chris guessed was in his mid-sixties walked in, followed by Goldin. He was wearing a blue shirt with the sleeves rolled up. The red suspenders he wore were a vain attempt at holding up his trousers. The overhanging belly seemed to be winning the battle against the suspenders. Chris guessed that it was Greco.

"Hello," the man said in a deep, rusty voice. "How are you today? I am Nick Greco."

"Yes, sir, great; very nice to finally meet you." Chris waited for Greco to offer the initial handshake. Greco walked over toward Chris and finally offered his right hand. Chris reached out and grasped it firmly. It felt weak and greasy. He gave it a brief shake and sat down.

Greco sat down directly across from Chris. "Well, tell me about yourself and why you think you can help us. Paul has told me that you are a computer guy that knows something about unions?"

"Yes, I have been specializing in union benefit systems now for, let's see, eight or nine years. I have been in business for myself since 1980. Prior to that, I was with IBM for over thirteen years. Advanced Computer Systems, the company I started, has a very competent and specialized team, and I am anxious to work with Local 4. I specialize in unions, and I think we can help."

"I understand that you do a lot of work with the unions upstate. Sonny is a friend of mine, and he told me that you wrote all of their software and installed their new computers." Greco glanced at Chris with cool eyes.

"Yes, sir. We converted all of the funds, the pension system, and annuities, and we also implemented the health and welfare fund."

Greco told Chris that they were experiencing problems with processing health insurance claims and the old software was going down on a regular basis. Greco pointed out that the software was unreliable, and they had finally come to the conclusion that they needed to find a new computer software vendor.

He continued to question Chris. "So you were the one who did the software for Sonny in Albany? You did the claims, right?" He spoke with broken English, despite the fact that he was born and raised in New York.

"Yes, sir. That was probably the biggest part of the job. We converted all their application files, but the health insurance claims process was a major success. They are doing very well. It was very smooth." Chris was now boasting and feeling rather good about his successes in Albany. "We had to train the staff on an entire new way of doing their job. As you may know, we converted the operation to a self-administered fund."

Smith interrupted. "Well, it is a bit different down here. We have over thirty-five people in the claims department, and about twenty of them are claims examiners. There is a very big dependency on keeping the system up and running. Right now, our main objective is just responding to problems and keeping the computer system up. All I do is run around the office and put out fires, so to speak. I have a small staff of computer operators and three contract programmers. They know the system very well and understand our operations. The biggest problem is that our software vendor did not provide us with the source code. So every time we need a modification, or an enhancement, or a fix, we need to call their boss in to fix it. He designed the software and is the only one that knows how it works. He is smart, but we have trouble getting him to respond on a timely basis. You know; you're in the same business. You are up in Albany, and you have other clients to support. Right? You cannot be at two places at the same time."

"Why can't your contract programmers handle the software changes? Is your union so different than all the others? Don't they know the system?" Chris asked, although he already knew the answer he was about to hear.

"Oh, yeah, they are okay, but they mainly work on the reporting side of the system. Union Systems Software is the name of the company. Our contract did not include the source code. The owner, who is also the chief programmer, Marty Bloom, wrote the software many years ago, and he is the only person that really understands how it works. The system works well when it is running, but there are a lot of changes, and every time he fixes something in one program, a problem occurs in another program. Besides, Marty is not very responsive, and we sometimes must wait two or three days before he shows up."

He continued. "Our claims system is a big problem for us, since it is just a check-writing system. Most of the work is performed manually by the claims examiners. We understand that your system automates the adjudication process. Our average daily claims volume per examiner is less than thirty."

Chris smiled as he jumped in. "Our typical daily production for examiners can be anywhere from 150 to two hundred. Our accuracy is over 99 percent." Chris continued. "Hmm, what do you do when Marty gets sick or goes on vacation?"

"Well, you hit the nail on the head, which is perhaps our biggest problem. That is why you are here today. He takes a lot of vacations," Paul replied.

Smith interrupted and asked, "Do we get the source code when we buy your software?"

Chris knew exactly where this was heading. The source code was his only protection that would prevent his clients from stealing his software. Without the source code, it would be impossible to maintain the software. He had always provided source code but recently lost an account when one of his union accounts in Syracuse had dropped the maintenance agreement. They hired a programmer who convinced them that he could maintain the software for a lot less than what Chris's company was charging. Chris needed to control the source code in order to lock in the client with a maintenance agreement. The challenge for a small software company was how to build and increase recurring revenue. This was done though the monthly fees he billed for his maintenance agreements.

"Yes, of course, we can provide source code in the appropriate situations, but don't you think it is wiser to have a software system that does not break and a software company that can fix any problem immediately? Our team updates our software on a regular basis and continually improves and enhances the software to reflect the changing requirements taking place in your industry. We can do a better job at a lower cost. We also do not have to be on-site to fix the problem. We sign on immediately remotely from our computers in Albany, so you never have to wait."

Chris had placed his briefcase next to his chair and reached down and pulled out his presentation materials, which he had in a manila folder. He placed it in front of him on the table and continued.

"Don't you think that it is better to have a system that you don't have to modify every week? A system that is reliable and at the same time satisfies all the needs of your union? And probably at a lower cost."

"We don't care about the cost; we just want someone who will give us what we want, period. And we want the source code, period." Smith turned slightly to his right and then looked at Greco, encouraging him to say something in support.

Goldin said, "Look, Chris, you come to us with a good recommendation, and I have seen what you have done for Local 290. I think there is a good fit here, and we understand there is a cost associated with your service, and of course, if we choose to purchase the source code, there would be an additional cost. But we need to know if you can work with us here in New York. You are three hours away, and when we need you, we are not going to wait a day or two for you to come down. We have a lot at stake and need your company's total commitment. This programmer that you assigned to Local 290—Williams, I think—will he be working with us? Can he handle this size union? We're big, probably ten to fifteen times bigger than the accounts you handle upstate, and we cannot afford to make any mistakes. We need a new system, and we would like to give you the opportunity. Price is important, but it will not be the deciding factor as to who we choose to do business with."

"Look, I would not be here if I thought even for one minute that I could not support you in an exceptional manner. We provide 24/7 support. I don't care if it is the middle of the night; you call, and we will be here. But the best part is that we build reliability into our programs. There should be no reason for you to call in the middle of the night, as long as we keep you up and running 24/7."

Chris continued. "Besides, we support you online. So we are not three hours away, just a telephone call away, and you connect our experts to your computer instantly. As for the source code, it will be our people who will be making the program changes, and we have the source code. Why would you want to hire an in-house programmer? That would cost you over $100,000 a year, maybe more. The system is very complex, with over one million lines of code. We have invested over $6 million in the software. Our technical team knows the system; they are the experts and wrote the software. They understand the rules and regulations, which are continually changing. We know the business and know what your needs are. If you ever get to a point when you feel you need the source code, we would be more than happy to provide it, but of course there is an additional cost."

Goldin stood up and gestured to Greco with a slight nod of his head toward the door. "Chris, Nick and I will be right back. We need to discuss something." He looked down at the watch on his left wrist, a shiny gold Rolex. "Give us a moment, and then we can discuss the job at lunch. There is a great little Italian restaurant on Seventeenth Street, Da Umberto. You will love it." He turned and walked out of the room, with Greco close behind.

It was no more than three or four minutes when Goldin returned to the room. Chris knew that he was to meet with Ernesto LaCola, the BA, and understood that he was the top executive at the union. He turned to Goldin. "Hey, Paul, when are we supposed to meet with Mr. LaCola?"

"Well, he is not back in the office today and Mary, his secretary, said that tomorrow would be a better time. You're going to be in New York for the rest of the week, correct?"

"Yes, I will be here through Thursday."

Goldin nodded. "That should work out fine. Now, let's grab Greco and go to lunch."

Smith stood up as Goldin began to walk out of the room. "Paul, I want to show Chris the computer room. When you are ready to leave, Chris and I will be in there."

Chris was now confused. He reached down to the folder in front of him, returned it to the briefcase, and followed Smith out of the room. He now came to understand that this was going to be a vastly different environment. There was no discussion as to the software's capability. The questions all seemed to be directed toward support and responding to emergency situations. But the biggest issue was the source code, with cost never entering the discussion. That was a good thing. He thought it had been a rather strange meeting. Here was the accountant, the fund administrator, and the computer manager, and there was never any question as to what the software did or what their needs were. They didn't care. It didn't matter. There were several funds, and they had given him little or no information as to their problems or their priorities. It seemed that Goldin was more concerned about lunch.

The best part of the meeting was that there was no question about the cost of the software. Chris was pleased and felt good. He would sell them access to the source code since he knew there would be more money for him, so he was careful not to give them too many reasons as to why they would not need it.

CHAPTER TEN

DA UMBERTO: CRISPY ARTICHOKES

APRIL 14, 1992

G RECO WAS OLD SCHOOL AND loved to play the part of a connected wise guy. He looked like one, dressed like one, and talked like one. Sonny told Chris that Greco loved Italian food and loved it when you took him to lunch. Sometimes he would wear the remnants of his lunch on his tie or the lapels of his suit jacket. He was tough and outspoken and had the look of a wiseguy. Although Greco took his orders from the business agent, he would serve in a critical role toward the success of Chris's business relationship. Greco had intimate knowledge of the inner workings of Local 4 and knew where all the skeletons were buried but was not well versed in computerization. Chris's first impressions of Greco were not favorable. Greco did not seem to be aware of what was going on with the computer operations, and his knowledge of the union accounting systems was nonexistent. He was not especially good with numbers unless you put a dollar sign in front of them. But this would be his principal account contact along with Paul Goldin, so Chris would have to accept it—even though he felt like he was aboard a ship piloted by a drunken sea captain who was navigating with no real sense of purpose or direction.

This was a new environment for Chris, and he was not sure that he could rely on any of his past successes. Leadership was lacking, and he was unsure of the staff's commitment of to the success of the project. They certainly wanted it to be successful but did not go out of their way or offer any assistance to make it easier. He was especially concerned about Smith's attitude. Smith treated it just like another job and showed little or no interest. Chris was smart enough to know that if he did not get the job done, they would toss him out of the building like an old pair of worn-out shoes, regardless of what they said about loyalty and trust. He would have to endure the pressure on his own. The account was his to own, and at this point, there was no running away from it. He immediately recognized that their computer operations were riddled with flaws, but he was not one that would ever disappoint his clients.

Chris had been looking forward to the restaurant ever since Sonny told him about it. But Sonny cautioned him and told him that he would be tested and he should plan on picking up the check. Chris was certain he would not have a choice and was prepared. Sonny told him to act like he was successful and act as though money did not mean that much to him. Sonny told him to always pay with cash and bring along several hundred-dollar bills to pay for the check. Wiseguys all carried a thick roll of hundred-dollar bills, which were held together with a thick rubber band. It was always better to be extravagant rather than to act cheap. If you were not paying for it, then what difference would it make? Again, this was just another additional cost of doing business in the big city with the big boys. He did not think about the check he would be expected to pay; he was thinking about the fees he would be collecting. And besides, Chris loved Italian food and was looking forward to the lunch. Quite a bit of business could be accomplished over a plate of pasta.

Chris was in the computer room with Larry Smith when Goldin returned. "Nick is going to meet us downstairs in the lobby. Let's go, or are you in the middle of something?"

"No, I am ready. Larry and I were just talking about the rate file and the problems getting accurate and timely contractor hours."

Greco had decided that they would walk to the restaurant, since it was only three blocks from the office and it was a perfect early April day. It was spring in New York City, and the thermometer was right at seventy-one. It was busy, with many passing cars and heavy foot traffic on the sidewalks. The three of them set out on foot headed north on Park to Seventeenth Street and then walked west just a few short blocks. Everyone seemed to be in a hurry and appeared to be walking with a purpose. Chris was amazed at how people approached the street crossings. Some seemed to have perfect timing as they approached the corner just as the red light turned to green. The girls were all out in full force, and with the mild temperature, there was little left to the imagination since they all had shed their coats and outer garments. Many were young, and many were very pretty.

Goldin walked on the street side with Greco closer to the buildings. Chris was in the middle. "Vincent, you are going to love this place. They have had the same staff since they opened twenty-five years ago. Everything is prepared to order, and all their pastas are homemade. And the veal is the best in the city."

After five minutes, Greco appeared to tire, and his breathing became more pronounced. He stopped and leaned forward and placed his hands just above his knees as he bent forward. The walk was pleasant for Goldin and Chris but proved to be a struggle for Greco. Chris was certain that they would need to take a taxi back if the lunch were anywhere close to what Sonny had described. Greco took a deep breath, stood upright, and then continued forward. It had been a few years since Greco had last walked to the restaurant, and his endurance was not as strong as it was just a few years ago. His cheeks were red. He was at least seventy-five pounds overweight, and his 250-pound frame was just barely an inch or two above five feet. "Did you know that there are over eighteen thousand restaurants in New York City? Most serve Italian food," Greco said.

"Yeah, pasta, and I think you have eaten at most of them." Goldin smartly replied to Greco with a big grin.

"Fuck you! What the fuck do Jews know about Italian food?"

"Probably more than you think. We love macaroni or pasta or whatever it is called, and the Jews eat it probably more than most of you Wops," Goldin snapped back at Greco.

Greco seemed to give in and looked over to Chris. "You are probably right. Anyway, Chris, are there any good Italian restaurants in Albany?"

"As a matter of fact, there are. Café Italia is great."

"Is that the joint that Sonny takes me to?"

"Yeah, that's it. Sonny loves the place. I think he eats there at least three times a week."

"Well, there you go; three times a week makes Sonny a Jew just like you, Paul. Ha! Three times a week." Now Greco was grinning from ear to ear. He was panting more heavily, and Chris could see that he was struggling to keep pace.

Greco was smiling and was pleased to find that Chris had a sense of humor.

The restaurant was located just east of Sixth Avenue in the heart of the Chelsea District of Manhattan and adjacent to the Flatiron District.

When they finally arrived, Greco was breathing heavily, and a neatly suited gentleman came out from around the bar as they walked in. The bar ran halfway down the right side of the restaurant. The man wore a tailored suit and a red bow tie. A red handkerchief was loosely fluffed and hung out of his breast suit pocket. The place was dimly lit, and there were about twenty tables draped in white linen. The bar along the wall on the right was filled with an almost endless variety of liquors and cordials in front of a mirrored wall. Chris liked the music playing softly in the background. Sinatra was singing, "Fly Me to The Moon." The far wall had a double-hinged doorway to the left, which was the entry to the kitchen. There was a large glass window to the right of the kitchen doors, and customers could look through the window directly into the kitchen. Chris was taking it all in and looking forward to the lunch. There were five or six framed scenic pictures of Italy hanging from the tan-painted walls.

"Good afternoon, Senor Greco. Where would you like to sit today?" asked the man, bowing his head slightly. The two approached one another and the waiter politely embraced Greco and leaned forward to place a Sicilian kiss first on Greco's right cheek and then on his left. "Hello, Mr. Goldin, and how are you today?"

"Fine, fine. How about the round table over there?" Goldin pointed directly at the third table from the door.

"No, no, no, we sat there last week. Too noisy, and I never sit at the same table two times in a row. How about the table in the corner?"

Greco redirected them to the corner table against the kitchen wall. He was always very cautious as to the table placement and always concerned about other people at nearby tables hearing their conversations. The manager waved his right hand as he pointed to the table against the back wall directly in front of the glass window looking into the kitchen. It was square and was pushed directly up against the windowed wall. As they were being seated, Chris hesitated for a moment and peered through the glass. There were four cooks in white chef's jackets, and he wondered which one was the head chef. The closest cook was an elderly white-haired man of about seventy. He was directly on the other side of the glass and hunched over the long table, rolling out pasta dough. There was a range hood on the right side and two other chefs stood on the other side of the window, one overweight and the other Black, both fully involved with the sauté pans on the stove. The fourth was cutting fresh vegetables on a wooden-topped table in the center of the kitchen. The kitchen walls were all lined with white tile. The kitchen appeared spotless, and orange tile covered the floors. The sauté line had a row of twelve or fifteen burners, and the walls behind were covered by stainless-steel panels. Directly behind the glass windows to the right were a large, gray dough mixer and a long table with several strands of freshly made pasta, which the white-haired man was rolling out. At the far end, there was also a large pasta-sheet machine that obviously handled the finishing end of the pasta-making process. Chris could see the blue flames flashing between the pans and the gas burners on the top of the stoves. They were receiving the full attention of the two men in white chef's jackets standing over them.

There were two chairs on each side of the table. Greco sat in the far corner chair, facing the door. Goldin reached over to the next table, pulled a chair over next to Greco, and sat down.

The waiter was there even before they arrived at the table. "*Buongiorno*, Senor Greco! Happy to see you today. If I may suggest, we have a wonderful beginning; hot appetizers are always prepared the way you like them, with wonderful surprises. Beggar's purse is also a good start. They are filled with goat cheese and pear in a light cream sauce with the perfume of truffle oil. We also have squid-ink ravioli. For the main dish, I have beautiful sea bass. It just came in this morning. Angelo bakes it in parchment with black olives and shaved fennel."

"Okay, give us a few minutes. But you can start with the cold assorted *antipasti* for the table. Oh, and bring us a bottle of the Santa Margherita. Gentlemen, is white okay?" Greco was asserting his leadership position for the table. "And yes, we will go along with your suggestion for the hot appetizer platter. Make sure there are some crispy artichokes."

Goldin picked up the wine list from the center of the table. "Maybe I will have a glass of the Chianti to start. Chris, red or white?"

Chris realized that Greco was calling the shots and thought it best to go along with Greco's recommendation. "The white is fine; thank you."

"Wonderful. I will get that going." The waiter, with almost a click of his heels, bowed slightly as he began to slowly back away from the table and then turned very gracefully and walked toward the service bar.

The three of them then turned their attention to the menu. It was broken down into four sections: *antipasti, primi, secondi,* and *conorni.* Chris realized that this was not going to be an ordinary lunch. This was the checking-out lunch, and Greco's objective was to size up this so-called computer expert from Albany. What better way than to loosen him up with a little wine and food? Under the *antipasti* heading, there were nine items listed, with a short description of the ingredients underneath. Under the antipasti, the first item was "*LacOrto,* market vegetables from our antipasto bar." Chris assumed that this was what Greco had ordered. But then as he gazed down, there were eight or nine other dishes, all with some element that could be included in the dish that Greco had ordered. The fourth one down was "*carciofi*: crispy artichokes, cherry peppers, aioli." Chris loved artichokes but thought it would be wise to go along with Greco's choice. There was a long way to go.

It seemed like an eternity, but no one said a word as they scanned the menu. Finally, after about a minute, Greco looked up at Chris. "Vincent, I don't know what Paul has told you about us, and I don't know how much you understand our business." He hesitated for a few seconds and then continued. "Sure, you know your way around the computer, and from what I have heard from Sonny, you can help us, but do you really understand what we do and why we do it?"

The conversation abruptly stopped as the waiter came over and uncorked the bottle of white wine. He pulled on the corkscrew and there was a slight popping sound, which broke through the silence as they all watched. Greco held out his glass and motioned for the waiter to pour. He sipped from his glass and nodded his approval.

Chris watched Greco and then realized that this was going to be the moment when Greco would lay down the rules. He realized he was correct as Greco began. "There is a war going on. It is between the oppressed class and the rich. This war has been going on for hundreds—no, thousands—of years. These two are on a collision course. The oppressed, the workers, those who have labored in pitiful conditions, versus the rich, the privileged. The big companies. Corporate America—and what is the purpose? To build their empires, so that the rich can get richer. Yes, it was done with money from the rich, but it was done on the backs of the oppressed. When the Italians came to America a hundred years ago, they were the people that built this country. The work was dangerous and barely enough to keep their families together. Working for pennies, barely enough to live. Conditions were miserable. In the tenements in the lower east side, in cold-water flats, in deplorable conditions."

Greco continued. "Some lived like dogs. Some had to work two jobs just to put food on the table. This country was built on the backs of the laborer, brick by brick. He worked on the docks, the railroad, the garment factories, the coal mines, and anywhere they needed a simple mind with a strong back. In Houston, Boston, New Orleans, Hartford, and in cities all across the country—and especially in New York—they came to work for a new beginning.

And the fucking government was all a part of the plan, because it was cheap labor. Did you know that there were close to five million Italians that came to this country from 1880 to 1924? They came to the new world because they were promised freedom, liberty, and an opportunity to build a new life for their family."

Greco hesitated briefly and gritted his lips angrily. He then looked down at his glass, picked it up, and brought it to his lips. But before he drank, he pulled it away and continued.

"They labored, sweated, suffered, and died. The organized-labor movement was the only voice that gave them hope. The only voice that allowed the oppressed to find some semblance of a decent existence. This union was built on blood, sweat, and tears and fought only for the oppressed. We built this organization so that we could transform lives. That was the beginning of the labor movement. My grandfather came to this country in steerage in 1890. He had seven dollars and a pocket watch that his father had given him. He had no job and no place to live. The only job he could get was loading the garbage barges, which were then dumped on Staten Island."

Greco hesitated and then directed a question directly to Chris. "Vincent, right? That is your last name, correct? Do you know what the fuck I am getting at? Do you know what side you are on?"

Chris was not sure what to say. "Sir, I am not sure what you mean."

"Look, there may be occasion when you will need to pick a side, and I want you to understand that the union always comes first." His face was turning red. "Do you get it?"

Chris was still not expecting the lunch to get so serious at this early stage, but he had been warned. "Mr. Greco, I understand, and I am with the unions and know that I will need to get the job done at all costs."

Greco was now shaking his head. "No, that is not what I meant." He then looked over to Paul Goldin. "Paul, please tell Vincent what I am talking about."

Paul put his glass down and looked at Chris. "There may come a time when you will be asked to do something that you may not agree with. There may be some risk, and you will need to accept that risk at all costs. You cannot walk on the top of a fence. You have to pick a side—and it is a tall fence, and you are stuck on that side to the end of the line. No jumping over to the other side. The fence is too high."

Greco cut him off and brought his hand up to the side of his face. "Vincent, you are either in or out, and things are done the union way—period. No other fucking way works down here. Once you are on our side, you stay on our side, regardless of the fucking consequences."

Greco was brought up in Brooklyn and had a fiery Italian temperament and exercised little control over his emotions. He was a New York City street-smart thug in some respects and would fly into a passionate rage at the slightest provocation. Chris could see that Greco possessed an iron-fist attitude when he spoke about the labor movement. None of his emotional outbursts were off limits. Chris immediately saw that Greco had a powerful and forceful nature and would go for the jugular if you crossed him. He used vile and obscene words without hesitation. Small beads of sweat started to appear on Greco's upper lip as he brought the glass back up to his lips and took a small sip.

"Good wine." With a small nod, he continued. "You see, Chris, immigration provided low-paying labor to build America. The dirty little secret is that it expanded the lower class and created government dependency. But they did not count on the unions to take over their job of helping the working man."

He smiled. "You see, Chris, they did not count on the labor movement to take advantage of the situation they had created. So, we compete with the government and actually do a better job of taking care of our families. We have a better retirement system, a better health plan, a vacation plan, and provide more benefits to the working man than Washington. Don't expect Social Security to take care of you when you retire. It is almost broke and can never compete with our plans.

"The government competes with the unions and would love to see us disappear if it were not for our votes. They are actually against labor and would like to shut us down. We elevate the oppressed working class so that they can have a bigger bite of the American apple, the American dream. We provide a voice that can be heard to improve working conditions for the guys on the bottom of the shit heap."

He paused for a brief moment and took a deep breath.

"Today, our union is over ten thousand strong. So you work for those ten thousand laborers, not me. If you remember who you work for, then you will know what side you're on."

His voice was now sharper and took on a rougher tone. "Last year, the health and welfare fund paid out over $35 million in health benefits. Thirty-five million dollars. And now the fucking government wants to take it all. They want to shut us down. Why? Because they want to control it all. The motherfuckers want to control our lives. Can you imagine what it would be like if the government was deciding which doctor you could see and how much they would pay? Can you imagine how fucked up the health-care system would be if they took over the health-care industry? Not just for unions, but for the entire country."

Greco's eyes started to squint, his thick eyebrows arched downward, and Chris could now hear the tension in his voice. "We have a health insurance plan that works. It was built on the backs of our members, and it's their money, and I will be damned if you think I would allow the government to take away what we have created. Our members deserve every penny that we pay out to keep them and their families healthy. Just so you understand, this is critical and cannot be compromised, so we are placing a lot of trust and faith in your company and in you, in particular."

He finally took a small sip of water from the water glass and continued.

"That fucking broad who thinks her husband is going to win the presidency. She thinks that once her husband wins the presidency and she becomes the First Lady, she is going to take over our health insurance program. Imagine that; we have put our members' money to work, and what do you think would happen to that money? We are in a fucking war, and we are not going to go down without a fight. We have to protect our membership and protect what we have created. The government has unlimited money, and the bastards don't care how long it takes or how much it costs. We are the working class and not going to merge our money with the tax dollars that pay for those who don't want to fucking work."

Chris could see that Greco was upset. "And we gave them a shitload of money from our PAC fund so they could win. Imagine that: they claim to be for labor, but it is all about them."

He again paused. "Chris, do you know what the word *unity* stands for?"

"Well, I think so; yes, it means together. Everyone is unified to provide strength," answered Chris.

"Yeah, that is part of it, but it goes much deeper than that. We send a lot of money to Washington and expect to be treated fairly. The damn politicians are nothing but leeches and cannot be trusted." Greco was now on a roll. "How the hell does he think that his wife, Hillary, who is a crooked lawyer, knows something about our health fund? We know what our members need, and we built this fund to help our members—period. And we are not about to let it get away from us."

Goldin decided he would add something to the conversation, since Greco was beginning to breath heavily. "Chris, the government is dirty and makes their own rules. We need to fight back any way we can. They are not as righteous as you may think. They play dirty, and we sometimes need to take the gloves off and fight bare fisted."

Goldin looked at Greco and saw he was nodding in agreement. "We sometimes get a little dirty as well, so be careful, and do not be so hasty to judge what or how we do things."

Greco caught his breath and continued. "It is the same thing Kennedy did after the unions in Chicago gave him the presidency. Unfortunately for him, he paid the ultimate price for betrayal."

He paused and took another sip of wine. "United is more than together as one; it is trust and loyalty. We are not fucking around. This is a very serious business, and we need business partners that we can trust. Yes, anyone that wants to do business with us must be with the fucking program. Our program. You want to be on our team, then you better play ball. You need to be committed to the labor movement, 100 percent."

Greco leaned forward with his belly finally hitting the edge of the table, which rocked slightly, all the while with his dark-brown eyes focused directly on Chris's. There was a silence. Then Greco growled, his lips squaring slightly, and said, "Do you understand where we are coming from? Loyalty is essential for unity."

"Yes, sir." Chris could feel Greco's eyes penetrating his very being. Greco now freely exposed a destructive mean streak; he was a gunslinger out for blood, and Chris could feel the meanness in the words.

"I understand exactly what you have said. My great-grandfather came over from Italy in 1897. He worked in the coal mines and died in a coal-mining accident. He lost an arm in a cave-in and died from an infection. My father ended up in an orphanage when he was five years old. He, too, experienced the hardships that you speak of. He was a water boy in a coal mine when he was just eight years old. Yes, I understand," Chris replied.

Greco looked directly into Chris's eyes. "Understand the first rule: you never, ever discuss our business with anyone on the other side. If you do, you will pay a big price. When you are asked to look the other way, you look the other way. And when you pick a side, you must remain loyal to that side. You cross over for good. We do not care about the cost, and you will be able to make lots of money if you do what we tell you to do and remain loyal to those ten thousand members."

Chris maintained his composure as he at the same time swallowed the obscenity that had flashed across his thoughts: "Do not care about the money, you fucking hypocrite."

Chris nodded in agreement, not certain how to respond.

Goldin wanted to throw the last shovel of dirt on the speech. "Chris, most people do not understand what a union is about, and I think Nick laid it out clearly as to our purpose and what this fight is about. I hope you were listening, because this fight sometimes gets a little rough. Sometimes, a little dirty."

Chris replied, "Loud and clear. I never looked at it that way, but now I understand." He turned to face Greco. "Thanks, Nick. I appreciate what you have shared."

Just then, the waiter appeared with a large oval platter. He placed the platter at the center of the table and began to spoon a small portion onto the plates which had already been set before them. There were roasted red peppers along with stuffed eggplant, stuffed clams, and shrimp. Then he saw them in the center of the dish: crispy artichokes.

Greco was ready and replied, "Yes, Anthony. I would like the truffle mushroom ravioli, and then the veal scallopini. Can you prepare the veal with the marsala and the mascarpone?"

"Yes, sir. And for you, Mr. Paul?"

"I think I am hungry for the cavatelli with the creamed corn. And can he prepare the chicken scallopini with the cream sauce?"

The waiter politely replied, "Wonderful. You want the mustard cream sauce. He can do that. Great choices."

Chris was ready. "Yes, thank you. I will have the same as Mr. Greco."

"Very well; I will place the order immediately." Head up and chin pointing forward, he took two steps backward from the table and gracefully turned and walked toward the register at the back bar.

Greco reached over to Chris and placed his right hand on Chris's left hand just as Chris was about to reach for the serving spoon resting across the appetizer plate. "Look, we have a little advantage. We can play politics too. The PAC fund is probably our most important weapon, and we use it for the friends of labor. And we have plenty of friends who protect us, so you have nothing to worry about."

Paul interrupted. "Chris." He dropped his stare toward the table as he looked across at Chris. He rubbed his thumb and forefinger together, back and forth.

Chris reached into his right-breast suit pocket and removed the envelope with the $10,000 check. He looked around, placed it on the table, and slid it in front of Greco. He breathed a silent sigh of relief and knew he had had just jumped over to their side of the fence.

Greco nodded and looked around as he placed his hand on the envelope. "Listen, I have checked you out, and you would not be here today if it was not for Sonny and Paul. I just wanted to let you know how we do things at Local 4. This thing goes into a shell company and is used for investments in real estate. Think of it as an investment of one dollar for each of our ten thousand members. The company makes lots of money, big returns, so do not have any bad thoughts about this. This represents your sign of trust and loyalty, and you have just become a stockholder."

"Thank you. I know there is a lot at stake, and I want you to know that I am fully committed to working with the union. I am with you 100 percent," Chris replied.

"You work through Paul." Greco picked up the envelope, looked around the room once again, and then slid it into his jacket pocket. "He will handle all the agreements and the money. He knows what the budget is, since he created it, so the pricing needs to be negotiated with Paul. You direct everything through him, including the fees.

He understands all this computer stuff. He will set up the next meeting and get our people involved. Everything is above board, and Paul has the contracts. You will be working with Larry Smith but working under my authority. Smith will introduce you to all the managers and the department supervisors. I run all the funds, including the health and welfare fund and the pension fund. You need to talk to Paul; he has my total confidence and will be the point man." Greco peered over to Paul, who nodded in agreement.

Goldin said, "Chris, tomorrow, you will meet with Ernesto LaCola. He is the business agent and the local president. He does not get too involved in the administrative side of the business but wants to meet you once we get going. Don't get me wrong; he is smart and knows where every dollar is spent. He has already approved your contract, so we want you to start immediately."

Chris nodded. He knew that he had passed the test but suspected that there would be many more. "Sure, let me know when you want to meet LaCola. Pete Williams is coming down tomorrow, and I will be here all day and through Thursday afternoon. We are going to set up the training terminals with Smith and start the data conversion. As a matter of fact, we will be on-site every week for the next several months, until we get the new system up and running. We will be here at least four days a week, probably through the end of the year. This is a big job."

Finally, the pasta course arrived. Chris looked down at the ravioli, three large, perfectly shaped pillows in a light-brown, creamy mushroom sauce. There were small sprinkles of fresh basil and a huge button mushroom in the center of the three pillows. There was a scattering of mushroom slices randomly sprinkled on the plate. Chris could smell the sweetness from the truffle oil, which was sprinkled on top.

Greco's eyes seemed to bulge out of his forehead as he stared down at the crispy artichokes on the platter sitting in the center of the table. Cracking a big smile, he said, "Let's eat."

Chris cut off a piece from the ravioli pillow closest to him and placed it in his mouth. It was stuffed with mushrooms and a sort of creamy cheese mixture that tasted like goat cheese. Not the best ravioli he had ever eaten, but it was delicious. The cream sauce was smooth and creamy. Chris thought it was exceptional. He was a numbers guy, and at twenty-seven dollars, he computed it to be nine dollars a pillow. He thought about his mom's ravioli. She would make one hundred at a time and they would feed the entire family for a week, and probably for no more than the nine dollars, the cost of one single ravioli sitting on the plate in front of him.

The lunch was terrific, and the pasta course was followed by the meat course. The veal was tender, and Chris easily cut into it with his fork. It was perfectly topped with a light white-wine and butter sauce. And then came the dessert. It was now close to 2:30 as the plate of fresh Italian pastries was set before them. Greco was the first to reach across his plate and grab a cannoli.

"Anthony," he said and looked up at the waiter, "can you wrap up half a dozen of the cannoli? I should bring some back to the office for the girls."

Just then, Clara walked in the front door and headed directly toward the table at the back. "Mr. Greco, your 2:30 has arrived, and I have a car outside."

"Great, okay. Well, Chris, I am looking forward to working with you. I know you will do a great job for us. Paul will be working alongside you and will work with you on the scheduling. I think that the first fund should be the annuity. It is pretty easy. Not a priority, but it should help to get you oriented with the staff and the way we do things."

Greco pushed his chair back and reached his right hand across the table to Chris. "Good luck, partner, and remember what we talked about. Trust and loyalty are the backbones of our family."

Chris stood up and clasped his right hand into Greco's. Chris thought his hand still felt clammy and wondered if it was just the cheese from the cannoli. Greco and Clara turned, and as they walked toward the door, the waiter handed Clara a small, white box neatly tied with white string. As if he knew that there would be a takeout box of cannoli.

Goldin looked over to Chris. "A word of caution: be very careful with what you say around Clara. She has been with Greco for over twenty years and has his complete confidence. No wisecracks, no looks at her ass or looks in her direction, no jokes, no off-color remarks, nothing. Just be very careful, okay?"

Chris replied, "Got it. Absolutely."

The accountant continued. "Actually, never say anything off color to the girls in the office. There is a lot of sex, and you never know who is banging who."

Just then, the waiter came over and placed a small, black leather folder directly to the right side of Chris's plate. Goldin did not say a word or move to pick up the check. Chris knew how the game was played and immediately picked up the folder and opened it. It was no surprise: $316.20. Chris reached into his pocket and peeled off four one-hundred-dollar bills. He counted them out loud to make certain that Goldin saw his generosity.

Goldin smiled as he sipped his espresso and said, "Thanks, Chris; next one is on me. I am going to take you to a place, and the steaks will knock your socks off."

He wanted to trust Goldin, and while there would always be some question as to the legality of union business, he would have to go along with it. It was too late to change directions, and he had too much invested in this deal and too much reliance on the union for his company's financial well-being. But Greco's speech did shed new light on the union's purpose and what he was about to encounter. It did not elevate his confidence or trust but gave him something to ponder.

CHAPTER ELEVEN

THE YELLOW ENVELOPE

APRIL 14, 1992 – EVENING

IT WAS ALMOST SIX WHEN the taxi pulled up to the curb in front of the Hilton Garden Inn on West Thirty-Fifth Street. The uniformed bellman immediately opened the back door and allowed Chris to step onto the sidewalk.

"Good evening, sir; how was your day?"

"Fine, thank you, fine." It was an automatic response, even though he was now tired and somewhat relieved after having met Greco at the 230 Park Avenue South building. He was not at all hungry but still felt some discomfort knowing that he still had the yellow envelope in his pocket. He was glad that he was at the hotel and would be able to secure the yellow envelope in the room safe. The introductory meeting with Greco had gone well and he was looking forward to the work ahead of him, even though he was not entirely comfortable around Greco.

"Can I get your bag, sir?" the cab driver asked as he opened the back door.

"No, I am good, and it is not too heavy."

He walked up to the registration desk.

"Good evening, sir. Do you have a reservation?"

"Yes, thank you. Chris Vincent." He placed his credit card and his New York driver's license on the counter and slid them toward the attendant.

The clerk answered, "Oh, yes; I have it right here. Just a moment."

He reached to his left and tore off the registration form from the printer on the back counter to his left. "Right here, Mr. Vincent. Please initial the registration and sign right here." The clerk pointed to the registration form, then looked up and nodded his head toward the man who was sitting across from the registration desk. He had on a dark-gray suit.

"I see you have not stayed with us in the past. The room number is in the envelope, and we have a bar and a fine restaurant that I hope you will enjoy. I have included a free-drink card, should you wish to join us for dinner. The elevators are just to your right. Mr. Vincent, I hope you have a pleasant stay."

"Thank you." He picked up the envelope and saw the room number was 847. He turned and was about to walk to the elevator when the middle-aged man in the gray suit approached him.

"Hello, Mr. Vincent. Would you mind if I had a brief word with you?"

Startled, Chris replied, "What is this about?"

"Well, Mr. Vincent, I am a friend of a friend. I work with unions and want to speak to you for a few minutes. I wanted to ask you about Local 4. I understand that you are installing new computer software to manage their funds. Is that correct?"

Instantly, Chris became very nervous. "Well, sir, I am under a confidentiality agreement and cannot discuss anything about the union. You will have to talk to them directly."

"I understand completely, and that is not the reason I wanted to meet you. I understand that you have something to deliver. Is that correct?"

"Well, I am not sure what you are talking about."

"Look, I understand that you own the computer-software company from Albany that we will be working with. Anyway, I did not want you to be surprised or concerned, since I meet with Mr. Greco and Mr. Goldin on a regular basis to review their operations. I help them out with their government reporting and wanted to meet you, since we may be working on some computer programs in the future. I understand that you are installing new software, and we may need your help as we go through their operations. We have not had any luck with their old software programmer, Marty Bloom, and he is the guy who we depended on to help us understand their software system. We spoke to him last year, and he was very helpful. He is the only knowledgeable person that we have worked with in the past, and he alone understands the system, or, I should say, their old system, so we are a bit handicapped. That is why I wanted to stop by," said the man.

Somewhat confused, Chris replied, "Do you work for the union?"

"Well, no, not exactly. I help them with their government reporting."

Chris was careful with his words. "Well, I suppose I can help you when the time is appropriate and, of course, if my client gives the okay."

"You see, although I don't work for them directly, the unions rely on many friends, since union accounting is very complicated. Since Bloom is out, we thought you, as the next-in-line computer expert, might be able to help us. Greco knows who I am, and I am also a friend of Sonny Russo in Albany. I came from the same town as him. I live in Poughkeepsie. Just wanted to meet you and let you know what to expect."

Chris was stunned. He did not know what to say. "Where did you say you are from?"

"Poughkeepsie, just up the river about ninety-five miles." He was smiling. "And how is Sonny?"

"Okay, Sonny is fine. As to Local 4, I will talk to Greco, and whatever he says is what I can provide. I am happy to cooperate, but I am not sure how I can be of help. I do not want to risk my client relationships and certainly do not want to disclose any sensitive information about their member records. I think you understand. But I am just getting started; today was my first day, and I know very little about their operations." Chris was confused and asked, "Am I supposed to give you something?"

"Yes." The man continued to smile. "Sonny gave you something—a yellow envelope, correct? That is for me."

"A what?"

"You have a yellow envelope for me that Sonny gave you, correct? And, you know, I told you that I am from Poughkeepsie."

Chris reached into his inside jacket pocket, and the envelope was still there. He nervously pulled it from his jacket. "Right here, and I have no idea what it is." He looked around to make sure no one was looking and passed the envelope to the outstretched hand of the man in the gray suit.

The bearded man nodded and smiled weakly. "No problem, I understand. I spoke to the accountant and he told me where you were staying, and I wanted to pick up the envelope. They are my friends as well, and I do not want to see them get in any trouble. I wanted to put you at ease. Remember, you need to know who your friends are."

Chris did not offer his hand and thought it was curious that this sort of exchange was done right out in the open in a hotel lobby in front of the desk clerk. "Well, thanks for the heads up; it was nice to meet you. I have just arrived and am just going to go to my room. It has been a long day, and I am ready to turn in."

"Well, thank you, and good night." He stood his ground and did not turn away as he watched Chris as he turned and began to walk toward the elevators. Before Chris had taken more than a few steps, the bearded man in the gray suit said, "Oh, Mr. Vincent, if you see Mr. Bloom, give him my regards. But I am guessing that he is fishing in Florida."

Chris turned and walked back toward the stranger. "No, never met the man. Sir, may I see your ID, or may I have your card?"

"Sure." He reached into his pocket, pulled out a business-card holder, and withdrew a card. "Here you go." He handed it to Chris, turned, and walked toward the hotel exit.

Chris looked down at the card with the man's name and title on the front. He then walked back to the hotel clerk as the gray suit walked out to the street. He turned to the desk clerk.

"Hey, pal, that gentleman who I just spoke to, did he tell you his name?"

"Why, no, but he did give me a business card. Actually, I just threw it in the wastebasket." He shuffled around a bit and pulled out a business card from the trash basket and handed it to Chris. The same name was on both cards.

CHAPTER TWELVE

BIG E

TUESDAY, DAY 2 – NEW YORK CITY

ERNESTO L**A**C**OLA** **DID** **NOT** **LIKE** the public limelight and preferred to conduct his business in the shadows of secrecy. He traveled in and out of the city to his home on Long Island on a private helicopter from Liberty Heliport, which was located at the southern tip of Manhattan, adjacent to the East River. It was only a fifteen-minute drive from Union Square via FDR Drive, and he was always chauffeured in a black Lincoln Town Car driven by Bobby, the seventh-floor guard and his personal driver. Ernesto LaCola may not have been a CEO of a Fortune 500 company, but he sure lived like one.

It was Chris's second day at the union, and he was anxious to begin work, even though he had not yet met the big boss, Ernesto

LaCola, the business agent. Chris was busy interviewing each of the department supervisors and taking notes regarding the process and workflows. He had already been given the go ahead by Goldin.

No time had been confirmed for the meeting with LaCola on the seventh floor, so Chris kept busy and dug into the workflows of the operations as he waited for Goldin to arrive. Although he was experienced and familiar with union accounting systems, he thought that the Local's computer software was the worst he had ever seen. It did not take him very long to realize that the conversion would be very challenging due to the lack of documentation and poor data structures.

Money flowed through the union trust funds like water over Niagara Falls. The accounting systems were complicated, and the biggest problem was keeping all the accounting up to date through the out-of-sequence workflows in the union offices. Despite the computer systems, the sequence and timing of events were all out of step with one another. Even with all the computerization, he began to discover that there was still a great deal of manual intervention required. Due to the lack of integration, tracking the money as it flowed in from the union contractors and into the union's bank accounts and eventually flowed out to the investment accounts would prove to be difficult. The workflows were inefficient and difficult to synchronize with what had taken place, despite the computerization.

The old system consisted of a series of transactions cobbled together with little or no logic and made little sense to Chris. These accounting methods and the timing of how the money flowed made it impossible to compare the actual cash balances in the accounts and the numbers that were reflected in the books for any given point in time. Those who ran the union preferred the process and did not want to make it easy for anyone on the outside looking in to discover how it all worked. But they finally realized that this made it easy for the people on the inside to help themselves. Money was all around, and it was so tempting for those who were close to it to grab some for themselves, with little chance for anyone to discover how it was accomplished.

Ever since the unions came into being, they discovered that the construction business in New York City ran afoul of the law. The mafia's involvement in the construction business had been commonplace since they began, and it was followed by infiltration with the labor unions. The unions controlled the labor force, and a delay of just twenty minutes could prove to be costly for building costs. If you wanted to play, then you had to pay. Bribery was so commonplace in the big city that it was viewed by many that it was not a bad thing. Everyone had their hand out in the real-estate and construction business. A little kickback never hurt anyone. *Bribery* was such an evil word that they substituted the words *kickback,* which did not have such an ugly connotation. Besides, because you simply marked up your price and gave some of it back, it was never a problem. Everyone was happy, and this was the way it was done. Everyone was agreeable since no one got hurt. The unions also realized that they were needed and supplied the labor, and they could get a part of the illegal markups.

Sal Barone's father ran the concrete business in the sixties and seventies and controlled all the concrete that went into all the new construction in the city. The Barone Companies produced the ready-mix cement and were involved with the organized-labor movement. Sal was a close associate with Ernesto LaCola. His projects included new buildings as well as the roadways and bridges, since they all were built using cement and concrete. The Barone Companies were the largest producer of concrete in the greater New York metropolitan area. It was a monopoly, and they sold millions of dollars of concrete every week. Sal grew up in the business with his father, and through the business, the family had amassed a small fortune. He had ties to organized crime, but even after numerous attempts by the government to incriminate him in illegal activities, they could never get anything to stick. He had business dealings with several Gambino-related companies and had on occasion been seen having dinner with John Gotti. In fact, he owned a few of the companies that shared ownership with Gotti associates. It was a known fact that the Gambino crime family received 2 percent of every concrete contract, but there was never any hard evidence uncovered to involve Barone.

Concrete and cocaine are both off-white powder but served two dramatically different purposes. Concrete helped to build the city, while cocaine was a highly addictive substance that only destroyed lives. When the government had to choose between concrete and cocaine, it always chose to go after the illegal off-white powder. Besides, The Barone Companies had too many political friends and paid off too many cops to be dragged down with the takedown of the five families. Construction was just too important an industry in New York City. Shutting down all the members of the "Concrete Club" would have been too big a cost for the New York City developers, and the building boom in the late eighties would have suffered severely. So, they escaped prosecution, and The Barone Companies continued to prosper. If you had the only concrete plant and controlled all the concrete trucks to deliver the concrete, then you controlled the construction projects. Too many businesses were depending on your product. It was just too important and too big to fail. When you were the only source for ready-mixed concrete, you could not be touched. Together with unions supplying labor, they now had the ability to devise sophisticated schemes that could go on undetected.

Sal Barone slipped through the cracks of the Justice Department, and as the issue of illegal bid rigging cooled, he shifted his attention to building other legitimate businesses. But the temptation was just too great, and he could not stay away from the rackets. The money was too easy, and besides, he loved associating with the syndicate and exploiting the opportunity.

Many of the club members were taken down, but the big prize was the Mafia Commission. The Gambino crime family decided who got to be included in the bid-rigging scheme: how much each would bid, who would get the contract, and how much each would share. But the unions needed to be part of the scheme, since they handled millions of dollars as the supplier of labor. They would be needed since they had the ability to devise a system for distributing the money back to the contractors. Goldin was the accountant, and it was he who devised the process to launder the money using the union computers. Eventually, many of the other trades, including the bricklayers, electricians, and carpenters, became involved.

Chris suspected that the secrets as to how the skim worked were hidden on the seventh floor. Ernesto LaCola's office suite was on the seventh floor and access to that floor was tightly controlled. Very few visitors had access, and only those who occupied an office on the seventh floor were given access. The elevators did not stop at this floor unless you had a special invitation. There was a private staircase in the back of the building that connected the sixth and seventh floors, but this was controlled by magnetic-card access. Once arriving on the seventh floor, you were greeted by an armed bodyguard. The only exception was when they conducted trustee meetings. These were held quarterly, and you needed to be on the list before Angelo the elevator operator would bring you up to the seventh floor. The rear staircase was seldom used, except when LaCola wanted to go down to the sixth floor to discuss something with Greco. LaCola, Stanley, Greco, and Goldin were the only ones who had card access to the back staircase.

Chris was waiting on the sixth-floor lobby with Goldin when he pushed the "up" button to call for the elevator. They could hear the hum of the elevator slowing as it neared the sixth floor and then abruptly stopped as it arrived and the door opened.

"Is he expecting you, Mr. Paul?"

"Yes, Angelo, thank you. Oh, Angelo, this is Chris Vincent. He is our new computer expert, and he will be spending a great deal of time here, so make sure you take good care of him, okay?"

Angelo turned to Goldin, nodded, and then turned to Chris. "How are you?"

Chris provided a return nod in response to the welcoming gesture.

"Look, Chris, just relax and follow my lead, okay? Ernesto is a pretty good guy, and I think you will like him. But he is sharp, and don't try to bullshit him."

They stepped in. The door closed, and the elevator jerked slightly as it moved up to the seventh floor. Angelo was very good at aligning the elevator door to the floors of each stop.

"Here you go, Mr. Paul. Seven."

The elevator door opened. Together, they stepped out into a large reception area paneled in dark walnut. A camera stared directly into the entryway, and another hung in the far corner of the room, peering out into the waiting area toward the two black-leather couches that faced each other in the center of the room. There was a large, circular coffee table in the center between the couches. There was a smartly dressed man of about six feet tall sitting at a desk, facing the front. There was a set of double doors in the middle of the wall to the left and another set of doors directly across the room on the right. The back wall was glass, and Chris could see that this was a large, formal conference room and thought that this was where the trustees' meetings were held.

The seventh floor was called the inner sanctum and was where Ernesto's office suite and the union accounting department conducted their business. Stanley also had an office on the seventh floor, along with auditors from Goldin's accounting firm. Access from the central reception area was to the conference rooms, a large boardroom, kitchen, exercise room, and the finance department. The finance department was comprised of a series of smaller executive offices, along with a large bullpen. Access to LaCola's office suite was through the doors to the left, and access to the finance department was through the doors to the right.

Finance was where the accountants and auditors would review and enter the contractors' reports and where the shop steward reports were reconciled. Goldin had six to eight accountants from his office working in that department under a special agreement with the union. The accountants were billing the union at one hundred dollars an hour.

Paul had called Mary earlier, and she had set aside eleven o'clock for the meeting with Ernesto, but the meeting was delayed half an hour since the business agent was still running on the treadmill in the exercise room adjacent to his office.

The six-footer rose from his chair and walked toward the entry doors to greet them. Chris noticed the small, black handle of a gun that was neatly held in a brown-leather holster strapped under the left breast pocket of his jacket. He had a magnetic card in his right hand.

"Good morning, Mr. Paul. Mr. LaCola is running a little late. Actually, he is still running."

"Hi, Bobby. Thanks. I want to show Chris the finance department. Tell Mary to come and get us when he is free." Paul pulled a plastic card from his wallet and inserted it into the access slot next to the doors to the right. It had a small brass plaque that read, "Accounting." *Click.* The door lock released and the two entered.

Chris and the accountant walked through a small hallway toward a large, open area. Near the end of the hall there was a gray metal door with red letters across the top that read, "HVAC Equipment Room." The accountant stopped, turned to Chris, and said, "Follow me."

Chris was confused at first but followed the accountant into the equipment room. The accountant flipped the light switch on his left as they entered. The small bulb from the hanging fixture over the center of the room barely lit it up. Chris could see that it was the ventilation and air-supply room for the heating and air conditioning for the seventh floor. The large blower motor was contained within a series of metal ductwork from floor to ceiling. There was a small bench in the corner with a red toolbox on top. A small fluorescent light hung down from the ceiling over the bench. Next to the desk was a large electrical panel with a series of circuit breakers, each neatly labeled. A clipboard was hanging from a hook on the wall and Chris noticed the lettering: "Maintenance Schedule."

"What the hell is this all about?" Chris asked.

The sound of the motor and the air movement almost drowned out the sound of his voice. Chris realized that this was where the air-handling equipment was operating for the heating and air-conditioning ventilation. The motor's noise and the movement of air was overpowering their voices.

The accountant brought his right index finger and thumb up to his right ear and pulled on his earlobe. He leaned forward toward Chris's right ear. His voice was barely audible as the sound of the whirling fans and motors moving the air through the ducts competed with their conversation. He moved closer to Chris and spoke directly into his ear.

"Listen to me very carefully; the building is bugged. This is one of only a few areas in the building where it is safe to have a private conversation. There are ears all over, and we must be incredibly careful. Since Giuliani took down the commission, there are some people who are paranoid about wiretapping. Do you understand?"

Chris nodded and quietly responded with a weak yes.

"Chris," he said and looked directly at him. "Your contract for the licensing fee was originally worth $300,000, right?"

Chris once again nodded. "Yes, that is for the software license. The implementation and the conversion are billed on an hourly basis, as we agreed. Williams and I are $175 an hour, and the others are billed at $145."

"Well, we have some more extra work for you, so we have budgeted $550,000. Your end is $450,000, and the other one hundred is for subcontractors. I will work with you on this, but we will have some extra responsibilities for you to perform. There is some extra money for unplanned expenses. The extra $150,000 is for you, and there is another $100,000 for CK Consulting. That ten grand yesterday was for the extra work. We both need to plan for unexpected costs. The extra money for you should cover the extra costs that you will incur. Trust me, this will work in your favor."

He continued. "It's a budget problem, so we had to move the dollars around. Do you understand? Are you on board? Because if not, then we may have a problem. If you have a problem, then the meeting is over right now. I have gone out on a limb for you, and we do not want to be embarrassed. So, it is your call; what is it going to be? Are you in, or are you out?"

Although Chris was surprised it was all happening so fast, he knew how the game was played. He nodded his head in agreement. He was in and had accepted the arrangement during that first meeting with Goldin on the golf course. It was confirmed yesterday with the $10,000 payment to Greco. He was cornered in this little dark room in a situation that was getting even darker. He finally realized that to back away at this point would be hopeless. There was not any chance that he could escape from the harsh reality of the way the union conducted business. "Yes, I understand."

Goldin continued. "Okay, remember: we must trust one another. We will need you to clean up the old system once we get the new software running. But as I said, this is only because we have had to move some expenses around in our budget. Our old software consultant is out for good."

He paused for only a moment and then spoke softly, as their faces were only a few inches apart. "Actually, we want no trace of the old system once we are up and running on your software. Look, that is not why I wanted to speak to you privately. I trust you; otherwise, I would not tell you this."

There was another meaningful pause. "Well, here is this thing. We have been under surveillance by the government. We get audited by the Department of Labor every year. That is a normal event for all unions, and they tear the system apart looking for any little discrepancies. We have been audited for the last several years, and now the FBI is trying to pin some wrongdoings on us. Did you know that the FBI and the DOL have informants that are well paid? Here is the other thing you need to know. We also have people on their side who are actually on our side. They are well paid by us. However, we know that there may be some people working for us who may think that they are running their own business. Simply put, they are stealing from our business.

"Our computer system is weak and has several holes in the process for money to leak out undetected. That is the reason why I have my accountants auditing the contractor reports against the shop stewards' reports. That is why the rate file is critical, and I have examined your fund-accounting process at Local 290. I did not go to Albany just to play golf; I spent considerable time digging into your software. Pretty tight code, and that is why we did not need any demonstration. We especially like the fact that we can change the rate file without the involvement of a programmer. It is date sensitive, correct?"

He hesitated slightly and looked directly into Chris's face. "So, we can easily adjust the rate file by job and by contractor. You see, each contract with the contractor is negotiated, and they are all different. I work directly with LaCola, and we do not want anyone on the outside to know what we do inside the union. And now we do not have to rely on the programmer to manage the flow of the money into the funds. My auditors can make the rate changes on the fly. So, we can keep the seventh-floor process on the seventh floor. Oh, and as for the extra modifications to the software: for starters, we will need you to remove the tracking of changes to the rate-file history, and that is part of the extra money we are allocating to your budget. We need your commitment, and especially your trust."

"Okay, I got it. But when do they sign our agreements? When do we start?" Chris asked.

Goldin looked surprised. "I thought you already started yesterday. Greco gave you his blessing and I gave you the green light. And by the way, I will tell you what to invoice for the payments. Everything is above board, so don't worry about anything. I will have the contract amendments to reflect the new prices by the end of the week. And by the way, the meeting with LaCola is just a formality. He has already checked you out and has talked to Sonny. He is comfortable and has authorized me to sign the software agreements. I wanted to have this conversation before we released any checks. We wanted to be certain that you understood how we conduct business, and you were on our team."

It was warm in the small equipment room, and Goldin wiped beads of sweat from his forehead with his handkerchief. He now understood the harsh reality of the situation he was a part of, which was created long ago from a shabby dream.

"I will go over how this works next week when you come down, but in the meantime, you need to trust me. Anyway, you should have some comfort in knowing that I have some friends at the Labor Department, so we always come out of the audits, worst case, only with a small fine. So, don't worry, this is all good, and I do not want you to worry about anything. Okay?"

"You're the boss."

Goldin continued. "Look, I do not want to put you in a spot, but Sonny gave you something. Was the yellow envelope delivered to our friend from Poughkeepsie?"

"You know about that? I was going to ask you about that."

"Look, I told you that we have friends that look out for us, and you keep passing the tests. So, let's go say hello to Stanley, and then we can meet with Ernesto." Goldin turned and opened the door, and they walked out into the hall.

Chris nodded and followed obediently. They continued to the right toward the door at the end. As they passed through the hall, they entered a large, open room lined with a series of small offices at the far end. On each side of the room were two rows of gray desks. There had to be at least six or seven desks in each row. There was a series of gray filing cabinets along the side wall. Just to the left of the file cabinets there was a large table, and on top were several stacks of red manila folders. There were six or seven auditors sitting at the desks with piles of red and green file folders on top. Each desk had a computer terminal with a display and keyboard. All the auditors seemed to be staring at the computer screens, moving their attention back and forth from the screen to the green and red folders. Alongside each computer terminal there was an adding machine, and the auditors were keying numbers into the adding machines and the computer terminals. Each adding machine had strips of white adding machine tape pushing out from the small, white rolls of paper.

One of the men sitting near the door looked up at the accountant. "Hi, boss."

Goldin turned and nodded. "My firm conducts the contractor audits. We usually have eight to ten auditors working here on a full-time basis. We have to reconcile all the hours reported by the contractors against the shop steward reports. This month is a little slow, and we only have seven working today."

"Why do you have to perform this step? What is with the colored folders?"

Paul walked over to the desk near the window and grabbed a folder. He opened it and pulled out packet of about six papers held together by a paper clip.

"Look, this is the shop steward's report. He is on the job site and records the hours worked for the week by each laborer. When the contractor submits his hours by man, we check to make sure that the number of hours the contractor submits with the shop steward's numbers agree. You know each benefit hour represents $16.25. Think about this: eight to nine thousand members working 140 hours a month. That equates to over a million hours a month. You do the math."

"Wow." Chris was stunned. "Let's see; that is about $17 million a month."

"Right. Actually more. How about a couple hundred million a year, and a 1 percent error represents a couple of million dollars," replied Goldin. He was now beaming, and as he nodded his head up and down, a broad smile crossed his face. "We usually find a couple hundred thousand a month, and isn't it curious, it is always to the contractor's advantage."

Chris was inquisitive. "What about the colored folders?"

Goldin's faced tightened. "Do not concern yourself with the colored folders. It is just audit stuff."

Just then a short, skinny man wearing a white shirt walked out of the corner office. His shirt sleeves were rolled up to his elbows, and he had a skinny black tie loosely tied around his open shirt, which was wrinkled and yellowing around the collar. Chris guessed he was about fifty years old.

"Hey, Stanley. How is it going? I know you briefly met Chris yesterday. Chris Vincent, he is the president of our new software company."

"Great, Paul, and our new guy is going to finally get our computer system straightened out?" Stanley smiled.

Goldin waved his right arm toward Stanley. "Meet Stanley Meckler, who is the controller and knows everything about the union accounting operations. He will be involved throughout the implementation." Paul continued and looked over at Chris.

"Chris, Stanley manages the finance department, and he can answer any questions you have regarding the fund accounting. He is our on-site CPA. I know you will want to get together to go over all of the rates and how the system works for the contractor reporting."

Chris reached out to a small, sweaty hand. Stanley had an old, leather-strapped Timex watch on his left wrist. "Hello. I am looking forward to working with you. I understand that your rate file is time and date sensitive and can be tailored to individual contractors and jobs. Is that correct?"

"Yes, that is correct."

The little guy was wearing gold-rimmed glasses and had a small mustache. Chris thought for a moment and then asked, "How many reports do you receive each month?"

Stanley looked somewhat surprised that Chris was so eager to go to work. He then looked to Goldin, as if to ask for permission to answer. Seeing no objection, he replied, "Well, it depends on the time of year, but we sometimes can get as many as fifteen hundred reports a week. We have lots of contractors. Sometimes, we may get over two thousand. It all, of course, depends on the economy. Right now, we are very busy. Lots of construction jobs and lots of contractors have jobs, and they all need union laborers. We have union laborers in all five boroughs."

As they were talking, Chris noticed that two men entered the room from a door on the back wall. There were bold, white letters on the door that read, "Emergency Fire Exit."

Chris looked toward the fire escape and asked, "What is that about? Is there a fire?"

Stanley smiled. "No, that is the fire escape, and that is where the smokers take their breaks."

Just then, a middle-aged lady walked into the room and approached them. "Hi, Paul. Ernesto is ready to see you." She then turned toward Chris. "Oh, hello; you must be Chris Vincent. My name is Mary, and I am Mr. LaCola's secretary." She reached out her hand. There was a large, green, emerald stone on her middle finger. Chris thought that it had to be at least four or five carats.

"I am very happy to meet you," Chris politely responded, along with a small head bow.

Mary turned and led Chris and Goldin through the reception area and through the double doors on the left. There was another hall, much larger than the accounting side. They then walked into a very large, carpeted room. There were three or four large, L-shaped mahogany desks along the sides. Each was in front of a mahogany door with gold letters painted on the doors. Chris could not make out the lettering. There was a glass-walled conference room to the left, with three crystal lights hanging over an oval table.

"Mr. LaCola will be with you in a few minutes. Won't you please wait in the conference room?" Mary motioned to the door that led to the conference room.

"Coffee or tea for anyone?" she asked. "Or water?"

Chris could feel his stomach growl once again. "No, thanks." He was still recovering from yesterday's lunch.

Paul smiled. "Thanks, Mary. I'm good."

They sat down next to one another, and Paul leaned over to Chris and quietly whispered in Chris's left ear. "Be careful what you say. Ernesto believes the place is bugged."

Chris looked startled. "Huh?"

"Shhhh." Goldin placed his right finger up to his lips.

The two sat there for about five minutes. No one spoke. You could hear the horns honking from Park Avenue seven stories below. The sounds of the trucks and buses seemed to bounce between the neighboring buildings.

It seemed like an hour, but it was just short of ten minutes when Mary returned. "He is ready, Mr. Goldin."

They stood and followed Mary to the double mahogany doors behind the biggest reception desk sitting in a small alcove. The gold letters above the door read, "Ernesto A. LaCola, Business Agent."

They walked through the doors, and on the far end was a large, marble-topped desk with sculptured gold legs. They appeared to be very old and looked like miniature Roman columns. To the right, Chris noticed a butler's pantry with a small refrigerator under a row of cabinets alongside a microwave oven and a sink. The marble counters matched the desktop marble.

LaCola was sitting behind the desk and immediately smiled when he saw the accountant. Goldin smiled and nodded his head as LaCola stood up.

"Ernesto, I would like you to meet Chris Vincent from Advanced Computer Systems. He is a friend of ours, and he is going to install the new software for us." Goldin swung his right arm toward Chris and then waved it toward LaCola as if to say, "It is okay to approach LaCola."

Chris bowed his head slightly out of respect and moved toward the desk. He was surprised, since LaCola was not at all what Chris had expected. He was at least six feet tall, maybe taller. He was well built, but not heavy. He had light hair that was rather short, with an athletic-style haircut. He had penetrating blue eyes and a warm smile. He was very handsome, with movie-star looks, and as he smiled, he flashed a set of natural, perfectly formed, snow-white teeth. He wore a gray jogging suit with "Mets" etched across the front of the jersey in large blue letters bordered in orange. He looked as if he had just come out of an ad from *Gentlemen's Quarterly* magazine. If it were not for the gray jogging suit, Chris would have thought him to be a CEO of a Fortune 500 company or a Wall Street executive.

"Hello. How is Sonny up in Albany?"

"Great, sir; he sends his regards." Chris stopped just a few paces toward the desk and waited for LaCola to reach out his right hand—which he never did, but instead abruptly sat back down in his chair. LaCola was not the typical BA; he was well educated, having graduated from New York University. His father was a union man and had been involved in organized labor for over twenty years, having worked his way through various positions throughout the union organization, which culminated in serving as the BA for over twenty years of his organized-labor career. LaCola's grandfather had been the BA before Ernesto's father, and it was just assumed that they could hand it down from father to son as if it were a family-owned business. Even though they had elections every four years, they were secure and held power through intimidation, fixed elections, bribery, or plain, old strong-arm tactics. Ernesto was healthy, big, and a solid-looking man, and as a business organizer had erased the lingering signs of crudeness from the past LaCola generations. When he spoke, he had a determined gaze, and his hand gestures seemed to model his words. Chris liked him immediately.

Chris thought the union business was not much different from that of the politicians in Washington and the famous Hollywood families. You owned it, and it was part of the family. When you have the power and the money, you can do just about anything necessary to accomplish your objectives. Ernesto was groomed to work in organized labor. His father insisted that he would go to college and then on to law school. And so, as expected, the young LaCola enrolled in New York University. He graduated with high honors in just three years and was accepted into the law program at Columbia. However, love intervened, and after two semesters, he exchanged the classroom for a family. He was immediately elevated to a position as a labor organizer in Local 4. It was preordained that when his father retired, he would be the next BA. He had been a member of the local since he was sixteen and had worked summers, not as a laborer but in the office. He was thirty-four when the plan was accelerated with the sudden death of his father. It was only expected that he would run for the position vacated by his father's death. It was not even close. He was young, smart, good-looking, and energetic, and it proved to be a landslide victory for the younger LaCola. He was now in his early fifties but looked no older than forty-five. He had now served as the BA for almost twenty years, and his position was very secure.

Ernesto walked around the desk toward the small, round conference table to the side of his desk. He sat down and motioned for them to sit down as well.

"Where are you from?" asked LaCola.

"Albany, sir." Chris replied as he started to relax.

"Oh, yes. That's right. Married?"

"No … well … actually, yes, kind of. Separated … let's see … almost two years now," Chris answered, although a bit annoyed that LaCola was probing into private matters.

LaCola looked across at Chris. "You're Italian, right?"

"Yes, sir," Chris responded, wondering where this was all going to lead.

"Good, good. We like Italians—and, of course, Jews." He turned his head toward Goldin.

Paul smiled and flashed a quick grin in response.

"I suppose you have been briefed about Local 4. I spoke to Greco briefly, and he told me that you have already started. I do not have to tell you this, but your work here is very important. Our members depend on this office. We provide them with their livelihood. We deliver an important service. And when the computer is down, it affects everything that we do. The computer keeps the dollars flowing in and out. We cannot afford a fuck-up. We have invested hundreds of thousands of dollars in our systems, and they are the lifeblood of our organization.

"But what is most critical is the information that we have in this office. We have over sixty years of data records in all forms of media. Punched cards, magnetic cards, computer tapes, and, of course, computer disks. We even have data in the form of three by five cards, ledger cards, and some on the old eighty-column punched cards. If you cannot get the job done, we are screwed and are in trouble—big trouble. Yes, you have been referred to us with strong recommendations."

He hesitated for a few seconds and then concluded, "And I am confident that you will be successful. I trust Paul's judgment, and we know you will do a great job. We have a system, and yes, I admit that it can be improved, but we cannot afford it when the computer system goes down." LaCola stopped and stared directly into Chris's eyes as he leaned forward.

Paul interrupted. "We have had a lot of computer crashes, and we know from experience that a system as complicated as ours can be problematic. That is why we have hired you."

LaCola continued. "Right. But the most important thing for you to remember is that everything is legitimate. The law requires that we keep this information confidential and secure. What goes on at Local 4 stays at Local 4. Look, I will make things simple for you. The government oversight is constant, and the reports we provide must be accurate."

He looked over at the accountant and smiled.

"The Department of Labor is the oversight agency and constantly looking into our operations. The liberals are screaming to increase wages for McDonald's and Walmart workers. They are screaming to pass health-care reform. They are screaming to increase benefits. The White House wants to provide more welfare benefits and redistribute hard-earned money from those who have earned it. Bush has been an okay president, but he is anti-labor. What do you expect? He is a Republican. The conservative politicians want to eliminate the unions. The Democrats want our money and our votes. No matter who is in power, we get squeezed. Our members work hard and are not on food stamps. We exist because we provide a needed service."

His delivery became more deliberate. "Chris, unions represent a powerful voice in our country and will play an even greater role in the future. It will take some time, maybe twenty-five or thirty years, but unions will grow significantly and will elect senators and presidents, and only when that happens will you see just how powerful unions will become. You and I may not be around, but what we do today will have consequences for the future. So, your work is important, and we are counting on you. Understand?"

"Ernesto, Chris is on our team. We have a signed contract, and he has agreed to our confidentiality agreement. We have discussed our budget problem and have a clear understanding of the fees. We are all good." Paul looked over to Chris and nodded. He made sure that LaCola saw him wink his right eye.

LaCola now stood up. "If there are any problems with any of the staff, you go to Paul. Understood? Remember that your job is critically important to the union, and I know you are aware of the Albany Life Science and Tech Center construction project. Do not forget that project. Everything is riding on that contract. For this union and our contractors, it provides the fuel for the liftoff of our future economic engine. There are many union families depending on that project. Keep that in mind. I don't know if Paul gave you the number, but I know you have talked to Sonny in Albany. Roughly speaking, it amounts to over $5 billion in construction work. Maybe six or seven. We need a computer that works perfectly. Especially when it comes to the reciprocity hours. But I have confidence in your ability, since you have come to us with good recommendations."

LaCola stood up and walked back toward his chair behind the desk. Goldin now realized that the meeting was over. It was LaCola's polite way of dismissing them. Paul stood, looked over to Chris, and waited for him to stand.

Chris, with a slight bow of the head, politely said, "Thank you very much, Mr. LaCola. I am looking forward to working with your people. You can count on me and my team."

Before he stood, he reached in his pocket and gave LaCola the white envelope, knowing that it contained the list of the senators serving on the Senate subcommittee who would be voting against the right-to-work bill in Albany. Next to each name were listed the amounts of political contributions the senators were expecting. Chris stood, turned toward the door, and followed Goldin out of the office. Just before he exited, he stopped and turned back toward LaCola.

"Oh, Mr. LaCola, Sonny sends his best regards."

Before reaching the door, Goldin turned and casually saluted to LaCola. "Ernie, I will see you after lunch. Actually, why don't we go over to Da Umberto's and grab some of those artichokes?"

"No can do. I have a contractor meeting in a couple of hours, but I will call you later."

Chris stepped into the elevator with the accountant. Neither spoke a word as they were ferried down to the building entry lobby. Chris followed the accountant to the sidewalk, and as they reached the corner, he turned to Chris.

"Chris, let's just say that the speech was not necessarily for your benefit. That was for the little rats with the big ears. The message for you is simple: anything you find, good or bad, you only discuss it with me. Got it? I think you now know that you will be well paid if you perform. This is a complicated business, and everything is riding on your success. As he said, many families are depending on the Albany waterfront project, and our success on that job will be tied to our computer."

"Yes, sir." Things appeared to be moving in a positive direction and Chris felt good about the project, but not so good about the people who he would be working with. He had met with both Greco and LaCola. He liked LaCola, but Greco, not so much. More important, he thought that they liked him, and that was all that mattered. Perhaps more important, he had delivered the three envelopes with no incidents, and he finally breathed a sigh of relief.

Goldin looked at Chris as he said, "Good job, Chris. We will need weekly progress reports and expect to have regularly scheduled status meetings every other week. I need to go back to my office and will be tied up for the rest of the week. Call me Friday and let me know your thoughts for a project schedule."

They shook hands as Goldin turned and walked to the corner, where there was a waiting black Lincoln.

CHAPTER THIRTEEN

MONEY TALKS

WEEK FIVE: NEW YORK CITY

IT WAS THE SECOND WEEK of May, and the computer implementation remained on schedule. It had been five weeks since Chris was first introduced to Greco and LaCola. Chris had assigned his team leader, Pete Williams, to the account, along with Frank Bevens, an accomplished programmer-analyst, to assist with the implementation. Frank had been working for Chris for over five years and was very familiar with union accounting systems and knew how the software worked. They were making good progress and were converting the history records. The new programs were loaded in the test library, and they were busy setting up the rate tables they used for testing. It all worked perfectly. Williams and Frank huddled together, peering at a computer screen. Williams was showing Frank a new subroutine in the claims system and pointing out how he had coded the routine. Frank, who was very detail oriented, was taking notes on how the new process worked.

Just then, Goldin walked in and sat next to Chris. "Hey, things are looking good for the new software. I just had a chat with Greco, and he tells me that he thinks this is all going very well. Once we get this up and running, this will be a big relief for the union. You know, I have a lot of other accounts that I have neglected lately, and I am spending an awful lot of time here. Just thought you might like to know."

"I know that. And I agree; it is a lot of work, but we should be able to get through this. I pulled Frank off our new-product-development team and have assigned him to this account full time. He is working on an hourly basis, plus expenses. It may not be cheap, but he knows what he is doing. And for every hour Frank works, you get exactly sixty minutes—no slacking off, and you get his full attention," Chris replied.

"No problem; we all understand. We told you that the only thing that counts is getting the job done and getting us to go live on the new system on schedule."

"Hey, Paul, will you do me a favor and talk to Stanley about cutting us a few checks? We never got paid for the first half of the licensing fee. It has been several weeks since we started, and according to the new contracts, we were supposed to get half of the licensing fee when the contracts were executed. There are also hourly services invoices that they should have paid. If Stanley needs to see me, I will be here every day this week through Thursday afternoon."

Goldin stood and motioned Chris to follow. "I will mention it to Stanley for sure. Actually, let's have a chat right now. Let me call Stanley and have him come down."

Chris stood up and dutifully followed Goldin as he walked toward the sixth-floor breakroom. They entered and approached a metal door in the far corner of the room next to the soda machines. Just then, Stanley walked through the door that had access to the private staircase that connected the sixth floor to the seventh floor.

Chris focused his attention on the magnetic card reader next to the door. "Hey, Paul, is that the private entrance to the seventh? You mean we need card access to go this way to the seventh floor? Why such secrecy? What is so secret about the auditors? I eventually will need to understand the process."

Goldin looked somewhat surprised, since he did not expect Chris to ask him about the auditors. He placed his right index finger to his mouth.

"You do not need to know anything about what goes on up there. Understood?"

His eyes immediately darkened as he looked directly at Chris. "But I can tell you this: the auditors handle that end of the business. Too much money to trust anyone. I think you understand that the government is auditing the union, and this is an annual event required by law. This year, they seem to be getting more aggressive, since they have pressure from Washington to find problems with our union. This governor from Arkansas, if he gets in, wants to hijack the health-care system.

"Our processing is a bit outdated, to say the least, but we have a great health plan, and we are well funded. They are looking to find fault with the administration of our funds, so if they can find inefficiencies, they will have reasons to shut us down. He is supposed to be on the side of organized labor, but no one should trust a politician. I think he has his mind on the ladies. Washington wants to take over the health-care system for the entire country. If they are successful, it will put you and me out of business. That is why we must get the new system up as soon as possible. We have a Cadillac health insurance plan and only want to improve our processing efficiencies. That is your only concern."

Goldin turned and greeted Stanley with a nod of his head. Stanley said not a word but obediently nodded back. "Stanley, let's talk; can we have a brief chat about money?"

Stanley replied, "Yes, but let's talk privately." He walked toward the fire-escape door. "Let's go out here."

Goldin followed as he motioned to Chris. "Chris, this way."

Chris reluctantly poked his head out the door and peered at the fire-escape platform. It was a typical iron-grated fire escape that was built when the building was constructed years earlier. Chris was visibly frightened as he looked at the iron platform and toward the concrete alley six floors below. The platform was rust colored and about four feet deep by roughly six feet wide, attached to the building wall. There was an iron railing on the outside of the platform and a series of stairs that went down to the floors below. From the second-floor platform there was a vertical ladder that could be lowered to the concrete alleyway at street level during an emergency. Alongside the staircase going down was another iron staircase connecting to the floors above. A cold sweat immediately overtook Chris as he gripped the railing tightly with both hands as he was about to step out onto the platform. He then stopped and turned back.

"Paul, I do not like this fire-escape thing. I mean, does this thing really hold all three of us up here?"

"Relax; relax. You want to talk money, right? This is the man who cuts the checks."

Stanley smiled and said, "Chris, I would have cut you the checks, but we only cut checks at the end of the month. But I also need authorization and a second signature for any amounts over $10,000. I also need to know what accounts we need to apply the payments to. I can write a check for $150,000 for the first half of the licensing fee but still need sign-offs. I can also cut a check for the hourly fees and the expenses but need the okay from Greco and LaCola. By the way, what are the new invoices for?"

Goldin spoke up. "Stanley, that is the budget problem we discussed last week, and it has been approved. We can pay them."

Chris's face tightened and turned white, and they were not certain if it was from his fear of heights or simply anger over the money they owed him. But he was not about to step outside. He could not look down at the concrete alley six floors below.

"What do you mean? Paul, the license fee is $450,000. So, I thought the first payment is $225,000." Chris turned to Paul Goldin, visibly shaken as his fear intensified.

Goldin replied, "Stanley, let's just write the checks. The licensing fee is $450,000, so you can pay the first half now, and the second half is due when we go live. We added some extra modules. I will get them signed." He turned to Chris. "How much do you need right now?"

"I have about $400,000 in outstanding invoices, and this only includes half the licensing fees. The travel and living expenses have me out-of-pocket close to $50k."

"Okay, Stanley will cut checks at the end of the month. And you need to send me the other invoices for the extra work, remember? One of the invoices should be made out to CK Consulting. That will cover half the $100,000 for the extra work."

The platform rocked ever so slightly, as the wind had gained some speed as it funneled between the tall buildings. Although Chris could see that perhaps there was little danger, he remained reluctant to step out onto the platform. He could not get his mind away from the possible disaster that he feared would take place. He thought he could hear bolts pulling from the brick siding and was certain the platform was going to break loose and hurl them to the pavement six floors below. Contrary to Chris's fears, the bolts held the platform securely to the side of the building, despite their rusty condition. It did not matter, as he remained deathly afraid of the imagined fall. Chris was now realizing the extent of his acrophobia and became dizzy as he looked out to the men on the fire escape.

"Paul, Stanley, if you don't mind, I am not comfortable out on that fucking platform. I don't smoke and would rather we talk inside, so excuse me."

Stanley looked over to Chris. "What is the matter? Do you have vertigo?"

"Well, it is called acrophobia. Sorry." Chris had had enough. He turned and was about to walk away, even though the discussion was about money.

Goldin and Stanley watched Chris as he turned away. They remained on the platform and continued to talk for a few more minutes while Chris regained his composure. He looked at the door and noticed that there was no lock. There was a small sign on the side of the door that read, "This is an emergency exit. Must remain unlocked at all times. By order of NYFD."

After a few minutes, Goldin and Stanley finally stepped back in from the fire escape. Goldin walked over to Chris and looked directly into his eyes. He had a serious look on his face, a look that Chris had not seen before.

"Just follow me."

They walked back to the computer room, and Goldin motioned for Chris to follow him next to the computer disk units, where a small hum came from the system fans. Goldin was the first to speak, in a very low voice so no one could hear what he was about to say.

"We can talk privately here. Chris, we had to know for sure that we could trust you and you were on our side. We know that the FBI will ask you about your business here, so we are extra careful, and your loyalty will continue to be tested. It is that simple. When they approach you, I need to know about it. They will threaten you and try to intimidate you, so do not let it get to you. You are on our team, and our team is protected. I wish I could share more information with you, but for now, just trust me. At some point, we will tell you what you need to know, but in the meantime, you need to understand that the FBI has always tried to intimidate us and any of the people we do business with. This is normal practice for them.

"I am not asking you to do something that you have not agreed to, but I am asking you to tell me when they approach you. It is just a matter of time. We will tell you what to say. Never—and I mean *never*—betray the family. You can never flip over to their side. They are bad news; you must never trust them, and you can never win with them. They will destroy your business and take you down. Just keep your mouth shut and trust us. We are protected because we have friends. Not just in Albany, but especially after the election, we should have some very powerful friends in Washington."

Goldin raised his hands in a calming gesture. "And for the good news, you will get paid all that I promised. I guarantee it. In fact, Stanley is cutting checks at the end of the month, and I will get the necessary signatures."

Goldin did not ask him if he had been contacted by the FBI or any other government agency, and Chris was unsure of what he would do if that occurred. He was just starting and although he suspected that there was danger ahead, he was still committed to the project and would remain loyal to the union. He did not have a choice. He was in too deep and needed the money.

"Look, I am simply following your instructions. I just want to be sure and do not wish to get involved in the politics or any of the union's legal matters. I am here to do a job and expect to get paid for doing the job. What is going on here? What about my trust in you? You know, trust is built, not given, and it seems that I am the only one doing all the giving."

"Chris, just do what we ask you to do. Get the new system up and running. Do not concern yourself with our government business. This stuff with the feds is not any of your concern. If you get the system up before the new year, everyone is going to be very grateful and very happy. It is that simple. We have a timeline that needs to be met."

"Well, I understand, but I need to know that I am going to be paid. As they say, bullshit walks and money talks. As you know, we are working here four days a week and the billable time is getting up there, and we are well into the job and have not seen a penny. You need to follow through with your end of this so-called business relationship. A little kick in the ass with accounts payable and Stanley will take some of the financial pressure off my shoulders so that I can concentrate on getting this fucking installation completed on time," Chris's speech was frantic as he looked away from Goldin. He then looked down and back up again before he continued.

"Paul, I trust you guys, but the dollar only goes so far. I need to know that the union is not taking advantage of my trusting nature. I run a small shop and am getting a lot of pressure from my bank. The union owes me close to $400,000, and everyone has told me money is not an issue. Well, show me. It is an issue with me, and when you are owed that much money, strange things happen. As you have said, a business needs extra money to deal with the unexpected."

Goldin looked across at Chris. "I understand completely. We can speak about this another time. It is in the works."

"Please just get me the money owed." Chris was feeling much better now that they were in the computer room. "And as for the fire escape, no, thank you; if there is fire, I prefer the elevator."

Paul now seemed more relaxed in his speech. "Chris, we have a man on the inside, and we are not concerned with the audit. You see, we are always one step ahead of them, and there is too much at stake and too many people involved. We have friends with serious connections. There is too much money and too many people in high places involved. So, we have protection. You might say, we have insurance. So don't worry about the feds."

Chris readily accepted his situation, since he was committed. He knew it was too late to turn back. He did feel some comfort in hearing from Goldin that he would get paid, but he also realized that the union was corrupted, and the people involved were very dangerous.

Goldin continued, "Chris, maybe I should not tell you, but both Sonny and I have gone out on a limb for you and have vouched for you, so you need to trust us. You will constantly be tested, so just keep passing the tests. We know that you will be asked to deliver certain things from Albany, so just do what we ask you to do, and keep your mouth shut. We are all in the real-estate business, and you are an investor. Your investments are going to pay big returns for you."

Chris looked at Goldin's face as he spoke. "I got it, but can I trust the union? My test is simple: I do the work, send you an invoice, and then you write a check. That is a basic test of a trusted business relationship."

"Trust me. I just told you some things that maybe I shouldn't have. Trust me. I brought you in on this, and you were told that I am the point man. Correct? I know about the yellow envelope, so relax. You were told not to say anything, and you did what was expected. You never said anything to me. You were simply following Sonny's instructions. As I said earlier, you will continually be tested, so be on your toes. I am your new friend, and I will need to know when anyone talks to you about the union business."

Chris nodded in agreement. "Paul, you keep talking about trust. Let's see some proof from your side."

"Yes, you are correct. But I need you to do something for me. It may sound a bit strange," Goldin said.

"Based on what I have seen so far, strange is normal in New York City," answered Chris.

"I need you to train my auditors on the rate-file setup. It looks easy, and you can check that task off your implementation plan. My people are familiar with the employer contracts, and it will be easier if they take care of the rate files. All the reporting is handled on the seventh floor by my auditors and is not anything you need to worry about. You mentioned that it is date sensitive, so we can apply the rates for each contractor agreement by date and job. Rates can change by job, so we can set it all up and not have to worry about the reports. That is one of the problems with the old system. Marty Bloom hard-coded the rates, and every time we needed to change them, he had to come in and change the program—that is, whenever he decided to show up. But when that happened, we had to wait for him to show us, and we could not enter the contractor reports."

"No problem; let me know when you want to set up the training session. I will do the training personally. We also have a training manual that covers the entry process," Chris replied and then looked across at Goldin with a serious expression on his face. "By the way, what happened to Bloom?"

Goldin replied, "History."

CHAPTER FOURTEEN

FBI IN THE BIG APPLE

MAY 16, 1992

M ARCO RICHARDS CLIPPED THE VISITOR'S badge to the lapel on his dark-blue suit jacket as the buzzer sounded, opening the second glass door.

He had studied the case file, had a planning session with Samples the day before, and was eager to get started. Samples had told him that the SAC review was a formality and there were seldom any changes or suggestions from the assistant director. Their only concern was to verify that the team had a written plan that would be followed. The review was a formality, and he was told that Macey knew exactly how it would all play out. Regardless of the prepared schedule, Samples expected Macey to shorten the timeline. She told Marco that they were only interested in results and timelines.

Samples had a prepared project plan with a list of scheduled assignments for each of the agents. She had also assigned dates to each of the tasks. Little had changed since their first meeting in Washington a week earlier.

Macey once again looked around the table and stopped when he came to Marco.

"Richards, I have a question I have been meaning to ask you. Hope you don't mind."

Marco, feeling more confident, replied with a bright expression on his face. "No problem, sir. Ask away."

Macey gave a questioning tilt of his head and asked, "How was it you were so successful in hacking into that Russian computer system?"

"I was ... well ... actually, lucky," Marco answered not so confidently, since he had not anticipated the question.

"Really? And how in the world did you get lucky?"

Marco had gotten hold of himself and thought, "Give them your standard line of BS. Talk over their heads."

Now he felt a bit more confident. "Well, I just hacked into their computer and was able to initiate a statistical approach to analyzing the available data. It involved parsing all the crap out of the data and then scrubbing, codifying, and normalizing the data into meaningful information and weighted rules. I then pulled the Medicare coding compliance data sets and ran the claims through our Medicare audit system. I compared what was paid to what should have been paid. Since I had applied values to each of the variables and assumptions, when I was through, the computer gave me a score. I looked at the score and then followed the money trail to the providers who were getting the payments above the benchmarks my program had established. Those were the providers with the high scores."

Macey interrupted. "Stop; stop; stop; I got it." He smiled as he looked over at Connie Samples. "Richards, I have a feeling that you will do just fine."

The gray suit, Charles Crowley, wanted to know more and asked, "But how in the hell were you able to break the process down in just a short time, when the Justice Department had been working on the case for over two years—and with a staff of over fifteen agents?"

"Well, sir, the standard statistical notation for investigative analysis tends to overemphasize the attention of the technical aspects of research." Now Marco had his chance to really snow them with a lot of gibberish.

But Macey cut him off. "Look, Charles, he is our man, and let's get the show on the road. I am confident he can handle the assignment."

Macey closed the second folder and continued. "Richards, we are going to send you to New York tomorrow, and I anticipate that you will do great things for us on this assignment. Remember what we discussed privately during our first meeting. Teamwork and dedication to the job will always get outstanding results."

With that, he placed the folders into his briefcase in front of him. "Oh, and one final word. I do not care how you do it, as long as you get the results we are looking for. Connie will see to all the paperwork, ensuring that it reflects FBI protocol and procedures. You're an analyst and can easily figure out what I mean. Good luck, and God speed." He looked across at Samples and smiled weakly.

Marco was excited, and although he had some questions that remained, he realized that this would be his big career-making opportunity.

"Yes, you can count me in. You can count on me."

The organized-crime task force members would focus on the Gambino side of the investigation and attempt to turn witnesses over to their side. They would exchange information with the New York team when they arrived in the city. Marco's job would be to find the forensic data within the union's computer systems to find out how they were stealing the money. They needed evidence, and they knew that the union's computer was what made it all possible. Local 4's computer held all the answers. They knew that millions of dollars were being siphoned out, and the team would be relying on Marco to unlock the door and figure out how it was accomplished.

The FBI was a field-oriented organization with over 12,000 special agents and another 20,000 support professionals, comprised of intelligence analysts, language specialists, scientists, and information-technology specialists. With over 30,000 employees, one could say it was overburdened with bureaucrats and a myriad of management levels. The organization was complex, with many departments disorganized and overburdened and prone to mistakes. It had nine divisions to provide program direction and support services to 56 field offices and approximately four hundred satellite offices known as resident agencies, four specialized field installations, and then there were another two dozen foreign liaison posts.

Career paths were complex, and while there were several opportunities for advancements even for the average agent, the process was fraught with politics and favoritism. To get along and have any opportunity to step up the next rung on the ladder, one had to put in the time and play the game according to the book, and you had to know exactly when and how to take hold of the next rung on the ladder. It was not accomplished by yourself, and you would need others to help you along the way. For Marco, he realized that this was a big break for him, and the next rung was now within reach—he had to immediately grab it when he saw it. That is, if he wanted to climb up. He was somewhat confused by what Macey had told him and was still uncertain if he was suited for the job as a field agent.

But this was New York, and there were hundreds of separate covert criminal investigations. It would be impossible to expect coordination with all the other police authorities, let alone across the spectrum of the entire FBI organization. Investigations were divided into several different programs, and there was considerable overlap among the various programs, since the criminal activity was vast and widespread. Individual cases in a particular program may receive extensive investigative attention because of their size, potential impact, or sensitivity, and this was one of them. The bureau's guidelines afforded centralized direction, which allowed for greater uniformity and control, but there was always considerable interpretation as it was passed across and up and down the various departments and levels.

The train was heading north to New York City. It was an express from Washington and would arrive at Penn Station around 4:00 p.m. Marco was thinking about dinner with the girl next to him. Connie was sleeping, and he could smell her perfume. He had no idea as to what kind it was, but he guessed it was French. Courting a female was too far back in his past. He tried to avoid the obvious stare but could not resist. Every ten or fifteen minutes, he would turn to make certain that she was still there in the seat next to his. Marco could not avoid peering at her moist, red lips and her perfectly manicured nails as they contrasted perfectly against her blemish-free complexion. She was very pretty, and he never had expected to be working with such a charming and beautiful girl. He knew she was in her mid-thirties but looked much younger.

He caught himself and thought, "Business, strictly business, and be and act professional at all times." That was what he had been told by many agents far more experienced than he. Marco came to his senses and realized that it was nothing more than wishful thinking and nothing would ever develop between them. She was a career agent, and her priority was the bureau. He saw that in the way she had presented the case file. Nevertheless, he had high hopes and was trying to come up with an approach but knew that he would never get to first base. Deep down, he had the uneasy feeling that he would not get any hits.

Marco was anxious to arrive in New York, dig his teeth into the investigation, and prove to them that he knew what he was doing. He believed that he would be instrumental in the success of the investigation and was excited about the assignment. This was Marco's first big field assignment, and he had the confidence that he would perform his duties well. But he remembered what Macey had cautioned him: "Expect the unexpected."

Marco was not officially a field agent but knew that this was his big opportunity. He was still a computer analyst and had been working under the policies and laws developed under the Computer Fraud and Abuse Act of 1986. These were policies and guidelines that required strict adherence as to how the government applied the law. He understood what Macey was saying and what he was inferring to as to Marco and how this investigation was to be handled. In many ways, it was in conflict with what he had learned while working as an analyst. There were many additional factors, and while he knew what was appropriate and what did not have legal authority, he now recognized that he would be walking a fine line that would zigzag across both sides.

He understood that in determining whether to bring a charge for violation under the act in a case involving obtaining information from a protected computer, consideration should be given to the sensitivity and value of the information involved and the potential for harm associated with its disclosure or use. The union's computer had a great deal of sensitive information, and much of it could not be disclosed to the public. It really didn't matter much, since the sensitive health history would be redacted. Marco was very familiar with the statutes and he liked his job. He decided he would play by the team rules but did not want to risk his career. He thought about it and realized he would be doing a balancing act on a high wire. If he were to look down, he would see that there was no net protecting his fall.

It was almost 6:30 when Marco checked in at the Roosevelt Hotel on Second Avenue. He remembered the scene from the movie *The French Connection*, when Popeye Doyle was shadowing the

Frenchman. It was a decent hotel in its younger days but was now dated and drab. The rooms were small and reasonably clean, yet the musty smell it emitted gave away its age. He was on the government contract, $89.50 a day, and there were few hotels in the city that still honored the rate, so he was left with little choice. Summer was fast approaching, and the weather was perfect. His room was on the sixth floor, and as he walked in, he could still hear sounds of the traffic from the street below his window.

Although he had gotten to know Samples a little better, there was no dinner that evening. She claimed she had too much paperwork and wanted to go straight to her hotel. She mentioned that she would interview the new computer specialist when the time was right and would attempt to coerce him into cooperating with them, but she had no confidence that this would be accomplished. She also told Marco that agents from the Albany office would interview him and accuse him of collaboration. She thought that they might be able to scare him into wearing a wire.

Macey and Samples had briefed Marco on the assignment and had provided extensive background on the union's activities. They had a tremendous amount of information consisting of surveillance videos and recorded conversation, both within the union offices and outside—but none that would incriminate anyone and none on the seventh floor that would work for them in a courtroom. Hundreds of photos and considerable circumstantial evidence were available, but there was little or no incriminating evidence as to how they were fixing the bids and skimming money from the contracts. The Department of Labor audited the union each year, and the actuarial reports, when compared to the benchmark data, indicated huge discrepancies. But most of it was circumstantial, and they needed much more before they could bring it before a grand jury. They also had several photos of union officials meeting with members of the Gambino crime family, and they even had photos of meetings on the fire escape on the sixth and seventh floor of 230 Park Avenue South. This was sufficient to allow them to obtain a court order for placing bugs throughout the building, but obtaining hard evidence of a crime proved to be difficult. Samples' presentation in Washington had been impressive, but there was much work to do since they needed hard proof of criminal activities. They had some early success by intimidation, but very little paper trail that they could use to connect the missing money to those who controlled the union.

This is where Marco was supposed to come in. His job was to penetrate their computer systems and identify exactly how the money was siphoned from the funds. His assignment was to unravel the computer programs and connect the dots. There actually were several cases that they had been investigating. It wasn't just the union and the labor leaders. There were also criminal activities, such as bribery and extortion that reached out to politicians and business leaders. No one would be immune, and their activities were to be tracked and recorded. According to Samples, there was a very extensive network of bad actors involved. *Bad actors* was the term she gave to them. The FBI investigation had revealed that in addition to the typical mafia activities of gambling, murder, and bribery, the mafia had successfully infiltrated the New York construction industry and union business.

He chuckled as he thought about it, sure this was just another computer hack job, but what would he do after he found the passwords? He needed to see the computer programs and interpret how they worked with the union data files. That would not be an easy task. The operating system was quite sophisticated, and he would need to find either a communications path or a hard-wired path. Not like the many breaches he had achieved with the PCs and the open-network systems used by many of PC network-based systems he had hacked into. Windows was a cool operating system and had considerable functionality, but it did have a big negative. It was an open system and was easy to hack into through the internet.

The IBM mainframe was a different story and would be a challenge even for a computer genius like Marco. He knew he needed to somehow get into the building or connect with one of the remote terminal connections. His work was cut out for him, but he was looking forward to the challenge. He thought about it. Maybe two or three weeks, at the most. That would depend on a lot of things going right.

Connie had scheduled a meeting the next day at 7:00 a.m. at the hotel coffee shop. She was staying at the Hilton. He thought, "I guess she has more time in grade than I do."

He was early; she was late. It was twenty after when she finally walked in.

"Hello; how is your room?" she asked.

Marco turned, and his face lit up with a brief smile. "Small and musty smelling. But it will have to do. Hopefully, I can get the hell out of here and into a nice hotel, like the Hilton or maybe even the Holiday Inn on Fifty-Seventh."

She slid into the booth across from Marco, and the slit along the left side of her skirt slid up slightly to reveal a perfectly formed left leg. She noticed Marco's gaze in the direction of her lower body as he tilted his head slightly to his right. She made no attempt to pull down her skirt over her bare thigh. For just a second or two, he thought, "Hey, maybe I do have a chance after all. She is advertising."

He smiled with a slight tilt to his head to let her know that he had noticed that she had done it intentionally and that she knew he knew it was intentional. He could play games as well. Maybe he could get to first base after all, even if it was an intentional walk.

She smiled back. "Okay, here is the deal. We have a friendly judge who may sign our court order, so we may be able to place a few bugs in several rooms at 2:30. But we cannot get anything up on the seventh floor. They scan every week, and the physical security is very strong. The phone taps are ineffective, since they have dozens of trunk lines and over eighty extensions. They have an IBM mainframe, an IBM AS/400, and the operating system, as you may know, is very tight. There are several levels of security. We cannot telecommunicate into their network. And to make matters worse, they are installing new software. They have selected a small software company from Albany as their new vendor, and from what we have learned about them, the software is excellent and has several additional layers of security. They have been installing the new software for about two months."

She continued. "Our Albany team is about to interview their company president; his name is Chris Vincent. Hopefully, they can scare him into wearing a wire for us. We even have a few pictures of him with our targets at the union. He is very close to Sonny Russo in Albany, who is also involved. We used the pictures to ask for a court order for the wire on Vincent. Hopefully, we can scare him into cooperating with us. We have the RICO Act to lean on, and this may be our best tool. We need to scare Vincent that we have evidence of his involvement. We have dates and times of meetings and even have some pictures that may involve Vincent. No one does business with the unions unless they play by the union rules. If he refuses, then we can put more pressure on him through scare tactics. Their old software programmer, Marty Bloom, is missing, but I do not think he is about to turn up. I think they got rid of him. We had several conversations with Bloom, and he agreed to cooperate, but we never were able to get his written affidavit. We put a lot of pressure on him and were just starting to turn him when he vanished. We'll simply ask Vincent to ask his union buddies what happened to Marty Bloom. He will get the picture."

She smiled at Marco and then continued. "We also have liberal judges that help us when necessary. But so do they. I think Vincent may be clean, but he is going to eventually get dirty. No one plays in their sandbox without getting some sand in their shoes."

The red soft-leather satchel that had been hanging on her right shoulder now rested at her side. She reached in and pulled out a black three-ring binder. It was about an inch thick. She placed it on the table, turned it to face Marco, and then slowly pushed it toward him.

"This is what we have so far with our linked-in binder. But we need hard evidence, and that is why we have called in a computer expert like you. We certainly would like to hear conversations on the seventh floor, but so far, we have not been very successful. That is why we would like to get someone to wear a wire. I have been working on this case for over two years and have a lot of background information, but nothing to bring it before a grand jury. Macey has decided to take a different approach, which is why you have been selected. We think the timing is good, with the new computer software and the new company from Albany. This guy, Chris Vincent, may be the key, and if you cannot break into the system, then we will need to put pressure on him. So you are onstage right now, and we trust you will be able to make some headway. If not, then we will need to turn Vincent."

She pointed to the notebook that she had pushed toward Marco. "Look this over carefully. It has a list of all the contacts our targets have made over the last two years. It has the dates and times. From the initial target list, we have expanded the investigation to several additional targets. We need to go over to the operations office this morning, at 249 Park Avenue South. We operate out of a small office on the third floor. We are fronting as a computer-supply company—you know, paper, ribbons, floppy disks. We can photograph visitors going in and out of 230, and we have a good angle to the fire escape on the seventh floor. But we cannot get any sound or get inside."

Marco opened the binder to the first page. It was indexed, and there were about thirty sections. He flipped over the first tab. The first page consisted of a numbered list of twenty-six names. Ernesto

LaCola was the first name on the list, followed by Nicola Greco and then Senator Vic Sano. The first page was followed by twenty-six indexed sections. Each of the sections had one of the names from the first page at the top of that section. It was a book of contacts with names, locations, dates, and times.

Marco said, "I don't understand, I thought that this was supposed to be all about the union. What the hell does a state senator have to do with all this?"

"Look, do not be so naïve. Albany is definitely involved, and there is a multibillion-dollar project that will flow hundreds of millions of dollars to the unions. The New York Technology Center in Albany is the big prize. Seriously, their reach goes well beyond Albany and maybe as far as Washington. We have a few pissed-off contractors who have been pushed aside and they have told us a lot, but we have no concrete evidence. They are all scared to testify." She laughed. "Ha, that's a good one, lots of concrete in the project, but no concrete proof."

Marco was not surprised at her direct approach to the matter at hand. There was no rapport building or small talk with her. She was all business.

Marco thought for a few seconds and then said, "Well, the mainframe computer is a tough nut to crack. Has never had a virus and not easy to hack. It is not as simple as a password, which can open the entire system. There are several layers of security, and then there is security in the application programs, the micro-code and the hardware. All of them play a role in securing the system from outside invasion. Even inside invaders. Lots of layers; it is just a series of fucking steel trap doors, and we will need to break each of them down, one at a time. But, there is always a way in, and if given enough time, I will find it."

Marco hesitated and viewed the binder before he continued. "Yes, I am thinking that we go underground. What I mean is, really underground. The city has a vast infrastructure network that is used for feeding the utilities into each building. We get an engineer from the telecommunications company and find the telephone lines that are connected to their computer. If that does not work, then you can always work on this guy Vincent. If we apply enough pressure, he is sure to break. But I can get into the computer."

Marco briefly glanced down at the binder's and flipped through the first few pages. "So, I see that you have already started a linked-in record from the surveillance. That's a good start, but I know you need hard evidence. So, you know who is meeting who and when, but is it hard evidence of a crime? I think you know the answer. No, all this does is broaden the number of people you are investigating and thin out your resources."

"Yes, yes, you are correct, but look, we had some cooperation before our assets disappeared from our radar screen. We really should not be discussing this here, but I can tell you a few things that we know about this union, and you need to understand. This union is dirty. They have connections with the Gambino crime family. There are quite a few leftover associates in that family trying to keep things going. What I mean is that they still have some powerful connections with politicians. Their money buys a lot of political connections."

She pointed her finger at Marco.

"And they reach far and wide. So we must conduct this investigation from all angles. We cannot discuss this with anyone outside our team. We especially need to be very careful with the Department of Labor. Crowley was not of our choosing. We were stuck with him, so be careful what you discuss with him. I do not trust anyone, especially Crowley, and I think some of the Labor Department people are leaking information to the *New York Times*. When it hits the papers, it tips off the union, and they become very guarded. We don't know who; we suspect, but we cannot be sure. One thing is clear: there needs to be someone tipping them off. They are always one step ahead of us."

Marco leaned forward and whispered across the table. "That aside, I think we can get access through the Fourteenth Street subway station, and we can get what we need through that station. In the meantime, why don't you have another chat with this guy from Albany, Chris Vincent, and put some pressure on him."

Connie replied, "When it comes to union computers, we know the computer is being used in their money-laundering scheme and is the key to how they are moving the money around. The computer programmers need to know how it all is put together because they have to write the code. They have access to all the data, and that is where this little kickback begins. We need to follow the money and the contractors are the first to handle it, so I believe that the contractors are also involved. And Goldin's auditors handle all the money as it comes into the union. They all have to be a little dirty; the contractors have to be in on it, and the union ties it all together. I agree: the computer is how they are doing it, and we need to crack the code or crack the programmers."

She continued. "The Albany field office plans to meet with Vincent soon. They have a few active investigations with the upstate unions and have informants. They will put the squeeze on Chris Vincent. From what we have learned, he has a good reputation, and we have not found anything yet. I think he may be clean—at least, maybe in the beginning, but we think he may have worked out a deal with his good friend, the accountant. They played golf in Albany in April, and Vincent and Russo are tight. Sonny Russo is definitely in with the boys from New York."

"How do you know?" Marco asked.

Samples looked across the table. "We know. We have informants in Albany. But we need corroborating evidence. Sonny recently cashed a union check from their PAC fund in the amount of $30,000, and we thought that this was not clean. We also recorded some interesting conversations between Sonny Russo and Paul Goldin. They spoke about the new tech center in Albany and the money that all the unions were going to make. Too much money to ignore. Goldin seemed particularly interested in the software and how Vincent's software handled the contractors' reports. But we need more, lots more, to nail them. This is where you come in." She paused. "So, can you get us into the computer?"

"Well, if I can get to the phone lines going into the building, that will allow me to hack into the system. The physical connection, that is the first step, the outside gate, so to speak. I can then get to the front door. I have a special program in which I enter background information and user profiles on the people that set up the passwords. Birthdays, names of pets, athletes' names, stuff like that. The program then creates over a million passwords based on the user profile. It runs for several hours and has never failed me yet. Once in, I can get to the data files. I know a little something about the AS/400 and will intercept the printer spool files so we can get copies of the reports that they send to their printers. Do you have the court orders?"

She was now smiling. "Look, Marco, don't worry about that; that is my department." She paused. "Hmm, the telephone lines?" She shook her head. "Well, we might be able to help. Let's go outside. I need to show you something."

Marco picked up the binder and placed it in his briefcase. He stood up and followed Connie through the door to the street, where there was a white Ford utility van with no windows in the back. "Con Edison" was painted on the sides of the truck.

"That's our baby right there. It is our portable set of ears and serves as our relay station." Connie walked over and opened one of the doors on the side. She held the door open and motioned for Marco to enter. Marco did not recognize the driver. He did, however, recognize the man sitting in the back behind a computer screen. It was Charles Crowley, and he was playing solitaire.

The electronics engineer sitting in the driver's seat was wearing Con Ed overalls. He gave Marco a brief introduction to the equipment and described its capabilities. Marco was attentive but already had some familiarity with how it was used. He was not terribly impressed, since they had more sophisticated, more up-to-date equipment in Chicago. Connie asked the engineer to drive to their covert office just one block to the south.

The van was equipped with highly sophisticated electronic surveillance equipment to surveil their targeted suspects. It included cameras, recorders, and relying equipment for eavesdropping on conversations and could record video and audio conversations. The antenna had the capability to listen and film meetings as far away as one hundred yards and, in some situations, could penetrate building walls. It was equipped with electronic cameras with telephoto lenses, listening equipment, and communications equipment that could relay all the data through encrypted government frequencies to listening stations in nearby buildings. The surveillance antenna on the top of the van could be directed in any direction and was controlled by computerized joysticks inside the van. The antennas looked like ordinary emergency truck lights.

Marco could not help but comment. "Wow, I like it. This should help us park right outside the union. It looks just like a Con Edison work truck."

"Well, actually, it was—that is, until we equipped it with $50,000 worth of our surveillance equipment."

The driver was a policeman who was on loan from the NYPD. He had an electronics engineering degree and knew how everything worked. "My name is Peter, and I can brief you on the setup anytime you want."

Connie directed Peter to drive to their office on Park Avenue South and park the van as close to 230 as possible. They were fortunate and found a spot just one block south of their covert office.

Marco and Connie had just entered the elevator as Connie pressed the third-floor button. The door closed abruptly and jerked upward. The elevator motor hummed with a low whine for just ten to twelve seconds and abruptly came to a stop. The number 3 lit up above the door. Connie walked out and to the left, with Chris following closely behind.

"This was about as close as we could get without getting inside. And it cost a small fortune. We have been here for almost two years, and the director is having a fit over the costs. Two rooms and five thousand a month, and we have nothing to show for it. Hope you can make some progress."

She stopped at the second door on the left; a small brass plaque to the left of the door read, "City Computer Supplies."

"Well, this is it; not much to write home about, but it has everything we need." She slipped the key in the door and turned it to the left. *Click*—the latch released. Connie opened the door and walked in, with Marco following closely behind. The office seemed perfectly normal. It had a reception desk with a multiline telephone, three chairs along the left wall, and a small table with a stack of outdated computer magazines. There was a bookcase, and on the far wall, several computer supplies were displayed. Chris noticed some ribbons, a few modems, and two or three wireless routers. There were a few small crystal award mementos on the top shelf. A sign hung behind the reception desk that read, "Supplying Technology."

"Hey, this looks pretty real." Marco turned to Connie.

Connie looked at Marco and said with a slight grin, "It should, because it is real; we have set up a real business. Last year, we sold some ribbons, but not much else. We could be profitable if we really wanted to make this work. We have set up a corporation and have a city business license. Nice little business."

She opened the door to the left and walked through a narrow passageway to another room at the end. As they entered, Marco noticed that there was a small window to the left that overlooked Union Square. There were two telephoto camaras mounted on tripods hidden behind a curtain. There was a cable that connected them to a computer terminal sitting on the table next to the window.

"Okay, here is what we have set up so far. It is up to you to figure out exactly what we will need. The network computer is in the closet on the right, along with the communications equipment. All the terminals are hardwired; everything is hardwired. We have a virtual private network connected to the bureau's back-end system in Washington."

There was a small, round table in the center of the room, and there were three computer terminals. Only one of the screens was turned on. Marco sat down and slowly pulled the keyboard toward his chest. The screen blinked, and he slowly typed in his ID and the password that had been assigned. The screen flickered for a few seconds, and then a menu appeared with several options listed.

"Okay, I am in the bureau's system. I am going to go into my private library and retrieve a few programs that should help. We are connected to a special library that we use for hacking. And I should be able to get everything I need and have access to some pretty cool programs."

Marco immediately pulled out the case file and began to review the handwritten notes he had scribbled the night before. He turned to Connie.

"Okay, let me play with this for a while. By the way, have you tried to sell the union any supplies?"

Connie smiled more broadly. "Hey, snoopy, you are pretty perceptive. As a matter of fact, I have made a few sales calls and have sold them some ribbons. There was a nice young man named Nick Greco, who happens to be the son of the fund administrator. I don't think he has a real job at the union, but he was in a meeting with their data-center manager—his name is Larry Smith—and young Greco insisted on taking me to lunch. Next thing you know, he called me the next day, and when I went over, he handed me a purchase order for $3,000 worth of printer ribbons. We had to scramble to get the ribbons he had ordered. We put a tail on him for a few weeks, but he rarely shows up at the office. When he does, he is never there for more than two or three hours. We checked the bank records, and he does get a very nice salary. His business card says assistant administrator. I think he is involved with the health and welfare fund. He has a title and gets a check, but from what we can tell, he has no official duties. I don't think he knows anything."

Marco nodded. "That's interesting. I may agree with you, and he is probably not much use to us." He hesitated for a moment. "But then again, what if we tap into the phone lines and screw up their communications system? Maybe you could sell him a couple of new modems."

"You're joking; of course, sounds complicated, and I know nothing about modems and routers." Connie sat down to the left of Marco and clicked on the terminal in front of her.

Marco peered to his left and watched her sign into the system. He could see that she was now smiling broadly. He noticed the reflection of her ruby-red lips bouncing off the screen. He thought she really was pretty.

Connie looked across to her right. "Oh, and another thing: I think our boy is on something. Probably cocaine. He drives a new BMW and frequents all the upper-east-side dance clubs. He is married, but that does not stop him from playing around with the ladies. And he is very open about it. There was one girl in particular. She was recently picked up with more than ten grams of coke. She is a sniffer, and he probably is as well. We know that there is white powder in all of the clubs he frequents."

"Well, maybe we should watch him more closely. We might be able to develop some leverage we can use against the old man. Maybe we can catch him with some powder," Marco said.

Connie shook her head. "That's not who we are after. We are looking to break the union down from top to bottom. We want his old man, and especially LaCola. LaCola is the only one who meets with the contractors, and that is where the money trail begins and ends. It has to be something to do with bid rigging. LaCola is the number-one guy at Local 4, and while we want Greco, LaCola is the brains behind it all. Him and the accountant, Paul Goldin. He is dirty, and the union is dirty. He is involved in all the dirty operations. We want the senators and the assemblymen, but not as badly as we want the union leaders. We want Local 4: the lawyers, the accountants, and the investment managers. They are all crooked; we know it, but we do not have the hard evidence or the proof.

"That is where you come in. We know all about the skimming, the kickbacks, and the money-laundering operation, and even though we have taped meetings and recorded their conversations, we still need to see how it is accomplished. Ever since Giuliani took down the commission with the wire taps, they have been careful. Right now, we have very little. We need to get inside their computer. And unless we have a clear money trail showing how the money goes in and out, we have nothing. I am hoping that we can get inside before they have cleaned it up with the new software. We are in a race."

Marco looked away from the computer terminal. He stood up and walked slowly to the window. He then peered across Park Avenue toward the Local 4 building. "Okay, I understand. But first, I need to find a connection into the system."

Connie looked across the table at Marco and asked, "What do you mean?" She walked over to the window and peered across Park Avenue. "If I understand you correctly, then you will use the Con Edison van, correct?"

Marco shrugged his shoulders. "Well, yes; it is a start. Last week, after our meeting with Macey, I contacted the city's engineering department and will have the plans for the telephone feeds this week. I can then get a connection into the computer."

Marco was scratching his right ear. "Wait a minute; why don't we just send Crowley over there and have him tell them that he needs to audit Medicare payments? That is what the DOL is supposed to be doing, right? And they know him, and he does occasionally meet with them."

"Well, you might have something there. But we never seem to be able to get anything from them when we use Crowley. I should not tell you this, but I am going to let you know. Macey never trusted him and put a tail on him. We have learned that he has been involved way beyond his duties and is taking bribes. Macey plans on going to the grand jury, and Crowley's career is about to end. If that is the case, then we will have the perfect asset, since he will want to trade what he knows to avoid prosecution."

Charles Crowley had worked for the Labor Department in the New York City office since 1985. He had been assigned to audit union trust funds for compliance with the laws and statutes for compliance with ERISA regulations. Although he seldom cited the unions for any wrongdoing, he was not well liked by the leaders who ran the unions. But that wasn't really the reason. Even though he would sometimes turn a blind eye to small violations, they paid him huge sums of money for information.

Charles was assigned to the case as part of the interagency agreement and the other team members could not get close to him. He stuck to himself and when the FBI became involved in the audit, he seldom offered an opinion that was contrary to the union's position. To some, it appeared that he was compromised and so they would withhold critical information from him whenever they could. He had established several relationships with the union labor leaders and knew how the system worked. They just went along, and even though he was part of the FBI investigation task force, they put up with him and kept his duties to a minimum.

Marco tilted his head and looked surprised as he turned away from the window. "Holy shit, this can work for us, but what if the union knows? Should he be put under protective custody?"

She answered quickly. "No, we don't think so, because he is law enforcement and Macey does not think they would risk it. Besides, we have not sprung the trap, and he does not know we are on to him. He is on paid temporary administrative leave due to a sexual harassment violation."

Marco smiled. "And who, may I ask, did he harass?"

Connie did not answer Marco. She placed her hands on her hips and swayed as a broad smile crossed her ruby-red lips.

CHAPTER FIFTEEN

PROTECTING THE
SOURCE CODE

MAY 21, 1992

THE FLATIRON DISTRICT WAS DIRECTLY to the north of Union Square and was especially interesting to Chris. The neighborhood was named after the Flatiron building at Twenty-Third Street, Broadway and Fifth Avenue. Built in 1902, it was one of the oldest New York skyscrapers. At the time, it was one of the tallest buildings in Manhattan, at twenty stories. Its triangular shape came to a point on the northernmost side on Twenty-Third Street. When you stood immediately in front of it and looked down the sides of the building, it was like this huge, tall tower building that appeared to be no wider than three or four feet, and when standing directly in front of it, you could not see the building. It was almost an optical illusion, with the building seeming to disappear as you moved up to it from across the street.

It was the start of a new approach to building skyscrapers, using steel skeletons rather than concrete. From an energy-conservation point of view, the building design was ahead of its time; today, one might consider it a green building of sorts. The narrow width had a purpose. The windows were recessed to reduce direct sunlight and heat, and the narrow design afforded cross ventilation. This was an important feature in the early twentieth century, since air conditioning was not widespread.

Most of the software implementation work involved the conversion of the old data, which had to be mapped to the new formats used by the new software. Most of the work had been completed successfully by Williams, and the team was checking to make sure that all the data fields were correctly formatted. Williams was very curious and had been examining the old claim records. He was particularly interested in the bad health-claim records he had discovered. He had the old data records and as he was mapping the fields, he first identified data anomalies he was eager to share with Chris.

This was Williams' seventh straight week in the city, and Chris appointed him to manage all the technical tasks. Chris took care of the business side of the implementation, while Williams addressed the programming changes required for the data conversion. They had complementary skills, and it was working well. Williams was in the computer room going over the conversion programs for annuity when Chris arrived. Williams was always very punctual and already had his head stuck in the computer terminal.

Larry Smith, the computer operations manager, and Williams were sitting at a small table to the left of the computer mainframe. They were looking into a computer screen, which was all lit up in green letters and numbers. Williams was focused on the screen but did notice Chris from the corner of his eye when he entered.

"Hey, boss, how is it going?"

"Great; how is the system behaving?" replied Chris.

"Larry and I are working on the mapping and data formats." Williams continued. "Larry is more knowledgeable than any other staff member and is a big help."

Chris held out his hand to Larry. "Hello. It sure is nice to see you again. We are all thankful that you are working with us. Pete tells me that you have been a big help in the conversion."

Smith was sitting down and at first did not stand or offer his hand. He briefly looked up at Chris and then brought his attention back to the computer screen. He had a yellow highlighter in his right hand, which he waved at Chris. "Likewise. This is a lot of work, and we have an aggressive schedule. I hope we can at least complete the file layouts and the data mapping that meets your implementation schedule."

Chris walked toward the window and turned toward Williams. "Pete, how about an update? Let's take a few minutes and grab a cup of coffee in the breakroom. I want to see how you are doing, and I have a few things I wanted to discuss with you. Larry, we will be back in fifteen."

They walked over to the breakroom toward the rear of the sixth-floor offices and sat down at the back corner table. "Look, Pete, this is our chance to make a big splash in the New York union scene. These guys are connected to all the other trade unions, and if—no, when—we are successful, we will get a lot more business. They are going to fall like dominoes. Paul Goldin has promised me that we will get as much business as we can handle, so we must play it smart. Smith may not be the smartest or friendliest guy in the world, but we need to work with him. We cannot make him look bad. Smith has no clue when it comes to the programming. He is an operator. He feeds the computer and punches the buttons. That's it. So we need to be very sensitive to his situation.

"And besides," Chris continued, "we cannot trust anyone here, especially Smith and some of the others who work on the system, especially their so-called contract consultants. They would love to see us fail. Our software is solid and is never the problem. We have proven software that we know works. It is always the conversion and the crappy data that we get stuck with. An even bigger challenge for us is to make certain we are not sabotaged, so we need to be very careful with how we work with the staff. We cannot trust anyone. What I am trying to say is that we need to protect our most important asset: the source code. They want to buy it and we have yet to work out a price, so we need to keep it locked down. At the same time, we need to win these people over, and the only way we can do that is to not get on the wrong side of them. We do not want to make them look bad, but I am not saying to make them look good at our expense. That is a fine line."

Chris stopped; he wanted to be certain Williams was paying attention to him. With emphasis. he continued. "Do you know what I am saying? We must cover our asses and document everything. We will not make Smith, or any other person at the union, look good at our expense. We must make certain that we get the credit and that our company comes out on top. So, just a reminder to document every issue along the way. Document, document, and document, got it? Although we may need Smith, just keep him in his place. I do not trust him. The source code is strictly off limits to anyone except you and Frank."

Williams was a natural-born analyst but an even better programmer. Although he sometimes overcomplicated an issue by overbuilding a solution for a simple problem, he usually delivered a good outcome. But he was flawed in some ways and had a few hang-ups. He never trusted anyone and always felt that he knew more about a problem than the user. Williams looked back at Chris with a weak smile.

"Okay, I get it. Look, I started to bring over the claims-paid file from last year, and I found something interesting. Looks like there is something wrong with the payments. Have not figured it out yet, but it looks like the pointers are all screwed up in the history file."

Chris's eyes lit up. "C'mon; are you serious? What do you think it is? Just what we need, another fucking problem. Are there any money discrepancies?"

Williams smiled. "Looks like there is $3 million out of balance. It is awfully suspicious, and there is a lot of money that they pay out in claims, so the health fund is a big opportunity for a new business venture. I am not sure, but we will know when I run the edits, which match the claims to the accounting side. But it does not pass the smell test, and it's not looking good."

Chris's faced dropped as he put a closed fist up to his forehead. "Okay, look; you do not ever discuss this with anyone, and this does not mean anything. If we do not need this on our side, then forget about it. The less we know about it, the better off we are. Pete, this is critically important. Please allow me to deal with this when I speak to Goldin. Everything is riding on this account, and we must not make any mistakes as to how we handle this. Just clean it up as best you can and bring the good claim records over. Not our problem, and we cannot get involved with their mess."

Chris shook his head in frustration. "What next? Pete, do you follow me? It's not our problem, and forget what you found. This is serious business, and we need to stay far away from this. But before you do anything, dump the old files to tape, and put the tape in my briefcase. Do not change anything and copy it over as is."

Williams had finished his coffee, while Chris had barely taken one sip. "Got it."

Chris looked at Williams and continued. "Pete, this account is perhaps our biggest opportunity ever, and I am counting on you to make it happen. We should make enough money to provide some nice end-of-year bonuses. They are paying for it, and this is our big chance to break the company out into another level. Copy all the old data to tape today. All of it. I want you to give the tape to me, and I do not want anyone to see it. Just put the tape in my briefcase. Make sure no one sees you do that. If Smith questions you, tell him we need to work on the conversion in Albany."

Chris held his right hand up toward the ceiling, with his right index finger pointing straight up.

"And this is perhaps the most important thing of all. Number-one priority, and I know I am repeating myself, do not leave the source code. Keep all our program libraries locked down, and do not give any of them access. We must protect our code. So, *secure source* are the two words that you must keep in mind. Got it?"

"Yes, I got it—but this is a bit unusual, don't you think?"

"Look, this is an unusual place, and I just want to tell you what we need to do to protect all of us just in case something goes south. Remember, do not allow anyone to know what you are doing, especially Smith and Stanley. We are almost at the point of no return, so they cannot go backward."

"Okay, will take care of it later." Williams shrugged his shoulders.

Chris went on. "We have to protect our investment, and these guys would think nothing of stealing our software. And one final thing. This is critical. Do not tell them anything about the problems you discover with the old system. We must confirm our findings, and then I will discuss them with the accountant."

Pete Williams nodded. "Okay, you are the boss, and I get it."

Chris's expression was now very serious. "Listen, I am going back to Albany late this afternoon. I will pick up my briefcase in an hour or so. You are working half a day tomorrow, so call me before you leave. I will be in the office all day tomorrow. We are almost where we need to be. None of this is any different or out of the ordinary. When Denise comes down next week, she will help with the testing and continue the training."

He paused for a moment and then spoke more slowly to make certain Williams understood.

"Also, we will need to train the auditors on the seventh floor on how to set up the rate file. They handle all the contractor reports. I will handle that personally."

William looked confused. "That is weird, don't you think? Why do the auditors need to know how to set up the rate file? What about Greco?"

"Don't worry about it. Greco does not get involved with any of that. They enter all the contractor reports on seven. So, they will be responsible, and it is one less task we need to worry about. The organizational structure of this place is weird." Chris finally began to drink from his coffee cup. "Awful coffee. I think I will grab a Pepsi."

Chris and Pete made their way back to the computer room and knocked on the glass door to get the attention of Smith, who was still sitting in front of the computer terminal. There was a small, black remote clicker on the table. Smith pressed the button and the door buzzer sounded, releasing the latch.

Williams sat down and handed Smith a cartridge. "Here, can you load this on tape drive number two, please? I need to load some of the files to bring back to Albany. I need to take a close look at the mapping this weekend."

Chris was observing the interaction and was pleased. "Okay, boys, I will leave all of this technical stuff to you guys. Sounds like you know what you are doing. I am going to make a few phone calls and will be waiting for Goldin to come by. We need to see Mr. LaCola for a few minutes." He placed his briefcase under the table in front of the AS/400 and left the computer room.

As they left, Williams went over to the tape-cartridge rack and checked to see that the tape was mounted. The cartridge was rewound, formatted, and ready to go. He then walked over to the operator console terminal and keyed in the system-control commands to copy the files. He then looked over his shoulder; even though he knew he was alone, he wanted to make certain no one was watching. He hit the enter key and looked at the screen and then the tape cartridge. It spun forward for just a second or two and then backward, as the system verified the format and the label, and then it began to rotate clockwise as it obeyed William's instructions and began to dump Bloom's data files to the tape. There was an ever so slight hum coming from the tape drive. He turned, looked under the table, and saw Chris's briefcase.

CHAPTER SIXTEEN

GIN RUMMY

MAY 22, 1992 – ALBANY

IT WAS FRIDAY, AND CHRIS was pleased to be back in Albany. He spent most of the day in his office checking in with other clients and meeting with the staff to get updated on other accounts. He had reviewed the financials with his accountant and had her prepare the invoices as directed by Goldin. Billing was strong, and he knew he would easily beat last year's revenue, providing the union paid him. But the collections had fallen way behind. Money was getting tight, and Chris was feeling the pressure. They had been working at the union for more than two months, and the billable hours were adding up to some very big numbers. But payroll never stopped in order to allow the cash to catch up. Most of his resources were committed to Local 4, and some of his other clients were feeling neglected. The company was small, and it was not unusual that when the checking account went dry, Chris would go without a paycheck. He had not received a paycheck in the last payroll period. Making payroll was once again of concern. Since Local 4 was where most of the billable hours were generated, his receivables were at an all-time high. He was getting nervous. He knew he would need to have another conversation with Goldin.

Most small businesses were undercapitalized, and it was no different for this small computer software company. Few banks understood the nature of the software business. Banks were asset-based lenders and typically loaned money for buildings and inventory; few bankers understood the value of software or how this asset could translate into real dollars.

While he would admit to some clients that they had at times experienced cash-flow problems, he made it clear that he intended to stay in business and that their account was vital to his business success. He learned that when he needed money, he had better success asking his best-paying customers for advanced deposits rather than the slow payers who owed him past due money. He understood the difference between good clients and bad clients. Good clients paid their bills on time. But slow pay was a business practice that he was forced to accept with Local 4. Even though this created troubling times, he was forced to go along since he had too much invested.

He accepted the bad with the good, and this was something he had to endure. Another lesson he'd learned over the years was to take responsibility for his actions. For Chris, it meant that when you said you would do something, then you had to be sure to follow up and do what you said you would do. This was a practice he followed, even for the slow-paying clients. He was responsible to his family, his company, and his clients. It was not about the money; it was about fulfilling his responsibility toward others, especially toward his clients, who depended on him. Responsibility was something he could never abandon—even for a slow payer like Local 4.

The implementation plan had to be perfect. He was fully committed to accomplishing the results he had promised. He was determined to help Local 4 be successful because he said he would. Chris was responsible, no matter what went wrong and no matter who was at fault. It was all on his shoulders; he accepted that responsibility, and he tried to convince himself that the money was secondary. That was the difficult part of it, because no client had ever owed him so much money. But then, the good part of the deal was the fees. When he thought about all that money, he smiled. The smile quickly turned to a look of distress as he thought about the possible bad outcomes.

It was almost the end of the workday, and Chris had returned all the missed calls and finished going through the mail that had been piling up on his desk. He paced back and forth in front of his desk and stared at the cup of black coffee sitting on top of it. He turned, brought it to his lips, and took a small sip. It was cold, and he realized that it had been at least twenty-five minutes since his secretary had placed it on his desk. He walked around the desk and sat down. He was especially troubled by the unannounced visit by the two FBI agents who were waiting in his conference room when he returned from lunch.

They were friendly and careful not to accuse Chris of any wrongdoing. But they told him that Local 4 was corrupted and that he would be putting himself in danger if he continued to associate with them. They warned him that he was playing with fire and that they were looking for the union's old computer software expert. They asked Chris if would agree to assist them and volunteer to wear a wire during his next trip to Local 4. They assured Chris that his cooperation would go a long way and that they were not investigating Chris or his company. Chris told them that he would need to discuss it with his attorney before he could agree to anything. He told them he had never spied on anyone, especially his clients, and this would destroy his company and all that he had worked for. They persisted; one agent took a small package out of a briefcase and handed it to Chris.

"Look, on your next trip to New York, take this and help us out, please. Some call it a wire. We will have someone meet you on the train to explain what it is all about."

"Well, I am going down next Monday in the morning. But I am not interested in getting involved. Certainly not interested in wearing a wire and spying on my clients."

They pulled out some pictures of Chris with the accountant and Greco. "Look, we know more than you think, and we are not interested in anything you have done or may be thinking of doing. They are not your friends and are using you. Don't think we do not know what is going on. We know that there are kickbacks and money sent back and forth. If you have any involvement, we will know, and you will be in serious trouble. On the other hand, if you cooperate with us, you have nothing to worry about."

They were polite but persistent. "Think about it. We surely would appreciate it if you would help us out just this one time. Look, Chris, these people will do anything necessary. They especially help their computer programmers to disappear. You need to be very careful and let us protect you."

Chris was scared and did not know what to think of the meeting earlier that day. He realized that he was already in over his head, but the thought of betrayal overrode everything else. He then reached over, picked up the phone handset, and dialed. After two rings, he heard a crisp female voice. "Michaels and Michaels Law Firm; how may I help you?"

"Hello, Ginny, may I speak to Gary please? This is Chris Vincent."

"Happy to transfer you, Mr. Vincent."

There was a short ring as the call was being transferred, and then a cheery response came from the other end.

"Hey, Chris, how are you doing?" his attorney, Gary Michaels, asked. "If you are calling about a golf game, I have a game for tomorrow, but I am looking for a fourth next Friday. We have a tee time of 1:22."

Chris leaned back in his chair and swiveled to face the window. He looked out and saw that most of the cold grays of winter had been replaced by the fresh, green sprouts of grass and the bright pastel colors of late spring and early summer. The buds seemed to be eagerly pushing out of the tree branches and turning into fresh, bright-green leaves, signaling that summer had just about arrived, and golf season was in full force at the country club. So much so that it was difficult to get a tee time on Friday afternoon and especially on weekends.

"Great, I am in, but can we meet sooner? I have a legal question and need your advice."

"Good," Gary replied. "I have Bobby and Frank for next week, and you will be the fourth. I am meeting them for lunch before we tee off. You want to join us, say, twelve o'clock? That's next Friday afternoon."

Chris felt a little better and leaned back in his chair. "Yes, put me down for the fourth, next Friday. But I need to see you as soon as you can; it is rather important."

"Sure, I am going to stop at the nineteenth hole later today about five, and I will buy you a beer. I just got out of court and am celebrating a ruling that went in my favor. I will call the pro shop and see if I can get a time for next Saturday morning as well."

"Perfect, I have a couple of questions about my New York situation," Chris replied and then held the phone close to his ear.

"Oh, how is that going?" Gary asked. "They can be a rough bunch down there, but there are lots of unions to sell to and they are all Italians, so you ought to be getting along with them. By the way, how is Sonny? I did not get to go to the party at the café, but I heard it was absolutely fabulous."

"Yes, it was; the party was fantastic. Best dinner party I ever attended. I will see you around five at the club. Thanks, Gary." Chris hung up the phone and spoke in a louder than normal voice toward his secretary's office. The door was open, and he was certain that she could hear him.

"Clare, would you mind getting me a hot cup of coffee, please?"

His secretary replied, "I will make a fresh pot. Give me a just a few minutes."

"Not necessary, I am okay with whatever you have, even if it just half a cup. Throw it in the microwave."

Chris sat back and muttered to himself. "I hope I am doing the right thing; this is certainly a strange and dangerous way to conduct business."

Chris took a few sips of coffee from the fresh cup Clare placed on his desk. It had been a tough week, and he realized that a stiff drink would be a better alternative. He needed to escape from the office and escape the world of computer software and erase the thought of the FBI meeting that had occurred earlier that afternoon.

It was 4:15, and he decided he would drive down to the club to meet Gary. He normally did not drink hard liquor, but this had been a difficult week in New York, so he ordered a Johnny Walker Black on the rocks at the men's bar at the country club.

It was the usual Friday afternoon at Wolfert's Roost's nineteenth hole, which adjoined the men's locker room and consisted of a men's bar, a large lounge area with several tables, and a big-screen television. This was the after-golf gathering place for men. It was also the perfect stopover for a casual drink after work. Eight of the regulars sitting at the long table near the entrance were playing eight-handed gin rummy. Eight-handed was a fast game; the four men on one side of the table were all partners and played against the other four on the opposite side. Most of them were retired and played golf four to five days a week and then followed with a penny-a-point gin game. Even though it was only a penny a point, when you considered double points for spades and blitz, which doubled the loss, it could get expensive. They also played Hollywood, which meant they were playing three games simultaneously. It was not unusual for one or two to each lose seventy-five dollars in less than an hour. It was interesting to hear the partners on one side or the other who had played their hand out before the other partners to provide encouragement to their partners still playing the hand. You'd hear things like, "Hey, Doc, we are holding eighteen plus gin, forty-three, so be careful. Knock when you can. We can sacrifice the fifteen points and still score and get on the third street."

The Johnny Walker was making Chris feel warm inside, and he was just starting to relax when Gary Michaels walked in, stepped up to the service bar, and addressed the bartender.

"Hi, Jack; how about a draft and a drink for that gloomy-looking guy over in the corner?" He walked over to Chris and sat down. "How is the New York deal working out for you?"

"Well, I am glad you asked, because it is not quite what I had expected. All they want to do is go to lunch or dinner. And the union guys never pay for anything, but that was expected."

"How is your new buddy, Paul Goldin? Is he involved in the process?"

Chris raised his eyebrows and nodded. "Is he? I think he is one of the senior partners. He is very involved and connected in just about everything. I think his firm must pull out $2 million or $3 million a year from these guys, and they act like this is a family-owned business to hand down from generation to generation. All the big shots have their kids working for the union, or I should say, taking a paycheck."

Gary smiled and took a long sip of beer from his glass. "Just like Hollywood and Washington. The politicians all think they are running a family business. Look at Governor Mario Cuomo; it will be no surprise if one day you see his son Andrew in Albany as the governor of New York. That is the way it has been and always will be. Anyway, cheers." He raised his glass and took a sip of beer.

"I suppose so, but thanks for stopping by, and thanks for the drink. I just have a few questions, so I am glad I can speak to someone. You can bill me as well once I get paid—if I ever get paid."

Gary rocked his head from side to side and chuckled. "No, the meter is not running, but don't expect any sympathy on the golf course next week. Anyway, what's up?"

"Look, this is not exactly a confessional, but … I think I am getting in pretty deep, and they have a tendency to push over the legal limits when it comes to money. I am getting an education, and it appears that to do business with them, they expect some form of kickback. Everybody plays the game, and it is something that is considered normal. What advice would you give—off the record, of course—to a friend? How should I handle them? I wanted to see you and ask for your advice because two FBI men stopped by my office today and wanted me to help them out. They asked me to wear a wire."

"Well, all I can tell you, as an officer of the court, is do not do anything illegal or anything that may have the appearance of being illegal," Gary replied. "Always document your meetings, and always cover your tracks to protect yourself. Do not trust any of them, the union guys or the FBI, because they would just as soon fuck you or shoot you. Oh, excuse me; that is just a figure of speech, an innocent expression, but you know that when there is money involved, people will get nasty. We see it all the time, not just in New York City, but even in Albany. So, document and have a paper trail when it comes to money to show it is legit. Make sure you have a written contract. Illegal kickbacks with a union are a federal crime, and you must be very careful. The feds like to dig at things that are not so obvious, so when there is an appearance to hide something, they will dig until they find something."

"Well, I am usually good at creating a paper trail, but I'm not entirely sure how to handle certain situations. The union expects me to deliver messages and envelopes, and the FBI wants me to cooperate. Betrayal is not something I am capable of."

"Well, I am not a criminal or trial attorney, but I would tell you: no cash deals. That is a slippery slope and is easily discovered. If you have to pay for something, then write a check and document what it is for. Make sure it is in your contract, and always put a cover letter in front of it. If they want to give you money and it appears that you are laundering the money, then it will be just that. Make sure you are billing for a service or a product. If you know what it is meant for, then issue an invoice and document the transaction. Make sure it is reflected in your financial statements and your tax returns. Make certain you have a good reason and can explain it, because they can always find it, and if they discover you are hiding something, that is when you get in trouble. The best advice I can give you when it comes to the FBI is to say nothing. Tell them you have an attorney and refer them to me. Even though my dad was the district attorney a long time ago, I still have a little juice."

"Okay. You are making me feel much better. I think it is either your words or the whiskey."

Gary replied, "Must be the Johnny Walker. They are Italian, right? And you know what those three letters, *FBI,* stand for?"

Chris looked at him questioningly. "No."

"Forever Bothering Italians." Gary paused briefly with a big grin on his face, then laughed out loud.

Chris was expressionless and did not appear to be amused.

Gary continued. "Chris, there is no law that requires you to wear a wire. If they had something on you, believe me, they would use it and would target you. So, it sounds like they are on a fishing expedition. Never lie to them, but do not tell them anything. Let them use their own bait to fish. Don't let them use you as bait."

Chris began to nod, as if he understood. "Interesting."

"You see, I am not telling you to admit an illegal act, but let's just say the union wants to pay you extra money, and then they want some back. Make sure there is a legitimate reason for it. Send them an invoice for money that they send you, and send a letter whenever you write them a check for whatever. Never—and I say, never—try to hide something. Your documentation must show that it was above board and appears legal. And by the way, if the FBI promises you something or wants to make a deal, then you will need it in writing."

Just then, Bobbie Lane walked in to join the two of them. "Hey, guys; happy Friday." He looked over to the service bar and shouted, "Hey, Jack, another round please," as he pointed to Gary and Chris.

He looked over to the older gentleman sitting at the end of the gin table. "Hi, Doc. Are you cleaning these boys out?" The man was expressionless, and his eyes lit up as he saw the discard. He then picked up the eight of diamonds that his opponent had discarded. He slid it into his hand and laid the ten cards face up on the table and proudly said, "Gin!"

Bobbie smiled. "That's what I thought."

Gary once again chuckled and said, "I wonder what it would be like to sit in his dental chair?"

Bobbie sat down and went along with the laugh. "I don't think he needs the income from his dental practice. Gin is his principal source of income."

CHAPTER SEVENTEEN

THE TRAIN

MAY 26, 1992

I T WAS NOT AS SMOOTH as the other station stops, and the train quickly came to an abrupt stop. The same familiar voice from trainman could be heard from the front of the car. "Croton Harmon; this is Croton Harmon. The next stop is Yonkers."

The trainman then stepped out onto the platform. "All aboard for Yonkers, Penn Station, New York City. All aboard!"

The sound of the trainman's voice awakened him from his sleep. He suddenly became aware that he had allowed his mind to play tricks He thought. "My God, I had dozed off for almost 2 hours. It was only 8 weeks from that first train ride, and he was worried when he got on the train not knowing how he would get out of the trap the accountant had gotten him into. He was thinking about the troubling events since that first golf game with the accountant. But for some strange reason, he now felt different. He was no longer worried. He now knew that he would find the right answers. He began to think more clearly about his options. Does he cooperate with the FBI, or does he stay loyal to the unions? What would he do once he arrived in New York? What would he do when he met the FBI handler? It brought Chris back to his old self and to the present moment and he felt a renewed inner strength. He looked out the window and saw that although it was still raining, the sun was struggling as the rays tried to break through the openings in the clouds. In some strange way, it was similar to what his mind was struggling with as he tried to find the answers. Chris had been thinking about the events that occurred from early April and once again realized he would need to face the situation that he alone was responsible for creating. He felt refreshed and knew he would find a way out. Not sure but with renewed confidence he knew he could handle it. Even though he would soon meet another FBI agent, he knew he would choose the right path. There was only one other stop after Croton Harmon. The wind was blowing against the window and although it was still a gloomy day, he felt more confident and reassured. It was a brief stop but slightly longer than the other stops, since this was the engine switch stop from diesel to electric. The Hudson River Line's local and express service marked the starting point of the third rail electrification on the tracks going into the city. He could feel the slight bumps as the diesel engine disconnected and the electric engine hooked up to the passenger cars. Just like his mind, it was now electrified with renewed energy. The beads of rain were now dripping down slowly from the top of the glass to the bottom. Chris was thinking about his next move once he arrived in the city. He had thought about the events over the last two months leading up to that moment and about the bad choices he made. He realized that they could not be changed. Yet he also remembered what his attorney had told him at the club: "Be careful, trust no one, and provide cover documentation to show legal intent." He was overcome with a strange feeling that would enable him to make the right choices. He was now more reassured and knew that, going forward, he would make better decisions to free himself from the jaws of the vice between the FBI and the union.

He gained his composure and with an iron-clad determination knew he could handle it. He calmly weighed the alternatives and knew that he alone was responsible for the situation he alone had created, and he alone would choose the right path to redemption. The decisions he would make would have severe consequences not just for Chris, but for many others. He thought about the words *loyalty* and *betrayal*. When he'd boarded the train, he was scared. But now he was confident and self-assured. Although he did not know exactly how he would escape from the trap he had knowingly walked into, he felt reassured that he would find the answers and a way out. He finally realized that he would be faced with many decisions going forward and could not predict where his decisions would lead. The path going forward would have many twists and turns, and the choices could only be made as he approached each turn. It would be just like a picture puzzle, just one piece at a time in the proper sequence.

As the train once again tugged forward from the station, a thin brunette holding a shiny, red patent-leather pocketbook walked straight toward him from the front of the car. Then, as if she recognized him, she abruptly turned and walked from the front of the car into the next car. Looking down at his watch, he saw that it was ten minutes to nine. They still had almost an hour to go before arriving in Penn Station. Lots of time and lots of red. He knew that she was the FBI contact who would meet him, and he wondered if she knew about the check he had given Greco. It was a kickback, but could they prove it? What about the handoff to Crowley? Crowley was supposedly on the union's side. Or was he?

The train was running out of stops, and he was running out of time. He was to be given last-minute instructions and discuss what they were expecting from Chris. Chris knew that anything was possible, and it would be dangerous regardless of the path he chose. He would trust no one and would find his own way. He wondered if Goldin had learned that he had been questioned by the FBI. Maybe he should tell him? They always appeared to be one step ahead of him. His loyalty would be continually tested, and he would need to be careful and remain on guard. Greco knew where all the money was and knew how they were using the computer to steal millions. Greco and LaCola had a good thing going and received extra money, lots of extra money, for sitting on each of the union's trust accounts, in addition to special expense accounts that would pay for the many dinners, travel, and union meetings.

There were lots of legitimate ways to get money, but that was small potatoes compared to all that money in the trust funds, and all within easy reach. Chris also wondered how much money they could be stealing and knew he needed to find out for himself. Yes, that was the first piece of the puzzle, and that would be the leverage he needed. At the same time, it looked as if there were others who had gone into business for themselves, and Chris wondered if Greco and LaCola were involved.

Chris did not understand why they were so generous with the extra software license fees and was certain that they would ask for something in return. But he did not know for sure what it would be. Goldin had mentioned payoffs and mentioned that the project in Albany was not to be put in jeopardy. He knew that the contractors would be making millions and knew that they were friends with the New York mafia, and they also had relationships with the New York politicians in Albany. He wondered who the consulting firm was that he had to make the check out to, and Chris was worried that the FBI had examined his bank records. Who was behind

CK Consulting? He had never seen any consultants at Local 4 other than those on the seventh floor, and they worked for the accountant. He wondered, was CK Consulting a real company with real people working there?

As the train began to accelerate from the station, the thin brunette walked back from the front of the car. She walked slowly down the aisle toward Chris and eyed the empty seat to his left. She walked past him and then abruptly stopped and sat down next to him. She placed the handbag on her lap and turned to Chris.

"I assume that this seat is not taken?"

"No, no. Be my guest. Wondering when you might show up." He was pleased and, after noticing the red handbag, was certain that this would be his handler, at least for the day. He had not been told anything other than to look for the color red. He turned to her and stretched his right hand across his chest.

"My name is Chris Vincent. It is nice to finally meet you."

"Hi. I know who you are. My name is Connie Samples, and apparently, you know why I am here." She tilted her head slightly to the right, but her stare remained fixed toward the front of the car.

"I work for the government, and I understand the boys in Albany helped set you up with the wire." She spoke in a low voice that was barely audible. "How do you feel?"

"I am not feeling very good today." Chris was careful and also spoke in a low voice so as not to be overheard. "You work for the government. What branch? The CIA? The Labor Department? The FBI?"

"Well, I am with the Federal Bureau of Investigation, and I work out of the New York City field office. I am what you might call your contact person with the FBI. In other words, I am a friend." She hesitated briefly. "And you are my friend. Can I call you a friend?"

Chris responded, "Not sure I need a friend."

"A new friend never hurts. Look, this should be very easy for you. Just go about your business, and hopefully you will have some interesting conversations." She turned slightly toward Chris and cracked a weak smile.

"Look, I am not very comfortable with the situation, nor am I comfortable with the role you people have asked me to play. My neck is on the line, and there have been people disappearing. You say it is easy; I assume there are several people within their organization that you can use to get what you need. I am just a small-town computer consultant running a small software company from Albany, trying to install new software. I would like to talk to the person in charge, because I have some concerns about wearing a wire, or whatever you call it."

"A wire, that is what we call it." She paused. "Well, I am the lead agent on the ground on this assignment, and if you need to talk to someone, you are talking to someone: me. I have complete control and authority regarding this investigation. Look, I need to know exactly when and how you became involved with these people. I need a list of all your contacts at the union. I also need to know who you plan to meet today. I think you know that we have some pictures of you with Mr. Greco and the accountant, Paul Goldin. We want to know more, specifically about the computer and how they are stealing millions of dollars, and, by the way, we know that you gave them money."

Chris was nervous and became defensive. "What is this, an interrogation?"

"No. You will know when it is an interrogation. I am not saying that you have done anything illegal, but I would like to know who this CK Consulting is and why you hire outside people. I need to know what is going on and what you guys talk about." She now appeared a bit annoyed and looked over directly at Chris. Her smile was replaced with a slight squint of her eyes as her lips tightened. Chris had at first thought she was very pretty but saw the meanness in her facial expressions and now thought she was not quite as pretty as when she first sat down.

Chris went on. "Look, I would like to know if I am a subject, or target, or whatever you call it in your investigation. Do I need an attorney? I have been told that I would not be prosecuted, regardless of what my involvement was. Your people have asked for my cooperation in your investigation. Right? I was told that I would not be charged, regardless of the extent of my involvement. Correct?"

"Yes, that is correct," she answered. "We do not have any interest in you, and you will receive complete immunity from any prosecution."

Chris looked back at her. "The FBI has threatened me and insinuated that they have evidence that I am conspiring with union labor leaders and politicians and have asked me for my cooperation. You want me to help you entrap my clients. Regardless of the legality. Is that true? You will not use any of this against me, correct? I assume that you have the courts' authority for all of this surveillance and that everything I do is not to be used against me."

"Calm down; you do not need an attorney. We just need a little help, that is all. We told you we are not interested in you and just wanted some questions answered. We are all conducting these investigations legally. Let me be clear: we do not have anything on you, other than the fact that you are hanging around with some very dangerous people. You write checks to New York City companies. You by now know how these people operate. Some may view you as a victim, since you have been dragged into their way of doing business. But you knew you were playing with fire when you chose to deal with characters like LaCola and Greco and, yes, your golfing buddy, Goldin. But you're a big boy and knew who you were dealing with, so don't give me the innocent little boy story that you did not know how these unions operate. I have heard this fucking victim excuse many times before."

She tilted her head and looked more directly at Chris. "Your friend Goldin is perhaps the dirtiest of them all. Let me give you some advice." She paused and then said with emphasis, "Be careful. When moths play with fire, their wings can get burned. Did you know that his accounting firm takes over $2 million in fees annually using his auditors? Yes, we know about that; we know more than you think. Goldin's firm has about seven or eight accountants reconciling the contractor reports with the shop stewards' reports at one hundred bucks an hour. Seems to me to be a neat little laundering operation. And ..."

She hesitated for a moment and then went on. "We have no interest in you or your buddy Sonny or the boys in Albany. We are big-game hunting, and we are not interested in any of the other unions. Local 4 is our only target, and our only objective is to collect evidence regarding their criminal activities. These people are stealing millions of dollars every year. We know about the kickbacks and the bid rigging. We know the computer holds the answers, and you can help us to unravel how they are getting the money out. We can only guess as to how much. We need the passwords for the computer, and we need you to identify the money trail. We are not stupid. After that, your job is finished, and no one will know where or how we got the information. We need proof, and we need the evidence to bring them to justice. That is where you come in, so we are asking for your help. Simply put, you help us and do what we ask you to do, and we will protect you. We would never ask you to do anything that would place you in jeopardy. But you know that people disappear at this union. We are after the big fish." Her lips had tightened, and Chris could see in her face that she was now determined to convince him by scaring him.

She continued. "Just to be clear and to address all your concerns: we have no interest in you, period. We do not care if you go out and rob a bank. Once we get a court order to seize their computer records, it is all over. When that happens, it is all over for you as well. So it is in your best interest to cooperate now that you have an opportunity."

Chris looked directly into her eyes and leaned toward her. He was careful not to be overheard by the other people in the train car. "You have asked me to risk a lot and to help you entrap Goldin and the others. You said it yourself: these people drag a person into their twisted web, and you are no different. The FBI has dragged me into this and threatens me and my business. I am just doing business, the same way other companies do business in the city."

He lowered his head and looked down. "What happens to me and my business is no concern of yours. Why am I wearing this wire? What do you expect to find out?"

She was all business as she returned the stare. She also began to believe that Chris was scared and would need more convincing. She replied, "Chris, whose side are you on? You need to pick a side, and you have very little time left. Sounds like they are getting to you. Look, we would just like to know about the conversations that you have with Goldin, LaCola, or Greco. We can then get a court order, and you are out of it. We need the passwords for the computer; that is it, simple. That's it." She hesitated for just a few seconds. "You can do that, right? If you fail to cooperate with us, any possible deal with you is off the table."

Chris was still on edge and did not trust her. He certainly did not trust the FBI. He looked up and then crossed his hands together and quickly pulled them apart, as if to say no with his hands.

"I wipe myself from this and absolutely am not comfortable. I am simply trying to run a business. I specialize in union software, and if that is a crime, then you might as well lock me up right now. That's it. I have friends that I have made in the process of building a business, and they trust me. They are my customers, and unions are my business. You are asking me to betray the trust that I have established with my clients."

"Look, don't be so melodramatic; it has nothing to do with trust. We are just asking for a little help with the passwords and want to understand how your software works so that we can look at their computer records. They steal and cheat from their own members. Can't you see? It is they that have committed the ultimate betrayal. It is the union who has betrayed the very people that they profess to protect, their own members. You need to be on the right side of this."

Chris shook his head and looked down. "Yes, I understand all that, but I just don't like the way you people sneak around and spy on people and look for a reason to put them behind bars. It seems that you are searching for a crime that you are not certain has been committed. You have no idea and are only interested in finding or fabricating a crime. I will be happy to give you my lawyer's number and send him what you have just told me and put any proposal in writing."

"Okay, okay. I am not here to argue or debate the issue. Just help us to monitor their conversations. We do not care about your involvement, and you will receive complete immunity from prosecution. I will have a written agreement for your lawyer, if that is what you would like. I have his number. Gary Michaels in Albany, correct?"

Chris tilted his head slightly and looked up to the roof of the car. He waited a few seconds. "Correct. But let me ask you a question. How would you like it if I recorded my conversations with you?"

"Wouldn't bother me in the least."

"I have asked you if I need an attorney, and you said I did not, correct?"

"That is correct; you can trust me, and you do not need a lawyer."

"I am sorry, would you mind if I went to the little boys' room? The coffee."

"Be my guest. I am not going to be the one to get in front of your bladder or other parts of your anatomy."

She appeared to relax. She now leaned her head back against the seat but did not stand as Chris stood and turned toward the aisle as he moved past her. His legs rubbed against hers as he squeezed in front of her. He could tell that she purposely did not give him as much room as she could have. He could smell her perfume and saw a weak smile on her ruby-red lips.

Chris wondered what she meant by her last comment. He looked down as he stood in the aisle momentarily and then turned and walked toward the bathroom at the front of the train car. He entered and calmly closed the door and slid the locking bolt to the left. Chris peered into the mirror over the sink. He took off his suit jacket and placed it on the hook on the back of the door. He then loosened his tie completely and raised it over his head, careful not to disturb the knot. He placed it on the same hook over his jacket and then pulled his shirt out and unbuttoned it. He had on a white V-neck undershirt. He pulled it up and stared at the reflection in the mirror. He realized that he not only was scared, but he now knew that this was a dangerous situation, and he could trust no one. He also knew that she could not be trusted. The device was small and thin, but size was not his big concern. He knew that the union was very sophisticated and possessed electronic detection equipment. He took no comfort in knowing this little detail of 230 Park Avenue South, which Goldin had shared with him. He was told that there was no bug that could go undetected, especially on the seventh floor.

The FBI handler in Albany told him that this bug had a radio transmitter and had a solid-state memory device to record the conversation. He was assured that the radio transmission could not be detected, since the FBI used an encrypted government frequency. He thought about the seventh floor and Bobby, who always carried a nine-millimeter in the holster under his left armpit. He knew that the union was a dangerous place and those who ran it would stop at nothing to protect their secrets. Two strips of white tape, each about a foot long, stretched horizontally across his torso and held the device to him. It was positioned just above his waistline on the left side of his stomach. There was a thin black wire protruding from the small black box, which ran up to a miniature microphone taped just under his left collarbone. The microphone was perfectly positioned so that the collar from his white button-down shirt would conceal its existence. He was warned to always keep his tie snug and always keep the top button of his shirt buttoned.

Chris could still feel the tape as it stretched across his torso and pulled on his skin. He first tore the tape holding the microphone and then placed the thin wire and microphone in his inside jacket pocket. He then reached down and turned the recorder to the off position and pulled the tape that held the little black device from his torso and stuffed it in the same pocket. He put the crumpled-up tape in the sink. He was careful and wrapped the tape in paper towels before he threw them into the trash container.

He calmly buttoned up his shirt and tucked his undershirt and his shirt back into his trousers and then buckled his belt. As he looked into the mirror, he then placed the tie over his neck and tucked it under the collar. He then straightened his tie and collar. He put his jacket back on. Chris then took a deep breath, turned, slid the lock to the right, opened the door, and began to walk back to his seat. He felt some relief knowing the device was safely in his jacket pocket and that the inside of his collar was now dry.

As he walked back into the car, he noticed that the thin brunette was still sitting in her seat. He squeezed past her and calmly sat down. Chris grinned and felt better.

He sat there for no more than a few minutes when she said, "Okay, we are all good. I think we understand one another. Can I assume that we have an understanding? We have a deal, correct?"

"Look, just call my lawyer and put it in writing."

She placed her right index finger to her lips. "Quiet; keep your voice down. Let's not broadcast this conversation. This is not the time to debate this. I look forward to working with you and will be in touch in the future. And my two associates sitting in the back are your friends, so be cool."

She stood up and walked to front of the car. She turned and looked toward the two men in the back of the car, and with a quick nod, she walked to the car in front with the briefcase with the bright-red handbag slung over her right shoulder.

Chris wondered if she would get off the train in Yonkers or Pennsylvania Station. At this point, he did not care; he now had another insurance policy.

"Yonkers! This stop is Yonkers. Next stop is New York City, Penn Station." Once again, he heard the familiar sound of the trainman, only this time, he was wide awake and alert. The next stop was the beginning of the end. Pennsylvania Station would be the stepping off place into the same New York City. But he now was a different person from the one who stepped on the train in Albany.

It would be less than ten minutes to Penn Station, and he was getting his thoughts together. He was feeling more confident and relieved that he did not have the little black transmitter attached to his body. He was more assured, and even though he did not know what he would face, he felt confident that he would make the right choices. He thought to himself, "Okay, so, New York City, here I come. I am fine, and I know how the game is played and I am ready to play."

He reached up with both hands and snugged the tie up closer to his neck. He breathed a sigh of relief. He was comfortable and now had an insurance policy as he peered out the window. This time, he was more relaxed and finally felt some comfort in knowing he could take control, regardless of what he would face in New York. He was finally looking forward to the unexpected and the opportunity to exact his revenge. On who, he was not sure.

Chris thought about what Greco had shared and viewed the union in a somewhat more favorable manner. They committed bad acts but believed that their actions were for the good of their organization. Others may have viewed the behavior as criminal, but to them, they only saw the good. They believed they were on a righteous path. They were powerful, and the acts, while bad, were necessary and were committed for the good of their members. The union was the family, and there were sacrifices that needed to be made. It was no different than what the politicians did once they attained power. While there was bad in the performance of their actions, in the long run, it was their only choice to maintain their power. The end satisfied the means. Chris wanted no part in it but knew he would not be the one to betray their trust. He knew there had to be a way to escape without betrayal. He knew it would be up to him to find it. Chris was about to step off the train once again with a renewed confidence, but this time, he was certain he would choose the right path.

CHAPTER EIGHTEEN

TRAIL BALANCE

JUNE 22, 1992 – WEEK 12

WILLIAMS HAD BEEN WORKING AT Local 4 each week from Monday to Friday. The work was wearing on him, and he had lost some of his enthusiasm. He was still fully involved in the work and now close to a go-live date for the annuity fund. He was running the trial balance programs to verify that he had moved all the transactions records over to the new system. This was the last step in the conversion of the annuity fund. After the numbers were verified, he could then move all the annuity files and programs to the operational library. Annuity would then be completed and ready to go live the first week of July. Timing was good and the project was ahead of schedule, which would allow time for any unexpected issues to be dealt with.

He sat with Al DiNapoli, the fund administrator for the annuity fund. DiNapoli had full operational responsibility for the annuity fund, which was similar to a savings account and used for funding vacation and out-of-work periods. A dollar and a quarter were deposited in each member's annuity account for every hour worked, and the fund total was close to $12 million. It was used as a savings and vacation fund. Stanley sat to the right of DiNapoli, smiling because all the account balance records were converted along with the transaction records. These held the balances for each member, and their total would equal the fund totals. Williams then added and subtracted all the transaction records using an audit program that verified the changes in the trust-fund totals from prior periods to the current period totals were in balance.

Williams turned to DiNapoli. "I noticed that there are a number of forfeitures in the annuity database. How are they tracked or recorded? I would need to know exactly how often the files are scanned and how often the money is transferred."

DiNapoli looked down at the racing form for Belmont, appearing distant and disinterested. He had been working for the union for over ten years and was a cousin to Greco's wife. DiNapoli was an avid horse-racing fan. He loved the ponies, but his real addiction was casino gambling in Atlantic City, which went far beyond the horses. He would bet on everything and anything. Although he played roulette and dice, his first love was poker. And the casinos in Atlantic City loved DiNapoli, especially when he played poker. He was hooked, and like clockwork, he would travel by limo to Atlantic City every weekend. He had several connections, and the limo and the room were always comped for him because he was a big better. He was what many would consider in casino parlance as a "whale," since he was a big loser.

Today, he was more interested in the racing form, but he did look across to answer Williams' question. "Rules are simple: we typically scan the transactions quarterly and transfer all of the accounts that have been inactive for the last twelve months or more and if they are below three hundred dollars, the money is forfeited. That money goes into the master annuity fund and eventually is redistributed to the active annuity fund accounts for our members. We use it to fund the interest. Reciprocity transfers are not a problem, since money follows the man. So you should not find any noticeable differences."

"I know that, but I can't get the trial balance numbers to balance. Unless I am missing something, there is at least $467,000 out of balance." Williams was shaking his head.

"Look, don't worry about it. We never depend on a trial balance. I can always plug in some adjustment transactions to get it to balance. It never has balanced, so why worry about it now? Bloom could never get it to balance." Williams now had gotten DiNapoli's attention away from the newsprint, and DiNapoli quickly put the paper down and walked over and peered down at the computer screen.

"Pete, look, there are too many transaction records that were never converted. All the early conversions were manually keyed, so there is bound to be discrepancies. Just let me take a look at the files. Let me know what the number is, and I can make an adjustment. Just don't worry about it. We were never able to convert all of the data over, and this fund has never balanced." DiNapoli now seemed to be a bit more interested. He put his fists up to his forehead and looked down at the floor. He hesitated for a moment and looked back up at Williams.

Stanley stood from his chair and walked around the table. He looked over Williams' shoulder and peered into the numbers on the screen. "Williams, how far back have you gone?"

Pete replied, "All the way back to ... let's see ... the earliest recorded date for the transactions was ... oh, here it is, 1984. Yes, that was when the annuity fund was started. Right? I think all the transaction periods are included. But the trial balance is only for the last three years."

DiNapoli now appeared to be annoyed. "Ah … look … look … ah, shit … toss that fucking trial balance and let's just get the new programs running. I will make the adjustments tomorrow or Thursday. The balances are none of your fucking business."

He walked back across the room and to the door. "I am going to go get a soda. These records have always been fucked up, so don't worry about it. It is what it is."

"I am just trying to do my job. We always run a trial balance as a cross check to ensure that we have transferred all the history records."

Stanley peered down and casually walked over and ripped the report from the printer. He then sat back down and studied the report as DiNapoli walked out of the room.

It was only a few minutes when DiNapoli returned with a can of soda in his left hand. "Hey, do you like Atlantic City? I am going down on Friday, and I have some connections. Free hotel rooms and free limo service. We leave about four o'clock."

"No, I am not big on Atlantic City, and my wife would shoot me."

"You don't know what you're missing. The shows are great, and the showgirls are fabulous." DiNapoli now had a big smile across his face.

"Thanks, but no thanks," Williams replied. His attention was now focused on the screen in front of him. "Hey, Al, what am I supposed to do with this file? I need to get it in balance." Williams was now more insistent.

"Fuck it. Don't worry about it. I will sign off on it. Stanley and I will work on it next week. I think there were some duplicate transactions that were included when we converted to Bloom's annuity system three years ago. We never could get the dollars to balance. We will need to make some adjusting entries."

"Alright. I just want to look at my program. I want to make sure it is clean. I ran into the same issue when I used it at the bricklayers' union in Albany and need to recheck the math. I would like to take a few minutes to think about it and then take a break—no, grab a beer, since it is almost quitting time."

Williams stood up and scratched his head. He was a perfectionist, and it was very unusual for him to just drop the subject and agree to something that he knew was wrong. He always checked and rechecked his conversion files by reconciling the starting and ending balances with the transactions. They always came within a few hundred dollars. They were never perfect, since there were always rounding problems associated with the interest calculations. It was almost impossible to identify how the pennies were rounded for each of the accounts, so there were always some minor discrepancies.

This was different. This file conversion showed $467,452 that had disappeared from the annuity fund. That was just too big a discrepancy to overlook, and Williams was not about to go out on a limb for anyone. He was a perfectionist and also weak when it came to accepting risk. Yet he was not about to let this go. Williams would wait until he had all the answers and confirm his suspicions. Few would stand up against a guy like DiNapoli, and Williams would follow Chris's instructions. He was not about to risk his job. Not for DiNapoli, not for Stanley, and not for anyone. He was convinced that something was wrong, and he was not about to let it go. He knew that he somehow needed to get the accounts to balance or bring it to Chris's attention.

Williams was facing the door and about to walk out when he abruptly turned and walked over to the window. He stared out toward the street below. He turned back around and walked over to the desk and sat back down. He clicked on the terminal, and the screen lit up with bright-green letters. He navigated into the program file and went down the list titled "Conversion programs – Local 4." He scrolled down and opened the annuity trial balance program. He then added a few lines of code and ran the RPG program. It did not take long, and after only a few minutes, he stared into the green screen. It showed the starting and ending numbers. He then subtracted the starting and ending numbers reflecting the number of transaction records. He looked at the count of the records in the program that were in the transaction file. There was a shortage of 2,068 records in the transaction file. This represented the number of missing reciprocity and forfeiture records that were unaccounted for.

He quickly sent another screen copy to the printer, then scratched his head and stood up. He ripped the report from the printer, folded it, and placed it in the pocket of his suit jacket. He quickly concluded that there was indeed missing money to the tune of over $467,000. He quickly calculated in his head that each missing transaction record amounted to approximately $225 dollars. He guessed that this was close to the average dollar amount of the forfeited annuity records.

"Hey, Al, one more question. What is the average amount of the reciprocity records that you transfer to the other locals that are forfeited?"

DiNapoli looked up. "I don't know, but it is usually less than three hundred dollars, because we run the transfers every month."

"How about the forfeiture records?"

"About the same—actually, a little less, maybe $200 to $250," DiNapoli replied.

"Okay, no problem."

DiNapoli had the racing form in his hand but was still troubled over what Williams had discovered. "Look, don't worry about the balance. I will take a closer look at the transaction file. Probably missing some of the transactions. I will take care of it. This is no big deal; the system has been screwed up for a long time, and that is why we are changing the software. I will talk to Marty, our programmer."

Stanley Meckler was sitting across the room peering into another terminal and had overheard the conversation. He walked over behind Williams and peered over his shoulder at the screen. He reached down and pressed the print key. He walked over and tore the screen printout and put it into his pocket. He then began to walk toward the door. He turned and said, "Al, come up to my office when you get a minute, and maybe we can unravel this discrepancy. Pete, run me a copy of that report." He then calmly walked out of the room.

DiNapoli was now fuming. "Pete, see what you started?"

"Look, Al, I am just doing my job. If you and Stanley sign off on the annuity, I am okay. I will look at my conversion programs. Maybe the rates are screwed up. The dates need to be correct, and I know that your rates are screwed up. Maybe that is where the problem is." Williams walked back to the desk and sat down.

Just then, Chris came in and walked over to Williams. He faced the terminal, leaned forward, and peered at the computer screen. It was now totally black. "How are we doing with the annuity files?"

Williams looked up at Chris, as he realized that he was pushing DiNapoli a little too hard. He quietly spoke to Chris, careful that no one else in the room could hear his words.

"Well, there seems to be a discrepancy. Out of balance by over $467,000. I am going to rerun the conversions and check against the fund balances again and will check the rates."

Chris tilted his head slightly and whispered back, "Aren't there transaction numbers assigned to each transaction?" He paused. "And I think they are all sequential and numbered."

"Yes, correct."

Chris had not programmed for many years but was an extremely accomplished analyst. He was really good at complicated conversion processes, since he had several years of conversion and accounting experience.

"Well, why don't you put a counter in the code and see how many transactions you have, and then look at the starting and ending numbers. That will tell you if you are missing any."

Williams looked directly at Chris and continued to speak softly into his smiling face so that he would not be overheard. He looked at DiNapoli and then quickly turned to Chris and winked. He now spoke so that the others could hear him.

"We are okay with it. Let us get the rate file transferred and accept the fact that there are a lot of errors in the old system."

Just then, DiNapoli, who was listening intently, came over and set his soda on the table. "What the hell are you guys doing? You are supposed to be putting in new software. This is not a fucking audit. The old software is fucked up, and that is the problem—plain and simple." He now appeared annoyed. His eyes were like two steel balls. "So why don't you do what we are paying you for and forget about trying to balance all the transactions. That is Stanley's job. Got it? The dollars never balance. Never have and probably never will balance, even with your fucking wonderful software."

Chris turned to DiNapoli. "Look, I am sorry. We are only here to do the job as best we can. If you want to sign off on the annuity, then we are fine with it." He turned to Williams and winked back.

"Pete, just bring the rate file over and update the member records. We are okay, and it is just as well, since we want to stay on schedule."

Chris then looked at DiNapoli and said, "Okay, I will check off the annuity trial balance on the project plan after you and Stanley initial it."

Williams flipped the terminal back on and then turned to Chris, looking somewhat annoyed. "Okay, we got it; we are good with the annuity. Let me sign into the system and run the rate-file conversion. The program looks good."

DiNapoli walked back to his desk, picked up the can of Pepsi, and took another sip. He then sat down and picked up the racing form.

CHAPTER NINETEEN

STATUS REPORT
JUNE 23,1992

T HEY WERE NOW FULLY INVOLVED in the implementation and training; all the new software had been loaded, and a big portion of the project was completed. Most of the data-conversion programs were written and tested and ready for the go-live for the fund accounting and then would be followed by the annuity and pension accounts. The contractor's reports were the critical entry point, as dollars and credits would flow into the union trust funds. Chris and Williams had trained the auditors the week prior, and they were already processing the contractor reports on the test side in parallel with their old system. Goldin had commented that it was going according to their plan and no major problems were encountered. The contractor reports were received every day, along with a check totaling the benefit dollars for the reporting period. Some were well in excess of $100,000. The union would often collect from $15 million to $20 million each month from the contractors.

Every other Tuesday at eleven, the project team would meet in the sixth-floor conference room for a progress report. Chris and Williams arrived exactly on time. Paul Goldin sat directly across from LaCola. Stanley sat to the left of Goldin, and Greco stood next to the pot of coffee chomping on a cream-filled doughnut, talking to Smith. DiNapoli was not in attendance; he had called in sick.

Goldin looked at his watch and began. "Hi guys, Mr. LaCola has decided to join us this morning and wanted an update on our progress. He has a trustees' meeting tomorrow, and he would like to provide the trustees with a progress report on the conversion. Chris, do you want to take a few minutes and tell us how we are doing?"

"Yes, thank you. Hello, Mr. LaCola, nice to see you again." He stood up, walked over to the foil projector on the far end of the table, and flipped the switch to turn it on. The white screen lit up on the far wall. He placed a transparency on the projector that showed the project-plan outline. Chris pulled out his laser pointer and was about to begin when LaCola interrupted.

"Hold on, Chris. What is going on with the annuity fund? Isn't that the first fund to go operational?"

"Yes, sir, we are still working on it. We have converted all the transaction records and are just checking out the balances. Software is working fine. Otherwise, it is all set to go live. We are just waiting for sign off from Stanley and Al," replied Chris.

"Is there a problem? Stanley tells me that he talked to Williams and there seem to be some discrepancies with the fund balances related to the reciprocity and forfeiture transactions."

"Well, we are sure we can make it work with what we have. We are checking the conversion programs and making sure we didn't miss anything," Chis said and paused for a moment. "We are also reconciling the reciprocities, withdrawals, and forfeitures. Al said he would sign off on the new process."

LaCola replied angrily, "Why aren't we going live this week on the annuity fund as planned? This was in last Tuesday's report. Is there a problem with the software? Where is Al?"

Williams interrupted. He was not about to take the blame for their old data problems. "Just a minute sir, the conversion programs work perfectly; it is just that we cannot get the transactions verified. The trial balance is off. I think it is the old data. That is the only thing preventing us from going live."

LaCola threw his hands up and almost shouted, "What the fuck do you mean, balance? Then he said softly, "Do you mean money balances or hours? Are there any money problems? How much is missing?"

Chris looked over at Williams and then back at LaCola. He was mentally shaken and felt trapped, not knowing exactly how to answer.

He then answered with some hesitation. "Well, sir, I can't say that there is money missing; the hours conversion has worked perfectly. All the numbers and our cross-checking reports balance. So, the front end of the conversion is solid. It is just that there are some transactions in the annuity fund that may be missing. We cannot get them to balance when we run the trial balance. We only convert the data that you have on the old systems, and some of the data loads in the past may be screwed up." Chris shook his head from side to side as he looked over at Williams. "We cannot verify the integrity of the data from the old systems going back three years. It looks like there are some transaction records that we cannot find. Al said he would make some adjustments to get us in balance."

LaCola stood up. He leaned over the conference table, placed his hands on the table, and looked directly into Chris's eyes. "How much? I know something about accounting and the operation of these funds. How much is out of balance? We had a perfectly balanced annuity fund three years ago. What is the number?"

Chris reluctantly replied, "About $467,000, but … but—" he stuttered and then abruptly stopped as Williams interrupted.

Williams was not about to take the blame and remembered what Chris had told him. "Four hundred, sixty-seven thousand, four hundred and fifty-two dollars." Then, with a slight hesitation, he added, "And thirty-one cents."

Chris looked over at Williams and gritted his teeth in disgust. "What the f—" he started to say and then caught himself.

LaCola shook his head as he sat back down and looked at Stanley. "Okay, I got the picture. Stanley, take a closer look, and make sure that DiNapoli can account for all the transaction records. I want answers. By the way, where the fuck is DiNapoli?

Greco answered. "He called in sick this morning and said he would be in tomorrow. He said he would work from home and was looking at the forfeitures. He thinks that is where the problem is. Forfeitures has always been a manual process, and it has never balanced in the old system. Al thinks he can get it in balance."

Stanley broke in. "Mr. LaCola, I am sure we will get to the bottom of this, and we will be able to find the problem. Not a problem with the new software. It is in the data. Looks like some of the transaction records have disappeared."

"Well, I want to see DiNapoli first thing tomorrow. No adjustments until we find the reason and get answers." Everyone could see that he was angry. No one was about to say anything further on the matter. He then added, "Disappeared … I will decide what or who disappears."

LaCola appeared to calm down but was not about to accept the explanations or drop the matter. "Alright, let's keep this implementation moving in the right direction. I want the annuity and pension systems up next week. I do not want any other fuckups.

Paul, you look into this with Stanley and let me know what you find." He then turned to Chris. "Chris, what else?"

Chris took a sip from his coffee cup and placed it down on the conference table. It was cold, just like the feeling he got from those in the room.

"No other issues so far; we are doing good. Everyone is cooperating. The staff is great, and we are going to start the training program for pension next week. Al is already trained on annuity. We plan to go live next week, and I do not see any red flags."

Greco interrupted and directed his question to Chris. "Anything else we should know?"

"No, sir; we are good with the schedule. Training and testing, all going well."

LaCola stood up, turned, and began to walk toward the door. He then turned to Chris. "Okay, great. Keep up the good work. I have another meeting and am not interested in the details. Stanley, Paul, I want to talk to you about this annuity problem." He then walked out of the room. Greco followed.

It was silent for a moment, but no one was anxious to break the silence. Finally, Goldin, appearing annoyed, looked directly across the table at Chris.

"Chris, I sure wish we had discussed this before we met with LaCola. He does not like surprises and obviously is upset over anything like this, especially when it comes to fund balances."

"Sorry, but I had no idea that we were going to get into this today. We are done with the annuity conversion, but this trial balance is not a problem for us. We just need your people to sign off on it. DiNapoli was supposed to check the reports and sign off on the data conversion. Paul, you need to talk to DiNapoli. I didn't know Mr. LaCola would be at the meeting. I was just answering his questions. And besides, it sounds like he was well aware of the problem."

"Alright, alright. Let's move on." Goldin stood up, walked over to the coffee pot, and refilled his cup.

Chris started to move toward the projector. "Well, okay, we are—"

Goldin cut him off. "Hold on, Chris. Why don't we just get back to work? There is a lot that we need to get done, and I think we have a pretty good idea as to where we are with the schedule. The weekly report you provided was very thorough. Just keep it on track. Okay?"

Stanley and Goldin stood and walked out of the room.

Chris waited until they were alone, and he then turned to Williams. He placed his hand in front of him.

"Hold on; since when do you decide on your own that there is money missing? I will address this sort of problem and discuss it with Goldin before any conclusions are reached. You must be careful what you say in front of LaCola and Greco. If you slip up and make accusations, then someone is going to get pissed off. You can screw this account up. Remember, you never discuss these issues without first clearing it with me. My job is to report to Paul. Your job is to do the programming and convert the data. We are now in a world of shit with LaCola. DiNapoli won't be very happy, either. He is in hot water and now will be sure to try and sabotage us."

"I am sorry, but Stanley sticks his nose in everything that I do. He came down and started to look at the reports. There was nothing I could do," Williams explained as he firmly stood his ground. "There were a number of transaction records that add up to a different number than the balances. I looked at the withdrawals, the reciprocity, and the hours and rates from the contractor reports. The accounts did not balance, and we always check the conversion files by tying in the transaction records with the starting and ending balances. That is the only way I know how to verify that all the transactions are brought over. You and I both know that there is money missing. When you steal from the forfeitures, you are not stealing from anyone. Money sometimes evaporates, and that is a hell of a lot of money to evaporate without someone's help."

Chris waved his finger at Williams. "I know, but going forward, you need to make sure Stanley is not interfering with us. Just keep him as far away as possible. He is LaCola's hound dog."

Williams was annoyed and fired back at Chris. "Chris, you told me not to take the rap for them. And that is exactly what I was doing, following your advice."

Chris was now concerned. He knew that going forward, the installation was not going to be easy, and he also had learned that the staff was not going to be very receptive to change. He wondered what he would say to DiNapoli. He thought that maybe the best thing to do was to work around him until things settled. Williams would need to find the problem with the data without DiNapoli knowing. He thought about his options. Perhaps there was nothing to worry about. Maybe it was just a problem of missing transaction records, or maybe it was simply a data-entry problem. He also came to the realization that it was entirely possible that $467,000 was now in Atlantic City.

Chris turned to Williams. "Okay, let's just move on."

Williams answered, "Okay, okay."

Chris thought that maybe DiNapoli's bad luck at poker had something to do with it. Not his problem. "Okay, lesson learned; don't share anything with anyone until you talk to me. And I won't share anything until I talk to Goldin."

Chris was still waving his finger at Williams. He then realized it was not William's fault. He turned his finger toward his head, touched his temple, and scratched.

CHAPTER TWENTY

THE RIDE

JUNE 26, 1992

DINAPOLI HAD NOT HAD A pleasant week when he returned to work on Thursday. He was immediately called to Stanley's office to explain the discrepancy. Stanley was fuming and told DiNapoli that he had better find the problem or he would risk losing his job. DiNapoli was insistent that the small amounts for the reciprocity accounts had not been counted and those transactions were not included in the trial balance. He claimed Williams' program did not identify those transactions and that he would look at the programs personally. But he could not produce any evidence to prove his theory.

There was a brief discussion between Williams and DiNapoli on Thursday, and Williams was insistent that the reciprocity sweep included the forfeitures and the transfers. DiNapoli disagreed and told Williams that he would bring in their own programmers the following week. Williams said two words in response: "Good luck."

It was now Friday, and after a stressful week, DiNapoli was looking forward to the weekend. It was almost 4:30 when DiNapoli walked up to the waiting stretch Lincoln Town Car. It was parked in the taxi lane around the corner from the union office on Seventeenth Street. There was a tall man of about thirty with a newly formed beard leaning against the right front fender. He wore a dark-brown suit with a white turtleneck sweater underneath. He held a stick in his hand with a small white sign attached to the top that read, "Trump A.C." DiNapoli stopped and looked over at the man.

"Where's Freddy?"

The bearded young man looked up at DiNapoli. "You must be my guy from the union, Local 4. DiNapoli, right? Atlantic City, right?"

"Yeah, that's right; how did you know? Where's Freddy?"

"He had another gig that was running late. I am just filling in for today. My name is Eric. Don't sweat it. I have made the Atlantic City run a hundred times, and we promise to take good care of you." He opened the rear door and gestured for DiNapoli to get in. "By the way, double duty today. My partner is driving, and I have to pick up a car in Jersey. Hope you don't mind."

DiNapoli slid into the back seat. Eric closed the door behind him, opened the front passenger door, and sat down to the right of the driver. Di Napoli looked up at the driver. "Thanks, and what is your name?"

"My name is Tony, and I am your driver for this trip. You are Mr. DiNapoli, correct?"

The brunette sitting in the back seat reached across and grabbed DiNapoli's left knee. "Hi there. You must be my ride for the weekend. My name is Fran, and I just love AC. However, I don't gamble."

"Hi. I thought that Inez was going to be with me this weekend. What the hell is going on??

The brunette moved her hand toward his left knee. She grasped it and moved it gently up his leg. "What's your problem, sweetie? I am a fun girl, and I promise you a good time. Same terms, okay? Twelve hundred bucks."

"No problem … it is just that I … well … ah," he stuttered and now looked directly at her face. DiNapoli surveyed her carefully, and although they were seated, he could see that she was tall and slender. She was not young, not beautiful, yet attractive to his eye. She appeared to be in her mid- to late thirties. He thought, "Maybe wearing a bit too much makeup." She wore a yellow sweater with the top three buttons undone. He could see that she was not wearing a bra. Her perfectly formed breasts were on full display, leaving little to his imagination. The orange skirt was well up her thighs. No panties as well. He smiled.

"Look, sweetie, I promise you a good time, and you may not want to go back to your regular girls. I know the score and am anxious to watch you play poker and other games." She reached for the open bottle of white wine and poured some into the two plastic wine glasses. Although he was at first hesitant, he now was looking forward to the ride. To him, she had passed the test, and he was looking forward to the weekend of gambling and sex.

"Okay, we are off and running," the driver said as he closed the passenger dividing windows. They were tinted and darkened to provide some degree of privacy for the passengers.

Di Napoli smiled at Fran, took a few sips from the plastic glass, and placed his hand on her thigh. The big Lincoln limo was headed south over the Verrazano Bridge when DiNapoli began to feel light-headed. He turned to Fran, withdrew his hand from under the orange skirt, and reached across to grab her right shoulder. He tried to reach her but just could not raise his arm. Several times, he tried to speak, to move, but could not. He was suddenly paralyzed and could not move as he slumped backward in the seat. His eyes were still open; otherwise, he was perfectly motionless. Realizing that he was not conscious, she pulled away and knocked on the tinted divider window.

As it began to open, she said, "Tony, I think our boy has connected. Now what?"

Tony continued to concentrate on driving while the bearded man in the passenger seat raised his hand. "Just relax; he will be just fine. He is no longer your problem; he is ours. We will be stopping once we get over the bridge, and we have a car. They will take you back to the club." He reached into his right breast pocket and pulled out a white envelope, which he handed to her.

She took the envelope and stuck it into a small black purse in the seat pocket in front of her. "That's it, twelve hundred bucks? That's it?"

"Actually, there is more. Much more if you understand and if you keep your mouth shut. We understand that this is not your first time and that you are a good girl that can be trusted. Understand that you never took this ride. And I don't think you want another ride. Okay?"

"Count on it." She leaned back, stared across at DiNapoli for one last time, and sat back in the seat close to the rear window. DiNapoli was spread out almost across the entire back seat, and she did not want to touch him. She could hear his breathing as she began to button up her sweater. She moved to her left, closer to the door. She was relieved that the ride would soon be over for her, even though she had been looking forward to the good time she would have had in Atlantic City.

They continued for another fifteen minutes, when they suddenly pulled over into a rest area. They drove around the back, where several trucks were parked. It was early, and most of the parking spaces were empty. The driver continued along the driveway toward the end of the lot and pulled alongside a large eighteen-wheeler.

Both the tractor and the trailer were black. There was no writing on the truck, but in small letters on the back of the trailer and on the driver's door, she noticed the words: "Private Coach, Not for Hire."

"Fran, that Caddy over there, the white one, is going to take you back to the hotel. Jimmy is with the driver, and you know Jimmy, right? So be cool, and don't worry. We are going to take our boy for a ride down to AC. Do not worry about him; the powder you put in the bottom if his glass was just a mickey, and he should come back around in about an hour. We just want to question him about something, and then we are going to drop him off. He will be just fine."

The back door opened behind the driver, and there stood a short, elderly gentleman who was no more than five feet tall. He had no hair and was wearing a gray jogging suit.

"Hi there. My name is Sam, and I was hired to take you to the Hilton on West Thirty-Fourth Street. Don't worry; it has all been paid for by the gentleman in the car."

She quickly jumped out of the back seat and saw her friend Jimmy waving to her from the back seat of the Cadillac. She quickly became at ease. She looked back at the men who had driven her to the rest area and saw that they were now opening the back of the black tractor trailer.

CHAPTER TWENTY-ONE

A FAMILY BUSINESS

THE ATTEMPTS TO ORGANIZE GROUPS of workers have always had varying degrees of opposing forces working against them. While these divisions were the result of societal and cultural forces, the process of unification took many forms. The early attempts to unify took many shapes, and there were many local, regional, and national organizations, some more organized than others. At first, the majority were literally hundreds of local affiliate organizations to provide a common voice for the rights of the worker. These were formed with the sole purpose to protect the working population from the abuses of employers. It was a banding together of the workers and a mechanism to organize the workers to oppose unsafe working conditions and low wages. When their objectives were accomplished, they were disbanded, since they lacked the structure and resources to continue.

The first effective labor organization that went beyond the scope of local and regional membership was the Knights of Labor, organized in 1869. The Knights believed in the unity and the interests of all producing groups and sought to enlist in their ranks not only laborers but everyone who could be classified as producers. They stressed centrality of free labor through cooperation with producers through politics and education, rather than through economic coercion.

In 1885, the Knights of Labor led railroad workers to victory against the Southwestern Railway system. That was followed in 1886, when they were trying to coordinate 1,400 strikes involving over 600,000 workers spread across much of the country with demands for an eight-hour workday. The strikes had spilled over from peaceful to violent confrontations in many areas such as railroads and coal mining. One of the strikes was at the McCormick Reaper Factory in Chicago.

The Knights were unable to handle the broad scope of the many strikes in so many locations, and as strikers rallied against the McCormick plant, a group of political anarchists, who were not affiliated with the Knights, tried to piggyback support among the striking workers. A bomb exploded as police were trying to disperse a peaceful rally, killing seven policemen and wounding several others. Although the anarchists were blamed and their trial received national attention, the Knights' reputation was permanently injured by the many false accusations that they had promoted anarchistic violence. As a result, many of the Knights' locals transferred to less radical and more respectable affiliated organizations or railroad brotherhoods. Although much of the early unionization of workers may have been temporary, they did set the stage for the longer-term creation of organized labor.

In the history of America's trade and labor unions, one of the most prominent was The American Federation of Labor (AFL), which was founded in 1886 by Samuel Gompers. At its pinnacle, the AFL had approximately 1.4 million members. The organization is credited with successfully negotiating wage increases for its members and enhancing workplace safety for all workers in most industries.

For Italian immigrants, learning the English language was the first—and perhaps the biggest—challenge. The Irish spoke the same language as Americans, so it was not a barrier. It was an advantage. Even for the Germans and for many other Europeans whose language was of a Germanic origin, the task of learning English was not as large a barrier as it would be for the Italians. Many Italians were illiterate, and when they arrived on US shores, their language was not Italian. They had certain accents and pronunciations that represented a dialect from the region or village that they had come from. The dialects were all different not just from the north to the south, or from city to city, but from village to village and from neighborhood to neighborhood. These differences were vast. To acquire a new language, it was necessary to start with a common base, which did not exist among the millions of immigrants who came from all regions and villages of southern Italy. In Italian, every consonant and vowel in every word was pronounced. In English, there were many words in which many of the letters were silent. How does one pronounce the sound of *th*? The Italian alphabet and the letters *J*, *K*, and *Y* did not exist. How would one learn this new and very different language when most were illiterate to begin with, even in their native tongue, which was comprised of numerous dialects with origins from the neighborhoods and conclaves from which they had come?

Most of the Italians who emigrated to America knew nothing about industrialization and trusted no one outside of their village. Since they had difficulties communicating, many had no choice but to resort to manual work. Their lives in the old country centered around their tiny plots of land and gardens, and when they arrived in America, they found few industries they were suited for. Those who could not find work in agriculture or in the coal mines found work in the garment industry or in construction projects and in gangs under bilingual foremen that were called *Padroni*. These men, many who came from the same village or neighborhood, could speak both Italian and English. They directed the labor and provided room and board for those who could not speak the language.

There were many organizations and societies formed for the purpose of helping Italians assimilate into the new country. One such organization during the immigration boom was The Order Sons of Italy in America (or, in Italian: *Ordine Figli d'italia in America,* OSIA) founded by Vincenzo Sellaro on June 22, 1905. As an Italian-American organization, its mission included encouraging the study of the Italian language and culture in American schools and universities; preserving Italian-American traditions, culture, history, and heritage; and promoting closer cultural relations between the United States and Italy. But in the beginning, their purpose had been to help the Italian immigrant assimilate into American society. One of their programs helped teach English and improve literacy for these immigrants.

During the early years, OSIA had at first been involved in promoting immigration legislation; assisting in the assimilation process; and supporting cooperation, trade, and diplomatic relations between the United States and Italy. They initiated social and fraternal events and encouraged educational achievement through scholarships. They brought the Italian immigrant communities together through a variety of cultural events. The order raised funds for local charities and provided low-cost financial investments and insurance. Some of these programs were hijacked and evolved into forced-protection programs, which had started in the old country.

In 1928, Sellaro was given the key to the City of New York in recognition of his social and medical achievements. In that same year, Ernesto's grandfather, Emilio, became a member of New York Laborers' Union Local 4. He helped establish a pension fund, and by the end of the first year, it had a balance of just over $1 million.

Emilio LaCola understood the value of literacy and attended the OSIA meetings and participated in the evening language classes. He was intelligent and outspoken and had met several like-minded Sicilians who were interested in social reform. Together, they would organize the meeting of workers on Sunday to discuss how they could work with union organizations to develop programs to improve working conditions.

As a *Padroni,* Ernesto's grandfather, Emilio, had several laborers and families that relied on him. Emilio LaCola was in his early thirties and was more than a *Padroni;* he was someone who could communicate, influence, and organize the workers. He was someone who could organize with a caring voice and unify the illiterate working man, while teaching them how to assimilate in American society. He traveled throughout the city and traded wheelbarrow handles for a bullhorn to become a leader of men, a labor organizer. Both his son and grandson would follow in his footsteps as labor organizers, and the family name carried into new generations, a name with respect that would enable his direct descendants to rise into leadership positions far beyond his dreams and aspirations.

The LaCola family name had become associated with great respect. The family name would become synonymous with the union as Local 4's power and influence grew exponentially. The union was viewed by many, especially the LaCola family, as a family-owned enterprise that could be handed down from generation to generation. Although they were regarded with suspicion in many quarters, their positions in the union slowly became a controlling influence in the New York construction industry throughout the twentieth century. A large segment of the population held that there must be something malevolent behind such growth in power and influence because of their associations with the New York crime families, who many viewed as crime-ridden organizations run by power-mad fiends. As a result, unions became the target of congressional investigations, the FBI, anti-trust legislation, and triggered numerous government regulations and oversight.

One of the most famous labor unions in history is the Congress of Industrial Organizations (CIO), which started under John L. Lewis and underwent a huge expansion during World War II. The AFL-CIO merger occurred in 1955, with its membership peaking in 1970.

Emilio LaCola had just turned fifty-two at the start of the Second World War when he was elected to the position of business agent for Laborers Local 4. The pension trust fund balance had just passed the $10 million mark. Emilio was a dreamer, and his dark-brown eyes always appeared to be gazing beyond reality, as if he might somehow find the answer to the purpose of his own existence. His call for unity and organization never wavered during his leadership tenure. The year was 1950 when Emilio was found dead at the age of sixty-one in his swimming pool on his estate in Long Island. He was an expert swimmer, and his death would remain a mystery. Many concluded that it was the result of the many opposing forces among the New York City crime families as they fought for control of the construction industry in the city.

Just two days later, his son Pasquale was appointed to serve in the position as business agent, and three months later, an election was held, which made the appointment permanent. At that time, their pension trust account had a balance of just over $50 million. Five years later, in 1955, Local 4 became the first New York City trade union to become affiliated with AFL-CIO. At age thirty-five, Pasquale was appointed to serve as a national board member and would continue to serve as a trustee on that board for the next twenty years.

In 1975, Pasquale LaCola suffered a fatal heart attack while attending an AFL-CIO conference in Miami. An emergency meeting was held, and Ernesto LaCola was elevated to the position of business agent for the union. At that time, the pension trust fund balance had just reached $150 million. The family's power within the labor movement would continue to grow substantially, along with their wealth and social position within the class system of American society. The family had amassed a multimillion-dollar real-estate portfolio, and Ernesto became a member of the social elite of New York society.

The outcome of historical conflict and differences among the many counteracting forces between the worker and the employer strengthened the LaCola family name. The road to what organized labor had become and the organizations that led the movement had dramatically changed against the backdrop of a changing political, cultural, and social values. The resulting government intervention influenced and forced changes to the methods and priorities of these organizations. Through the years, there was conflict and differences that would eventually lead to physical injury and injustices, which created even further conflict between workers and management.

Little by little, organized crime began to establish a foothold within these organizations. At the same time, the public demanded social justice, equity, and fairness, resulting in more oversight by the government. These new laws and regulations created complex operating environments and sophisticated accounting systems that could only be managed by computers. While freedom of speech and protection of the worker became a part of the American culture, the power of the unions' voice sparked interest from the political landscape and established a foothold in government. The worker was no longer working for himself but was now working under a different two-tiered system—no longer apprentice and journeyman but now employee working under a more organized corporate structure. That corporate structure was built around capital, and the end means was profit.

In America, there was an influx of immigrants in need of work who could not speak the native language, or who did not understand how to exchange or add up the nickels and dimes that went into a dollar. An expanding immigrant population resulted in worker abuse, lower wages, and a greater need for organized labor. The question remained: was it an opportunity for the immigrant worker, or was it the cheap labor to support the capital structure?

Organized labor was built on a foundation of unity. This was often the call to organize that which was expressed to all workers: unity among all members. It was necessary to build strength in the organization and a requirement that each member look out for the interest of all other members. It was a brotherhood, and aptly so; many of the newly formed organizations had *brotherhood* in their name. Collective interest for the union would override the individual interest of each member, since they were one and the same. There was a disdain for the elite, and the only way to attain justice and fairness was through the collective rights of the organization. This would only be accomplished through unity.

Unity was the means to achieve equality, and this had to be accomplished through any means available. Often, it was through convincing dialect and powerful voices speaking for those who could not speak. On some occasions, it was through violence and threats. Labor leaders and organizers discovered that when they were united, they had power. Whatever the means, they must be unified, and this gave them a voice that was heard and an enabler of power. When they were together, this enabled them to make threats and to call upon their members to strike or walk off the job. This ability to stop work was perhaps their greatest weapon. Work stoppage cost employers money and gave the unions the ability to make threats and coerce management to give in to their demands.

During the eighties and nineties, the union became a controlling force in the New York City economy. As membership grew and they became more organized, so grew their power. With power came money. With money came corruption. As the interaction with government became more prevalent, the corruption spilled over into politics. More members meant more votes and more dues flowing into the unions, as well as more influence in the electoral process. Unions had the membership and had a collective voice in who and why they supported a political candidate. Just as elected officials produced regulations that would influence industry and commerce, it made sense that organized labor would vote for those politicians that were aligned with the labor-movement cause.

But just as the unions gained power, there was a sense of empowerment from many labor leaders that led them into corruption. There was just too much money to turn their backs on. They recognized that they not only had a say; they also had the money that reached far beyond their labor force and could influence laws and regulations that would enable them to gain more power over industry. They could yield power well beyond the employer and management and could influence political outcomes and change social and economic culture. With the power, they demanded more money and fewer hours, but with better retirement benefits, better health-care plans, and all sorts of benefits far beyond the simple demands of the early unions, which were a fair day's wages for a day's work.

It was 1992, and the journeyman in the union would earn over $27 dollars an hour. For each hour he worked, the employer would contribute an additional $16.25 in benefit dollars. They had indeed accomplished their purpose: a fair day's wages for a fair day's work, and much more.

The administration of complex multiemployer benefit plans by the union required accurate and efficient record-keeping systems. At the same time, the government created new laws to ensure that the workers were protected. Bigger unions meant more complicated regulations and laws creating more government oversight, on the pretense that it would protect and benefit the public. Crime families gained a foothold while huge amounts of money flowed in and out of the unions. The need for improving management systems and more advanced computer systems intensified, and with these advancements, the unions turned to outside professionals. The unions were running a multimillion-dollar, multifaceted business, and the principal role that Chris and Goldin would serve was quite clear: help them manage all that money while maintaining the power held by the family. The year was 1992, and the pension trust fund alone was now close to $500 million.

Ernesto's grandfather was not just a *Padroni*; he was a visionary, an organizer and was one of the first to recognize that unity could be expanded among all the building trades. His views contributed to the formation of cohesive bodies of organized labor, helping to grow the role Local 4 played in unifying the worker, while at the same time, creating the family business.

CHAPTER TWENTY-TWO

JUDGING PEOPLE

YOU CAN GET A PRETTY good indication of a restaurant well before any of the food has been served. You can judge how the entire meal will taste, even before the first bite. Just walking in and looking around at the tables provides several indicators as to the food and the service. How crowded is the restaurant? How many empty tables are there? Is there any food on the tables? What do the dishes that were plated as they came out of the kitchen look like? Are the customers eating, smiling, and talking, or are they just sitting in their chairs, silently waiting for the food to arrive? Usually, the louder the chatter, the more pleased are the patrons, the better the experience. And then, of course, how does the bread look? Is it fresh? Is it warm? And, of course, how does it taste? That is perhaps one of the most important tests and provides an early indication of the meal to follow.

Why is it that something so simple can be so complicated or difficult for so many restaurants? You don't need to make your own bread, since there are so many good choices that can be purchased from numerous food suppliers. If they cannot place a fresh, good-tasting bread in the basket on the table, something so simple, then how is it possible to improve on the anything else coming out of the kitchen? It is the little things that make a big difference when you judge the quality standards of a restaurant. The bread is one of the first tests of quality when you are out to dine, and first impressions tell the story of what is to follow.

The same applies to people. It is that first encounter that is so telling—the first meeting and that first impression you come away with. The dress, the suit, the tie, and, yes, even the color of the tie and the way the knot is tied. That first greeting and the expression on one's face. The face provides a good indication of the person behind it. That first handshake. Was it bold and firm or sweaty and limp?

Chris had immediately disliked Greco, regardless of how much he wanted to like him. He was witty and told funny stories. And, of course, he was old-world Italian, just like your old grandpa. Chris grew up in an Italian family in an Italian neighborhood and was at ease and comfortable with the culture. He was proud of his Italian heritage and loved the people. He enjoyed doing business with the unions. He especially enjoyed the labor leaders who ran the trade unions, particularly the laborers' and bricklayers' unions, since most in those trades were Italian. He was comfortable doing business with Italians and enjoyed just hanging around with them and listening to their stories.

But there was something about Greco that gave Chris an uneasy feeling. Greco continually talked about unity, trust, and loyalty, and Chris wanted to believe that there was some truth in what he had said, but he still could not bring himself to like the man. Maybe it was the handshake; he thought back and remembered that it was sweaty and limp. But that wasn't it. He remembered the spots on his wide tie that looked like a pattern on the material that you would drape from the windows in his Italian grandmother's parlor. No, that wasn't it either. Maybe it was the way he ate at the restaurant on Seventeenth Street. He was crude and, in some respects, ignored all table etiquette. He actually was a pig and devoured the food as if he were a person on the run who had not eaten in ages. Maybe that was the reason? No. Perhaps it was the way he just assumed that Chris would pick up the check? No. Chris even did not mind the $10,000 that he'd had to give him. When you added it all up, it was certainly cause for anyone to dislike Greco. But what truly takes the cake was when he jumped up and had the nerve to take the extra cannoli. That was it; that was the breaking point. He crossed over the line with the cannoli, and that was perhaps what had triggered Chris's dislike of the man.

Chris had devoted much of his resources to the account, and the expenses were mounting up. New York City food and lodging was expensive, and he had Williams, another programmer, and two trainers assigned to the account almost full time. He had asked to see Greco to discuss the billing and Greco had put him off for the last two weeks, refusing to talk about it. He had simply said not to worry and that he had to check with Goldin. He said Goldin needed to sign off on all the invoices over $10,000. Chris knew that this was a delay tactic. He was losing all faith and confidence in the entire project. He was fuming; they had put so much effort into the account and after the first eight weeks had over $50,000 in expenses alone, which he had billed but was still waiting to be reimbursed. He was still waiting for a $225,000 check for the first installment for the software and then another $150,000 in billable hours.

It was getting out of hand. Chris knew he had to work with Greco but realized that Greco had no understanding of the computer's inner workings. He did not care about Chris and did not care about Chris's money situation. If he could take advantage of a situation, he would, so Chris finally decided it was time to confront Paul Goldin directly about the money and the outstanding invoices. He recalled that he was instructed to discuss all money matters with Goldin. They agreed to dinner on Wednesday. He knew that Goldin was a food junkie and was always available for a free dinner. Only this time, it would be different, and Goldin would be picking up the tab. It would be catch-up time for Chris.

There was a status meeting every other Tuesday, and Chris was not comfortable bringing up money matters at those meetings. Paul was the go-to person, and he recalled that first meeting in the equipment room on the seventh floor. Paul told him that he would make lots of money and there would be an up charge of $150,000 for the software. Chris was not stupid and knew that there was something wrong and not entirely legal. He realized that it was a bribe and that he could go to prison. He also knew that there were other charges that he would bill and pay to the consultants. He would be ruined if he were caught. He wanted no part in it, but he was already in too deep, and there was no way at this point to back out.

He was committed and still believed he would find a way out. Chris had too much at stake and too much invested. He needed the money, and the bank was not going to allow him to draw any more from his credit line. The clients in Albany and Syracuse were complaining because he was not giving them the attention that they were normally accustomed to, and the maintenance fees were chicken feed when he compared it to the fees he was charging for the work at Local 4. Things were slipping in the wrong direction, and he now realized he would need to address this head-on with Goldin. Paul had gotten him into this, and Goldin was going to fix it. Right now, his goal was to get the money today and worry about tomorrow's problems tomorrow.

CHAPTER TWENTY-THREE

WHERE'S THE MONEY?

JULY 20, 1992

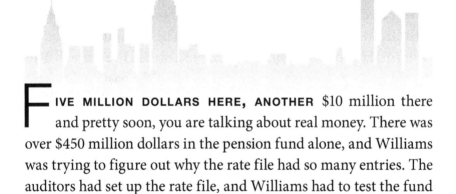

F IVE MILLION DOLLARS HERE, ANOTHER $10 million there
and pretty soon, you are talking about real money. There was
over $450 million dollars in the pension fund alone, and Williams
was trying to figure out why the rate file had so many entries. The
auditors had set up the rate file, and Williams had to test the fund
accounting process. He then had to provide reports to the auditors
to verify that his programs were working correctly. All seemed to
be going well, but the auditors were not quick to provide feedback.
They simply said thank you.

Williams was very thorough but was also very inquisitive and
went beyond what was necessary for the job. When he ran the audit
reports that matched the dollars to the hours that were reported,

he was pleased that the hours and the dollars all balanced. He was surprised at first, since this is where most of the money flowed into the funds. He thought it was curious that everything seemed to balance. But then he realized that there were several auditors checking all the reports before they were entered into the computer. He was pleased and felt good that Goldin's auditors were on the seventh floor.

His purpose in converting the data was not to determine if the data was correct; he just wanted to verify that his programs were bug-free. He did not care about the hourly credits and how they worked in Bloom's programs but was pleased that he finally was able to verify that good data had been converted over to his side. He checked his math and ripped the report off of the printer and was ready to mark "complete" on his project plan. Like most new implementations, the challenge was always the conversion of data and not the programs. Even though there would be new software, they still needed to convert all the hours over and match the hours, benefit credits, and the changes in the balances in each fund. Union software was different in that regard. The software needed to perform the processes going forward but also had to ensure that all the old history records were correct and that the past credits were in balance. He ran a test program, and when he used the converted data records, he needed the assurance that the process worked perfectly. The auditors did not share any information, other than to comment that they liked the process and that the new system was an improvement over the old system. He thought, "We are good on our side, and my audit program proved that we converted all of the data correctly."

Williams was satisfied and looked directly into the IBM terminal as he turned his attention to the health and welfare process. He peered down at the old paid-claim file and saw that there were problems. He knew his programs were good, and he immediately could see that there was something amiss. He was not about to say anything to anyone except Chris until he was sure. He didn't care and thought about the last time he'd opened his mouth and spoken about the data problems he had uncovered. "We are here to install our software and to convert the data, regardless of the quality. Not our problem and not my responsibility to evaluate the old system," he reminded himself.

Williams finally looked over to Smith, who was not paying attention to what Williams had discovered.

"Okay, Larry, we are getting close. I am close to move the paid-claims history file over. The contractor reporting is clean."

Smith was not a programmer and didn't know how the conversion program worked, but he was happy to hear Williams' comments.

"Great. Stanley will be tickled, and I know that Greco and LaCola will be very pleased." He pointed to the screen. "What is this screen telling us?"

Williams, with a broad grin, looked back at Smith and also pointed to the screen. "Well, it tells me that electrons are green. See, all the numbers are green."

"Yeah, that's funny stuff, but really, what are the numbers telling us?"

"No, we are good. We have a few hundred dollars' difference, but that is simply the rounding problem of pennies after we calculate the interest earned. See, it's less than five hundred dollars." He was lying.

"Yes, this was one of those things that drove us nuts for a long time. Chris came up with the algorithm, and he is the boss, and besides, it passes the litmus test. See, it is green. That is nothing when you compare that to the millions of dollars of paid claims each year."

"Well, that is pretty cool. I know that Goldin will be happy to hear about this. He is a CPA, and I don't think he ever looked at the numbers in that way."

"Yeah, but the big deal—and the problems—are yet to come." Williams looked at Smith, his broad smile turning into a frown. "No problem; it is just that the health-claims set-up process is going to be our next challenge, but we can handle it. No problem," he repeated.

Just then, Chris walked into the room and peered over William's shoulder.

"Hey, how is the paid-claims file looking? Let's get the claims software tested, and then we can start training. I would like to start testing the claims adjudication process using their plan setup. Do you have the claims history mapped and converted? This is critical and is not going to be easy. We can expect to run into some issues."

Williams looked up at Chris. "We were playing around with your benchmark test, and it is okay. I have the rate file loaded and have started to test the crosswalk over from the contractor reports to the various funds. I think it looks good going forward. Stanley wants to look at it. I cannot test anything until we get the sign-off for the hours' entry process from Stanley and the auditors. But my cross-check balances. I used our test data with their old rate files, and the balances are all perfect."

Chris's voice was now sharper, and Williams could tell he was annoyed. "Why does Stanley need to look at it? We are supposed to have Goldin sign off on the conversions. Goldin told me not to worry about the old rates. Just go forward and test using the new rates. The data you have should be good. Goldin is upstairs and we should get him down here, but I will talk to him tonight. We are supposed to have dinner. He has about six or seven accountants up there, and they said that our programs work perfectly."

Williams stood and turned. "The more I get into the conversion, the more problems I find. The contractor audit is fine, and we have no issues. But we still have some work regarding the paid-claims history."

Chris motioned Williams to come over to the window. "Pete, what is bothering you? What about the paid-claims file? Let's go across the street and get a decent cup of coffee. I might even buy you a bagel."

They both walked to the door of the computer room and opened the secured glass door. The buzzer sounded, and as they exited, they both peered up at the camera and smiled as they passed by.

As they walked across the street, Chris noticed a Con Ed van parked directly in front. There were three bright-orange curb cones to the rear of the van. He also noticed the small, yellow bubble light on top. He had no idea that it was the camera lens.

Connie was the first to notice from inside the van.

"Hey! There is our boy, number-one software guy, and he is with his number-one techie."

She sat in front of the computer terminal in the center and looked up at the middle monitor. There was a black gentleman in a dark-gray T-shirt seated to her left, and he immediately began keying into the keyboard sitting before him. She continued.

"Can we get audio in the coffee shop? Looks like they are going into the diner."

The yellow light on the roof had a 360-degree video camera that could be rotated in a full circle and pointed to their surveilled target. It was controlled by a joystick within the van in front of the middle computer screen. It also contained a small parabolic antenna, which could pick up sounds and conversations in its pointed direction. There was a smaller screen at desk level that displayed where the audio antenna was pointing. This was controlled by the computer mouse.

"Okay, aim the audio antenna at the window and see if we can pick up the conversation," Connie said.

"Well, let me see what we can do. I think we only can get the tables next to the window. It is just too crowded right now, and there is too much noise to pick up any of the conversations, or to filter them."

The young black agent moved the mouse and pointed the antenna at the diner window across the street. He stopped it and adjusted the distance using the plus and minus keys.

Chris and Williams entered the small coffee shop, and Chris walked to the rear corner. It was noisy, and there was a small line of five or six people at the front end of the counter waiting to pick up their order and pay. It was close to 4:00 p.m., and the early dinner crowd was just beginning to enter.

Chris was first to speak. "Hey, do you think we can get lucky and find a table? I need to go easy on the food because I have a dinner meeting tonight."

Chris could not immediately find a table but then noticed a man who stood up from a table next to the front window and was about to walk out. Chris walked over and sat down and motioned for Williams to join him. Williams walked over and sat across the table directly facing him.

"Look, you mentioned that everything was looking good, except what? What is the problem?" Chris asked.

Williams leaned toward Chris and said in a low whisper, "I am okay with the contractors' reporting system data. It all looks good, and the hours balance with the dollars. Our programs are all perfect going forward. I also have started to transfer the paid-claim records from Bloom's system," He smiled as he looked across at Chris. "But the history file is all screwed up. There are claims payment records that are screwed up. Here is the big problem: there are several paid-claims records that have bad pointers. The check file is also screwed up, with missing records. This does not make any sense. I checked the provider master file, and some of that data does not match the claims records. Someone is ripping the health and welfare fund out of a lot of money."

"Careful—there may be some of the union people in here, so let's be sure no one overhears our conversation, okay?" Chris now spoke in a lower voice and had raised the menu up over his face to be certain that no one was reading his lips.

The engineer in the van was the first to speak.

"Hey, I think we might get lucky. Look who is sitting next to the window."

He had earphones covering his ears and was listening intently. He could barely make out the conversation that was vibrating from the window.

"I am getting some distinctive conversation, but there is quite a bit of noise and other talk mixed in."

Williams replied to Chris. "What the hell is going on here? Every time we bring data over, we find more problems. It seems that everything in the old system is screwed up. I can see why Goldin is involved in everything that we do. Greco is useless, and he comes in at about ten o'clock and leaves for lunch about 11:30. When he does return from lunch, it is never before two, and then, if he comes back at all, he leaves about three. Smith is a nice guy, but he is just an operations guy. He has no clue as to what is really going on with the system. Do you want to laugh? Smith has a degree in computer science from SUNY Albany."

Williams raised both hands with his palms facing upward and looked up at the ceiling. His motions were in the form of a question as he shrugged.

"Chris, our conversion programs are clean and work perfectly. The auditors will sign off on the contribution system. So, just when we think we are getting ahead, we run into another problem. These people think it is their own private bank account. I hate to say this, but I think we should contact the authorities."

Chris answered, "No, no, we are in too deep, and they will turn it on us. What are you saying? Just look at this as another job, and …" He trailed off and paused for a few seconds. "We are not going to get involved in their problems. Keep all this to yourself. Do you know how much money this account owes us? I will handle the political end and cover our ass with Goldin and the others. You must never say anything to anyone. Goldin is the only one who understands the system and the accounting. He is in charge and put this deal together for us. He is at the helm and steering the ship on this voyage. Greco and LaCola are on the bridge, but it is Goldin who has his hands on the wheel.

"We do not care where the ship sailed last year. I am only concerned that we end up in the right port chosen by Goldin. They have a screwed-up system, and we are here because of that. Goldin is the brains behind this operation. But first, let me say this. The contractor reporting audit is good news. We cannot fix all of their old problems. I will tell Goldin both the bad news and the good news. He needs to know about the claims problem. If he is not surprised or not concerned, then he is involved with the skim. If he is surprised and was not aware of the problem, then we will know there are others on the inside who have gone into business for themselves. It will be up to him how he wants to handle all of this. Forget about trying to clean up their problems with the old software. Just put it in writing in your weekly report to me and this will keep us clear of their problems. Remember, document."

Chris continued. "The old software is crap, and it was all hard-coded. That is why they have the auditors on the seventh floor processing all the contractor reports. Be thankful to Goldin's auditors. He runs the show, so we do not care what happens on the seventh floor, only what comes down to the sixth floor. It is none of our business and has nothing to do with anything we are doing. Our priority is to convert the data and get our software working with the converted records. Then we can collect our fees and go back to some sense of normalcy in Albany. They owe us over $400,000, and we are out of business if we throw in the towel at this point in time. Pete, relax; I am covering our ass with our documentation."

Chris was still curious about the colored folders and still suspected that something was not right on the seventh floor. But he was pleased that Williams' audit of the contractor reports ran smoothly without identifying any problems. He however was concerned that the claims history records were screwed up.

"Hold on; here comes the waitress," he said. "Hi. Two coffees, and I would like a toasted onion bagel."

Williams turned and looked up at the waitress. "Coffee and a piece of apple pie."

She turned and walked toward the counter. Chris watched her as she walked away. They now spoke in an almost whisper.

"Pete, what else? What can you tell me about the claims history?"

Unknown to Chris and Williams, the van was continuing to focus its audio antenna at the window. They could not see through the glare against the window.

Samples looked over at the engineer. "Martin, what have you got so far?"

He grinned. "So far, onion bagel and two coffees. That is all I could pick up clearly."

Williams reached into his left breast pocket and pulled out a folded piece of computer paper.

"Take a look at this. Do you remember when we discussed the paid-claims problem a week ago? Well, I verified my program and ran the edit program, and guess what? They are definitely out of balance with the accounting system."

He unfolded the paper and stared at the numbers. "Well, let's see, in the first six months of last year, there were 458 claim records all over five grand, and the total amount is just under $3 million."

He pointed to the number shown on the far-right column as he pushed it across the table for Chris to see. It read, "$2,944,940."

Chris looked down and stared at the numbers. He then picked up the report. "So, what does it all mean? What do you have? What do you think happened? What does this prove?"

Williams replied, "Strange things are happening. There are 458 records screwed up. That is the rather curious thing; there should be a few records with common provider numbers. There were a few other data fields that were all blank. So, statistically, it is impossible to assume that there were unintentional errors. This leads to only one conclusion: it is on purpose, and someone is helping themselves to a few dollars—actually, a few million dollars from the health and welfare fund."

Chris shook his head in disbelief. "You got to be kidding. Every time we think we are good, something else pops up. Are you sure about this? I will need to discuss this with Goldin and want to be certain. If someone has gone into their own business, then Paul needs to know."

Chris folded the report and stuffed it into his breast pocket. "Are there any other clues that can help point to who is responsible?"

He knew that Williams was not going to stop short, with only half the problem solved. Chris waited for Williams to continue and said, "So?"

Williams replied eagerly, "Well, I can tell you this. The terminal used was DiNapoli's terminal in the annuity department. And it was the last week in July of last year when the data was scrambled."

Chris frowned. "Do not speak to anyone about this. Especially anyone across the street. But wait a minute; DiNapoli told me that he always goes to Saratoga the last two weeks in July. Remember? That was when we went live with the pension fund, and DiNapoli was on vacation."

Williams looked across at Chris and tilted his head to one side as he shrugged his shoulders. He was a perfectionist and remained upset. "This was last July. I do not like this place, and we keep seeing more and more problems. I guess there are just too many opportunities to get at the money."

Chris grinned and replied, "Pete, it is no different than all the other unions we have converted; they are all messed up. Look, this is their problem, and it is up to Goldin to fix it. This is not our problem; this is our opportunity. The old system sucks, and we cannot do anything about that." He then said forcefully, "Forget about it. And keep this between you and me. Document this in your weekly report but be sure to sound a little vague. Never speak a word of this to anyone."

"Look, Chris, at least the contractor reporting history records balance."

Williams smiled back at Chris and raised both his hands as if he were throwing something up. He remained calm and did not show any signs of his uneasiness to Chris. He was now more forceful and wanted to have Chris think that he was past all the uncertainty and that he could not be fooled. In some way, this was an opportunity for exacting his revenge and to demonstrate that he was the brains that made it all possible..

Chris shook his head from side to side.

"This account is a gift that keeps on giving. No wonder they wanted to desperately install new software. We have a job to do, and we are not auditors. Pete, as long as we avoid any wrongdoing on our part and perform according to our contract, then we are doing the job we were hired to do."

Inside the van, Samples directed her question to the man sitting to her right.

"What do you think? Anything?"

"Well, Chris Vincent is the main guy, and if either one of them have any information to share, we are not getting it at this meeting."

Martin was an FBI electronics technician and had expert knowledge of the electronic apparatus contained within the van.

"I can run the tape, and maybe I can make something out of it if we send it to the lab, but I doubt that we can get anything. Maybe we can get a voice print when they come out, but I do not think it is going to help. Too much street noise is interfering."

Connie shook her head. "I think we need to have another talk with Mr. Vincent. That might be our best bet to get the passwords and find out what is really going on. They are pretty sharp and know what is going on under the covers."

The young black man spoke next. "I still think the programmer knows more."

She shook her head noticeably. "You may be right, but Williams is too unstable. He could not handle it and would probably shit his pants if we ever spoke to him. I am going to have another meeting with the little Italian. Vincent is our guy. We had the Albany guys talk to him in May and I personally met him on the train, and he knows we are on to them."

Marco sat near the rear door. He wore gray coveralls with the Con Edison logo imprinted on the front and back and a bright-orange plastic vest.

"Look, we have been here for … let's see … almost a week, and isn't it about time that Con Edison fixes the electrical problem under the sidewalk? We do not want to compromise the van. It is time we moved out of here since we are not getting anything useful. I have the telecommunications feed into the computer and should have the passwords in a few days. My program has never failed me." He hesitated for a few seconds and then added, "Yet."

Samples directing her next words to Marco. "I am going to give it another week or so for you to get into the system before we go to plan B. If you cannot come up with something, we will have another talk with the little Italian. Maybe a talk with Williams. Why don't we put out a couple of slices of pizza as bait? Vincent is sure to bite."

"Funny stuff. Cut the crap." Marco was not amused. "Hey, hold on," he said and pointed to the video screen. "Wait a minute; here is the black Lincoln, ready to pick up our number-one guy, LaCola. Right on time, 4:30. Why don't we put a tail on him and see where he goes if he does not go downtown to the heliport? He is very careful in the office, so he must be conducting business outside the office, and we may have a better chance."

Samples shook her head. "Don't bother; we tried that a few months ago and followed him for two weeks, and it was a dead end. He always leaves at 4:30 and gets driven down to the heliport. Let's stay focused with plan A, and let's see if you can get under the covers of the computer. That is what you are here for, right?"

They waited another twenty minutes before Chris and Williams walked out and crossed the street to enter 230 Park Avenue South. The two men did not speak a word to one another. With that, the electronics expert moved to the front behind the driver's wheel and started the engine. The young black agent put on an orange Con Ed vest and exited from the back and took the three traffic cones and threw them into the back. He went around to the right side of the van and climbed into the right front seat. The van slowly pulled into the traffic with its yellow light blinking.

CHAPTER TWENTY-FOUR

SISTINA

JULY 20, 1992

B OBBY OPENED THE DOOR FOR LaCola.

"Hi, boss, the chopper?" The car would normally be double parked, and the driver usually waited in the limo with the engine running and flashers flashing. Today, he found a spot and stood outside of the big Lincoln.

LaCola answered as he stepped into the limo. "No, not tonight. I have a dinner meeting. Sistina—do you know the address?"

Bobby pulled out into the traffic. "Yes, I think it is just below Eighty-First Street. It is on Second Avenue."

LaCola sat in the back seat, opened his briefcase, and pulled out some contracts to review. He also withdrew the folded piece of paper Chris had given him from his pocket.

"You got it. You have a pretty good memory."

"Well, Mr. LaCola, we have been there before, and I remember you told me you sat next to Beverly Sills and Barbara Walters. That is Walters' favorite restaurant, and she is a regular. Supposed to be one of the best Italian restaurants in the city."

LaCola looked up toward the driver. "Yes, Bobby; now I remember. Beverly Sills. She was often called the queen of American opera."

"Really? Who is Sills? Why is she called that?"

LaCola continued. "Well, that is because she gained notoriety for her rise to stardom without the benefit of European training. She paved the way for other American-trained singers to succeed without the normal Met certification."

The driver concentrated on his driving while he listened to LaCola. "Interesting."

"Yes, she was really something, and she was very pretty. She was a blonde with a very warm personality. Her parents were Jewish immigrants from Odessa Ukraine, and she spoke several languages. She grew up in Brooklyn and was known by her friends as Bubbles Silverman. Anyway, her friends called her Bubbles."

It took well over an hour to travel uptown, since the traffic was heavy. The reservation was for 6:15, so they would arrive with time to spare. LaCola wondered if he would see Beverly Sills again at the restaurant.

LaCola was dropped off in front, and the maître d' opened the door.

"Good evening, sir. Welcome."

"Hello. I believe that there is a table reserved for Sal Barone."

"Yes, sir. Welcome, and right this way; you are the first to arrive. Mr. Barone called and said he would be arriving around 6:30."

Barone was very wealthy and one of the most successful contractors in the city. He controlled the concrete business, and every real-estate construction project needed concrete. He was very flamboyant and generous and always picked up the bill. Barone had a special house account, and the bill was sent to his accountant at the end of each month. He never looked at the bill, nor did he know exactly what the cost was. It did not matter, since he did not care. Some thought that he was worth at least $100 million to $200 million. Barone's fortune was acquired through the special construction projects he performed with collaboration of the unions and the New York City politicians. As the largest and most exclusive concrete producer, he was involved in all the construction projects, and he could influence the pricing and contractor selection. He was tough as nails, although he had a friendly and generous outward demeanor. He also was involved with the Gambino crime family and close to all the union labor leaders. Price fixing was the game, and he knew how to play the game to his advantage. He was definitely a friend to the organization.

Sal Barone often bragged and would tell his friends that his bill at Sistina was well over $10,000 a month. He could afford it, since it was buried within the hundreds of millions of dollars of contract work across the many projects that he was involved in. Barone never complained about the service or the price. He was a multimillionaire who did not play golf, and although he was a member of three country clubs, most of his entertaining was done at Sistina. He was a special customer, and they always made it a point to take special care of Sal Barone. They never disappointed him, and he received the best possible service with perfectly prepared food. Everything Barone ordered was special. He never looked at or questioned the bill. The menus for his guests did not have any prices on them, but it did not matter, since they knew Barone was picking up the tab. The waiters would take orders without writing anything down, and then from memory key the order into the point-of-sale terminal.

Whenever you went along with the waiter's suggestion or accepted a special that was not on the menu, there would be an upcharge. Sistina had quite a following as a restaurant serving uncompromised food quality delivered in an exceptional manner. But it was expensive. You might say the menu was electrifying. The food quality was never in question. However, after the meal, when you saw the bill, you were in for quite a shock. But quality was never compromised, and it was more than worth it. It was far more than a dinner; it was a memorable experience.

Hey, this was the upper east side, and Giuseppe Bruno was the chef owner and was reputed to be the best chef host in the city. When he was in the kitchen, he did not cook; he directed and saw to every little detail. No dish ever left the kitchen unless it underwent the personal inspection and strict scrutiny of Giuseppe. He did not cater to the rich; he catered to the super rich, and in the city, there were plenty available. He had operated one of the finest restaurants for many years and cared about those customers who cared about fine dining more than they cared about money. It was quite popular with the rich and famous and had wonderful décor and well-placed tables for special business meetings. The restaurant had all the bells and whistles and all the amenities that went far beyond the elegant dishes, including white tablecloths, candles, fresh flowers, a great wine list, and delectable desserts.

This was New York City, and it was perfectly acceptable. Actually, it enjoyed a powerful following with the jet-set crowd who lived in the upper east side. The owner ran the restaurant like a well-oiled machine and delivered excellent and uncompromised service with grace and care to his upscale clientele who appreciated quality.

"Jack will be right with you, sir, and may I suggest a wine or provide you with a cocktail?"

"No, just bring me a Peroni in a chilled glass, please." Ernesto had already decided that he would let Barone order for him since he knew the menu intimately.

"Right away, sir."

It was less than thirty seconds when the waiter returned with the beer, and he gracefully placed the glass in front of Ernesto and poured the Peroni into it.

"May I get you an appetizer to start with?"

Immediately to his right was a shorter waiter in a white jacket who placed a crudité tray down on the center of the table, accompanied by a plate of Italian bread and small container of breadsticks. LaCola noticed that there were three place settings and wondered who else Barone had invited. He expected someone from the contractor's association but was not certain who it would be. He assumed it would be Micky Rugerri, who was the business agent from the concrete workers' district council. Mickey was involved in the negotiations and had connections with all the New York City trade unions. He had a very high-profile job like LaCola, a millionaire in his right with a salary of close to a million dollars annually when you added up all the funds he had his hand in. They touched every construction project in the city. He also had an exorbitant expense account and very exclusive tastes in watches, cars, and clothes. They even paid for his country-club membership at Winged Foot and a Lincoln Town Car.

LaCola looked up at the waiter, who wore a perfectly tailored black suit with a gold tie.

"No, thank you. I will wait for the others to arrive."

He was relaxing and enjoying the beer and the time he would have to himself. It was peaceful, and he was relaxed and comfortable. He reached for the small plate at the center of the table, took a green olive, and bit into it. He could taste the Sicilian olive oil; the flavor was bright and rosy. He then reached in and removed a small piece of Italian cheese. It was parmigiano-reggiano. His favorite.

It was almost 6:30 when he spotted Giuseppe at the front entrance in a sparkling white chef's jacket. It had a gold collar and gold ribbons sewn to the sleeves. He knew immediately that it had to be Giuseppe Bruno, the host/owner who had been selected by Zagat as the "host of the year." His name and chef title were embroidered in red on the front of his spotless chef's jacket. He oversaw every aspect of the operation from the front to the back and would often personally greet his patrons.

Almost with perfect timing, a white Rolls Royce pulled to the curb, and the rear door opened. A short, stout man of about sixty emerged, dressed in a light-gray suit. He was followed by another man who was younger and a bit taller and was dressed in a gold and tan checkered sport coat. His attire was sharp and complemented by perfectly shined Italian loafers. He had on a light-brown silk shirt with a broad collar that hung outside the narrow lapels of the sporty jacket. The door was opened immediately, well before they could arrive at the door. LaCola could faintly hear Bruno as he greeted his guests.

"*Buongiorno*; *buongiorno*, Mr. Barone. Welcome, and *buongiorno*, Mr. Rugerri. Nice to see both of you."

The shorter gentleman responded. "Hello, Giuseppe. Nice to see you. I have another guest; has he arrived?"

"Yes, yes; he is sitting at your table."

"Great. We are very hungry and looking forward to another great dinner."

Bruno turned and escorted them to the back-corner table, where LaCola was sitting. As he passed the other tables, he bowed and repeated the same welcoming words.

"*Buongiorno* … nice to see you … yes, *buongiorno* … hello … thank you for coming."

When they arrived at the table, the short man wore a broad smile. He almost lit up the entire dining room.

"Well, well, well, happy to see you, Ernesto. I am sure you know Micky Rugerri. I think you know him from the district council and from the Greater New York Contractors' Association."

"Yes, of course. He was one of our trustees on our pension fund. I think it was four or five years ago. Hello, Micky. Glad to see you. I love the jacket; where did you find it?"

Bruno held the chair back for Barone, and the waiter came over to assist with seating the others.

"Well, I discovered this little old Italian tailor in the Flatiron District who imports about fifty bolts of Italian silk from Sicily every month. He called me when he received this pattern. When I saw it, I could not resist. It reminds me of the jacket that Fredo Corleone wore in the *Godfather II* movie. Of course, this is much flashier, and I like the standout colors. Feels like it was made especially for me."

Barone interjected. "Well, it was made for you, correct?" He wore more conservative attire, but you could tell immediately that it was tailored Italian silk and very expensive.

"What, don't you like my suit? It was made for me."

LaCola was not about to be disrespectful, even though he knew that Barone was kidding. But they were friends. "Yes. It is beautiful, even though it is bulging a bit in the midsection."

"Well, it is about to get a little more bulging once you see what we are going to eat tonight. I purposely skip lunch when I plan to have dinner at this joint."

Barone's face beamed with a broad smile. There was no handshaking since they all knew one another, and they all seemed to have greeted one another with their broad smiles and brief nodding of their heads, which was apparently sufficient. The table was round and slightly larger than the rest. It was in the far corner and spaced slightly away from the other tables surrounding it to provide more privacy. Bruno thought of every little detail, and that made a big difference to Barone.

Just as they began to get settled, a bottle of red and a bottle of white Italian wine appeared, and another black-coated waiter began to pour wine into the glasses sitting in front of them.

"White or red? This is from the special wine cellar and is Mr. Sal's favorite," he asked.

They were very cheery, and Sal decided it was time to order when the waiter came over for the third time.

"Well, Mr. Sal, may I assume you are going to order for the table?"

Barone had tucked his white cloth napkin into his collar to protect any food splashes from violating his tie.

"Yes. I might as well order for the table. Let's see; for the appetizers … hmmm, can he make the globe artichokes with the fava beans, and a hot antipasto chef's choice? Make sure there are some shrimp and scallops. Also bring a plate of crab salad. Make sure there is enough for the three of us. And maybe some lobster as well."

The waiter nodded, opened another white napkin, and motioned to Barone. Barone understood completely and leaned back to allow the waiter to drape the napkin over his lap.

"I will get that going and will come back and give you a few minutes before I take your order for the pasta," the waiter replied.

Barone jumped in again. "No, you know what I like. The risotto with the asparagus and mushrooms—oh, excuse me, the morels."

He turned to LaCola to get his agreement. LaCola smiled and nodded. "And how about some of the homemade truffle pasta? Just don't put it in right away. We have lots of business to discuss."

"Yes, Mr. Sal, right away. Perfect. I will also bring some jumbo shrimp for your guests. They are colossal."

"Great, Jack. Perfect." Barone once again took charge, and LaCola and Rugerri simply looked at one another and nodded.

They each followed Barone's lead and raised their wine glasses to toast one another. Again, Barone took the lead.

"*Salud* … to good health and to good and profitable business."

LaCola and Rugerri replied, almost in unison, "*Salud,* and God bless."

They sat there with a look of complete contentment, sipped their wine, and engaged in some small talk when Ernesto decided it was time to discuss what was on his mind.

"Sal, can we talk openly here tonight? Is this place clean?"

Barone looked a bit disappointed in the question as he tightened his lips, tilted his head slightly, and frowned.

"Ernesto, this place is as secure as a confessional booth at the Vatican. We ran a scan here at four o'clock today, and Bruno is always very careful. No one will know what we talk about, for sure, and there are no bugs in this joint. I have an inside person who always tips me off. So we are clean. But if they did hear anything, we are only talking business. Right?"

"Just wanted to ask because I have some good news, and I am sure you both have heard. The Albany project is a go, and the groundbreaking was a great success. We are all excited because our boys in Albany will be relying on us for the general contracts. We will control most of the work since there are no other New York State firms big enough to handle the job. We have friends in Albany who have made it clear that this will be built by New Yorkers. It was in the RFP that New York State contractors and union contractors got extra points. We lobbied like a son of a bitch, and the politicians are true friends of labor.

"As you know, we have reciprocity agreements, and this should put us in a good position to spread the jobs out to several downstate locals. Of course, upstate as well, including Albany and Troy but as far west as Buffalo. I also have some real good news, Sal. Good news for you: the committee is going to select your company to manage all the concrete and masonry work. I know that it has not been signed by the governor yet, but even though you are not going to be the low bidder, you will be awarded the contract as the general contractor for the site work and, of course, for all the concrete. Micky, we will need the other contractors to play ball, and there will be some spillover for all the trades and most of the contractors in the association. There is just too much work for any one company, and most of the work will be on a cost-plus basis similar to the South Mall project, which made Sal's father a lot of money," Ernesto concluded.

Barone nodded in agreement. "Yes, that project put us on the map and paid for our cement plants ten times over, not to mention the thirty new concrete trucks. The South Mall was the best thing that ever happened in our state. The only part that was difficult was the transporting of the marble and granite from Vermont. That was difficult, and we could have made a lot more money if we had gotten the stone from Georgia. We still have connections in Brazil."

Rugerri represented several contractors. He looked around and spoke very quietly as he leaned over the table. "And the club members will be very happy. Hey, we cannot be greedy. We all made out, and we will make up for it with the new waterfront and the elevated interstate along the river. Sal, that calls for a lot of concrete."

"So, how do we put this all down into contractual language? What is the process we-"

He paused as three waiters began to place plates of food in front of them.

Rugerri was the first to comment. "Wow, this sure looks good." The black-coated waiter came over and handed a clean plate to the white-coated server on his left.

"May I help you with your plate, Mr. Barone?"

"Sure, go ahead."

The waiter spooned a little of each delicacy on a plate and repeated the routine for both LaCola and Rugerri. A large platter holding several giant shrimp was placed in the center of the table. Five lobster tails sat in the center on top of several King Crab legs. There were small bowls of sauces on another platter in the center of the table. There would have been no space for the platter on one of the regular-sized tables. LaCola now had a better understanding of Bruno.

Ernesto said, "What's for dessert?"

Rugerri laughed and replied, "Brioschi, for the digestive tract."

Barone looked at him as he stuck his fork into one of the lobster tails and transferred it to his plate. "You ain't seen nothing yet."

"Well, as I was saying, what are the next steps, and how do they guarantee the bids?"

"What kind of a question is that? How do we always do it?"

Rugerri replied, "We break a few bones."

LaCola shook his head. "No, maybe that is the way our fathers used to do it, but you know that has all changed. We do it through our connections and with green paper. In this case, we will need to make some campaign contributions to the usual suspects, and we have to buy a few new cars. Albany had chosen the lobbyists who had been working on the request for proposals. The RFPs have all been written to conform to your company's capabilities. We will split the front-end cost proportionally. The consultants and the lobbyists will cost us close to $3 million, but that is a drop in the bucket when we consider the size of this project. At a minimum, it will run up to $4 billion, maybe five or six.

"What do you think we have been working on for the last two years? Our engineers and architects have been working hard, and we have completed the design and specifications. We are all in; the numbers have all come together, and by the way, we all have to kick in for our friends in the Senate up in Albany. Sonny sent this down."

Lacola pulled the small piece of paper Chris had delivered from Sonny out of his suit jacket.

"This is what is expected of us for the Senate committee members. We can count on their vote to nix the right to work bill. I am meeting with Sonny and Sano next week, and they guarantee it. We will confirm the numbers and then send them money from our political-action accounts."

LaCola continued. "Sal, looks like the State of New York is going to build you guys another cement plant, but this time, it is in upstate New York."

"Well, I am glad to hear that this is finalized. I was beginning to wonder why I spent all this money with the consultants and the lobbyists."

Barone dipped pieces of the lobster meat into a small cup of melted butter and chomped away. "This has a tiny bit of truffle oil mixed in with the butter, and it tastes so sweet. Crazy stuff."

Rugerri did the same. "You are right, Sal, different and delicious."

All three reached in and focused their attention on the lobster and crab meat. LaCola noticed the head waiter looking across the room from the entrance to the kitchen. As he peered over, Barone looked up at him and nodded his head. The waiter acknowledged and left to order the kitchen to begin cooking the pasta course.

Only half a minute had passed when a short, white-coated server brought a large plate of mixed antipasto. It had lettuce, fava beans, slices of heirloom tomatoes, provolone cheese, roasted red peppers, and mozzerella. The artichokes were in the center of the platter. Another white coat followed with a small cart. There was a bottle holder on the side that held a selection of salad dressings. On the cart was a large bowl of gorgonzola cheese, which he placed on the table. He also had a stack of clean, white plates.

"May I serve some salad, gentlemen, or would you prefer that I leave this here and return in a few minutes?"

Sal was orchestrating the meal and replied. "No, we are moving too fast, so come back in a few minutes. No, I will let you know."

"I will leave this here for the moment; the gorgonzola is wonderful. We just received a few wheels from Italy yesterday."

Another two bottles of wine were placed on the side table. Sal continued with the business discussion. "So, Ernesto, what are the next steps?"

"We have to send money and sign the contracts after our lawyers have reviewed them. I brought copies with me tonight and have copies for both of you. Silverman has already reviewed them and made a few comments and notations. Nothing major, he just wants to justify his fees. This is a copy of the split Sonny received from our friend in the Senate. My end to the committee is $300K, and you guys need to decide where the rest comes from. So bring your checkbook. And by the way, your lawyers have all been involved and are aware of the terms of the deal. The management portion and some other front-end costs must be guaranteed, but that is less than 2 percent of the contract, so there is little or no downside risk to this project. Sal, the management end alone is anywhere from sixty to $100 million over the course of the project. I am talking about just the management piece."

Rugerri was enjoying the crab legs. "This has to be a cost-plus, because it is impossible to provide a fixed price for a project that runs five, maybe six years. I am glad that they agreed and have worked it all out."

LaCola put his right hand on his temple. "I have to give the lawyers credit. The contracts that they have developed and reached agreement with the state will be signed next week."

Ernesto continued. "Yes, and the governor want to make a big deal out of it. He has a new slogan: 'Build New York.' You will need to come up or send a representative. Sal, by the way, Sonny said thank you for the equipment you provided for the groundbreaking event and for the dinner at Café Italia."

"He is most welcome. Please tell him I am happy to oblige. How was it?"

"I could not attend, but Sonny said it was fabulous. He has sent the bill to your controller, Steve, and I think it was already paid. It was a good investment for you, and you will reap big returns."

Rugerri leaned back and looked down at his coat to make sure he had not soiled any part of it with food.

"Wow, when do we rest? I know that there will be a lot of deals that we have yet to make, but I spoke to the boys from the contractors' association meeting last week and they are comfortable with the deal."

He stood and took off his jacket. No more than ten seconds had passed before one of the waiters arrived with a wooden hanger and said, "Please allow me to take this back to Mr. Bruno's office."

"Okay, thank you."

Just then, two large platters arrived. There were two white coats, each holding one of the platters. They were about to serve the pasta French style and Jack, the head waiter, came over with a large serving spoon and a large fork. He stood in front of LaCola.

"Sir, I have homemade pasta with a light tomato and truffle sauce. I also have risotto with asparagus, morels, and fresh peas. May I serve a little of each to start?"

The three of them were in awe as LaCola responded, "Yes, thank you, a little of each."

He transferred two spoonfuls of each dish and then shuffled sideways to Ruggeri and then to Barone with the same manner of politeness. Sal was now ready to order the entree.

"Okay, Jack, how about some veal chops and some of the dover sole?"

"Yes, sir, right away. Is there anything I can do for you, anything I can get?" He waited a few seconds for a response. Hearing none, he went on.

"I have a couple of bottles of Pellegrino coming over. Are there any questions, gentlemen?"

"No, perfect." A big smile crossed Barone's face. "This is great, isn't it? What a country."

As they began to sample the pasta, Giuseppe Bruno came out from the kitchen in his flashy, spotless white chef's jacket. He looked to the front and the head waiter came over with a bottle of Dom Perignon champagne. LaCola noticed the year on the label: 1966.

"Gentlemen, I would like to personally thank you and would like to join you in a toast. I hope you like my choice." The waiter popped the cork and the champagne bubbled slightly as it was poured into the three glasses on the table and the glass that Bruno was holding.

"Gentlemen, to your good health and prosperity. Gentlemen, *salud*," Bruno said.

Barone was pleased; Bruno knew how to treat his special customers.

Another thirty minutes passed and three new large platters arrived. The first one had three different veal dishes with three different sauces. They reflected the colors of the Italian flag. Bruno arrived at the table and began to describe the dish.

"Gentlemen, this dish is a tribute to a famous Jewish soprano. In particular, I have created three different tastes and honor Beverly Sills and the Italian operas that she pays tribute to. Hope you enjoy."

The second and third dish arrived soon after. The second dish had three perfectly frenched rib veal chops.

"This is a veal chop *oregonato*. It has a slight wisp of sherry wine and butter and, of course, fresh oregano." Bruno pointed to the third dish that was placed in the center of the table. "This is 'the Atlantic and Pacific,' dover sole prepared with a lemon butter, and this is a traditional spicy Tuscan-style sauce with anchovies and a touch of fresh tomatoes. Enjoy."

They all raised their glasses, clicked them together, and said, "*Salud!*"

It was just past 10:30 when they were finally finishing the celebration. The champagne bottle was empty, and the sixty-year-old bottle of brandy was half full. This time, it was Ruggeri that looked down at his shirt to inspect whether there were any bits of food that may have violated the special silk material. It was still perfect, and he was pleased. As for Barone, the white napkin stuck in his collar held small traces from each of the courses, providing a road map of the dinner.

The waiter came over one last time. The dessert platter in the center of the table held remaining pieces of half-eaten Italian pastries.

"Mr. Barone, we have put the bill on the account. I have also prepared a box of pastries for your lovely wife. The box is in the car. Gentlemen, I have called your drivers, and they are waiting out front. I want to personally thank you for allowing me to be of service tonight, and I hope to see you again soon," he said and then bowed and took two or three small steps backward, turned, and walked to the front. There were still about thirty patrons enjoying a late-evening meal. LaCola had noticed that throughout the evening, none of the adjoining tables surrounding their table had been occupied.

Barone spoke. "LaCola, Rugerri, I salute you, and we will be in touch. I assume that you will be meeting with the boys downtown and dealing with that end of the business."

Rugerri nodded and looked across to gain LaCola's attention. "Ernesto, look, nothing must interfere with the project in Albany. I can assume that you will guarantee that."

He tilted his head forward as he peered at LaCola. His eyes were rolled up toward his forehead and his stare became more concentrated.

"We are family, and we all must work toward the same set of rewards. We will make a lot of money, and this is an exciting time for both contractors and unions when we work together. We will need the accountant's auditors on the seventh floor to process the reports. Same split. We cannot allow anything to get in our way. Oh, and by the way, how is your new computer software guy doing?"

LaCola did not say a word, but his expression left little doubt as to his meaning. He nodded and pressed his lips together to communicate that he understood. "I think he is doing great. I think we can count on him for a long, long time. He is on our team, and Paul and Sonny swear that he is trustworthy."

The response from Rugerri was short and to the point. "Good to know. Anyone has to be better than that fucking Bloom. Glad we sent him on vacation."

They all rose and began to walk to the front of the restaurant. They walked to the door, and Bruno came out with Ruggeri's jacket and handed it to him, hanger and all. Ruggeri did not bother to put it on. The white Rolls and a black Lincoln limo were directly in front of the restaurant. Their drivers were leaning against the rear fenders and stood erect as they saw their passengers walking from the restaurant. The Rolls driver had been smoking a cigarette and when he saw Barone, he quickly dropped it to the sidewalk and put it out with his left foot. He opened the rear door in a military fashion to allowing his passengers to enter. LaCola's driver did the same. LaCola leaned back, closed his eyes, and felt as though he had just run a marathon. It was just ten minutes past eleven.

"Bobby, take me to the apartment. I am going to stay in the city tonight," he said.

CHAPTER TWENTY-FIVE

FACING THE TRUTH

JULY 24, 1992

T WAS NOW THE FIFTEENTH week of the implementation, and they were approaching a critical point in the conversion. It was late July and getting muggy in the city. It was just past two o'clock, and Chris was testing the claims and the pension programs. He was running the reports and testing the newly programmed eligibility system. He had also designed a user security system that had three levels of security built into the application. The first level only provided entry into certain programs, based on the user classification. The claims examiners were only allowed entry into limited menus that were used by examiners. Each menu was tailored and only allowed access to specific functions by user type. Each user had established levels of authority that limited their access to specific fields within each of the database records.

There were global settings for each department and settings for each individual user. This would allow the administrator to manage access to sensitive information by both level and departments. It was all quite sophisticated and advanced. Once into a specific area or database, there were security levels for controlling access to specific fields within the records. These were all well beyond the typical user sign-on and password-protection processes. But perhaps the best feature was the logging of all transactions, with each data change logging the date, time, and user. The software had over one million lines of code, and Chris had invested over fifty man years in the development to bring the software to its present state—which was well beyond any other union accounting system. Chris was very proud of his accomplishments and very protective of the software that he had created.

Chris was sitting at a long table across from the racks that held three IBM computer terminals. Two laser printers sat on the left side of the table. A high-speed printer was placed to the right of the computer racks. The racks were all lined up squarely in the middle of the computer room, and it reminded Chris of a row of soldiers standing at attention. He thought back about the early computers. He was impressed over the progress that had been made from advancements in technology. Everything had gotten smaller, had more capacities, and was faster. In the old days, they measured capacities in megabytes. Technology had advanced at lightning speeds, and now the measurement was in gigabytes. When he first went to work for IBM, they had eighty-column cards, and capacities were measured in bytes. One of the first big advancement was the ninety-six-column card, which provided 20 percent more capacity, with a punched card one-third the size.

A low humming came from the disk drives, and in the background, air hissed softly from the computer room air-conditioning vents. The AS/400 processor was on the first rack to the left, adjacent to the rack that housed the disk drives, and the tape cartridge backup drives followed to the right. They all were neatly secured to the series of standard nineteen-inch racks, which were all organized in a neat row, and to the extreme right of the last of five were the communication controllers, modems, and the cross-connect wiring circuits that connected all the terminals to the system. There were at least eighty-five computer terminals connected to the computer, which were located on every desk in every department throughout the union's office.

All the cabinets were painted a soft beige color, each with four numbers and the IBM logo on the front in the traditional IBM blue. Chris felt very good about his accomplishment, although in the back of his mind, he was troubled by the problems he was encountering at the union. It was not the process; it was the people. It was the environment and errors that they had discovered during the conversion. It made him feel very uneasy. He needed to find a way to correct them while at the same time bringing the new system up to a trouble-free state. Something was going on inside the building and especially on the seventh floor, which made Chris uncomfortable. He could not understand who and what they were about.

He was beginning to question his judgment and wondered whether it would all be worth it. He realized that he remembered all of the little decisions he had made and all the lessons he had learned long ago. He was now trying to forget all the big decisions, the mistakes he had recently made. He stared at the computer-disk drives and listened to the humming as they spun their story of corruption. All those little bits and bytes would tell the true story and would provide the evidence the FBI was looking for. Chris knew that the FBI would eventually find the means to get at the data, and even though he needed to erase the truth, it was still a crime. The old system was riddled with flaws. They used Bloom, and when they no longer needed him, they threw him aside. Now they were using him. Loyalty, unity, and trust were just words that had no real truth or meaning, and once they no longer needed Chris, he, too, would be expendable.

The computer-room door swung open as the buzzer sounded, and Goldin walked in.

"Hey, Chris, going okay from what I hear, but we need to go upstairs and have a small talk. I need an update."

"Is there a problem?"

"No, no, we just have a few questions regarding the conversion. LaCola wants an update." Goldin motioned his head toward the door and said, "Follow me."

Chris stood up and followed him out the door. The buzzer once again sounded as the door clicked open. They walked past the conference room and into the sixth-floor breakroom. Goldin took out a plastic card from his wallet and inserted it into the card reader next to the door to the staircase. They entered the small platform and casually walked up to the seventh-floor door. Goldin, with the card still in his hand, inserted it into the slot next to the door. There was a quiet click, and Goldin pushed the door to allow entry into the seventh-floor breakroom.

Chris observed the process curiously. "Paul, this is pretty cool, but what is with this private staircase, and who gets to use it?"

"This is a special staircase for use by Stanley, LaCola, Greco, and me. We built it about ten years ago so we do not have to go to the front elevator to go back and forth between the sixth and seventh floors. A few extra steps up, but a lot easier. Ernesto does not mind the stairs, but Nick always takes the elevator."

They walked past the auditors and approached the equipment room. It was not locked, and they entered. Goldin reached for the light switch to the left. The small bulb hanging from the ceiling lit up the back portion of the room as Goldin flipped the switch.

Goldin turned to Chris as they walked over toward the ducts where the fans were running and said, "Chris, do you remember when we first had a meeting in this room?"

"Yes, I remember."

It was noisy with the fans and motors running. Goldin stepped closer to Chris and faced him directly. Although it was noisy, he still tried to speak slowly and deliberately.

"Good, so let's be sure that we understand one another. We are somewhat in a jam. Marty Bloom, the so-called expert programmer, is the only person who knew—I mean, knows—the internals of his software and has not been seen for quite some time. Obviously, they are going out of business, and that is why you are here. As far as I am concerned, they are out of business here for sure."

Chris looked surprised. "Well, I got the impression that something was not quite right."

"I just want an update on what you have found before it surprises Ernesto." He went on. "We know all about the corrupted data files in the old system, and we do not want to go backward. Don't look back; look to the future. We are only interested in the future, and there may be some data problems that may give some people the wrong idea. You are a pretty smart guy, and this Pete Williams is pretty smart too, but we need a clean system going forward and will need to fix any of the problems you discover. The FBI is looking at us, and we need to get our system cleaned up."

He saw a look of bewilderment on Chris's face. "Chris, what is bothering you?"

"Well, besides the money you owe me, we have found another problem."

"We will get to the money a little later, and maybe we can talk about it at dinner tonight. You didn't forget, right?" Goldin asked.

"Paul, I need to get paid. My bank is knocking on my door."

Goldin nodded. "I understand, and it will be taken care of this week. I promise. Look, Chris, you are doing a great job so far. And it looks like you are going to make our implementation schedule by several weeks. We all have confidence in your team, and we appreciate it, but we don't need you to audit or fix the old problems. We can always go back and fix whatever you find. We do have some other consultants we can call on. Remember CK?"

He placed his right hand on Chris's shoulder. "Look, I am your friend and I recommended you. I know that we will be successful, but only when we work together. Here is the problem. We are being audited by the Labor Department, and we have learned that the FBI is also looking at us. So we do not want to help them. Understand?"

The computers' fans hummed softly muffling their conversation. Chris and Goldin stood close to one another, careful that no one in the room could overhear their conversation.

"What is going on with the claims conversion?"

"Look, Paul, I am glad you asked. There is money that has leaked out. Someone has intentionally messed up several claim records, and we have found that there was roughly $3 million in claims-payment records that have been changed. Missing pointers, missing payment records, and missing providers. Nothing balances in this place, and the health fund is missing money to the tune of about three million bucks."

Goldin did not look surprised. "Chris, we knew there was a problem, but we could not put our finger on it. We suspected that it was our software expert, Marty Bloom."

"Well, Paul, it had to be someone who knew the internals of the software, and apparently, he is the only one who knew how the system was put together. He actually was the one who put it all together, but he must have had a partner. Bloom fixed the data, but someone paid the claims." Chris shook his head. "If the old system was fucked up, then it is not my problem. It is your problem, but that doesn't mean I am supposed to ignore it. Should I just convert the bad stuff over to the new system? Maybe you get a faster system, but it will still be a bad system that is a little faster. I cannot pay claims unless I have clean history records for the duplicate payment process."

The accountant quizzed Chris. "What can you tell me about these claims?"

Chris was not just defensive; he now became angry. "Paul, we do not know for sure who it was, but they used terminals in the claims department and the annuity department. The deed took place the last week in July of last year."

"Did you say the last week in July?"

"Yes, that is when they screwed up the claim records." Chris shook his head.

Goldin looked puzzled. "Hmmm, that is strange, because DiNapoli takes his vacation the last two weeks in July and goes to Saratoga to play the ponies. But then again, we have not seen him since LaCola canned him, I think because of the annuity problem."

Chris was now asking the questions. "Paul, I am talking about last year."

Goldin looked up as he thought about the question. "Hmm, I think that was the week our friend Crowley helped us with our audit. He always worked with Greco in Al's office."

Chris replied, "Well, there is your answer. I guess you need to talk to your friend Crowley. Maybe Greco as well."

"Thanks for letting me know, but I will need this thing cleaned up. Can you fix this?"

Chris frowned. "Paul, what are you asking me to do?"

Paul grinned. "Can you clean up the old system? You know, wipe it clean. Chris, remember when we had that discussion about extra work? Well, this is one of those unplanned situations—think of the extra fees that we have allocated to your company. What do you think we are paying you all that extra money for?"

"Yes, but ... but—"

The accountant cut him off. "No buts about it. We need you to cleanse the old records and create what you need in the new system.

You know, erase, clean, or whatever you need to do. We don't care; just erase the bad crap and bring us a sparkling new system. The government has unlimited resources and money. They have the time, and the FBI has unlimited resources as well, so if they are looking to find something, they will find it. Do you think they will ever give up without finding something? This is what the FBI does. It does not start with a crime; it starts with a suspicion, and then they search for a crime. Give the bastards the annuity problem. We don't even care about the claims problem."

Chris looked surprised. "What are you telling me? You know about the health fund?"

Goldin tilted his head slightly and smiled. "Of course we know. And we know that they will never give up until they find something. Right, then why don't we give them something? We know who grabbed the money and we put a stop to it long age, correct?"

Chris shook his head. "Well, the old system was fucked up, and Bloom was the only one capable of manipulating the data. He was the only one who had the knowledge. He also never gave you the source code."

The accountant now smiled. "Great, then how the hell can they link anyone to the problem? We do not have the ability to get under the covers of Bloom's software, and DiNapoli was the only person running the annuity operations. We fired both, and they are on the run and hopefully will never be found."

Goldin nodded and continued. "Well, I have discussed this with Greco, and he agrees that we are at a point where we need to clean things up. Tidy things up a bit. And you are the only one who we can depend on for that job."

"Paul, I am not sure I can do this alone. You want me to get them off your tail and then give them a scent that they can follow. Look, you have more experience than I do with this sort of thing, and I will need to show some legitimate documentation. I need to get Williams to do the dirty work. I need to tell him what to do without him suspecting anything."

Goldin was surprised at Chris's response.

"Well, I am glad you understand. We need to need to think this through. I will need to discuss it with Ernesto and the boys across town." He looked at the door. "Anything else?"

"Well, yes, I think that your auditors may be able to help. Let me look at it more closely and see if we can come up with a fix. Your old data records are all screwed up. I do not care how you used Bloom, but I think it is about time that we both leveled with one another. The thing is, I always thought that there was a problem with the contractors' reporting. But the process looks very clean, so my suspicions were misguided. Maybe your auditors can fix the old data manually; there are several utilities that are standard with the IBM system. I will have Williams provide some training to your guys. Or maybe you start a fire in the warehouse or lose the old records. You need to feed the FBI something that they will chase. Maybe the annuity thing. Maybe the claims problem."

"Chris, this is complicated, but I think the annuity may be all that we give them for now. We do not want to go too far."

Chris was now leading the conversation. "Well, for starters, I would clean up the paid-claims file. Maybe we give them the converted claim records, since we have a two-thousand-byte record and can throw a lot of new fields into the file. Since the problem was with last year's records, we do not need them for our duplicate claims check process."

Chris went on. "One other thing, Paul. I think someone has breached our firewall, and we saw some activity from our communication logs. A few of the phone connections show that someone has gotten through to the operating system through the back door. The good news is that there is no source code, so they are chasing their tail. Has to be the FBI. It is just a matter of time before they find out. You, Greco, and LaCola should be careful about what they may find in the old system, so we are fighting the clock. Look, from our analysis, we think that the reporting is clean and that the problems we have found are not unusual. This is a complicated process, and tying in all the balances together is almost impossible. Bloom's software was really bad, and you had to change it. In fact, it was so bad that they will never put the pieces together."

Goldin stared at the ceiling and then looked back into Chris's eyes. He was deliberate with his words. "Okay, I will have a meeting with LaCola, and we will decide what we want you to do. I will also discuss this with my auditors."

Chris smiled. "Look, Paul, give them a little taste. Give them the annuity problem. We can fix the claim thing. Let them chase DiNapoli and Bloom, or whoever was responsible. Give them the old software problems, and show them that you have plugged the leaks with new software. Give them the old mistakes. As long as the mistakes implicate people from the past, and as long as they will never find any audit trail, you just might get them off your ass. After all, you cannot be put in jail for a crime committed by someone else."

Chris could see that the accountant was thinking and pondering what they had discussed. Goldin then said sternly, "Let me straighten you out. We know there have been breaches in our system, but the clock is ticking. We need to get the new system up before the end of the year. Maybe by Thanksgiving. We are running out of time, and this is a race between us and the FBI. We are counting on you. Understand?"

"Paul, I think I understand. Just give them enough to get the dogs on the scent of a different fox. I am just a software guy from Albany, and I have no idea how the feds work. However, I do know that if they get a court order, they can seize all your records and programs. You know that is where they are heading."

Goldin now looked up at the ceiling, and Chris could see that he was pondering his suggestions.

"Well, it is not my decision, but maybe we should consider an approach like that."

He folded his arms and then said, "For now, just let me know everything you find. Chris, these guys play hardball, and we need to clean this system up, quickly. If we can stall them until the next year, we have friends in high places who will shut this whole investigation down. There are millions of dollars in play, and there are too many people that have a stake in this business. It reaches many people, far and wide."

Goldin pressed on. "Chris, how much did you say the claims problem is?"

"I don't have the report in front of me, but it is around $3 million, and that is only for the first six months of last year."

Goldin continued. "Get me the details on what you need to fix it." He shook his head. "Son of a bitch. I never thought Crowley would turn on us. Especially after all the money we greased his palm with."

"Okay, but speaking of money. The union owes me a lot of money, and if you want me to keep going, I need to get paid. I cannot wait any longer. My bank line is at its max. Paul, I need to get fucking paid. It is a matter of trust, and I think I have passed all the tests so far."

Goldin replied, "Chris, I got it." He took a step backward. "Okay, I promise I will get you some money tonight."

"Look, Paul, the old system is fucked up, and people have been robbing you blind. Right, so give the feds something to get them off your back. You get rid of the old problems, and I give them a squeaky-clean new system."

Goldin placed his right hand up to his chin. Chris thought that it was possible that he would consider what they had discussed. "Well, I will need your help."

Chris smiled and said, "Well, sometimes, you have to outsmart them. I think that if we can rebuild the claims for last year and rebuild what we need for the duplicate claims process from the manual records, and we ditch the bad claims ... hmmm ... and if we create clean history records in the new formats. And the manual paper records get lost." He stopped and looked at the accountant. "Just might work."

Goldin took his hand from his chin and pointed to Chris. He smiled in agreement. "This is a little tricky, but it just might work. Maybe we put them on the trail of another fox with a deep, deep hole."

Chris was getting warm from the heat emitting from the computer fans. "Paul, it is your business. I just want to finish the job and get paid. I have been thinking about it, and I will sell you the source code, but I have to think about a fair price."

"Chris, I knew you were smart, but I never realized until this very moment that you are also very clever." Goldin smiled. "Does anyone know about the claims problems?"

"No one except Williams and me. Now you."

"Good, good, good. Let's keep it that way. Make sure that you talk to Williams, and make sure he keeps it to himself," Goldin replied.

Goldin looked up and nodded. He turned and began to talk to himself, but Chris did not hear what he was muttering. Chris stopped and placed his index finger below his right eye and pulled downward. It was an old Italian gesture. He then looked directly at the accountant's eye.

"Paul, this means we see each other eye to eye."

Goldin responded with the same gesture, and Chris now felt more secure in knowing that the accountant understood.

"Like this?"

A small grin crossed Goldin's face.

"Okay, let's go see LaCola, and don't ever bring this up again—ever—certainly not with Greco or Stanley. I will do all the talking when we go into Ernesto's office. Just get me the reports, and I will

314

review them with Stanley. And then LaCola and I will decide how we are going to proceed." He paused and then said to himself in a low whisper, "Just might work."

They walked to the front elevator and were bought up to the seventh floor. They were surprised to see Mary sitting behind the desk in the front reception area. "Hello, Mr. Goldin, Mr. Vincent. Ernesto is expecting you and will see you immediately. He is not in a good mood, so I hope you have some good news for him."

Goldin looked up. "Thank you, Mary." He stood and walked into LaCola's office. Chris dutifully followed.

Ernesto sat at his desk. On the granite top were several newspapers. He wore a dark-blue blazer and a light-gray dress shirt with a silver tie.

"Guys, please sit down."

As they sat down, LaCola picked up the *New York Times* from the top of the stack. He picked it up and threw it across his desk in front of Goldin.

Lacola in a load voice said. "What the fuck is going on? What the hell is happening?"

Goldin turned it around so that he could read the front-page headline: "FBI Investigates Laborers Local 4."

LaCola angrily shouted across the desk, "Who the hell is leaking information to the *Times*? Who is leaking information to the FBI? We better find out! We know that they are always on our ass, but this is clearly intimidation."

He grabbed the stack of papers, picked them up, and then slapped them back down on the granite.

"And it is not just the *Times*. This is not good. Not good."

Goldin looked at the headline and shook his head. "I did not read the papers this morning. Ernie, I don't know what to say."

"Those motherfuckers. Well, Paul, I need you to find out what you can. Our people at the *Times* apparently are not very dependable, but call them and find out who. I know that the FBI is looking at us, and they have leaked it to the papers just to scare us. But of greater concern beyond that is …" He paused. "What have they got? They have turned someone, for sure."

Chris looked at Goldin. "Paul, the invoices for tonight?"

Goldin looked back and nodded.

"Ernesto, can we go for private talk? Chris, we will be back in a few minutes. I just want to have a private word with Ernesto. Mary will get you a coffee or a drink or whatever you like."

They stood and walked out of the room. Chris knew where the private conversation would be held. He was now worried and wondered what would happen with his contract. So much was riding on this account. But this was the do-or-die moment, and he desperately needed money. He was fully involved and knew he had to force the issue, even though he had jumped into a deeper hole. Chris was now preparing himself for a bad outcome.

Goldin and LaCola were out of the room for almost twenty minutes before they returned. LaCola was smiling and was the first to speak.

"Chris, I have Stanley cutting a check for what we owe you. Sorry we have been a little slow, but we wanted to be certain that the new system would be working. I know that is not the way normal companies conduct business. But we have a lot of people we answer to. It is not just the trustees; we have ten thousand members who depend on us."

He sat down behind his desk. "Getting back to the news. Paul, there is only one group who would leak this to the *Times*. Someone here is trying to make a deal, and he has been talking to the FBI. The leak, of course, is coming from a mole who is passing information to the FBI. I think we both may know who that is. But for now, let's get up to date with our new friend Chris. Get him paid. We need him more than ever and need to clean up the system so we can get back to building buildings. Too many problems in the old software, and I think Bloom made it too complicated. We must move a little faster with the new system; if it costs us more, then that is okay. There is too much at stake and we have too much to lose if we cannot get the system up by Thanksgiving. I expect things will change next year, once the election is behind us."

He turned to Chris. "Chris, I need you to get us fully operational by Thanksgiving. I do not want any of the same old problems. I want it finished. What do you say?"

LaCola was a very crafty person. Chris realized that once LaCola decided to do something, it happens.

LaCola pointed to Goldin. "Paul, I have been thinking. We need the new system up and running as soon as possible so we can start the new year with a clean slate. Vincent, can you do that for us?"

He motioned with his hands, again pointing across to emphasize the words. "Look, the problems are all computer related, and that is why we have brought you in, Chris. There may have been some mistakes in the past, so let's put that behind us. This is a complicated business to run, and we depend on the computer. We need to take the necessary steps to fix these problems and want you to know that we run a clean operation. We hide nothing, so if you find problems, then let Paul know. Your job is not so simple, but your goal is simple." He paused. "Deliver new software that helps us improve our operations."

Chris could see that Goldin had discussed the idea with LaCola and they both were onboard. "Yes, sir; I think we can make it happen."

LaCola did not need any time to think it through. He recognized immediately that they were in too far and needed Chris to complete the job. LaCola cracked a smile.

"I need a guarantee. There is no other option for us if we are all to come out of this clean. So let's keep up the good work, and Chris, you be sure to let Paul know if you run into any problems. We are counting on you. Paul will update Greco on the new timeline. And Paul, let's make sure we get Chris up to date on his invoices."

Goldin broke in. "Chris, we have a lot of confidence in you, so please do not let us down. Stanley is cutting a check this very moment."

"Well, thank you; that is good news, because I cannot continue without positive cash flow. We can meet a more aggressive schedule, but a lot will depend on your people. I think it is entirely possible, but we will need to compress a few tasks and put more resources on it. I brought Frank down a few months ago and pulled him from our development team to work on this full time. I think we can assume more responsibility and make it happen. I think it is possible. We will get it done for sure."

LaCola walked around his desk and sat down next to Chris. "Vincent, I know this may cost us more, but I want a clean system going into next year. There is too much at stake. I am depending on you, so let us know what you need. I can assure you that Paul, Nick, and the rest of the staff will give you anything you need. If you need to put more people on it, then that is okay with us. Paul's team, and the other consultants will also be available to help."

"Great, thank you. I won't let you guys down. I run a small company, and I can assure you that this account is critical to our future success, so it will have my complete attention and commitment."

Chris recited the script from his playbook. He was confident it could be done but did not want it to sound too easy.

Ernesto stood, and both Chris and Goldin recognized that the meeting was over. They both stood and said their goodbyes and walked out through the reception area into the lobby. They took the elevator down to the sixth floor.

Chris began to think about the meeting and finally realized that Goldin and LaCola were way ahead of him, and this was not a result of Chris's suggestion. They had planned all along to give the feds something and were simply playing Chris all along. Chris smiled to himself as the thought raced through his mind, "Those clever bastards. He thought; "They were involved with the claims skim of $3 million."

CHAPTER TWENTY-SIX

SMITH AND WOLLENSKY

JULY 24, 1992

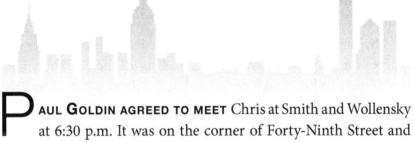

P AUL GOLDIN AGREED TO MEET Chris at Smith and Wollensky at 6:30 p.m. It was on the corner of Forty-Ninth Street and Third Avenue. It first opened in 1977 and was a majestic-looking two-story building nestled in the midst of towering skyscrapers. It not only survived; it prospered.

Chris had had dinner there about four years earlier when he had gone into the city to make a call on the bricklayers' union. However, back then, he'd had no connections, and while he did not understand it at the time, he now realized that he had absolutely zero chance to sign up the account. This time was different; he had the reference from Sonny, who connected him to Paul Goldin, and that was all that was required. The restaurant was known for their aged prime steaks. It was very successful and very crowded. He assumed that Goldin had made reservations, since it would be crowded with all the big-city yuppies. There were gold-digging girls fresh from their offices and still clad in their shiny patent-leather shoes, with their walking sneakers of course now hidden in their handbags.

The name of the restaurant had been randomly pulled from a phone book. The book was opened, and the first name pointed to was Smith. The second time the phone book was randomly opened, the name pointed to was Wollensky. Success is not often found by chance or luck, but this is the way it sometimes happens. For these restauranteurs, it proved to be fortunate.

Chris arrived early and noticed that there were stars on the waiters' and servers' jackets. They were located right on top of the jacket pockets. Some had one star, a few had two stars, and then there were a very few that had three stars. The number of stars denoted the length of service for their employees. For every five years, they would earn a star.

The steaks were USDA prime, dry aged in-house at thirty-six degrees for four weeks. Everything was cut in their kitchen, and this aging resulted in a very tender and delicious but expensive steak dinner. To some, the quality was unmatched. At any given time, they would have anywhere from seven to twelve tons of beef in their aging cooler. Chris enjoyed a good steak dinner and was well prepared, and he knew that Goldin would be picking up the dinner check. He arrived early, and as he had expected, Goldin had made a reservation for a quiet table in the rear.

The maître d' stood very upright and immediately escorted Chris to a corner table in the rear of the restaurant. It was perfect, quiet and away from the noisy bar in the front. He was comfortable with the location, since he felt he could have a private and direct conversation with Goldin.

"Sir, your waiter, John, will be right with you. I will escort Mr. Goldin when he arrives."

He hesitated for a moment and stood directly in front of Chris, perhaps thinking that Chris would pass him a ten or twenty. Chris looked down at the menu as he took a ten from his now thin pack of folded bills and passed it to the maître d'. He responded with a polite, "Thank you," and then turned and walked back to the front.

"Hello; my name is John, and I will be your server this evening. May I get you a drink?"

Chris was startled, as he did not see the waiter standing in front of him. "Yes, I would like a Heineken."

The beer was cold, and Chris was sitting facing the front when he saw Goldin walking toward the table. Chris was pleased because he could see that he was alone.

"Well, there's my computer expert." Goldin stopped and grabbed the back of the chair. "Glad you could make it. LaCola and Greco are happy that things are rolling along quite well. I never expected anything less than excellence. Certainly expected, but it seems that you are far exceeding our expectations."

He quickly held out his right hand. Chris stood up and grabbed Paul's hand. "Hello, Paul; happy to be here and hope we can keep moving forward."

Goldin sat down and turned to the greeter who had escorted him to the table. "The usual, please."

"You got it, Mr. Goldin," the waiter replied as he immediately turned and walked back toward the service bar.

"Well, you will really like it here. The union boys love the joint. We eat here almost monthly. In fact, we have had trustee meetings here in the winter. They have a private dining room, and they really treat us special." Goldin took the napkin, unfolded it, and placed it neatly on his lap.

Chris looked down at the menu and then up at Paul. "How is the food here? What do you suggest?"

"The steak—it's the best in the city."

Chris laughed. "Ha! I know about this place; I was only pulling your leg."

The sommelier arrived with a chilled bottle of Santa Margherita wrapped in a white-linen napkin. He very expertly took the corkscrew from his left jacket pocket and went about the business of expertly removing the cork. Chris noticed that he had three gold stars on the breast pocket of his jacket. He poured a small amount into Paul's glass and waited for the usual ritual of smell, taste, and acknowledgement that all was well with the wine. Paul brought his nose to the glass, took a small sip, and looked up at the sommelier.

"Great, great, as usual."

He nodded politely and turned to Chris. "Sir, may I?"

"Yes, absolutely," Chris replied and then turned to Goldin. "Thank you, Paul; this is very kind of you to treat me to such a fine meal."

Chris was no fool and was simply spiking the coffin with one final nail to affirm who would be getting the check. This was a technique that he had learned from his friend Tony, who sold over three hundred cars each year at a dealership in Albany. Tony used this technique to confirm to the buyer that this was a deal you could not back out of. He sold the car and then always resold the car with a nail in the coffin. That technique was a way to seal the deal, since the spike made it very difficult to "open the lid," or give the customer a chance to change his mind. Chris raised his glass and lifted it toward Paul's. They clicked them together and said, "*Salud.*"

"Well, you wanted to discuss something, but let's first order something." Paul apparently was quite hungry. "I am suggesting either the crab-meat cocktail or the lobster cocktail."

"I am in; I think I will go for the crab meat."

John the waiter returned to the table. "Well, may I suggest something to start? I recommend the crab or lobster cocktail, both delicious." They grinned as they looked across at each other.

"John, bring us each the crab-meat cocktail. Thank you."

"Yes, sir, Mr. Goldin. Great choice." John turned; he didn't write anything down, since he could rely on his memory to place the order. His three stars indicated that he had been there for at least fifteen years.

"So, I believe we are making good progress, but there is one little matter. When do I get paid? I am owed over $350,000. As you know, I run a small company and am not a bank. I cannot afford to keep this up for very long without getting paid." Chris looked across the table at Goldin, who noticed the firmness in his facial features.

Goldin began to nod. "Chris, please understand that we could not discuss this matter within the confines of Local 4. Your contract is at a level well above Stanley's pay grade."

He continued. "Chris, they trust you, and you need to trust them. I told you we have a deal. We will pay all your invoices, but you we will need to change a few things, especially after our little talk with Mr. LaCola. We are both very impressed with your analysis. You are finding quite a few problems that we would have never discovered. This was quite a surprise to us, but it is all good. Just want you to know what we think about your work. So, listen to me first before you get excited. The expenses are all good and in line. They have been approved, and the software licensing fees are good as well. You now know the importance of your role at the union, and so does LaCola. You have earned our trust. You will be paid for everything, and we are going to decide on the source code once we know that everything works according to what we discussed.

"But then there is another $100,000 that you need to invoice for the extra consulting work that we had to contract with the consultants here in the city. The consulting invoices are to be invoiced by your firm, and it is included in our written contract. These will be in two installments at $50K each. Those invoices must show the services provided by CK Consulting. They are subcontracting under your name. These boys will do most of the cleanup work based on what we discussed. Then, when we are up and running, you bill for the second half of the license fee, which is another two and a quarter. CK Consulting needs to be billed for the second half of the other hundred—that is $50,000 in each invoice. Simple: you pay CK Consulting once the union pays your firm. It is all according to our contract."

He stopped and leaned forward toward Chris, now lowering his voice and turning around slightly to be certain no one was listening. He then turned his head and directly faced Chris, moving as close to him as possible without appearing too obvious.

"And the good news. Look, Chris, I have something for you." He reached into his pocket and pulled out an envelope. "Here."

Chris took the envelope and opened it. He pulled the check out and saw his company as payee: Advanced Computer Systems. But his eyes immediately moved to the amount column, and he smiled as he saw the total: "$387,456."

Chris immediately broke out with a broad smile and began to nod. "Thanks, Paul. I think that Local 4 is fast becoming my best account."

Paul smiled as well. "Chris, LaCola likes you and trusts you completely. But he only wants to limit the disclosure to the annuity problem that our friend DiNapoli was responsible for. But as to the claims problem, we will take care of that ourselves. Do not discuss this with Greco. He must not ever know anything about the claims problem. We will discuss with him. The annuity might be just enough to get the dogs off our ass, and we, of course, will need your help. And if you get us up and running by the new Thanksgiving deadline and your little suggestion gets them off our scent, then there is another $50K as a bonus. That is directly from LaCola. We will put the new timeline in the form of a letter agreement. Worst case for us is January first. After all, something for nothing is worth nothing, Right?"

Chris smiled and then looked more serious. "Paul, I need to tell you something. I have the information that you requested concerning the claims problem."

He now had the accountant's attention. "What do you have?"

"Well, it is the data that is telling us that there is a few million dollars in bad claim records for the last two years." He handed the report over to Goldin, who looked down at the number.

"Chris, this is not something you should talk about. We can fix this data, and you only need ninety days of history for your duplicate claims routine, correct?"

"There is something else that has been bothering me, Paul. The delivery to this guy, Crowley. What the hell does he have to do with you, and why does he get money from Sonny?"

Goldin hesitated. "Chris, let me level with you. Crowley is on our payroll and helps us to get through the ERISA audits. He cleans up our system for us, and he also helps some of the other unions, even Sonny's local. He is just a messenger boy, so don't worry about him. Relax; this is how it is done."

"Why did you have to get me involved in the delivery? You put me at risk."

"Chris, relax; we had to test you and bring you over to our side. This is the way it is done. And you passed the test."

Chris was still uneasy. "Well, we just found out about it a few days ago, and Williams ran the reports, which show where the checks went. I will get more data. We do not know who, but there is definitely some programming involved to mess up the claims file."

Goldin now spoke with more authority. "Okay, here it is. Chris, I need to know what you can find out about this claims problem. I want you to dig. This is one of those unexpected things that we discussed and why you are being paid extra money. Remember?"

"Yes, I remember, but I still don't like this situation with Crowley. Can you trust him?"

"Chris, I am a lawyer and know how to set up these deals so that no one gets exposed or hurt. I spoke to Greco and we have also decided to purchase the provider-network management module that you originally pitched to us. I can get you paid on the same day that the invoice is presented; that is, if you make the go-live deadline of Thanksgiving."

"Paul, you are pulling me in further, and that is not what I expected. I am okay and just doing a job. Perfectly normal. Paul, so long as you know, we will not be able to install the network-management software until early next year, since we are still testing it."

Chris realized that he was in deep and there was no way he could back out. All that he had worked for could be at risk, but it was more money than he ever imagined. And it all sounded like it was above board. Well, at least the paper trail would be out in the open and above board.

Goldin continued. "I have been working with the unions, and this one in particular, for over twenty-five years, and we have everybody's ass covered. We put a little pressure on you and you did not cave in, so we now are good. There are lots of others who would have walked long ago. I don't care when this provider-network management software is installed, if ever, as long as the new claims system is running by Thanksgiving. Clean—squeaky clean. We have the connections, and the money flows way beyond my firm and the union. Everybody gets a little taste, and the unions are all connected, all the way to Albany and even all the way to Washington. We do not need to steal money from our funds, from our members; there are much easier ways to make money in this business, legitimately. Prostitution loan sharking, gambling, and all those other schemes are gone.

"We even cleaned the skim from the health fund three years ago. At least, that is what we thought. Whoever is doing that is not part of our approved side businesses. The union makes money from construction and real-estate investments. We also loan money—big money—on big jobs like hotels and hospitals and waterfront projects. It is all perfectly legal. That is the way things are accomplished. If LaCola wants more money, he gets more jobs and can get a raise any time he wants from the trustees. We let the feds look for stuff, and they can never find it because we have people who are on our side."

Goldin clenched his lips together, pointed his finger at Chris, and continued. "Chris, you have been reading too many crime novels and watching too many movies. The old ways are gone. Think about this for a moment: The Hudson Valley Life Science and Technology Center is going to cost $5 billion, probably much more. Can you guess how much money is expected to flow through the unions? There is a lot at stake, and we are depending on you. You can act naïve, but do not think that this is uncommon. This is the normal way of doing business in New York. The IBMs, the AT&Ts, General Electrics, and the contractors all play the game, and they do not teach you how it is done in business school. Even China is a partner. This is how it is done, and if one goes down, we all go down. It's called capitalism. That is the secret that no one wants to tell you."

The waiter arrived with the crab cocktails and placed them on the table.

"Chris, here is another secret: more work means more jobs. More jobs mean that we can raise the rates and collect more benefit dollars. The more money we collect, the more money we get to manage. We are in the construction business, and when we build buildings, roads, and bridges, everybody wins. We control the flow of business, and our money allows us to invest in those projects. Investments—that is the secret. And it is all legitimate. Do you see anything wrong with that?"

Goldin smirked and then smiled broadly. "We like what we see with the software, but you are more important than the software. We like and trust the people installing it."

Goldin was the first to dive into the food. "Wow. Does this look good or what?"

Chris was glad he had skipped lunch earlier that day as he stared down at the appetizers. Three different sauces accompanied a large mound of crab meat that sat on a bright-green lettuce leaf. He stuck his fork into a piece of crab meat and dipped it into the lemon-butter sauce. He slowly lifted it up to his mouth and bit into it. It was tender, juicy, and full of the sweetness of delicate, cold-water crab meat. His appetite had immediately returned.

"Oh, and one final thing: Williams does not need to know anything we discussed. Got it? Never. Since this is between you and me."

Chris sat back and tilted his head slightly with his lips pressed together. "Okay, I understand."

They both raised their glasses at the same time and their wine glasses met once again with a clink. "What is it you Guineas say? *Salud*," Paul said.

They both smiled and Chris replied, "*L'Chaim*."

John came over and stood in front of them. "And Mr. Goldin, would you like to order the entrée?"

"Yes, John, I think we are both together on this one. We are going to share the porterhouse steak for two, medium rare." He paused for a moment and looked over at Chris. "You okay with that, Chris? That fucking thing is forty-four ounces and about as tender as mashed potatoes, and John, the usual sides: hash-brown potatoes, creamed spinach, mushrooms, and, of course, before you place the order, salad. How about the classic wedge salad? What about you, Chris?"

"I am going to go along with you, Paul. Only along for the ride. But as for the salad, I would like the ugly tomato with the burrata."

"Excellent choices. I will put it in; thank you. Mr. Goldin, I will bring some blue cheese on the side for the wedge. Is that okay with you?" Goldin nodded.

The waiter stood erect, and again with no need to write it down, he backed away two short steps and smartly turned and walked toward the service bar, where he keyed in the order.

Only two minutes had passed when two servers came over, each holding a salad. Not a word was spoken as each placed the correct salad in front of Chris and Goldin. "These guys are pretty good; nothing was written down, and yet, the two servers knew which salad we had ordered. Pretty good, Chris, don't you think?"

"Yes, it is all about quality, organization, and service." The accountant smiled.

"That is exactly my point. You see, they have a system, and it only works when the system works and people use the system. It's just like our new system at the union—foolproof."

Maytag blue cheese was on a small plate in the center of the table. There were tomatoes, crumpled blue cheese, and bacon bits with a generous portion of blue cheese dressing over the top. He cut into the wedge and took a large piece on a fork and brought it to his mouth. He leaned back as he bit into it and savored the taste. Chris could hear the crunch as Paul's teeth bit down into the lettuce. But Chris was busy himself; he sliced into the soft burrata cheese and watched as the soft center of cream began to slowly creep out from the center. He then cut into a small piece of the ugly tomato.

"Wow, tastes like it just came from the homegrown gardens that we used to have growing up."

The two were more relaxed, since they both were comfortable with the agreement they had reached. They continued to focus on their salads, and each had another glass of wine. Two assistant waiters arrived and placed the potatoes and spinach along the side of the table, and the head waiter brought a sizzling platter on top of a wooden board. The porterhouse was almost talking and was sliced into several one-inch-thick portions. The aroma emitting from the platter was incredible as the meat sizzled.

"May I serve some on your plate? This is really one of our best cuts, and I know it will not disappoint. Is there anything else I may get you gentlemen?"

He placed three pieces of the beef from the sizzling platter on each of their plates. "Gentlemen, enjoy."

There was little conversation as they spooned potatoes and spinach onto their plates and began to eagerly attack the food. It was difficult to hold back their enthusiasm and difficult to consume the entire porterhouse steak. There was a considerable amount still on the sizzling platter in the center. The platter had cooled, and the meat was no longer talking to them. Finally, one of the waiters came over. Goldin looked at him and nodded.

"Would you mind wrapping this up for me? It is not for my dog; it is for my wife, and please throw in the remaining potatoes and spinach in a separate container."

"Yes, sir, immediately. I will get you fresh spinach and potatoes. And an extra salad and bread."

Goldin was a professional diner and a regular at the restaurant. He ended with the New York cheesecake. Chris was completely full and decided to pass on the dessert but did have a cup of coffee.

"Thanks again, Paul. I am fully committed, and you can count on us to get this done and on time. And thanks for getting Stanley to finally cut a check; my banker will be very pleased." He stood and reached out to shake hands with Goldin.

"Well, you are very kind to treat me to this wonderful dinner. Thank you again. I buy next week, since I expect I will be able to afford it."

Chris was pleased with himself that he was able to throw one more spike into the coffin. He thought about it for a brief moment and hoped he was not the one trapped under the lid—not just for the dinner, but for the new deal he had agreed to with LaCola and Goldin. At the beginning of the evening, he did not understand why they were so eager to part with their money. What were they looking for from Chris? He now had a better understanding of what was at stake.

CHAPTER TWENTY-SEVEN

THE HEAD FAKE

C HRIS WAS BACK IN HIS office on Friday and spent the morning preparing the invoices and the paper trail with his accountant. He was following his attorney's advice, but he was still uncomfortable. He did exactly what Paul Goldin had instructed him to do and signed the letter agreement and gave a copy to his secretary so she could file it. He felt especially good about the bank deposit and met with his friends at the club for lunch, followed by golf. He played well and won sixty dollars. Apparently, the size of your bank account made a difference in your game.

He took the 7:00 a.m. express the following Monday and went straight to the union. He was to meet Goldin to present the invoices for CK Consulting, along with a cover letter that outlined the additional work. It was similar to the format that he used to present his invoices for his team. He would spend the day testing with Williams after he met with Goldin. That was good, since Chris's time was also being billed to the union. Williams had not arrived yet, since he was to take the later train.

Upon Chris's arrival, Greco came into the computer room and approached him. "Chris, I need to talk to you; it is important."

"Sure, Nick. What is going on?"

"Let's go over to the computer-disk drives. I want this to be a private conversation." He walked over to the computer, where the fans emitted a low humming sound. Chris followed.

Greco then moved close to Chris and whispered in his ear. "What the fuck is going on with the health fund? I understand that Williams found some bad claim records and is suggesting that there may be some money missing. What do you know about that?"

Chris became very uncomfortable. "Mr. Greco, I know very little. It is just that we found some bad claim records, and I mentioned it to Paul. I really think you should talk to Paul."

Greco looked angry but continued to speak very calmly and deliberately, showing no emotional outbursts of anger.

"Paul Goldin works for me, and I am the boss. So you need to answer my questions." Now he began to show some signs of anger. "What the fuck is going on?"

"Mr. Greco, you told me to report everything to Paul, and I am following your orders. We have not reached any conclusions, but the old data is all screwed up. I am simply converting the data, and the old system is all screwed up. This Bloom character really has taken you guys for a ride. That I know for sure. I am doing all I can to get you off the old system and running on a system that you can depend on."

Greco eased up slightly. "Look, Vincent, I understand and am not blaming you for anything. I just want to know what the problems are. You were very helpful to us when you identified the annuity thing, and now it looks like there is a problem with the health fund. I just need you to let me know when you discover something. Fair enough? I am the boss, and my ass is on the line. I want to speak to you when Paul comes in after lunch. I will call you in. We need to have a private conversation. I am happy with your work but need to stay in the loop." Greco raised his hands in a questioning gesture.

"Nicola, you are the boss, and I am here all day. Just call me when Paul arrives." Chris nodded to show his agreement.

"I received a call from our friend Crowley, and he tells me he is off the union account and has been reassigned. He wants to meet me for lunch, and I just wanted to have a word with you to find out what problems you have found with the conversion. I will call for you when Paul arrives. But I think it will be sometime after 2:00 today. Okay, that's it. Keep on pushing. But remember what I said: I am the boss." He turned and walked out of the computer room.

Greco went back to his office, and as he walked by Clara, he then stopped. "Clara, would you get me a car and driver? I have to go out for a lunch meeting. Say about 11:15 on the corner of Seventeenth Street out front. Be sure to get me Sam; he is a good driver, and I always feel safe when he is driving."

Clara smartly replied, "Yes, sir. I will take care of it right now. 11:15."

The dark-blue Lincoln pulled to the curb at the intersection of Seventeenth Street and Park Avenue at exactly 11:15, just as Greco was crossing Seventeenth. He looked around and quickly jumped into the back seat and said, "Hey, Sam, how are you today?"

"Great, Mr. Greco. Where can I take you?"

"Well, I have a 12:30 meeting in Little Italy, but I want you to drive around as if we were being followed, so the usual route, if you don't mind. I want you to eventually drop me near Mulberry Street and Canal, and I will let you know when to stop. Fair enough? Stay in the area, and I will have Clara call you to give you the pickup point when I am ready to be picked up."

Sam looked out the window and waited to see if there was any suspicious movement from the parked cars on Seventeenth Street. He saw none and timed the red light to jump in front of the northbound traffic.

The Con Ed van saw what was happening outside and immediately called the surveillance team that was sitting in the dark-gray Ford sedan parked three cars from the corner.

"Joe, Greco just jumped in the Blue Lincoln Town Car at the red light."

The red Ford looked like an ordinary, private, for-hire car and was perfectly suited for the job as a covert chase car. Special Agent Joe Romano sat behind the wheel and to his right sat Dan Crowther, another special agent, who both were assigned by Macey to follow Greco. There were three cars on the chase team, all different colors—one red, one white, and one blue—to avoid detection, and they would alternate as they followed the blue Lincoln.

Romano, behind the wheel in the red car, shouted into his radio. "Son of a bitch! He just pulled out in front and jumped in front of the bus. But I am not going to lose him."

The speakers in the two other chase cars blared out Romano's words. The white Ford responded. "White here; he is heading up Park Avenue in a dark-blue Lincoln stretch. Just went by. Do you copy? Let me know if you pick him up, and we will try and continue to chase, but the bastard is in a big hurry. I am blocked by a double-parked bakery truck."

The white Ford was double parked and stuck his left arm out the window as he squeezed past the bakery truck, but it was too late, as the blue Lincoln sped past. It was now almost a block in front of the white Ford. The red car was almost 2 blocks to the rear. The blue Ford double parked at the next corner pulled in front of a taxi to enter the chase. The taxi blasted the horn as the driver shouted profanities.

"You stupid motherfucker! Where did you learn to drive?"

The white Ford was now well behind Greco's Lincoln and was not certain where the turn-off would be. "I will take Seventeenth Street east, and you cover Twenty-Third Street. I am guessing that he goes east toward Williamsburg Bridge."

"Blue, we will need you cover behind us and watch if he goes west. If not, we still do not know if he is going uptown or downtown. My guess he is going uptown."

The radio blared. "Bullshit, downtown for sure. I think it is downtown. If he does not go west, I will follow up to Twenty-Third Street. He is definitely trying to lose us and is going somewhere in a hurry. Probably lunch with some bimbo."

Romano looked over at Crowther. "I agree; the son of a bitch is in a big hurry. He—"

Crowther interrupted. "Got him; he has turned east on Twenty-Third and just went through the red light."

"This is blue; I will pick him up. You guys go to Madison and see if he runs north. Red, go to Lex and see if he runs south."

"Roger that; this is red. You guys go across Twenty-First to Lex, and see if he goes past you south on Lex."

Greco loved the chase and now knew they were being followed since he saw the big white Ford jump out into traffic in front of the taxi.

"What do you have in mind, Sammy?"

"I am a little busy, sir, but I have always had good luck going up to the Fifty-Ninth Street Bridge and then looping back on the bridge from Sixtieth Street back to Manhattan. Both one way and less traffic. We can then go across town to Sixth Avenue and then loop around the block to Twentieth Street and then back up Madison and then turn on Twenty-Second Street to Lexington Avenue about ten miles over the speed limit in the outside lane. When we get to Gramercy Park, they will be scratching their heads wondering what just happened. From there, I am done with the loops and take a straight shot and pick up the pace back on Sixth Avenue down to Houston. The cross streets change from numbers to letters to street names below Houston, and they will be scratching their heads again.

"The Dutch settled in the southern end of Manhattan near Battery Park, and many of the streets still retain the Dutch names," Sammy continued. "I always lose them below Houston because it is confusing, and they can never remember the names of the streets. In about three minutes, those guys will be playing with themselves and wondering what just happened. Then we go down to Canal, and when we get close to Mulberry Street and are in the Diamond District, I will turn the corner, and you jump out. I will then drive around for about another hour in Chinatown until I either pick the assholes up again or get the call from Clara. If I do not get the call, I will see you at the drop-off point in about two hours. I was thinking: if they pick me up, maybe I will take them to Brooklyn or Queens. They will not be able to see inside the car and will think you are still in the car. Especially when I continue with some evasive moves and go through a few more red lights."

Greco began to relax. He laughed, smiled, and turned to look out the back window. He did not see any sign of the Ford sedans behind them. "Sounds good to me. Don't you just love driving in New York? These one-way streets are sometimes a real blessing."

Romano and Crowther looked both ways on Twenty-Third Street; they were beginning to realize that they had lost the big Lincoln. "Hey, guys, anybody see them? Got any ideas? The son of a bitch is good and knows the one-ways. I got suckered into Fourth Avenue, which is that fucking short avenue and runs into Fourteenth Street and dead-ends. Fuck, I forgot about Fourth. I should have known."

Greco was still smiling as they reached Canal and proceeded east. "Sam, how do you do this?"

"Well, Mr. G, I was born on Houston Street and grew up in Manhattan. I never had a car until I was almost thirty and walked the streets almost every day. I also have a good memory and practice at least once a week. I have about five different routes that I use, and they have never failed me."

"Well, Sam, you did good today. You earned your pay. Thank you; nice work."

As they approached the Diamond District, Sam made an abrupt turn north and stopped. Greco quickly jumped out of the Lincoln; he thought it wiser to walk up to Grand and then over to El Fornia at 131 Mulberry. He was a little early but saw that Crowley was sitting in a back booth. As he walked over, Crowley nodded and gestured for the Sicilian embrace. As he did, he ran his hands along Crowley's torso to check for a wire. Then he placed his cheek up to Crowley's and ran his hands up and down his sides and chest.

Greco looked at the restaurant host and said, "Hello, Charlie. Would you mind if we sat over in that corner, away from the window in the booth next to the kitchen?"

Crowley stood, and Greco went over and again openly ran his hands up near Crowley's neck. It was not a very good pat down but provided sufficient confidence that Crowley was not wired. Crowley got the message.

"Nicola, what do you think I am? How long have I known you? Be serious; do you think I would ever—"

Greco cut him off. "Look, Charlie, if you are in trouble, then we are all in trouble. What the fuck has happened to you? Why the hell have they reassigned you to another district? I hear you are on administrative leave. What have they got on you?"

"Nothing, Nicola. I got a hard-on over this broad, and when she made a few moves, I said something that I should not have said. It is just a sexual harassment charge. Nothing to get too excited about. My union lawyer is taking care of it. In the meantime, they have moved me off the team. Worst case is that they ship me back to Poughkeepsie."

Just then, a short olive skinned waiter came over to the table.

"Gentlemen, what can I get you today?

"Two Peronis and two broiled veal chops with the oregano and breadcrumbs in the dark sherry and butter sauce. Both medium, and both with a side of angel hair." Greco looked across at Crowley. "Is that okay, Charlie?"

"Perfect, how did you know?"

"Easy, the best in the city, and the second choice never comes close." Greco continued. "So now what? What can you tell me about this FBI thing?"

"What can I say, other than I cannot help you anymore. They will protect my pension and, worst case, they put me out in the street. They do not know anything about the claims thing, and they have not found Bloom. We are in the clear. Bloom cleaned it all up."

"Are you kidding? Our new guy spotted this almost immediately. Bloom was an amateur. The boys downtown have become very worried about you."

Crowley's face turned red. "What the fuck are you talking about? Money? I got very little from that thing and took a big chance. You and Bloom got it hidden somewhere in some stupid upstate real-estate scheme. I got no assurances that I will ever see my end."

Greco continued. "Charlie, Charlie, you made your bed, and now you have to sleep in it. Just remember how the game is played. We know that you took a cut off the top before you passed the money back up to the lawyers in Albany. We are not stupid, and you will be able to get out of this hole that you dug if you do what we ask. Look, understand; I am just a messenger, and our past dealings have nothing to do with our friendship or our personal relationship. It is out of my hands, so you will need to provide some assurances to prove that you are still with us and will not talk. That is all that I am going to say for now. And we need a copy of the case file, for starters."

Crowley was visibly shaken. "Are you serious? That just drags me in deeper, and if I get caught, I go to prison."

The waiter placed their beers on the table in front of them, and they each began to drink directly from the bottles. Another short waiter came out of the kitchen and placed the plates of veal and pasta on the table. Greco's eyes widened as he saw the chops.

"Charlie, we are willing to provide you with a little going-away travel money. Say, a couple hundred large. It ought to be easy for you to disappear south, or north or wherever. That is, if you play it smart and continue to help us on this investigation. Retire and go fishing or something. The choice is yours. Make a deal on this sexual-harassment problem and retire before the boys get nervous. You have your twenty years in and have your time and grade for at least one hundred a year, correct? As a friend, that is the best advice I can give you. We will have a safety-deposit number and key at the same bench, same time next week, and do not forget the FBI case file. Charlie, come on; you're safe, and you know that we cannot touch you because your badge protects you. Oh, and Charlie, we still have some very clear pictures of that little girl that disappeared three years ago in Poughkeepsie. How old was she? What was her name? Yolanda or something like that?"

Crowley shook his head. "You bastard. That is what dragged me in, and you were supposed to clean that up for me. You bastards will stop at nothing. You are no friend of mine."

Greco had delivered the message and said what needed to be said. He cut into the veal chop sitting on the plate in front of him. "We did clean that problem up for you, but the problem never goes away."

"Charlie, this is not personal. It is strictly business."

Crowley stared down at the table and looked at the chop. "You are all no good bastards." Although he could smell the sweet oregano sauce that the chop was sitting in, he suddenly lost his appetite. He stood up looking at Greco while his head shook from side to side, then turned and quickly walked out the door to the street.

CHAPTER TWENTY-EIGHT

THE BUST
SEPTEMBER 17, 1992

THERE WAS AN EARLY WINTER chill in the air that had begun to push the mild and muggy breezes of autumn aside. It was more winter than fall. They had their prey in their sights and were ready to spring the trap. The flashing light from within the restaurant flickered across the street and flashed through the windshield of the Buick. It was one of those "Open" signs that flashed on and off, but the *p* would not light up, so it simply flashed, "O en." Its lights mixed with the refection of the streetlights on Canal Street just one block to the north and also with the red and greens from the flashing signs in the Chinese restaurant windows along Mott Street.

The lights from restaurant windows bounced back toward the unmarked police car. The scene would all bear witness to the event that was about to take place as the two detectives sat nervously in the black sedan. It was almost 9:30, and the city was about to enter the second half of the evening dinner hours for New Yorkers. The drama that was about to occur would affect the lives of not only the union leaders but would ripple up to the state capital just 150 miles to the north, in Albany. The stage had been set, and the trap was about to be sprung on the unsuspecting target.

The city was at war with the drug traffickers, and tonight they were hunting big game. The two cops sat in their 1991 Buick four-door sedan, awaiting the moment in which they would witness the exchange of four kilos of cocaine. There was an eight-man backup team of police from the drug squad that were also part of the trap poised to join them once they received confirmation in the earpiece stuck in their right ears. The two detectives slid over close to the doors of the Buick. Detective Keegan sat in the back seat directly behind Marty O'Brian, who sat in the driver's seat. Keegan had his gun clasped in his left hand and hidden from view while resting on his lap under today's copy of the *New York Post*.

The .32 caliber short nose was the backup weapon of choice he normally carried in his ankle holster. The revolver had little chance of jamming that was typical of the city-issued Glock 9-millimeter semiautomatic. The short-nose revolver had plenty of kick and could stop a charging bull dead in its tracks. But it was the noise that made it so scary. They had just been through their routine to check their weapons and make certain they were loaded and ready. Keegan leaned forward and whispered softly into O'Brian's right ear.

"Marty, is that him?"

Marty turned his head slightly toward the back and said softly, "I think so, but let's hold on for a minute and be absolutely certain. Wait for our spotter to come out."

The little old Chinese ladies were shuffling past, grasping tightly to their evening dinner in little orange plastic bags. Their footsteps shifted uneasily past the Buick, and the detectives could hear them pass as their heels clicked an imagined staccato accented against the murmur of the passing traffic and the anticipation of the drama that was about to occur. It was a daily Chinatown occurrence for the Chinese mothers to buy food sufficient only for that day's supper, contrary to the weekly trip to the supermarket enjoyed by most suburban housewives. This was repeated each day as they canvassed the shops for a small portion of fish or meat. The vegetables would pretty much be repeated, but the dishes that were created in the small upstairs kitchens throughout Chinatown would yield an endless variety of tastes reflecting old-country Asian dishes, depending on the evening protein and spices that were married to the vegetables.

Lin's Chinese Garden had excellent food at reasonable prices, but the mixed aromas emitted from the kitchen did not always attract strangers who were unfamiliar with the mix of Chinatown smells. When you married all the various Chinese preparations and spices together into one single cloud of odor and mixed it with the unsavory fumes of the dirty pavement, it was not very appealing to the tourists. In fact, it was not at all appetizing and drove many would-be diners across Canal Street toward Little Italy just one block to the north.

"Boy, does this stuff smell so unappetizing. I am just not a big fan of Chinese food," uttered Keegan as he nervously began to take in short breaths.

O'Brian smiled as he directed his words at Keegan. "Actually, the food here is quite good. The kitchen needs a little fumigation, and if you can get by the wallpaper, it is one of the better places to eat in Chinatown."

Keegan stiffened in his seat as he peered out the open window and looked across the street.

"Yes, yes, that's him. He has a small bag under his left arm; that has to be the money bag. Okay, our spotter just walked out and lit a cigarette."

They were parked directly across from the restaurant facing to the west. The red flag pointed straight up in the small window of the parking meter. They obviously were not worried about getting a parking ticket, since they played by a different set of rules.

Small groups of customers began to enter the restaurant. The detectives placed their guns back into their holsters, quietly got out of the car, and walked across the street. They tried to be discreet and unassuming, but their mannerisms gave them all away. Nevertheless, their mark did not notice them as they walked in and sat down at the table near the window. The door was immediately to their left. The restaurant was not very busy, and they were pleased that their information source was accurate.

There were two unmarked cars, one just east and another Buick west of the restaurant with backup members of the drug-enforcement squad from the Fourteenth Precinct. This was not their first arrest, but nevertheless, they understood the danger. This was not an everyday occurrence, and small beads of sweat formed on Keegan's upper lip, even though the temperature was just nearing sixty outside.

Across the room at the far table against the wall were two elderly Chinee men sitting next to one another. There was food on the table, and they obviously had been eating for some time. There was a large platter in the center of the table surrounded by three or four smaller plates. The large platter in the center of the table appeared to have a half-eaten fish carcass.

O'Brian looked across at Keegan and whispered, "Grouper or yellowtail?"

Keegan was now annoyed, and his impatience was showing. "Cut the crap, and focus on why we are here. But it is grouper for sure. Too large for yellowtail."

"Okay, I am just trying to lighten the situation a bit, that's all."

Keegan growled, "Look, this is not the time to fuck around. We have a job to do, and let's not get too relaxed. I would like to go and get a plate of spaghetti after this is finished. I am hungry and not especially in the mood for this Chinese food."

They had been given a one-hundred-dollar bill for the meal, and Keegan decided not to use any of it in Chinatown.

They had to order something, since they expected it would take some time before they could witness the exchange. They had been sitting for only a few minutes when a waiter came over. He was a young Chinese man no older then eighteen or nineteen and spoke in perfect English.

"Good evening, gentlemen. Can I start you off with a drink?"

Keegan took the lead and looked up at the waiter. "Yes, a couple of beers, and we don't care what kind. How about Bud?"

The waiter did not reply but bowed, turned, and walked into the kitchen. The two detectives, although trying to be discreet, paid careful attention to the table against the wall. The young Caucasian man with the small package under his arm had now placed it on the table. He was in mid-thirties and well dressed. He slid the package toward the older of the two Chinese men who sat directly across from him. They did not notice any other package on the table. Keegan was the first to notice.

"Where is the junk? I don't see anything. Four kilos is almost ten pounds, and it has to be visible. Where the fuck is it?"

"I don't know, but I can tell you with great certainty that he is either leaving with his money bag or the junk. That, I guarantee." Again, O'Brian whispered.

The older man opened the money bag and looked down into it. He looked up at the young man sitting across from him and cracked a smile. He offered a quick, short bow of his head.

Just then, a waiter came from the kitchen and walked over to the table against the wall with a large, white plastic bag and placed it in front of the older Chinese man. He said something in Chinese. The Chinese man opened the bag, peered in, briefly nodded, and then smiled. He carefully folded the top of the bag and pushed it across the table.

"Those clever bastards. It is a to-go order." Keegan now smiled as well.

The waiter returned with two bottles of beer and placed them on the table.

The young man at the other table peered into the bag, bowed his head slightly, stood, picked it up, turned, and began to walk toward the door when the two detectives quickly jumped in front of him. Their guns were drawn, and O'Brian was the first to shout.

"Okay, freeze, and do not make a move or you are dead!"

The young man froze and dropped the bag. It made a thump as it hit the floor. He slowly raised his hands. Keegan quickly ran over to the table against the wall and pointed his gun at the two Chinese men as he shouted, "Do not move!"

He had his radio open to the backup units outside, and it was no more than ten or fifteen seconds when five uniformed policemen ran through the door. They each wore a bulletproof vest with "NYPD" printed on the back in large letters.

O'Brian reached down and picked up the white plastic bag. Inside were four neatly packaged bricks of powder tightly wrapped in plastic. He smiled at Keegan. Keegan reached down and picked up the canvas bag that sat in front of them on the table. He opened it to inspect the contents. He could see that it was packed with several banded packages of one-hundred-dollar bills. He could not imagine how much was in the bag but knew that it was several thousand just by the look and weight of it. The uniform policemen guarded the door to the outside and the door to the kitchen.

It was no more than another ten seconds when the room became full of policemen. A captain walked over and nodded toward Keegan and O'Brian.

"Nice work." He then turned to two other detectives. Both wore suits, one brown and the other dark gray. "Okay, arrest the three of them, but first, read them their rights."

He turned toward the two arresting detectives.

"O'Brian, Keegan, you have the evidence, and do not turn those bags over until you have the chain-of-evidence forms signed. Take out a sample and test it in front of a uniform. You need to be present for the count and for the testing and weighing of the stuff back at the station. It then goes directly into the evidence vault. Now, don't forget to pay for those two beers. Oh, by the way, someone go back and get the waiters. Line them up, and I want to talk to the one who dropped the bag on the table."

O'Brian was quite pleased, since it had gone much easier than he had expected.

"You are under arrest; you have the right to remain silent. Anything you say can and will be used against you. You have the right to an attorney. If you cannot afford one, we will provide you with one. Do you understand your rights? Now, if you please, face the wall and hands up high." He placed his gun back in his holster and frisked the young man.

"He's clean. Now, please place your hands behind your back. Do you mind if I ask you for your identification?" O'Brian continued.

The young man slowly moved his right hand out and down toward his back pocket. He pulled out his wallet and handed it to the detective and then placed his hands behind his back. "You guys are way over your head and making a big mistake," he said.

"Shut your fucking mouth, and do not move." O'Brian motioned with his head to a uniformed policeman to join them. "Officer, hold this bag, and stand right here beside me. Watch him carefully while I cuff him."

The uniformed policeman came over with his gun drawn.

"Sir, please do not move, and face the wall." O'Brian handed the officer the bag. "Holster your gun. This is evidence, and be careful. You are now wedded to my side until we check it in. Do you understand?"

"Yes, sir."

Another uniformed policeman stood near the door. He was a bit older than the other policemen. He was not allowing anyone to leave. Keegan and the two other detectives had the two men against the far wall and were frisking them.

O'Brian slowly opened the man's wallet and noticed that there were several hundred-dollar bills.

"I have your wallet, and I am going to keep it in my possession for evidence. It looks like you have about twelve hundred dollars in your wallet, and this patrolman is going to witness what I am doing and will sign an affidavit as to the amount when we book you. Understand?"

There was a small pocket and two or three credit cards in the wallet. Then he found it—a New York State driver's license. He pulled it out and peered down at it. The name on the license was clearly visible and surprised O'Brian.

"Captain Reilly, you better look at this," he said as he handed the license to the uniformed policeman with the two silver bars on his shoulders. The captain took it from Keegan and looked at it as he began to shake his head from side to side.

It read, *Nicola Anthony Greco, Jr.*

"I think I better call the chief."

The New York City Police Department (NYPD) was the largest and one of the oldest municipal police departments in the United States, with approximately 35,000 officers and 19,000 civilian employees. It had seventy-seven patrol precincts, with patrol officers and detectives covering the entire city. It was impossible to coordinate all the police activities in a city like New York with the FBI. The captain knew immediately that this was going to be problem for the department, since he was aware that there was an FBI investigation taking place and Local 4 was a target. The union was on the FBI's radar but had not been involved in this sting. He had no idea that their target tonight would be someone directly connected to the union, and knew he would need to get the chief involved. He went directly to his car and radioed the chief.

Most people caught drinking a beer in Central Park or jaywalking would not be sent to Rikers Island, but it was possible. And most people accused of murder are not allowed to walk free, but that is possible too. Caught red-handed buying or selling four kilos worth of drugs was a very serious situation, even for those who were connected. Greco Junior had had the juice, and his family was well known in the city. The captain decided that they would hold the young Greco at the precinct for the night before he was arraigned and booked. This was the smart move, since there would be serious ramifications if he made the wrong decision. The chief was very clear and advised Captain Reilly to hold off until morning.

"Do not involve the assistant district attorney until they can discuss the situation in the morning," he said.

Getting too far down the line would complicate matters. Rikers Island was not a pleasant experience, even for the most hardened criminals, and the captain had some latitude to hold everything until morning. The chief simply said, "Throw him in a holding cell at the precinct until morning."

Nicky had used his one phone call, and as with the many difficult situations he had previously gotten into, that call was to his father. He was nervous and frightened and had never been in so serious a situation. But he knew that his father would need to get involved if there was any chance at getting out of it. His father had the right connections, and he knew he would do whatever was necessary to get him out of the jam. Family was family, and even though his father would be mad at him, family would always come before anything else. His father would always say, "Blood is thicker than water." That is what counted most, and he knew that he had a family that would always stick by him. He felt some comfort in knowing that they did not arraign him and did not cart him over to Rikers.

New York City's criminal-justice system was rigid and rule-based in many ways, but every player in the system made some choices. Police officers, and certainly police captains, could often choose whether your infraction was worth a ticket or serious enough to run you through the system. Captain Reilly understood the gravity of the situation and was not about to risk making the wrong decision. He knew that this decision was well above his authority. No way was he going to risk his career or pension for a simple blunder or misjudgment. And besides, the average time from arrest to arraignment was close to twenty hours, so he knew he was within a safe time window before he made any bad choices. Seven or eight hours would make little difference.

CHAPTER TWENTY-NINE

MY BLOOD

SEPTEMBER 18, 1992 – EARLY-MORNING HOURS

IT WAS NOW **1:30** IN the morning, and the phone was ringing. It startled Nicola and his wife, Marie. He was an early-to-bed person and a deep sleeper. But when he heard the ringing of the phone, he had an uneasy feeling that something was wrong. He could not reach the phone from his side of the bed, and Marie lifted the handset from its cradle and said, "Hello."

"Hello, Mom; everything is cool. Sorry for the late call, but I need to speak to Pop."

Marie, like most Italian mothers, could sense that something was not right.

"Nicky, what is the matter? Are you in trouble? Why are you calling so late? Your father is asleep."

"No, no, I am okay. I just need to speak to Pop. It is important."

Marie handed the phone over to her husband. He still had his head resting on the pillow and had barely moved.

"Hey, what the hell are you calling me at this time of night? Did you get in an accident? Are Gracie and the kids okay?"

Junior replied from the other end of the line, "Everyone is okay. We are all just fine. I just got in a little trouble and need you to bail me out. I cannot talk about it yet, but I will need a lawyer tomorrow morning. You know, that criminal lawyer from the Bronx—Silverberg or Silverman? You know, the lawyer that the international uses, our union lawyer."

"Speak louder. I cannot understand you. What has happened? Where are you?" Greco Senior was now frantic. "What kind of trouble are you in?"

"Look, Pop, this is not a big deal. I am at the Fourteenth Precinct. You need to call in the morning, first thing, and ask for Captain Reilly. Call after seven o'clock. We can then straighten it out. Now go back to sleep. Remember, Fourteenth Precinct, and ask for Captain Reilly."

"Fucking kids give you nothing but heartaches," Greco said to himself and then said into the handset, "Okay, eight o'clock, Captain Reilly, Fourteenth Precinct."

Greco handed the phone back to his wife, who placed it to her ear. "Nicky, what is the matter? Are you in trouble?"

Nicky tried to not sound scared, but he was shaking. "I am all right, Mom. Just be sure to tell Dad to call the lawyer in the Bronx and call Captain Reilly at the Fourteenth Precinct in the morning. Good night, Mom, and don't worry. I am all right." *Click.* The phone fell silent.

"God bless you, my son. We will take care of it." She hung up the phone and began to sob softly. Greco was already fast asleep.

Little Nicky was at first thrown into a holding cell with eight or ten others, most of whom were either drunk or arrested under a disorderly conduct violation. A small middle-aged man came over and said, "Hello, my name is Tony DiPapa. I think I know you from somewhere."

"Not a chance, I am from New Jersey," replied Nicky, since he knew enough not to give anyone information. He suspected that this Tony was in the union and probably recognized him. He thought better and decided to keep him guessing.

"Well, you look a little uncomfortable, and if you need someone to stand guard, let me know. It is always best to team up and when one sleeps, the other stands guard."

"I know the routine, but I don't think I am going to be here that long. And besides, I can assure you, I am not about to take a nap." He turned away and walked to the front of the cell. He did not sit down or face away from the others.

It was approaching 7:30 when two uniformed policemen approached the cell. One of them had captains' bars on his shoulders. He recognized him as one of the policemen who was at the Chinese restaurant.

"Mr. Greco, I am sorry for the bad night, but we need to talk. I would like you to come with me."

The other policeman unlocked the door, and a buzzer sounded that opened the electronic lock. He swung the door open, and Greco stepped out of the holding cell.

"Please turn with your hands behind your back. Procedure."

Young Greco turned and placed his hands behind him. "No problem."

The captain then placed the handcuffs on Greco. They walked to an open area where there were several hallways. Down each hallway were several cells, and he could hear the chatter of the inmates making idle conversations.

They passed through a secured door that was opened electronically. There was a camera and bulletproof glass at the door that allowed the door guard to open the door from the other side of the glass. The door slid inward into the wall on the left. They then entered a large room with several doors and several glass windows. The windows all had security screens built into the glass. The lobby had three elevator doors.

Captain Reilly pressed the "up" button just as the middle door opened. They entered and Captain Reilly inserted his magnetic card into the reader and pressed the "5" button. They went up to the fifth floor and entered a large reception area with another uniform policemen sitting at a desk in the center of the room. The uniformed policemen handed the captain a small magnetic striped card.

"Hey, Cap."

The captain picked it up. It read in large, black letters, "Interview Room 508."

"Got it, Sergeant. Thanks. When the others arrive, just buzz me. Right this way, Greco."

Room 508 had a gray table that was bolted to the floor and four metal chairs standing along one side of the room. There was a camera hanging from the ceiling in the far corner and a large mirror that obviously was a one-way. He pulled a chair to the table.

"Greco, you sit right here." The camera pointed directly at him. There was a small console on the table with four buttons and a phone. "I am not going to talk about last night, but I must tell you that we are recording this conversation and you do not have to discuss anything or say anything that might incriminate you. Do you understand?"

Greco nodded.

"I must ask you to please tell me verbally, yes or no."

Young Greco replied, "Yes, I understand."

"Do you wish to speak to an attorney?"

"Yes, my attorney should be here shortly, and I have nothing to say."

"Very well. You made a call last night, so hang tight until your attorney arrives. In the meantime, we are just going out to the room next door. You are being monitored, so make yourself comfortable. Do you want a cup of coffee?"

"Yes, but how do I pick it up? With my teeth?"

"Joe, get him a cup of coffee. Black?" He turned to young Greco. "Someone will need to stay with you until your attorney arrives. And Joe, get him a doughnut, maybe two."

"Yeah, black is fine. And doughnuts would be great. I am starved."

The uniformed policemen went to the back of the chair and removed the handcuffs. There was a weak knock at the door, and another uniformed policeman was buzzed in and placed a cup of coffee and a paper plate with two jelly doughnuts on the table.

Greco looked up and nodded. "Thanks." He took a sip and immediately sat up erect in his chair. "Owww, that is hot coffee! You guys are torturing me."

They were all quiet. Only fifteen minutes had passed, but it seemed more like an hour when the phone on the wall began to ring. The captain picked up the handset.

"Reilly, 508 … yes, fine … send them in."

After another five or six minutes, the door buzzer sounded, and the two men entered. One was dressed in a dark-blue suit with a green tie. The shirt was a dull olive color. Nothing seemed to match. He had thinning hair and metal-rimmed glasses. It was Morris Silverman, the attorney. He was carrying a black briefcase. The other man was old-man Greco, and he had on a pair of gray slacks with a dark-blue shirt. He was wearing a dark-blue sweater over the shirt.

"Son," he said, "this is Morris Silverman, and he is going to represent you."

The young Greco stood and immediately greeted his father with a powerful embrace. "I am sorry, Pop. I was doing someone a favor and was set up."

Silverman interrupted. "Nicky, please. Captain, may we have some privacy? Can you turn off the recorder and camera, and can

I assume that the room next door does not have anyone in it to witness our conversation? We need to speak privately."

The three policemen walked out of the room. They then heard over the intercom: "You guys are good to go. All clear." The small red light on the wall went dark.

"Nicky, first, we do not discuss anything here today other than bail. You do not breathe a word about what happened last night. Our discussion here this morning is only … only about getting you out of here and keeping you from Rikers. That is it. I spoke to the assistant district attorney, and they want to arraign you today. This is a very serious matter; from what I have learned, you are accused of buying four kilos of cocaine."

"Those bastards, they told me it was supposed to be five kilos. Never trust anyone."

"Nicky, what did I just say? Be careful of what you say. I never trust these rooms."

He continued. "Well, that makes little difference at this point, but regardless, if convicted, you are facing a minimum of twenty-five years to life. We may have some pull if we can plea this down, but the ADA is pretty adamant about this arrest and does not want any plea deals … so we are in a real pickle. The priority now is to get you bailed out. I think we can get the judge to go for a $50,000 bail. Your dad is ready to write a check, so first things first, at the arraignment, you will plead not guilty. Understood? The ADA meets with us at ten and then presents the case to the judge for arraignment. We will get you out today, and we can meet Monday or later today after we get you out of this place to work out a defense. Are you okay with that?"

"Yeah, sure. Hey, Pop, I am sorry, and I appreciate your being here for me."

"You are my son. A father can never abandon his son— remember that. You are my blood."

"Okay, that's it; we can stay in here for a little while, and we can wait for the ADA. Do not say a word, and I will do all the talking. Hopefully, it will not be a long wait."

Old-man Greco was very upset and near tears. "This fucking place gives me the willies. We have to get the hell out of here." He finally could no longer hold the tears back, and they began to flood his cheeks.

"Pop … Pop … we will get through this. I am okay, and I need to call Grace. Did you call her?"

"Yes, your mother called her about two a.m. and told her not to worry. When we get you out, you will come over to the house. Your mother called Grace, and they are coming over with the boys. Your mother is going to make us breakfast."

Silverman said, "Look, our first priority is to get you bail. You are not going to Rikers Island; it is a living hellhole and no place for any human being."

"No fucking way," Greco Senior added.

Old-man Greco was tired and had not slept very well since the phone call. He grabbed a chair and placed it next to his son. He sat down and closed his eyes. They were still wet, and he pulled a handkerchief from his back pocket and wiped the tears from his cheeks. His eyes were bloodshot, and his cheeks were red from his ordeal. He had been taking blood-pressure medication, but this morning, he forgot.

They sat quietly for almost twenty minutes before the buzzer sounded. The door opened, and in walked a young man in his mid-thirties.

"Hello; my name is Richard Rowlands. I am with the New York District Attorney's Office and am an assistant district attorney. I have been assigned to this case. Do you mind if I sit down?"

He grabbed a chair and sat across from old-man Greco and his son. Silverman was standing in the corner. There were no pleasantries and no handshakes. He had a manila folder, which he placed on the table in front of him. He opened it and looked at the pink-colored typewritten page that had been stapled to the inside of the front cover.

"Okay, I did review the file, and I expect that Mr. Greco will be arraigned this morning." He looked at the older Greco and then turned to the younger one. "We are on Judge Luciano's docket this morning, and it should be sometime around eleven. First of all, you do not have to say anything. I think you understand that anything you say can be used against you in a court of law. I know your attorney is present, but it still applies. You do not have to say anything. Do you mind if we have a short talk about how you will plead, and then we may be able to discuss bail?"

Silverman took the remaining chair and brought it over to the end of the table. He sat down and peered over at the ADA. "Well, he is going to plead not guilty, and of course we will ask for bail." He paused. "Do you have any objections or any idea as to what amount you will suggest to the judge?"

"Well, Mr. Silverman, I was thinking that this is a pretty serious charge, and the normal amount of bail is somewhere north of two hundred."

Silverman was ready. "This is not normal; my client is married and has a family that he needs to support. He has a job, and he is an upstanding member of this community. I was thinking … somewhere in the neighborhood of ten or twenty. He is not a flight risk, and I think you know that."

"The judge will never go along with that."

"Look, I don't want to get into a pissing contest, but this judge knows the family and has always been fair and reasonable. My client is not a flight risk, and this is a nonviolent offense." Silverman's voice was firm and assertive. "And if you look at the arrest report, he was fully cooperative and put up no resistance to the arresting officers."

The older Greco decided he would have a say. "Young man, I have borrowed from my pension plan, and I can write a check today for $25,000. Please do not send my son over to Rikers, not even for a day. He is a good boy, and he is not going to jump bail or do anything crazy. Our family has deep roots in our community. You have my word as a father."

He added, "I don't know if you have any children—but if you do, then you will understand."

"Well, I think if we can agree on, let's say, fifty; that is, if you agree right now, and then there may be other areas where we may reach agreement on some other issues," Rowlands replied and nodded.

Silverman began to nod his head as well and reached over to confirm the deal with a handshake. "Nick, $50,000 is fair, and besides, you will be getting it back."

Greco was pleased. He thought Silverman was doing okay so far, but he also recognized that the real work was yet to begin.

CHAPTER THIRTY

NO TURNING BACK

SEPTEMBER 19, 1992

T HAT EVENING, CHRIS AND WILLIAMS were working late and
waiting for the results from the parallel test. This was the big
moment and would determine if they could go live with the pension
system tomorrow. Summer had ended, and he had no appetite
and was thinking about all they had gone through the last several
months: the meetings, the drama associated with labor leaders, the
dinner parties, the lunches, and the FBI encounters.

He stared across the table at old-man Greco. He was sleeping,
and they were waiting for the report that the pension system was
ready. He began to think about the mystery on the seventh floor as
many questions ran through his mind.

"What are the deep, dark secrets on the seventh floor? How much money are they skimming? The computer audit process was clean, but what the hell are the colored folders used for? It just does not add up. Who is involved? How do I protect my position from these people? How can I gain leverage to protect myself?"

Chris thought about all that was going on and how he would put the pieces of the puzzle together. He knew that if they went down, they would take him with them. Maybe you could not trust the FBI, but it was clear that you could never trust the union. LaCola, Greco, and Goldin only cared about themselves. The annuity fund was not a big deal, and the Medicare skim, although more money was involved, was not a surprise to Chris. If they discovered a betrayal and knew who was responsible, they would be eliminated. Trust was all they talked about, but he knew that there was no honor among thieves. They would agree to cooperate to save themselves.

DiNapoli had to be punished and set an example for others. Bloom, who knew too much, had to disappear. The FBI was not stupid and knew that Bloom's sudden disappearance was not voluntary. Chris knew it would not be the pension fund. That is the first place that the feds would look. The math was easy, and the pension fund was too big. The feds always looked for the missing money from the largest funds, when in fact the skim occurred in the smaller funds with lots of transactions. The annuity and the health and welfare fund were better ways to steal and more easily covered up. The feds were always looking in the wrong corners. Goldin must have known it was Bloom who was needed to fix the skim. But he needed an accomplice.

Was it DiNapoli and Greco? Maybe both. Chris wanted to find out who and how. Who else could manipulate the data in the computer, and who had access? Bloom is the only one who knew how it all worked, and he was too close to DiNapoli and Greco for them to ignore. The programmer was clearly involved and there was plenty of money in the annuity fund and the health and welfare fund. So these were the side jobs that may not have been approved by anyone. But as he thought about it, he suspected that they knew. But the big-money skim must be on the seventh floor. It was complicated, and there were several ways to get money out undetected. And yet, Goldin and Greco were so eager to give them DiNapoli and Bloom.

More questions began to haunt Chris, but the big one was, what would happen to him? Would he go to jail, or would he end up in the East River? Chris knew they had lots of money, but he never could have imagined the extent of the power, influence, and corruption. The International Labor Union Local 4 was huge, with big multimillion-dollar trust funds and big bank accounts. He knew there was a big secret on the seventh floor and that they would stop at nothing to protect that secret. Chris just could not let it rest, and it was gnawing at him. He needed to find out and to get leverage on them to protect himself. What were the colored folders for? The shop stewards' report had to be a fabricated story to throw them off, a diversion. But was it? It had to be a cover story to the real scam. Chris was guessing that it was the big-money operation to launder money back to the contractors and the syndicate. The auditors could change the rates, and no one would be the wiser, except perhaps Bloom. His stare moved to the magnetic badge attached to the lapel on Greco's jacket.

He knew what was happening but realized that the Albany project would be an important part of the scheme going forward. It would be much more money than the skim from the claims and annuity. Not millions, but hundreds of millions were at stake. Goldin was quick to throw in another $150,000 without giving it a second thought. Chris now realized that he did not fool Goldin or LaCola. They were pulling the strings and knew Chis had to go along. He was easily bought and paid for as an accomplice.

He was in too deep and could not run away. They had sucked him in with the envelopes and tested him. He had to get the evidence to protect himself. He could never betray the union but knew they would not think twice about betraying him. He no longer trusted the accountant or LaCola.

Time was running out, and he would have fewer opportunities once the work was completed. This was his opportunity to learn what was in those colored folders. He suspected but needed the hard proof. He needed to gain an advantage over LaCola and Greco, and especially over Goldin. They knew that he would be loyal; he was tested and had passed, but he needed protection from them because he knew that they could never be trusted. Chris was never one to go on instincts, but this time, he had a strange feeling that he knew the truth and needed to act to get an insurance policy to prevent the union from betraying him.

The more he thought about it, the pieces started to fit together. These people were not good people, and they always would try and leverage their relationship. They were takers and always wanted to be in total control. They were not just thieves; they were murderers. The extra $150,000 was protection from betrayal by Chris. But what prevented them from betrayal? He knew that if push came to shove, they would quickly throw him to the wolves. They did not care about anyone other than themselves. Both sides were closing in on him, and he realized that this was the only way. He had to act, and this was his opportunity.

He kept thinking about the seventh floor, Goldin's accountants, and the colored folders. He needed proof so that he could trade if necessary. The red and green folders contained the hard proof that he needed for protection. Tomorrow was the go-live day, and time was running out. They were going to transfer the test library to the operational library. Tomorrow would be a big day, if the Williams transfer worked.

Larry had gone with Goldin to get sandwiches, and Williams was running the edit programs in the computer room. Greco was still fast asleep in the chair at the other side of the conference table.

It was almost eight o'clock, and the staff had all gone home for the day.

Chris eyed the magnetic card clipped to Greco's jacket draped over the chair. He had to decide. He quietly walked around the table and unclipped the badge from the jacket. He knew he had only a few minutes and walked out of the conference room and back to the breakroom. There was the door, painted in dark gray. Painted on the door was, "Private." It had a magnetic reader on the right side. He inserted the badge and could hear the latch release. *Click.* He opened the door to the back stairway, and just beyond a small platform was a staircase going up. He was not sure he was doing the right thing, but it was too late to go back. He was committed. He quickly ran up the stairs to the dark-gray door with the number 7 on it. He quickly inserted Greco's badge into the badge reader. There was another click, and he could hear the latch release the lock. He was careful to open it slowly and peered in through the opening. He was relieved to see that no one was in the office. The room was dark, other than the small red light from the exit sign above the fire-escape door. He could just make out the row of gray desks along both sides of the room.

He cautiously walked in and saw the long tables alongside the file cabinets. He knew immediately that he was in the auditors' bullpen in the front of the accounting office. He walked over to the row of gray metal desks with the folders on top, then to the table next to the file cabinets. There were several stacks of multicolored folders on the tables. He noticed that there were some folders held together by large rubber bands and had been stamped "Complete" on the outside. He took one of the bundled sets that had been stamped, which contained a red, a green, and a manila folder. He quickly took off his jacket and stuck the bundled folders between his belt and backside. He then put his suit jacket back on. He quickly turned and walked back out to the back staircase door and inserted the plastic card into the reader. The latched released, and he quickly but quietly went back down to the sixth floor.

When he reached the sixth floor, the door was locked. He inserted the plastic card into the card reader and waited for the latch to release. No click. Nothing happened, and the door remained locked. He was frozen for just a second and felt trapped. Wait, maybe he had inserted the card backward. He took it out and tried with desperation to insert it from the other direction. Still nothing. He inserted it again with the stripe on the right side. It did not work. Chris thought, "Fuck, I am screwed; how the hell can I get back in?"

He stood there for a moment when it came to him. He was now frantic and realized that he was trapped. A cold sweat overtook his body, but then he regained his composure and thought about possible escape routes. Then it came to him. He quickly ran back up the steps to the seventh floor. He once again inserted the badge into the card reader and entered the accounting area. He was trapped and tried to think of a way to get back down to the sixth-floor conference room undetected. He knew the camera would record his exit if he were to try and walk out using the front staircase or elevator. He remembered that there was the fire escape along the back wall, and this was where the smokers would go for a cigarette.

There it was: the red door. It was his only way out, the fire escape. He gritted his teeth and knew he would need to face his greatest fear. He gathered up all his courage as he thought about it but knew that the fire escape would be his only chance to escape undetected. Feeling uncertain, he reluctantly approached the door and noticed that there was no lock on it. He nervously opened the door and stepped out onto the metal platform. For a moment, he was paralyzed. The noise from the traffic below echoed off the nearby buildings. He thought, "Thank God for the smokers."

It was windy, and the platform rocked back and forth as he forced himself to take the first step out on the platform. He moved cautiously forward to grab the hand railing. He inched forward as he closed the door and could hear a faint scraping noise as he carefully walked toward the metal stairs. He moved slowly and was bent forward, almost on his hands and knees, almost touching the bottom of the platform to steady his movement. He edged forward inch by inch toward the open metal staircase. It sounded like fingernails scratching on a blackboard as the platform rocked from side to side. Chris imagined that the sounds he heard were from the anchor bolts as they tore from the mortar that held the platform to the side of the building.

He was shaking but gained strength and newfound courage with each new step as he forced himself to continue. He had never been more frightened in his life and was gasping for a breath of clean air. The platform held securely, and he remembered seeing two or three smokers at a time on the platform. He realized that this was his only way back, and he forced himself to continue. There was no turning back, and he prayed that the emergency door on the sixth floor would not be locked. He was terrified and had to ignore the height. He thought, "Please, God, no lock. Please, God, no lock. Don't look down; do not look down; you can do this. Be calm and don't look down."

He grasped the handrail tighter with each step he took and slowly and carefully walked down the metal staircase. One step at a time. He could see through the steps to the concrete alleyway below but had to ignore his fear. He could feel that his heart was beating at well over 150 beats per minute, and he thought his heart would jump out of his chest. "Think of something else. Anything but the fall." He forced himself to look down at each of the steps before placing his foot on the step below to advance down to the platform below. "Almost there, just a few more steps, almost there," he thought and then finally, he was on the sixth-floor platform. He took a deep breath and now moved more quickly, his confidence gaining strength. He thought about Greco in the conference room as he finally reached the emergency exit. He said to himself as he pulled the door open, "God, thank you. Thank you." No lock. He opened the door and finally felt relieved as he stepped into the sixth-floor breakroom.

His legs shook and he was barely able to walk. He stumbled toward a chair and sat down to calm himself. Chris sat motionless for a few seconds, since all his energy had drained from his body. "Whew, I did it. Think; think; what do I need to do next? Greco's badge. I need to get it back and calm down." Slowly, he began to gain his composure. He stood, walked over to the soda machine, and inserted a dollar. There was a *clunk* as the can of Pepsi rolled out at the bottom. He then inserted another bill and punched the button again, and another can rolled out. *Clunk*. One for Greco.

Chris stood and knew that the worst was over. He never thought it would be possible, but he had overcome his fear on the fire escape. He did it. He quickly walked back to the conference room. He thought, "Almost there," and as he opened the door, he was startled and surprised to see that the room was now empty. He did not see Greco. Where was Greco? The jacket was now gone. He turned around and could feel his heart pounding again. He turned around and looked up. There he was; Greco stood at the other door of the conference room.

"Where the fuck were you?" As Greco sternly looked across at him.

Chris was startled and not sure what to say. "Huh? I was just in the bathroom and then got us a couple of sodas." He reached toward Greco and handed the Pepsi to him.

"Thanks. Hey, did you see my badge? I always have it on my jacket, but I cannot find it."

"Your what?"

Greco was now wide awake. "The magnetic badge. I am always losing that thing."

"Where was your jacket? I saw it last on the chair and you were fast asleep."

"Hey, I guess so." Greco looked confused.

Chris immediately dropped down to his knees and started to look under the table. He reached into his pocket without Greco seeing him and tossed the badge under the table to the other side. "I think I see something over there on your side, Nick."

Greco looked down and dropped to his left knee and peered under the table. "Aha! There you are, you little bastard. We need to get a better system; these things are ruining my jackets, and they are too small to keep track of." He casually clipped it back on to his lapel.

Greco was about to stand when Goldin walked in with Smith. Smith was holding a large brown bag and Goldin had a larger plastic bag that apparently held two six-packs of Coors Light.

Goldin's white teeth were showing from his broad smile. "We have some nice Jewish deli sandwiches Nick, and some ice-cold beer to go with them. Now, this is what I call a good, old-fashioned Jewish dinner."

Chris smiled, as he felt somewhat relieved. "Hey, why don't we buzz Williams in the computer room and see if we have cause to celebrate. I am taking bets that we are good and the balances match."

Chris had spoken to Williams earlier, and they had confirmed that the edit programs all worked perfectly.

Goldin placed the bag of beer down on the table and walked over to the small refrigerator. He took out a tray of ice and brought it back and threw the ice into the plastic bag. "It's still pretty cold, but here is some ice. Hey, Larry, get the bucket and let's ice these cans up."

He then flipped the top open on the can of beer in his hand and took a long sip. "Chris, as I was telling you, Katz's Deli … best pastrami in the world. None better."

Just then, Williams appeared and stopped at the doorway before he entered. "Okay, men, we are good; it all came over and no error messages … and …" He hesitated and then said with a big grin, "The total numbers matched between the old and the new from running a week of parallel operations. All benefit credits matched perfectly between the old system and the new system. We are ready to go live with pension and claims tomorrow morning."

Chris reached over and grabbed a can of beer. He was relieved, and he was not sure if it was because of the conversion, the pastrami sandwiches, the beer, or the badge now clipped to Greco's jacket. He handed a beer to Williams as he peered at the others who were all smiling. A weak smile came across his face. He was careful as he sat down remembering the colored folders sandwiched between his belt and his backside. He breathed a long sigh of relief and thought to himself, "Finally, another insurance policy."

CHAPTER THIRTY-ONE

VERRAZANO

SEPTEMBER 20, 1992

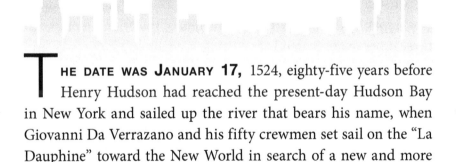

THE DATE WAS JANUARY 17, 1524, eighty-five years before Henry Hudson had reached the present-day Hudson Bay in New York and sailed up the river that bears his name, when Giovanni Da Verrazano and his fifty crewmen set sail on the "La Dauphine" toward the New World in search of a new and more direct route to the Pacific Ocean.

His ship was the only remaining seaworthy vessel from the original four that had started the journey from France. The other three were the victims of a storm soon after their departure earlier that year. His belief was that he could find a more direct way through the Northwest Passage to Asia. He was welcomed by the natives in present-day North Carolina's Cape Fear in mid-March of that same year. After a brief and friendly visit with the natives, he sailed south for almost two hundred miles reaching the northern most point of the Florida coastline, and when he was unable to find a suitable harbor to land, he turned back to continue his journey north.

He continued on a northerly route up the coastline in his search of the Northwest Passage and with it, an open channel to the Pacific Ocean, and then on to Asia. He continued his journey and in mid-April of 1524, he and his crew sailed into New York Bay. He was the first known European to sail into New York Bay. It was a friendly encounter with the natives, who welcomed him and gave him and his crew food. His journey would continue north as he explored the Long Island Sound in New York, Block Island, and Narragansett Bay in present-day Rhode Island.

His namesake bridge, the Verrazano-Narrows Bridge, was officially opened to traffic on November 21, 1964. The Staten Island to Brooklyn Bridge is a thirteen-lane bridge that is 13,700 feet long. Designed by Othmar Ammann, it is a behemoth double-deck suspension bridge. At its completion in 1965, it was the longest single span in the world. The completion of the bridge, along with three other major Staten Island bridges, enabled rapid growth and new and more efficient ways commuters and tourists to travel by car between Staten Island, New Jersey, Manhattan, Brooklyn, and Long Island. These new pathways enabled significant opportunities for growth in both commercial and residential development.

Staten Island, although the least populated of the five boroughs of New York, is the third largest borough in land area of the five boroughs comprising the city of New York. Rosebank is a neighborhood located in the northeastern part of Staten Island, with more than half of its population of Italian descent. It enjoys the reputation of being the most Italian-looking city of Staten Island. Nicola Greco had built his house in Rosebank in 1968, and it was no exception to the look, feel, and influence of Greco's Italian heritage.

Silverman was on his way to Greco's home on 9635 West Wellington Avenue, Staten Island. Their meeting was scheduled for 3:00 p.m., and Silverman had already received a call from the ADA. He expected it and wanted to have a sit down to discuss possible options regarding how the government would proceed. The ADA had informed Silverman that the FBI had been notified and wanted to talk. He also told him that the FBI was interested in the case and that they were in the process of an investigation into union affairs. There was the possibility of working something out, so he thought that was good news in one respect but bad news in another respect. But he thought that perhaps they could work out a plea deal for young Greco if there was cooperation. They requested a sit down with old-man Greco. Silverman was reluctant and knew that the FBI would be more than willing to make a trade for inside information. He was hoping for the best but knew he first would need to know exactly what the FBI was looking for so that he could put limits around the discussions.

The house was a typical one for an Italian family in Staten Island. It was a two-story house situated on a very narrow, yet deep lot. There were barely fifteen feet of space between all the houses on the street. It had a basement, half of which stood at least six or seven feet above grade, and the front façade of the house was Italian marble with red brick along the sides. Any passerby knew that the family occupying the residence had a last name ending in a vowel. There was a broad staircase of stone leading up to ornate double-glass doors on the second level.

There was a transit above the doors, and he could see through the oval glass window that the hanging chandelier was lit. There were two Roman columns on each side of the double doors, with two carved lions sitting there, one on each side, as if to guard the front entrance. They were made of stone and stood at least three feet tall. He pressed the bell and could hear the chimes ringing out an Italian folk tune. No question, the house was inspired by a deep Italian influence. Greco had purchased the lot in the early sixties and had built the house to his specifications. He had put $40,000 into the initial construction but had a number of upgrades in the last ten years, including a new kitchen and an upgrade to the three bathrooms. He had received considerable material and free work from his intimate dealings with the many contractors and crews who were associated with the union, and the value was pegged at well over half a million. He even had one of the contractors send over one or two landscapers each week to cut the grass and trim the shrubbery.

"Hello, Mr. Silverman." Marie Greco had been crying, and her face was still moist from the tears as she greeted Silverman. "Please come in. We are in the dining room, and I have some cannoli and coffee."

He walked through the foyer to the dining room, which had a large mahogany table surrounded by eight matching chairs. Nicola Senior sat next to Junior at the far side of the table. There was a silver pitcher with what he assumed was coffee sitting in a silver tray with two smaller bowls containing cream and sugar. There were several china cups on small saucers near the center. There was a large platter filled with Italian cookies and several cannoli and other Italian pastries.

"Please, help yourself. I just made a fresh pot. I hope you like regular," said Marie.

Goldin sat at the end of the table. "Hey, Morris, how are you?"

"Good, Paul; glad you are here." He then turned to Marie. "I will have a cup of coffee; thank you."

Nicola Senior looked up at his wife. "Mama, would you excuse us for a few minutes so we can have some lawyer talk?"

She nodded her head. "Yes, honey." You could tell that she was disappointed for not being included in the discussion, but she gave in like a good Italian wife and walked into the kitchen.

Silverman faced Greco and said, "Okay, so, here it is. I just got a call from the ADA, and there may be a deal here. Apparently, the union is being investigated, and the FBI wants to trade something. I don't know too much about it, other than they told me that they are looking at a few things in the union. They want to talk to Junior first and then to you, Nick."

Greco then looked back. "Morris, what is it that they are looking for?"

Silverman replied, "Same fucking thing that they are always looking for. This crap never stops. They want you to give up your associates. Doesn't matter if it is true or not; they just want to take over the union. Same crap every year." Silverman could see that the older Greco was becoming very upset.

Greco Senior continued. "Look, Nicky does not know anything, and he is barely involved in union business. Yes, he gets a check and has a title, but he does not know about any of our business. The Department of Labor is involved, and we had a meeting a few days ago and our friend, Charles Crowley, cannot be depended on to do anything for us. These sons of bitches just want to throw all of us out and give control to the government. Fuck these bastards, no more PAC money for anyone who does not want to help us."

Silverman answered, "Nick, you know what they are looking for."

Greco angrily answered, "Screw them. Same crap every year."

Silverman looked across the table at Greco. "Well, they want to dig into the computer records, and they said that they wanted to look at the pension records. They also said they were involved in a Medicare audit and wanted to look at all your claim records. So, if you are clean, then what is the problem?"

"Morris, we are in the process of putting in new software, and there have been some problems with the old system." Greco paused. "We did discover that there was some money missing from the annuity fund. It was the annuity fund administrator, and he is now gone. We fired him as soon as we found out."

"Nick, how much did he steal?"

"About $465,000," replied Greco.

"Okay, let's see what they are asking for first, and then maybe we can decide what we can give them. What about Ernesto LaCola?"

Goldin answered. "What about LaCola?"

Silverman continued. "Well, we would need to get him into the discussion at some point, assuming that you have nothing to hide."

"Of course, we have a lot to hide, and you know it. We have to be sure we are not getting the short end of the stick. Maybe we can give them a little taste, but not to the extent that it breaks us apart. You know that if they want to put us away, they have the ability to do it."

Silverman took a sip of coffee from his cup. He looked at both of them. "Twenty-five years to life is a big bargaining chip that they have, and it sounds like they are ready to go all in."

Young Greco said, "Well this is a big pot, and I can agree to cooperate, but I don't know anything, and if I did, I would not say anything."

"It does not work that way; they want to see the size of your bet before they will make any offer." The lawyer was now talking. "Let me go to work, and in the meantime, Paul and I will go over this and see if there is something that could work. In the meantime, let me review the case and the evidence and see how strong their case is. We need to work it out before we set up or agree to any meeting. We have to place barriers on the outer limits of any deal. We first must find out which judge will be hearing the case. We might get lucky. In the meantime, I am leaving you with our retainer agreement. Look it over, and sign it if you are okay. The union's legal fund handles some of the fees, so it won't be too bad after my discount."

Greco Senior asked, "Morris, what if we work within the drug case and if Nicky throws his connections under the bus? Maybe we do not work with the Labor Department or the FBI. Is that a possibility?"

"Yes, of course, anything is possible, but we are just getting started. That does not make the union situation any better. We may be able to use this to our advantage. They also are conducting a Medicare review. Is there anything that you can give them from the health and welfare fund?"

Young Greco leaned forward and placed both hands on the table and said, "Pop, I do not think that I can throw these guys in. They are pretty serious players, and this could loop back to the union regardless. It could hurt everybody. I got involved with this girl, and she asked me to do the pickup. It was a setup for sure, so she could save her ass. That little bitch. This could wreck my marriage, and I now realize how stupid I was."

The older Greco had his hands against his head, and his lips were clasped together. He leaned back slightly and said softly, "Let us examine our options. Then we can decide how to proceed. We won't know until they make their play. Morris, you need to see what they have and what they are looking for. Fair enough? Let's find out what they want, and then maybe we can make a trade. That is the way I see it. We have some very powerful connections, and we can also use them. We can use the papers as well." He looked over at Goldin. "Paul, you need to decide what if anything we can give them to take the heat off."

Goldin was there mostly as an observer but answered. "Nicola, you are correct, but the FBI is involved, and you know the reason. They want to take the union down. All of you, LaCola, me, you, and even the lawyers and the accountants. They can play you against one another and want to tear the union apart, but we have political connections and have the votes—lots of votes—so, let's not move so fast."

The old man replied, "All right, then we all agree that we let Morris go to work and see what he can find out about the case. They have to tell us what they are looking for, and then we can decide if we are willing to play along. We have been working very hard for the last five years to fix our accounting systems and legitimize all of our outside business activities, and we do not want to go backward."

Greco Senior put his left hand on his son's right hand. "Nicky, are you okay?"

Young Greco looked down at his hands, which were still resting on the table. He reached over to the silver pitcher of coffee and poured some into his cup. He brought the cup to his mouth and took a long sip. "Too cold."

His father spoke. "Hey, Nicky, this is your ball game. Are you good with the approach?"

Young Greco was quiet for a moment. "Yes, fuck it. Morris is the lawyer, and I go along with him. I …" He paused and then said, "Do we have the time to clean up all the loose ends in the union? You know that if they want to find something, then they will find it or create it."

The older Greco nodded. "Look, we have this new computer guy from Albany, and he has agreed to clean up our system. Paul and I have had a talk with him, and I think he is onboard. He has found a few things that we can attribute to mistakes. We have some independent consultants working on a cleanup of the old system. So, if we can stall the FBI and the Labor Department for awhile, our new guy ought to be able to clean up our operations and make it impossible for them to figure out what was going on. They cannot put us in jail for mistakes or being sloppy. This is a complicated business, and we are certainly trying to eliminate all the problems and mistakes of the past that were made by others. We may be able to work a trade and give them something that takes the heat off the union. As long as it points to someone else."

Greco continued. "Okay, Morris, see what you can find out. Call us when you need to meet again, and thanks for getting Nicky out with the judge and the ADA. No way was he going to Rikers."

CHAPTER THIRTY-TWO

THE TRADE

SEPTEMBER 21, 1992

M ACEY KNEW THAT THE COURSE of the investigation could take a few turns for better or worse. And he knew that a favorable outcome would depend on today's meeting with the district attorney. It would come down to whether they would be successful in making a deal involving the drug charge against Greco Junior. They had significant leverage and would need to work a compromise with the NYPD and the district attorney.

Drug trafficking was a serious crime, and Macey knew that the only way to get Greco to cooperate was to have the DA drop the drug charges against his son. The city had thousands of drug-related arrests each year, and they could easily afford to trade this one arrest, especially when they could bust a criminal conspiracy that could yield several dozen arrests. Four kilos of cocaine was worth about $100,000. The numbers didn't work because Greco only paid $50,000. The Mexican cartel was not that stupid and would never sell any at that price. No big deal, when he had the opportunity to crack a criminal enterprise that was stealing millions of dollars each year. He knew that Greco would do anything for his family. And the drug charge was the leverage he could use. The twenty-five years to life was something that he would use, but he would need to get the district attorney to go along with him. After all, it was only cocaine, and half the city was using it.

The Manhattan district attorney's office was in the courthouse building just a few blocks from Chinatown, and the meeting was scheduled for ten o'clock. Macey, Samples, and Richards were to meet with the Manhattan district attorney, the ADA, and the chief of police.

At exactly 9:58, Paul Sullivan walked in, followed by Mark Hulbert and Rick Rowlands. Captain Reilly followed them into the room just a few minutes later. A court transcriber was already seated at the far end of the conference table.

"Good morning, ladies and gentlemen, and thank you for coming this morning. I am Paul Sullivan, and I am the NYPD chief of the Narcotics Division. This is Mark Hulbert, the Manhattan district attorney, and this is Rick Rowlands, the ADA who handled the arraignment. This is Police Captain Reilly, who was present during the arrest." He pointed to his right at the captain.

As expected, Macey took the immediate lead. "Thank you, Chief, gentlemen. I am Colonel Macey, and I am the special agent in charge of an investigation into union corruption. This is Agent Connie Samples and Agent Marco Richards, who are here as observers. Of course, it is obvious that the reason we are here is to work with you folks and come to an agreement as to how we can best use this situation to our mutual advantage. We are always anxious to cooperate with the local police agencies and of course understand that we need to work together so that we all can best accomplish our mission. But first, let me say, we appreciate it that you called us before it got too far down the line. We appreciate the opportunity to have an open discussion today so that we can decide how we can best move forward."

Chief Sullivan replied, "Thank you, Colonel; we always cooperate with the agencies according to our interagency agreements and want to work openly with full transparency. Why don't you tell us what you have in mind?"

They all sat down, with the FBI agents on one side of the conference table and the city officials on the other side. A large bucket of ice in the center of the table held several bottles of chilled water. There was a tray of plastic glasses alongside the water.

Macey replied, "I think we can all agree that we have an unusual opportunity before us. We know that young Greco may have some connection with the union, which is on our radar screen. But he is the son of a key target that has information that can break their criminal conspiracies wide open. This is an unusual opportunity. We know that his father is the fund administrator and is likely to do anything to save his son from a long stretch in prison. So … we would like you to trade the drug charge so we can bring the old man over to our side. He is old school and will not be brought over easily. But we think he may provide valuable information to break our investigation wide open. Our deal is pretty simple: you drop the charges on the drug case, and we get a cooperating witness who may be able to support the evidence we have. We make a trade."

District Attorney Hulbert asked, "What makes you think the old man will go for it?"

Macey grinned. "Simple. It is his son, and as an old Sicilian, it is always about the family."

Chief Sullivan said, "Mark, I think this is a question that only you can answer, but before you do, I would like to know what assurances the colonel can provide. What have you got that will push him over the edge, besides his son?"

Macey did not give Hulbert a chance to answer. "Chief, with all due respect, you know that nothing is a sure thing. We have some hard evidence against the old man, and we have an inside person that is helping us. We will give him a pass, or he will do some time. We have a few cards up our sleeves that we can play to put more pressure on him to come over to our side."

Hulbert now seemed more interested and looked directly at Macey. "Can you share that information with us?"

Macey pulled a cigarette from the crumpled pack of Camels in his breast pocket. "Well, I can tell you this: we have a few things that we know about the union but cannot speak about them at this time. We have been collecting quite a bit of information from our people to retire the old man and convince him that he has no choice. So, you see, we have an ability to go at him in a couple of directions. You might say we expect to squeeze him."

The district attorney leaned over and said something in the ADA's ear. He then looked over at Macey. "Well, Colonel, we will agree to drop the drug charges but of course will want to be a part of the follow-up investigation and play some role yet to be determined—even if it is just a minor role."

Macey lit the Camel with his worn Zippo lighter and continued. "Look, guys. You know that this was a friends and family buy and the kid was set up, so your open-and-shut case is on some shaky ground. The cocaine was from Thailand and was not from the southern border. The kid is an amateur, and he has no connection to any crime family or drug cartel. This was amateur night for the kid. Tell me, where did you get your tip? Who was your source? Was this a sting? Come on, the fucking deal was in a Chinese restaurant in Chinatown. He had $50,000 in the bag for the buy, and even if it was cut 50 percent, it was still undervalued. This shit did not come over the southern border from Columbia, and you know it."

District Attorney Hulbert replied, "Well, Colonel, don't oversell yourself. We will go along with your offer, but we will need to get an agreement from the court once the judge is assigned. Are we clear?"

Rowlands looked across at Macey and could no longer hold back his thoughts.

"Look, Colonel, we are fighting drugs and crime in the city of New York, and we have a construction industry in the city that we are not happy to turn upside down. It is also our job to protect the public and keep the peace. We do this by protecting our economy. We need the real-estate industry; thousands of jobs are generated from this sector. We cannot destroy the jobs or the construction industry. And by the way, most of those jobs are union jobs. So there may be a little kickback here and there, but it is the way things get done."

"We fight crimes like drugs, murder, extortion. robbery, mugging, and assaults," he continued. "We fight crime just as you do, but our priorities are different because different types of criminal activity produce different results. There are always some unintended consequences, so we must take those into account. We do not necessarily have any problem with the union, because they are not involved in drugs, and that is the scourge of mankind and will destroy our cities. The unions help to put people to work, and our crime prevention requires that we engage the people within our communities. We protect the public by working with the members of our communities. How do you think it would look if we allow a drug dealer to walk? Or worse yet, break apart union organizations that remove over seven hundred thousand tradesmen from the unemployment lines. We are builders of communities, and we have a mission as well. We protect the public in many ways that may not be apparent to most of the bureaucrats sitting behind their fancy mahogany desks in Washington."

Macey could not resist the opportunity and wanted the last word. "You have the first black mayor in the city, and what has he done? He pledged to be tough on crime. Did you know that the first day when he began to serve as the honorable mayor of your great city, nine murders occurred? Tell me, how many of those murders did you solve? The reality is that he is soft on criminals. That is not what I would call a law-and-order administration. You give the criminal an inch and they will take a mile, as the saying goes. You have to nip it in the bud."

Rowlands looked disgusted and said, "I agree that all criminal activity needs to be addressed. When you overlook something as minor as shoplifting, eventually they will break the storefronts and help themselves to what is inside. Once you start to get sympathetic to those who are committing minor offenses by giving consideration to the offender, then you might as well defund the police departments and remove the bars from the jails. It would be just as easy to eliminate bail and ignore prosecution. Hey, this is not a game of Monopoly where you receive a get-out-of-jail card for passing go—is it? We cannot afford to turn our backs, and neither can you, so while we may understand our differences and agree with your deal, we do not necessarily appreciate your comments."

Chief Sullivan looked bewildered as he stared directly into Macey's eyes. "Colonel, your earlier comments are not an accurate representation of the NYPD. As you said earlier, our missions and our approach to crime prevention may not be entirely aligned with yours, but we both need to recognize that we both have our priorities set by others. We report to Mayor Dinkins, and he establishes our priorities. You report to Washington and the Justice Department. Let's face it; you report to the president, and don't tell me that it is not political."

Hulbert had had enough and knew he had no choice. He could no longer hold back the obscenity. "Fuck it; sure, we will agree to your plan, but we would like to have a role in this arrangement. And let's see how it all works out."

Macey stared directly back. There was no backing down. "Look, guys, we look forward to working with you and appreciate your time. I think we have said what needs to be said and are pleased that we have a deal."

Macey, Samples, and Marco stood and pushed their chairs back as they began to walk to the door. Chief Sullivan and the others remained seated, and the chief meekly responded, "Colonel, we will be in touch."

The chief then turned to the district attorney. "Mark, can you call Silverman and make the arrangements?"

"Yes, Chief. Will do."

CHAPTER THIRTY-THREE

ORGANIZED CRIME

OCTOBER 8, 1992

ONE MAY EXAMINE ORGANIZED CRIME as compared to a Fortune 500 company. Organized crime is a big business. According to Justice Department estimates, organized crime generates income in the range from $50 billion to $100 billion dollars annually. No one really knows for certain, because these criminal enterprises do not file any income tax returns or pay any taxes.

It was common practice in New York and many other large American cities to pay for business. This could be through direct kickbacks, price fixing, inside information, or any number of schemes all designed to benefit those who had a role in the scheme. Not every scheme was illegal or unethical. On the other hand, if everyone did it, then it was considered normal. In New York City, it was so embedded in the construction business that it was considered normal and had been tolerated. Up until the early sixties and until Robert Kennedy became attorney general, Hoover's FBI had paid little attention to organized crime. In 1959, there were only four agents in the New York City office assigned to organized crime. There was a more intense interest on domestic communism; that team numbered over 150 agents.

By 1962, under JFK's administration, the FBI organized-crime task force grew to over four hundred. Organized-crime syndicates were getting more attention, and those within the inner circles of the corruption were becoming more creative. Their schemes were more sophisticated and took on the appearance of a legitimate business. The unions had the money and the political connections and could legally provide kickbacks in the form of political contributions. It was just another form of taxes, only paid directly to those in political power.

Bennie Aiello and Ernesto LaCola sat quietly at one of the four tables in the restaurant. Aiello was an underboss of the Gambino syndicate, and LaCola was just considered an associate. The two would meet at least monthly to discuss union contracts in the city. Next to the door was a small counter where you would pay your check. The restaurant was one of the many small ethnic eateries that catered to the lunch crowd who did not have the privilege of a full hour for lunch. Their customers only had twenty or thirty minutes for lunch, and Ron Raposa understood their need and would get them in and out in lightning-fast time. Most of the orders were to-go orders and were called in ahead of time. Located just a half block south of Thirteenth Street on Second Avenue, it was a quiet and safe place for a private conversation.

Two o'clock in the afternoon was an especially good time to have a private discussion, since the lunch crowd had already cleared out. The owner was a short, balding Portuguese immigrant who was cleaning the sandwich board in the back of the display cooler that was loaded with several Portuguese salamis and salads. He had conveniently turned the open-closed sign hanging on the door to the closed position and slid the latch on the door. He may not have spoken good English, but he understood the nature of the meeting and the need for privacy.

The two men sitting at the small wooden table closest to the small kitchen in the back could hear the clatter of the plates and the pots and pans as Ron's wife, Angie, washed them. There was no dishwasher, and this was a daily routine for the couple after lunch was served.

Aiello leaned forward and looked at LaCola. "Ernesto, we may have a big problem, and we may need to take care of this."

"Look, Benny, the kid does not know anything. Nicola has kept him in the dark and never wanted him involved in our deals. I don't think we have to worry about him."

The man across from LaCola was fifty-five-year-old Benny Aiello, a swarthy mobster who still had a full head of black hair. He was often called "Bennie the Grease" because he used a greasy hair cream to hold his straight black hair in place. Aiello had been arrested at least half a dozen times but never was indicted and never served time. He lived in Staten Island and drove a new Mercedes Benz 550 SL Roadster. He traded the car in every year for a new model. They were always black with red leather interior. If the weather was clear and the forecast was for no rain, Aiello could be seen driving around Manhattan with the greasy hair cream holding his straight hair in place. He was principal arranger for the Gambino family that worked directly with union business.

"Ernesto, I am not worried about the kid; it is the old man that causes concern. I know that he is likely to do anything to keep his son out of jail, and he knows a lot."

LaCola turned around and checked to see where Ron and Angie were to make sure they were out of listening range.

"Benny. I have been working with Nick for over twenty-five years, and he is loyal to all of us. I have a new guy putting in new computer software, and he is helping us to cover the tracks. We found a few of the problems from the old system that we can feed to the feds. And yes, Greco may have been involved in some of the problems."

"Yes, I can go along with that, but we have to make certain that Greco does not go too far. And this Crowley thing is even more troubling. We have a lot at stake, and my people will have to take care of things if we see anything moving in the wrong direction. I took care of this DiNapoli thing for you, and I also took care of the other computer guy; what's his name? Bloom. So I expect that you will need to stay on top of this. I suggest that you have a nice, quiet talk with Greco and straighten this thing out. The fucking FBI is getting very aggressive, and we thought this would be fixed in the same old way. I like the old man too and do not want to see anything happen to him. As for Crowley, I couldn't care less. Maybe Nicola should think about retiring. It's up to you, but remember, if things start to go bad, we will not risk it. Ernesto, how is your math?"

"What do you mean?"

"Well, I sometimes think you need to use a calculator. But 2 percent of $5 billion is $100 million. That is what is at stake. The old man is in control of his own destiny. And another thing." His face tightened, and his look grew more serious. "This guy from the Labor Department. What does he know? Get as much information out of him as you can, quickly."

LaCola answered, "We have been paying him for a long time and he knows a little, and he was close to Bloom and DiNapoli. I also think he is scared. Nicola met with him and delivered the message. We still have some leverage over him, but I think he has outlived his usefulness."

Aiello responded, "Well, I am not concerned with that. I am worried that he may have been giving them information."

"Bennie, we own him, and we keep him in the dark. He knows very little. He helps us out with the annual audits, and we do not share any inside information. He gets a nice little bonus from us every once in a while and delivers things for us."

"Look, Ernie, we have reason to believe that the FBI has an informant, and they have a mole. Isn't it obvious to you that maybe this guy is Crowley and he is not what he says he is? After all he is a cop."

The greasy-haired man was now smiling and pushed the paper plate toward the center of the table. Scraps from a half- eaten salami sandwich still sat on the plate. His cold, dark-gray eyes were affixed on LaCola's eyes.

"Okay, listen to me. We know he was friendly with Bloom. They were connected, and it was a little too cozy."

LaCola looked surprised. "What are you saying? Do you have any proof?"

"Ernie, we have our informants as well. We know more than you think. Look, we know that he has some information on the old man, and that may be enough to push him over the line. Let me ask you this: why would the Labor Department talk to Bloom without you knowing about it? Did you ever think that he was playing you all along? Maybe he is a ... what do they call these guys? What's the term?" He hesitated and looked up. "Yes, a double agent."

"Well, he gets clean and untraceable cash payments from us. But he should not be talking to anyone. All of our meetings are in the office, and I do not recall if Bloom has ever met him, certainly not in our office. But ..."

Aiello nodded and smiled. "No buts about it. Our information is reliable. You see, we got it right from the horse's mouth, your boy Bloom and Crowley. They were partners, for Christ's sake. Where have you been? And Greco was involved as well."

LaCola shrugged his shoulders in acceptance. "Bennie, then I guess you will need to handle it. I will call a meeting."

"Look, Ernie, how is the new computer guy from Albany doing? He apparently knows a lot. Can you trust him to keep quiet?

LaCola looked across at the greasy-haired man. "Bennie, I think we are good with him. We are paying him serious money, and so far, he has passed all the tests."

"Well, be careful, and make sure that he stays with our program. If the feds get to him, we are cooked. We have too much to lose if he breaks. So watch him very closely."

Bennie paused for a moment and then raised his glass but then placed it back on the table. "I can tell you this. We will give you another couple of weeks, but we will act quickly if we see this going in the wrong direction. The jury is out on Crowley, but the old man is on shaky ground. If you cannot straighten this thing out with the old man, then we will handle it. Understood? Let me just say: a canary with a broken wing can't fly—but a dead canary cannot sing."

LaCola reached for his wine glass and made a motion to Aiello. He raised it in a toast but did not drink from it. "By the way, how is the boss doing?"

"John is as tough as nails and as hard as Chinese math. He wouldn't sing if they stuck a glass rod up his dick and broke it into little pieces. Not like that motherfucker Sammy the Rat. Can you imagine? He gets five years for confessing to nineteen murders, and they give John life without parole on a bunch of trumped-up charges under RICO. They got him in solitary confinement somewhere in Illinois, but we still communicate. You see, it is about self-esteem. It is about knowing who you are and about how you feel about yourself. John knows who he is and is not about to change that person inside of him. He will stick to who he is until the end of the line," Aiello replied.

"Well, we all wish him well and appreciate him for his toughness. Benny, he sure is one tough son of a bitch." LaCola finally reached for his glass and drank from it.

"Okay, I hope you realize what is at stake. I have another meeting with the boys over at the club, and I think it might rain. I have the top down and would give you a lift, but ..."

"No problem. Bobby is out front with the car and will drive me back. Benny, let me speak with Nick, and do not worry about a thing. We will talk; I think we can handle it."

"I sure hope so, because if you don't, I will."

LaCola took out a wad of money from his right pocket and peeled a fifty-dollar bill from it and placed it on the table.

"Thank you, Ron. Bye-bye, Angie," he said as he turned toward the kitchen and smiled at the chubby brunette wearing a soiled white apron. She smiled back as she pulled her hands out of the sink. She waved and then plunged her hands back into the sink of pots and pans. She returned a faint smile and said, "Tank a you, Mista LaCola."

They walked out and onto the Second Avenue sidewalk. It was a one-way street, so Ernesto carefully crossed over Second Avenue, where his driver Bobby was waiting with an open back door to the Town Car. He heard the screech of tires from Benny's accelerating Mercedes convertible.

CHAPTER THIRTY-FOUR

THE BENCH

OCTOBER 4, 1992

T HE **DEPARTMENT OF LABOR WAS** comprised of countless departments, agencies, and governmental units spread across every state, county, city, and township. The department's leadership was fighting for control within most of the sections and departments. Within many of the agencies, it was getting to the point where it was impossible to monitor, let alone manage effectively.

Some, like Charles Crowley, took advantage of their inefficiencies and had side jobs. What started as an act of friendship to help his union buddies work through the annual audits slowly turned into nefarious alliances. They initially returned favors with a free lunch, dinner, Yankees tickets, or a night on the town. But eventually, the stakes grew, and they could ask for more, and the currency they traded grew into real money and resulted in alliances that could not be broken. It slowly escalated as greed took over and the currency that was exchanged began to add more zeros.

There was too much money for the taking, and the temptation was too great to turn away. Crowley had hedged his bet and was collecting information for the FBI. He was comfortable and playing both sides to his advantage. He had worked a deal with Greco and Bloom and had a piece of the health fraud. That was one of the side businesses that fueled his bad habits. He felt safe knowing that he could still help the union and they would never eliminate a law-enforcement officer with such a high profile. He knew that they had gotten to Bloom but was unsure if Bloom had told them about their secret partnership.

The note he received had the time and place and was in the usual format of past meetings with the messenger. At the meeting, he would always receive another envelope, providing that his information was useful. The writing on the note read, "Same bench. Same time. Next Tuesday."

Although Central Park was not as dangerous as most people thought, it was 840 acres of darkness and emptiness at night. It was election day, and Crowley took a cab to the same corner and walked the three hundred yards to the bench. It was close to eleven, and there were no pigeons in sight, although he thought he could still hear their cackle in the bushes as he sat quietly and waited. He watched the young man as he casually walked over from the other direction.

"Hello, Charlie. What have you got for me?" The man in the white turtleneck and blue blazer walked over and casually sat down beside him.

Crowley replied in low whisper to the man sitting to his right. "How is it going? Are you kidding? You called the meeting and probably know more than me."

The young man said, "We need to know what they have on old-man Greco. Have they shared anything with you?"

Crowley replied, "Well, all I can tell you is that they are prepared to go all in with him, and they expect to break him."

The man sitting next to Crowley asked, "Charlie, what does that mean? What do they have on him?"

"Nothing, except the thing with his son. That's it."

He leaned toward Crowley and said, "Charlie, come on; are you trying to tell me that they have nothing? Nothing except the kid?"

"Correct. They are bluffing and have no other concrete information that they can use on the old man. They have nothing to go on other than a hunch. The SAC from Washington is bullshitting them."

"Look, Charlie, we know about the little business you had going. We know all about the partnerships. You know what I am talking about, don't you? The little thing amounting to $3 million. We know all about it, and you can keep the money you skimmed off the top. You either tell us, or your friends at the FBI might find out about your little Poughkeepsie problem a few years back. We don't care about the money. You can keep it. We just want some answers. You owe us information. Did you bring anything with you that Nicola asked you about? The audit must be cleaned up, so we still need you. Unfortunately, you are going to have to prove your loyalty once again."

Crowley was now visibly shaken, and he became very tense. "Here is the file." He handed the young man a manilla envelope. "I am working on it, and by the way, I don't have any answers. I have always protected the union. If the department finds out what I did for the union, I would be finished."

"Come on, Charlie; stop the bullshit. You are just protecting your ass, trading assets, and we are protecting you, correct? So it all depends on what you do next. This all depends on what you can provide. We know what you did, and it depends on what you can do for us going forward and what you can tell us about the investigation. What does the FBI have?"

"They are fishing and want to squeeze Greco and the new computer people. They do not have any conclusive evidence and need to get a court order for seizing the computer records. But the union owns the judge. I cannot help you when it comes to Bloom. He is the mastermind, and I only did some of the setup with Greco. I got very little out of the arrangement and am just a water boy sitting on the bench. I am nothing but a go-between, and the bureau keeps me in the dark."

The man in the turtleneck looked over at Crowley. "Charlie, you have been married for what, almost twenty years? Three nice teenage girls. How many trips have you taken with DiNapoli and Bloom to Atlantic City? We counted four, at least, that is what the pictures show. And that thing from Poughkeepsie? Well, that is another matter."

"You motherfuckers would stop at nothing." Crowley was now frantic and looked down. "Leave my family out of this. I am telling you everything, and I am on your side. Bloom engineered the entire thing with Greco and is the brains behind it all. Ask Marty Bloom. You are getting me nervous. Where is the key that Greco said you would deliver?"

Crowley did not see the man in the black shirt who suddenly jumped out from the shrubs behind the bench. The man could hear every word that was spoken and had heard the code word to act: *Poughkeepsie*. They knew they would not get any more information and had to carry out their principal mission.

Crowley heard the movement of the bushes behind the bench and turned. He saw the raised arm holding the crowbar as he vainly attempted to block the blow with his hands. It was too late. The strike was partially deflected to his left but landed on his left shoulder and snapped his collarbone. The bar caught his thumb on the way down and ripped it out of the joint. The force was so severe that a small strip of skin was the only thing holding the thumb to the hand. His mouth was open with a look of horror as he looked at his disfigured hand. He saw the four fingers pointing straight up. His body stiffened just as the man to his right withdrew the knife from its sheath and lunged to his left as he attempted to thrust the six-inch blade into Crowley's chest—but it missed its target and found the soft flesh just above his waistline.

It was a disabling blow, and in an instant, all the energy drained from Crowley's body. He tried to stand as he fought off his attackers, but it was too late. His heart rate went from normal to supersonic in an instant, and he could not move his left arm. He pushed on the bench with his right hand and tried to stand. But the two men were much younger, and their strength easily overpowered him. Crowley had no chance of repelling the onslaught. Both men continued with another strike in less than a second. This time, the knife found its target on the left side of the chest. There was a faint popping sound as the blade found its intended target and entered the left side of the chest just below the rib cage. A short burst of blood spurted from the wound as the blade was withdrawn. The crowbar came from his left and stuck the side of Crowley's head, crushing his temple. The sound of the strike was horrifying, and the blood splashed out in all directions.

It was suddenly quiet, and they could hear a low moan as Crowley slowly exhaled the breath of air he had taken just a few seconds earlier. The men knew immediately that this was the last breath that would be taken by the man in the gray suit. Crowley's head had been thrown back in the attack, and his lifeless body was now slumped backward, yet still in a sitting position on the park bench. His head was tilted back, and his eyes were open. The muscles of the lifeless body relaxed as it slid back. It was as if he was calmly sitting on a park bench looking up at the stars. If not for the blood that poured out of his wounds, it looked perfectly normal.

"Quick, pull him back in the bushes and take his watch and wallet. It needs to look like a mugging. Cut the ring off his finger," the first man said.

"Okay, okay. I know my job. He was a little surprised, don't you think? The bastard was not going to give us anything. The double-crossing rat bastard. Thought he could play both sides."

"Shhh, keep your mouth shut. Let's just finish this job and make sure there are no footprints. Make sure he has nothing on him. We need to take everything. Oh, shit, my turtleneck is soaked with blood. We need to keep the knife, but the crowbar can get lost, but wipe it first. No fingerprints, remember. Wipe them down clean. Throw the bar in the lake, and make sure it is wiped." He pointed to a small pond across the footpath. "Wipe the bench too. Let them work for the evidence."

"I am wearing gloves, remember? Let me pull his pockets out and make sure that we leave nothing."

With precision, the two men went about their business efficiently and professionally and made certain that they left no clues. They had not brought any loose change, worn jewelry, or had anything in their possession other than their weapons. Each knew exactly what to do and had performed their assignment in less than a minute. After dragging Crowley into the shrubs, they calmly walked down the footpath a few hundred yards to the waiting van and entered the rear, where they stripped and placed their garments into a black plastic trash bag. The driver turned and asked, "How did it go?"

"Like we planned. Take us back so we can shower and get into some new duds. I am hungry and would like a big steak."

This was mob justice and was carried out with efficiency and permanence. They did not need a prosecutor, judge, or jury. They handed out the sentence with no mercy. Crowley may have thought he could play both sides and thought that his badge would protect him, but unfortunately, he had made a fatal error in judgement and paid the price.

The union affiliations were far reaching and often relied on crime families to carry out justice. The rules for betrayal were clear. When it was time to apply justice and carry out the sentence, their courtroom would not have any chance for an appeal.

CHAPTER THIRTY-FIVE

THE OFFER

NOVEMBER 6, 1992

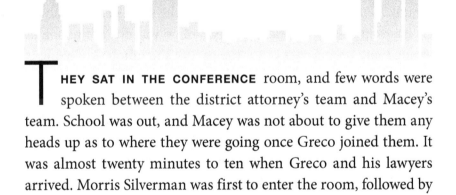

THEY SAT IN THE CONFERENCE room, and few words were spoken between the district attorney's team and Macey's team. School was out, and Macey was not about to give them any heads up as to where they were going once Greco joined them. It was almost twenty minutes to ten when Greco and his lawyers arrived. Morris Silverman was first to enter the room, followed by Greco, Greco's son, and then Silverman's partner, Bernard Simon. It reminded Marco of protective custody, with the two Grecos in between the two attorneys.

At first, few words were spoken as they each greeted the others without any customary handshakes. The district attorney was the first to speak as he rose from his chair and walked over to greet the visitors.

"Good morning, Mr. Greco. Thank you for coming by this morning. We appreciate your cooperation and want to have a chat about your son, Nicola Junior. To my right is Colonel Macey and two members of his team." He pointed to each as he spoke their names. "This is Connie Samples, and this is Marco Richards; they work for the Federal Bureau of Investigation. The purpose of today's meeting is to review an agreement worked out by your attorneys and our department, and if you approve, we will execute the documents. We are here today to review the terms of that written agreement and discuss the disposition of your son's case."

Greco Senior did not look happy. He wore a perfectly fitting black suit and a neatly pressed light-blue shirt with a silver tie. The tie was spotless.

Silverman returned the greeting. "Thank you. We are pleased to be here today, and we hope we can reach a favorable arrangement. Mr. Greco is here today in the spirit of cooperation. He has volunteered to help, but this is in no way any admission of wrongdoing on his part or on the part of the union. My name is Morris Silverman, and to my right is Bernard Simon. I represent Mr.Greco, and Mr. Simon represents the union."

Macey was going to waste no time and threw the first verbal punch. "Mr. Greco, thank you for being here. I want you to know that we believe we might come to a compromise with regard to the charges that have been brought against your son. Twenty-five years in a cage is not a good outcome for your boy. I think you know that the union is the subject of an investigation, and we understand that you are making a genuine effort to clean things up with your computer system. We also know that there have been suggestions of potential problems regarding the old computer system. I think … th—"

Simon immediately cut him off. "Hold on, Mr. Macey." He intentionally did not want to give him any stature by calling him colonel. "What are you inferring? We are here to talk about Mr. Greco's son. Mr. Greco has not been accused or formally charged with any crime. Nor has it been suggested that he is under an investigation, so please be careful. Where are you going with this?"

"Look, I am simply referring to certain evidence and past associations with certain people who have disappeared and certain information that has come into our possession that suggests there may be some union problems. We want to talk about Mr. Greco's son and his case, but let us be perfectly candid. We are investigating the disappearance of people and money, and we would like to know what Mr. Greco knows and if he would like to help us. It's that simple. We are prepared to make some concessions regarding his son's charges, and the district attorney has agreed that he may be willing to drop the charges based on the extent of Mr. Greco's cooperation."

"Well, let's be careful. I am not going to allow Mr. Greco to answer any questions today about any union matters, but we are willing to listen to any offer that could help Mr. Greco's son. We are here today to review the documents, and if they reflect the terms that we discussed, and after our legal team has reviewed them, I will present them to Mr. Greco for his acceptance."

District Attorney Hulbert looked at Silverman. "Mr. Silverman, we have a pretty good case and are ready to go to the grand jury, and as you know, his son ..." He paused for just a moment as he directed his remarks toward old-man Greco. "His son is facing many years in prison. Many years of hard time. The deal we are willing to make depends on the extent of Mr. Greco's cooperation." Hulbert was reminding them of a potentially bad outcome and emphasized the words *hard time*.

Macey was impressed and pleased that Hulbert was on the same track. "Look, there may even be immunity for Mr. Greco.

Nick, how old are you? I think you are well past retirement age, and maybe it is time for you to relax on a sandy beach in some nice warm state—Florida, Arizona, or maybe even California." He stopped momentarily. He made some gestures with his head. "What do you say?"

Bernard Simon now spoke. "Gentlemen, I do not think that Mr. Greco can help you out in any of these matters, and I do not think he is aware of anything you may suggest regarding any criminal wrongdoing within the union. Mr. Greco certainly wishes to cooperate and of course wants to help his son, but he has no information with regard to missing people or missing money. I suggest that we proceed and go over the agreement, particularly the outline and the questions that we would agree to. You must provide any exculpatory evidence, as stated in the agreement. I thought we all went over this. Mr. Greco will cooperate with your investigation and provide every due consideration it deserves. Right now, I would like to see the court's acceptance and the judge's signature agreeing to immunity of prosecution."

Silverman then added, "We have a pretty good chance at an acquittal based on what we see so far, so I am not certain that this deal can be finalized today."

Macey once again wanted to get in a word or two. "Gentlemen, we have asked you here today so that we could find a way to help Junior. We know that he has two boys that he would like to be with and would like to see them play Little League baseball and take them to a Yankees game. Take a picture of the boys and the dates when they would go to the high school prom. If there is something that we can work out, then we as well want to cooperate and help. We just want to reach a win-win arrangement."

Connie watched Greco with keen attention to gauge his reactions. She noticed that he made a faint motion with his facial expression to her, indicating that he would consider a trade.

Macey was now ready to make the offer. "Look, if Mr. Greco agrees to cooperate, we are prepared to provide immunity for him and drop the drug charge completely. It is all in the agreement. Of course, Mr. Greco would be stripped of his position as fund administrator and would not be allowed to participate in any union activities for twenty-four months. It is that simple. But we would want full cooperation. We are only interested in the union's activity about their association with organized criminal enterprise. We have framed our inquiry only to those involving union operations."

Silverman answered, "We did not discuss this at our last meeting, and we will need to look it over very carefully. Put it in writing, and we will need to know exactly what the specific areas of your interest are. We will only answer written questions and only regarding specific areas of the operation. These must be clearly defined in advance, before we agree to anything. Mr. Greco gets a complete waiver of prosecution, and there are no proffers and no 'queen for a day' deals. All charges and related charges against Mr. Greco's son will be dismissed."

Macey happened to see Greco's facial expression, and it momentarily caught him off guard. "Well ..." He paused, now staring directly across the table at Greco. "I think it is pretty clear, and we are happy to put it in writing, but upon Mr. Greco's signature, he must agree to answer the questions or suffer penalties if he reneges on the deal."

Simon responded, "We don't expect much to come from it, but we will look it over and advise our client. We can say that Mr. Greco has always cooperated and has nothing to hide but may not be willing to step aside at this point in his career. We will review the agreement, and we will need guarantees that the parties will abide by anything that is agreed to in the written agreement accepted by the FBI, the Southern District, and the district attorneys' office. Clearly, Mr. Greco does not want to see his son incarcerated. But be advised: he is not willing to implicate anyone in any criminal activity or any made-up case that threatens the ongoing operation of the union. We both understand the law but may have different interpretations of the facts as presented. We have a different definition of criminal activity and what you define as corrupt acts.

"We recognize wrongdoing when it is so obvious. We see many instances when a law-enforcement agency investigates a suspected crime, even when no crime has occurred. We do not want to be a party to any of your ill-conceived suspicions. You must be prepared to show us the evidence. And, I might add, Mr. Greco must be assured that should he cooperate, he will receive every consideration from the government for the protection of his family and, of course, his pension and any accrued or future benefits that the trustees may wish to provide. We are not going to participate in a fishing expedition."

Simon continued. "Let's be clear; you are asking for Mr. Greco to place his life and his family's life in danger, if there is even an appearance of cooperation. The implication or suggestion or appearance of cooperation to implicate members of any organized syndicate, such as the Gambino crime family, is a death sentence. We are not suggesting that he has information. It does not matter; just the appearance of cooperation is a death sentence for Mr. Greco's family, so you are asking an awful lot."

Silverman was handed the agreement in a manila folder and was the first to stand, followed by Greco, his son, and Simon. Greco thought he should say something.

"Thank you, gentleman," he said as he walked out of the room with his son and the two attorneys.

After they left the room, Macey was the first to speak. "Well, just as I thought, he is ready to make a deal, so we need to agree on our offer. I suggest that we have no choice but to give the kid a pass. That is the only way he will cooperate."

Hulbert was taking notes and looked up. "I do not have a problem with that. I may not like it, but we know we have to give in to Washington. We are okay with the trade and will sign off."

Macey was pleased. "Okay, so we are in agreement. I hope you did not mind that we would drop the drug thing. The case was weak anyway, and the twenty-five-year thing was stretching it a bit, don't you think? They do have a few judges in their corner."

From their faces, it was apparent that both Hulbert and Rowlands were not pleased. They both shook their heads, and Hulbert looked across at Macey.

"Did we have a choice?"

Macey grinned and answered with one word. "No."

CHAPTER THIRTY-SIX

THE DEAL

OLD-MAN GRECO WAS IN A tough spot, and he knew that he would be squeezed hard. There were too many illegal schemes that the union had been involved in. While some could be overlooked or even tolerated, Macey was intent on finding something. They were out to break him no matter what and now were going to bring the full force of their power to work him over. Silverman had discussed the format with Greco and cautioned him on his conduct. He was especially careful and had coached him on how he should answer questions. He went over a few simple rules.

The first one was to read and listen to the question and make certain that he understood what they were asking. The second rule was, if he did not understand the question, then he should say he did not understand the question. Ask them to repeat it or restate it until it was clear and he understood. The third rule was to only answer the question. Never babble on about other matters, and never offer anything extra. Only answer the question that was asked and no more. The fourth and final rule—and the one that Silverman stressed—was to never tell a lie, and only tell the truth. He also advised Greco that it was okay to say he did not recall. He told Greco that he should always be mindful of the word *recollection*.

"Keep in mind the words *recollection* and *recall,* since these are safe words that could be used to fall back on and used in some cases when you are evading the question. They cannot interpret your thinking. Do not evade or hide the facts, that was the danger, so it would depend on the question," he said.

Greco remembered what Silverman had told him: "Nicola, if they push you for an answer, just tell them that you cannot recall. You cannot remember, or say that it does not ring a bell. It is okay to blame your memory, or lack of memory."

During the interview, Silverman and Simon would be right beside him, and they encouraged him to lean on them before he spoke or provided an answer he was not certain of, or one that would provide incriminating evidence against him or his colleagues. They had prepped him well with several practice questions and rehearsed answers. They also prepared a written statement for Greco to read when they thought it was the right time. They did not want to take any chances, and they would be managing the process.

The meeting was to take place at the office of the US attorney of the Southern District of New York, located at 1 St. Andrews Plaza in Manhattan. Two other staff attorneys and a court reporter would be present. Today, they were to review the written agreement and execute it, and then the interrogation was to follow the first week in January.

Greco was nervous before; however, one might say that he was now on the verge of suffering a stroke or heart attack. He realized what he was up against and knew this was going to be a difficult battle of mind and conscience. He was sweating profusely, and the moisture rolling down from his upper lip gave away his state of nervousness. Silverman turned to his left and whispered into Greco's right ear, "Relax; you're good. We will take good care of you. Relax. The agreement looks fine."

The US attorney gave the others at the table each two minutes to provide opening remarks. There was very little evidence presented by the FBI, and even if there was, this would not be the forum for disclosure. They were there to see how far Greco would go to make a deal to get his son out of the meat grinder. When it came for Greco to say a few words, he did exactly that: "I'm Nicholas Greco."

Once they were all seated, Colonel Macey delivered his opening. "Good morning. Let me start by first saying that our negotiations have not been easy with the New York attorney general's office, and I am sorry to say that when a crime is committed, there is always a cost associated with repayment. Mr. Greco, we are interested in both sides of this matter, in the hope that you will assist us in our investigations of corruption in the construction business. This is the only offer that we are going to make with regard to the charges against your son. I am not looking to harm your son, and while he may have a clean record, there is a strong case against him.

"The parties are prepared to offer a win-win deal to benefit both you and your son. We will provide you and your family with protection, and we are prepared to offer you the witness protection program, if necessary. There will be no loss of any of your union benefits, and whatever they may wish to provide you with in the form of a pension or an exit buyout will be tax free. For your cooperation, you will receive a complete waiver of prosecution, and we will provide you several good options for relocation if necessary. In the agreement we have provided, we have framed the specific areas of our interest. It is focused on illegal kickbacks, and we have also provided you with a list of questions that you will be required to respond to. The deal we are offering is quite unusual and something that is seldom offered. The second element of our offer is that all charges against your son will be dropped, and no further charges will be brought against him regarding the matter. Do you have any questions?" he concluded.

Greco looked over at Silverman and nodded. Silverman then rolled raised his right hand for Greco and motioned a rolling forward with his hand.

Greco looked down at the table while he spoke. "Sir, I would first like to read a prepared statement for the record."

Greco knew that Silverman and Shay would not allow him to disclose any information until he had a written agreement. It was a shell game and not much was expected to happen, and there was little hope that anyone would gain any advantage. They were there to sign the agreement. Both sides knew what to expect and had planned well for the meeting. It would be a dance for the first part of the meeting, as they were expected to trade barbs and innuendoes back and forth in the hopes of disarming their foe.

Finally, Silverman and Simon decided to allow Greco to read his prepared statement.

Greco opened the folder which they handed to him. A small bead of sweat could be seen on his upper lip as he looked down at the papers in front of him. He then cleared his throat as he began to read.

"Gentlemen, thank you for this opportunity to discuss a possible arrangement to cooperate with the government in cleaning up corruption in the city of New York. My goal as fund administrator is to improve the operation and delivery of benefits to our members. Our number-one priority is to protect and preserve the benefits of our members and their families' health and welfare. As fiduciaries, we hold the concept of trust above all else, and I am here today, while it may appear to help my son, but first and foremost, to continue to serve the interest of our members and the people of New York. I have volunteered to help and do the right thing and seek ways to improve the relationship between organized labor and the government.

"The laborer is a well-trained tradesman that has acquired many advanced technical skills through the professional and formal training programs delivered by Local 4 and our affiliated organizations. The laborer has more than a strong back that many may think just carries the cement blocks to the masons. He is trained in the complexities of construction across many trade disciplines, including carpentry, engineering, steel fabrication, cement-concrete formulas, and many other trades across many building disciplines. He provides an essential and critical set of skills that is essential to the New York construction industry ..." he hesitated momentarily as he wiped the moisture from his upper lip "... driving our economy forward.

"I am here today because I wish to cooperate and wish to make our unions better, and if there is any outside illegal influence that takes us from our mission, then I am certainly willing to help open the books and provide full transparency concerning our processes. There are countless families that depend on our union to provide the necessary jobs that sustain their livelihood while giving them security. Laborers' Local 4, coupled with many other organized labor groups for the building trades, employs over 700,000 tradesmen across the state of New York and serves a vital role toward helping build our economy."

Greco continued. "We are not just builders of hospitals, schools, bridges, and roads; we are builders of families. Local 4 creates a needed livelihood for over ten thousand workers—ten thousand members of Local 4—ready to put their strong backs and minds to work, so that they can create a better life for their families and for the families of our great state and for future generations. I am here today because I am a good citizen and willing to make any small contribution in that endeavor. Thank you."

Clap, clap, clap, clap. Macey clapped in an act of rudeness and defiance and said, "Nice speech. Who was that for? There are no television cameras here, nor are there any reporters. I assume you are running for—"

He was immediately cut off by Silverman, who jumped up in a rage with outstretched hands and shouted across the conference table. He looked first at Macey and then turned to the US attorney at the head of the table.

"Sir, I object. That is most uncalled for, and I ask that Mr. Macey apologize. That outburst was a rude and unconscionable attack and is representative of the government's treatment toward organized labor. My client came here today on his own volition. Mr. Greco has not been charged with any wrongdoing, nor is he under a subpoena. He has volunteered to cooperate, and if this is an indication of how Mr. Greco is to be treated, then I am going to suggest that we end this meeting at once. Sir, I demand that the gentleman apologize at once."

The ADA tapped the table with his fist and said, "Gentlemen, gentlemen, may we please have order? I agree with counsel, and the comments were uncalled for and most inappropriate. I insist that we all conduct ourselves with the proper decorum."

He hesitated and looked around the table. Macey realized that he should have remained silent and was looked down as he listened to the US attorney.

Hulbert continued, now that it appeared he had everyone's attention. "Colonel, would you like to say something to Mr. Greco?"

Macey continued to look down for a moment. He had anticipated that there would be some outrage toward his comments, but this was expected. This was simply a tactic to disarm Greco.

"Yes, I would like to say something." He looked up and directly across at Greco. "I am sorry, Mr. Greco. I apologize. My actions and my comments were uncalled for, and I am as well truly interested in working to improve the relationship between organized labor and government. We have been assigned a task to fight organized crime in our cities, and as we all know, over the years, there have been some bad actors that have infiltrated the construction industry. I am looking forward to working with you and am hopeful that we, together, can improve our relationship and clean up any of the illegal influences that prevent outside forces that may get in the way of organized labor's mission to provide benefits to their members. We both have job to do, and hopefully we can work toward getting them into alignment."

Connie Samples had scribbled a message on her notepad and passed it over in front of Marco. "Is that an apology ... was he planning on making that comment.? Watch and learn. He just wanted an opening to make his speech"

The US attorney decided that the room needed to cool down. "Okay, folks, I suggest that we take a short recess, say, fifteen minutes. Let's take a bathroom break and be prepared to resume the meeting at, let's say, ten of. Today, we need to review the agreement, and if we can all agree, then the parties can execute it and establish a schedule to follow up with the terms outlined."

Macey motioned to Marco and Connie with a nod of his head to join him as he walked over to the far corner. He whispered to them, "Look, get to the computer guy, because we need more leverage to open Greco's mouth. We will need collaborating evidence."

After the break, the meeting resumed for another two hours as they reviewed each term within the agreement. Part of the agreement was that Greco would agree to meet with Macey's team at the union office and allow the FBI to examine the computer reports and that he would demonstrate his willingness of transparency by allowing their people to meet with Chris Vincent to provide an overview of the new system. This was not within the context of the formal agreement.

Greco was encouraged and was anxious to get back and get the blessing from Paul and Ernesto. He knew it was risky and he would be walking on a fine line but was willing to take the risk for his family. But he was quickly realizing that it would be either him or his son. He also understood that there was more than one family involved.

CHAPTER THIRTY-SEVEN

BAGELS AND COFFEE

NOVEMBER 9, 1992

L ACOLA KNEW HE WOULD NEED to call an emergency meeting.
He called Greco and the sequence would be in series, with
each party calling only one other party in the chain until the
participants were all notified. He picked up the phone and pushed
buttons on the old-fashioned intercom: *1 0 2*. He could hear the
click on the other end as Greco said, "Yeah, Ernesto, what's up?"

No words were spoken, only the following numbers: "6153213."

"Okay, I got it. 6153213." The line clicked.

It sounded like a phone number, and the agents in the van were
jumping with glee. They had bugged the office intercom.

"Hey, maybe it is a phone number. Run it through the system. No area code, so run it through them all." This was Tim Robinson speaking.

The other agent was already keying the numbers into his computer terminal. "Roger that, Tim. I am on it."

They did not realize it was not a phone number but rather a coded message, a sequence of numbers to identify the time and place for the private meeting. The first three numbers indicated the time plus 45 minutes, so the time of the meeting would be 7:00. The fourth number would indicate the location. They all had prearranged to meet at one of ten hotels, and each number represented a specific hotel. The last three numbers indicated the room number. So, it would be seven o'clock, number 3, which was the Carlisle Hotel, and room 213. These secret meeting were always held the following Monday. They needed to discuss their options for their next move. It was now not a game of checkers, but more like a game of chess. The players were smarter than the FBI had imagined.

It was up to LaCola to call the special number and notify Bennie and Goldin that they would need to attend the meeting. The agents were busy in the van and intently stared at the line of numbers rolling down their screen.

"No hits around here yet, I did get a hit in Pocatello, Idaho. That does not make much sense. It is a Mexican restaurant."

Suddenly, there was a knock on the back door of the Con Edison Van. "What the fuck ... who the hell is that? It is a little early, don't you think?"

Robinson opened the rear door, and there stood a delivery boy in a white apron holding a white bag.

"The guys upstairs sent these over for you guys," he said. In big, blue letters on the bag were the words: *THE JUG ... best bagels in the city.*

Robinson took the bag and said thanks. He brought it over to the desk and opened it in front of the other agent. There were three cups of coffee and half a dozen bagels. "Those lousy bastards. We've been made."

Greco and LaCola rode in separate Town Cars and were driven in a sinuous route to make certain they were not followed. They were early and went straight to the elevator and pushed the "up" button. Each of the attendees were extremely careful and made certain that they would be alone in the elevator car. They would push all the floor buttons, just in case.

Greco was the last to arrive and entered room 213 at the Carlisle Hotel on East Seventy-Sixth Street. As he entered, he turned and locked the door. He also flipped the security latch. Bennie and LaCola were standing near the window. The drapes had been drawn.

Goldin was sitting at the table with a small bottle of wine he had taken from the service bar in the room. He poured it into a paper cup. It was a two-room suite, and there was a bedroom, bathroom, and an adjoining sitting room with a table and four chairs. Goldin stood and walked over to Greco and gave him a bear hug. He then turned and went back to the table and sat between Bennie and LaCola.

"Hi, Nick. How are you holding up?" Goldin asked.

Bennie jumped in. "Nick, how did the meeting go with our friends?"

"Well, what I think is tha—"

Bennie quickly cut him off. "Nick, I am not interested in what you think. I am asking you what they said. What the fuck did they want? How did it turn out?"

"Relax. I am the one that is in the hot seat, and I am getting to that. We had a very short and to the point meeting, and I did exactly what my attorneys told me. I said absolutely nothing and only read the written remarks that Morris had prepared. Paul, you also had a hand in the statement. I am the one in their sights. My son is the one that is getting squeezed, so give me a fucking break ... please." Greco's tone of voice reflected his frustration.

"Nick," LaCola shot back. "We are here to find out what they know and what they want. Maybe Bennie can help us."

"Have they assigned a judge to Junior's case yet?" Bennie jumped back in.

It was now Goldin's turn to answer, since he had someone in the district attorney's office. "Yes, it looks like our friend Angelo Solomos, the little Greek from Queens. That is the good news."

Bennie continued. "So, Nick, what did they want?"

"The usual bullshit. They want to make a deal and asked me to roll over."

Bennie continued, "And?"

"And what? They were very specific as to the areas of their investigation. You have a copy of the agreement that I had to sign, and they have agreed to drop the charges against my son for my cooperation. There was some discussion about the things that were mentioned in the annuity fund and the claims, but nothing else. The good news is that the US attorney's office has no interest in jumping into this investigation. Their boy Giuliani is going to run for mayor next year, and I think he will win. They are now more concerned with the changes he has promised.

"They are in a holding pattern until January. There may be a big shake-up in the NYPD. That is good news. This FBI guy, the SAC from Washington, was very aggressive and would be in charge of the interview with me. As we discussed, we will show him just the crap we found on the old system, and anything new is off limits. Nothing specific, and I said absolutely nothing. If it gets bad, then I will give them permission to look at our new computer system with our software guy. It is super clean, and he is on our team."

Greco looked down. He momentarily hesitated, then looked at LaCola and Bennie, who were sitting directly across from him. "Look, guys, Silverman has tightened the scope of their inquiry. At first, it was too broad, and he wanted to prevent them from going too far back into areas that could hurt us. You can trust me on this: I am never going to throw anyone in. We have it framed very tightly. I am only going to answer written questions, and from what we have learned, they don't have anything to hang their hat on, so we are going to be able to direct them to matters that do not matter. And the good news is that our friend from Arkansas is going to be in the White House in January. We will have friends in the Washington. New attorney general and maybe even a new FBI director."

Bennie tightened his jaw and said, "What about the computer guy? What do we do with him?"

Goldin quickly held up his hands in front of him. "Bennie, what the fuck do you want to do? Do we kill them all? We will always need the computer and always need software. I have tested this guy from Albany, and he has passed all the tests. He knows a lot, but we still can use him. I do not think he knows about the seventh floor. If he did, he would have used it by now. He is on our team and is as good as it gets, so we let him finish the job. We are paying him well, and we have no other choice. He is gone in January, and we have the software and hired one of his guys. He is happy to get out clean and not about to do anything foolish. And he has agreed to sell us his source code. So, he will be out of the picture next year. We will own him"

LaCola nodded. "I agree with Paul. This guy Vincent seems okay in my book, and we can use him. We still need computer software, and I can assure you that I am not going to take up programming anytime soon."

Bennie's facial expression was still hard. "Well, okay, I may go along with your recommendation. But if it gets out of hand, I will do what needs to be done." He looked over at Goldin. "Paul, I can go along with you, but remember, he is your friend and not ours, so you are his sponsor. Do I need to remind you what happens to sponsors that lose their friends? You go down with the ship if we lose him. So, if I can make a suggestion, you might want to let him know what is at stake."

Goldin replied, "Bennie, I am not worried about it and am not worried about him."

Greco now spoke and was beginning to relax. "Well, there are a couple of things that we may be able to trade, and it won't cost us much. That DiNapoli thing. That is a small thing by our standards. And then there is the claims thing. That was about three million. I don't think we have to worry about that one either. No more coconspirators or witnesses. Thanks for taking care of our perverted friend from the Labor Department. He worried me. Our new computer system has insulated us from the past. Our operations are nice and clean. This guy from Albany has done us a great service, and he is in our corner.

"The new system has gone live and is working wonderfully. We are in great shape. He has delivered for us and beat the Thanksgiving deadline. He has the reports all documented, and it should be all sealed up like we planned." He stopped and looked over at Goldin. "Right, Paul? Everything leads to a dead end, and the old system is gone—gone forever—so there is no way they can find anything in the past beyond what we give them. The new system is clean. Paul, what do you think?"

Bennie was asking the questions. He had taken charge, and no one would dare question his authority. The decisions going forward were his, and the others knew it.

"Well, that could work, but we have to outsmart those bastards. We need to be absolutely sure. We cannot take any chances. And Nick, you may have to be prepared to take a short vacation if this does not work. They will always want more than what they agree to. They would like to nab somebody, and it sounds like you may have to take a little heat yourself. You are on vacation for a couple of years. As you know, we are family and need to protect the family at all costs. Maybe you should retire. Maybe they will settle for knocking you out of your job and the union because you made a few mistakes—of course, nothing criminal, just incompetence.

Your family will come out okay, and you can take some relief in knowing that your family will be secure. Your pension is secure."

Greco replied, "That is embarrassing. I would rather leave with a reputation as a crook rather than an incompetent buffoon."

Bennie said, "If you don't know what to do … then you should do nothing. That is always a choice. What do they have, other than Junior? Nick, we owe you, but what the fuck is the matter with your son? He knows the rules, and he just can't make them up as he goes along. He got himself into this mess, and he may have to live with the consequences. No junk in our thing, and that goes for the associates as well. And for a broad, of all stupid reasons. There is an awful lot of free pussy in the city, and he has to pick a floozy who sniffs cocaine. He needs to grow up and take responsibility."

"Bennie, it is my son, and he is family. We are supposed to be family, and nothing will affect our arrangements. We should be able to get through this. We would do the same for you if it were your son." Greco's face turned red.

Bennie nodded. "Alright, alright, but I don't have a son. Here is what we will do. First, let's see if we can fix the rap with the DA. Also, I like the idea of giving them a little something. Paul, just the annuity thing. You work it out, and make sure your new computer guy does exactly what you tell him. The computer will provide the evidence to support what Nick tells them. We tie it all together. And you, Nick, everything is riding on how you handle it. Do not offer anything other than what we decide. Nothing beyond what is in the agreement. We take it one step at a time and only feed them little pieces. The FBI needs two things. They need evidence from the computer, and they need a witness to corroborate the evidence. Without both, they have nothing but suspicion. We need to beat the clock, since things will be better next year when we have our friends in Washington."

LaCola also nodded. "Maybe they will get on DiNapoli's trail. Also that fuck Bloom, who was taking us for a ride for the last two years. I doubt they will find either of them. And maybe they can chase a little money that has leaked out by our former friend from the Labor Department. Give them clues to lead them to Atlantic City. Paul, if you trust your computer guy, then make sure he is on our team and does exactly what you tell him to do. You did it many times in the past. I will let the contractors know that we have to shut it down for a few months—maybe three or four months, until this thing cools down and they are off our backs. Clean up the seventh floor immediately. We cannot risk it."

Goldin looked up. "Already taken care of."

Bennie wanted to make one final comment. "Paul, make sure you handle this new computer guy. Understand? You have a decision to make. I do not want to get my people involved, so let's see how you handle it. Otherwise ..."

Goldin laughed. "We can handle this. No problem, and our computer guy is smart. More importantly, I got to know him, and I think he can be trusted."

Bennie added, "Okay, Paul. As long as you understand that he is your responsibility. Do you get my drift?"

LaCola nodded. "Okay, thanks, guys; I think we all understand."

Greco rubbed his stomach. "I am hungry. Say, let's go downstairs and grab a steak. It's on me."

Goldin added, "You mean, it is on the union."

CHAPTER THIRTY-EIGHT

SHAKY GROUND

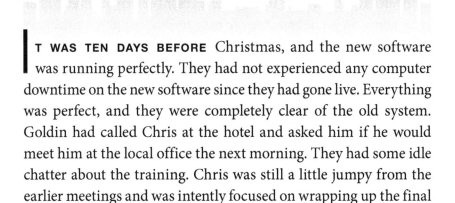

T WAS TEN DAYS BEFORE Christmas, and the new software was running perfectly. They had not experienced any computer downtime on the new software since they had gone live. Everything was perfect, and they were completely clear of the old system. Goldin had called Chris at the hotel and asked him if he would meet him at the local office the next morning. They had some idle chatter about the training. Chris was still a little jumpy from the earlier meetings and was intently focused on wrapping up the final training tasks. He knew that the deadlines would be met, and he was relieved.

From experience, Chris knew that the last 10 percent of the implementation was the hardest, and he had a rule of thumb that he preached to his staff: the last 10 percent of a project usually takes another 90 percent of the time. Problems usually occur at the last minute and never give a fair warning, so he was always prepared for the worst. They had one thing in their favor: they had several successful implementations under their belts and had no reason why they would incur any surprises.

Chris had arrived earlier and was looking at the plan setup with Frank, who had been staying with his daughter but was looking for a six-month rental for a small studio apartment. They had agreed that Frank would work at the local full time at least through June of next year. It was good insurance when considering the costs and provided added assurances in the event of any unforeseen problem. Chris did not think it was necessary, but the union was insistent and was willing to pay for Frank's time at $135 per hour.

Goldin was cheery and in a good mood, or so they thought. "Hi, guys. Tell me some good news."

Frank looked up at Goldin. "Hi, Paul. I will let Chris tell you, but we are in good shape. Just ran another batch of our test claims through, and the claims are perfect. One last task to perform for the health fund. We have to load the text for the denial letters. That takes about an hour, and then we have to load the precertification rules. That should be completed by tomorrow afternoon."

Chris smiled. "Paul, looks like we are all done. We have most of the training completed, and all the department supervisors have signed off and are happy. We ran parallel for the three weeks, and it looks great."

"Good. Everyone appears to be very pleased."

Goldin walked over to the corner and took a bottle of water from the small fridge. He walked back and said, "Chris, look, the problems that you found with the annuity and the provider records. We want you to document what you found and back them up with the edit reports that you ran from the conversion programs. We want to get to the bottom of this, so we want to make certain it does not happen again. You can also give us your opinion on the cause. The important thing, however, is to clean up everything and make certain that there is nothing that can point to the people here at the union. So make sure your status reports only include what we discussed. Also, one last thing: show Smith how to clear the old data libraries. Get rid of all the old crap."

"Okay, I will have something for you, but give me a couple of days. I will need to call Williams."

Goldin sat down next to Chris and leaned forward, almost in Chris's face. "Chris, about the source code. The local wants to purchase it. Ernesto and Greco had a talk with the trustees, and they do not want to take a chance. They do not want the same thing to happen that happened with this Bloom character. I know we talked about some numbers, and I think I can get the trustees to approve it."

Chris shook his head. "Paul, what the hell are you going to do with the source code? Smith is an operator and could not program his way out of a paper bag."

"We would have Frank."

"Yes … but what do you plan to do in July and beyond?"

Goldin hesitated for a moment and then looked down. "Well, that's the thing; we are going to hire Frank."

Chris turned abruptly toward Frank, who was looking down and could not look at back at Chris.

"I am sorry, Chris." Frank now spoke up. "But you know that I wanted to move to the city. My daughter is here, and this is an opportunity for me. This is a good fit for me. I am sorry; you have always been good to me, and ACS is a great little company … but—"

Goldin butted in. "Chris, this is good for you. We are going to continue with the maintenance fees for the next three years and the hourly fees for Frank according to the contract. We will have the union sign the necessary nondisclosure agreements. This is the best thing that can happen—and you get to bill for his fees for the next six months, so you come out way ahead. You have given the source to some of your other clients, and you have not made a big deal out of it. Going forward, this is best for both your company and the union."

Chris turned to Frank with a look of embarrassment. "Well, there is not much I can do about it. This is a free country, and if that is what Frank wants to do, then I guess I don't have much else to say. It is Frank's decision to make." After a slight pause, he began to shake his head. "I am just a little surprised; this is not something I ever expected."

"Well, Chris, there are many more unions down here, and when they hear about the great job you have done for us, you are going to be very busy for a long, long time."

"Paul, thank you, but right now, I think I want to go back to Albany and rest a little. Maybe play golf and have some dinners at Café Italia."

"I understand, Chris. Anyway, let's go grab lunch this afternoon. I have to go upstairs and meet with Ernesto; he is in the accounting office. We have been talking about the cost for the source code. We have the approval from the trustees."

Paul walked to the private staircase and slid his card into the reader, and the door clicked. He then entered and walked up the steps to the seventh floor.

He entered the accounting area and saw LaCola looking over the shoulder of one of the auditors. LaCola immediately waved to Goldin to follow him. They walked to the back past the reception area and into the accounting bullpen. There was a metal door on the right of Stanley's office. LaCola pushed the door open. It was the fire escape exit.

"Let's go out here, Paul, where we can talk."

Goldin followed, and they walked out onto the fire-escape platform. LaCola closed the door behind them. It was in the back of the building, and there were similar iron-grated structures hanging against the walls of all the nearby buildings. Most of the fire escapes were brown from the years of rust that had accumulated from the weather. No one was in sight, and the street sounds were muffled and barely audible.

LaCola felt secure that no one could hear them. "Okay, I wanted to talk to you privately. How did you make out with Chris Vincent? Is it all set?

"Yes, he is okay with Frank, and I believe we are safe. He has beat our schedule and has done what we asked. The old software is gone forever. He has cleaned up a lot of the old problems, and we are in good shape. The system is squeaky clean. He will sell us the source code, so we do not need him anymore. I think we bought ourselves out of this one. Yes, he is smart, and I think he is in our corner."

"Paul, why do you think he can be trusted?"

"Ernie, we can't make everybody disappear. I cannot answer that question but we have tested him, and he is on our side. He has too much to lose. He is very loyal to Sonny, and the FBI has nothing on him or us. He cleaned up a lot of things, and he created the documentation to support the fees. He knows nothing about my auditors and has no real evidence. He could have sunk us long ago if he had. If I was to worry about someone, I would worry about Nicola. I know he is old school, but with him, the family comes first. The original deal was to let the kid off, but it means early retirement for Nicola. Crowley has not helped us at all, and that matter has been settled. He never gave us any useful information beyond the audits. He only found a few minor things, but I never liked the guy. Sooner or later, they would catch up with him, and he would roll to save his ass. The pension on the new side all looks perfect."

LaCola looked back. "Paul, I don't think we have to worry about Charlie anymore. I am more concerned about Nicola as well. They are going to put him through hell, and he will protect the family at all costs. He is tired and worn out and should like the thought of retirement."

LaCola began to shake his head and looked across Thirteenth Street. "Paul, Nick is weak, and he won't hold up under the pressure. Our friends will go to plan B if he caves. It is not up to us; it is now out of our hands."

Goldin had his left hand clenched to the railing. There was a slight wind blowing, and the platform rocked slightly.

"Our new computer man, Chris Vincent, is okay. He is only interested in saving his business and has put too much into it. The new software is running perfectly, and we shut the operation on the seventh off until the heat is off."

LaCola turned and faced the accountant. "Well, we may not have to go too far to get Nick out of the firing line. Bennie said they may have something going that can blow the drug rap completely apart. But that is not a sure thing. Bennie does not like loose ends and is getting pushback from his friends. We made the right decisions a few years ago to clean up all the other loan-sharking and gambling. But we never counted on DiNapoli or Bloom going into business for themselves. We should have known that they had a partner inside."

Paul tried to be reassuring and made a calming motion with his hands. "Well, that is water under the bridge. Our boy from Albany has made sure that the computer trail leads to a dead end. Vincent only has information on the annuity and claims, and nothing leads back to us on the seventh floor.."

"Good. I hope you are right. But you need to know that if he flips, he will follow Bloom. In the meantime, you are responsible. So you better be sure about him. Also, let's see what Bennie comes up with and if he can get to the DA and the judge. If Nick has to lay low for a while, the Department of Labor sends a trustee in to take over the position of fund administrator until we have our election." LaCola started to laugh. "Guess who thought he was going to get the job and sit behind Greco's desk?"

Goldin looked down at the alley. They both began to laugh and LaCola said, "Crowley—that son of a bitch. He sure thought he knew how to play it. Nothing like letting the fox into the hen house."

Goldin shrugged his shoulders. "Could be worse, at least it gets the fucking DOL off our backs for a while. But you know that sooner or later, we had to take care of that Crowley thing."

LaCola tilted his head slightly and gritted his teeth. He waved his right hand in front of Goldin with his forefinger pointed up to make a point. "I don't like to say this, but this is Nick's problem, and he may not come out of this. Sometimes you have to operate on the patient, and it is necessary to amputate an arm or a leg to save the patient, but—boy, I love him like a brother—but we may have no choice."

Goldin replied, "Ernie, I understand."

LaCola looked at Goldin. "Paul, I hope you also understand that Vincent is your responsibility. So for your sake, I hope he remains loyal. It is in your hands."

LaCola turned and opened the door so they could enter back into the building.

"I hate to say this, but I don't think Nick will have any more meetings on this platform. The ground he is now standing on is a lot shakier."

CHAPTER THIRTY-NINE

PUBLIC RELATIONS

THE PURPOSE OF THE MEETING was to demonstrate cooperation and have Greco sign the FBI agreement. It was just a few days before Christmas, and the meeting format was structured around a social event and all sides were invited. They viewed it more like a public-relations call, since they decided to provide the FBI with a tour of their operations. It was a sell job all the way, and they would need to be very careful and stay on the script they carefully rehearsed. Goldin had asked Chris to meet him the day before, since he wanted to brief him on what was about to take place. They planned carefully and were not about to take any unnecessary chances.

The meeting with the FBI was a like a show and tell, but very little inside information was actually revealed. Everyone, including Greco, LaCola, and Goldin, was careful and cautious. They met in the seventh-floor conference room, and Stanley gave them an overview of the accounting operations. They had cleansed the accounting area and the auditors' area and would throw nothing but curveballs. As they walked past the accounting entry area, there were the same gray desks with a few clerks keying in the contractors' reports. Marco asked a few questions and inspected a few of the manila folders and saw that the deposit slips matched the check amounts printed on the contractors' reports. The colored folders were nowhere in sight.

LaCola was at the meeting and gave them a quick walk through of his office. He said a few words about the union's purpose and his role at the union. It was unnecessary, since the FBI had a folder on LaCola at least four inches thick. They knew where he grew up, his education, and all his associations with all the legitimate and illegitimate labor leaders in the Greater New York area. The FBI had surveilled him for over two years and had him on tape but had very little to implicate him directly in any illegal activities. They knew he had several dinner meetings with members of the Gambino syndicate but had no hard evidence of a crime. Nevertheless, Macey wanted to give the impression that he did not view this meeting as part of an FBI investigation. He knew it was presented as a public-relations event, even though their real purpose was to intimidate Greco. LaCola and Goldin viewed it as an opportunity to confuse them and throw them off the trail.

After the accounting department, they went down to the sixth floor. During the tour, there was an occasional question by Marco to a few of the staff members. Most praised the system and provided little inside information or secrets. They saw how the contractors' reports were entered into the computer, and Marco questioned Chris about the rate file setup. Marco was impressed and thought that the transaction reports were accurate and provided a solid audit trail that could hold up to any government review. Stanley showed them how he matched up the deposit slips with his accounting system.

They then went to the fifth floor and walked through the claims department. There were about twenty claims examiners all busily keying in provider claims. It was the second week on the new system. Marco was particularly interested in the claims process, and the department's lead claims supervisor processed three claims in less than five minutes. Marco was very impressed and saw that the new system functions were very advanced. The new system was performing flawlessly, and Marco could not find any fault in the operations. Marco looked over at Samples and Macey and provided a nod of approval. Chris was very pleased and at one point had been asked to explain where he had learned about the medical-coding policies.

Chris's answer was clear and concise. "We get them from Medicare. We get updates every quarter and load them into our computer. We also receive monthly bulletins from Medicare and also subscribe to the Federal Register, just to keep up with the rules. Our medical-coding rules are integrated within the framework of our adjudication process."

He could see that everyone was impressed. Although few understood the extent of the software's sophistication, Chris knew that Marco understood. They finished the tour in the customer-service department and then retreated to the computer room, where Smith gave them an overview of the IBM computer system.

Marco and Chris were sitting in front of the computer terminal when Goldin walked by, pretending not to be paying attention. But he was close enough to listen to the general theme of the discussion. Chris was showing Marco how the Medicare edits worked. Marco was nodding in agreement, and Goldin was very pleased with how Chris was diverting their attention to all the positive features of the new software.

Across the room, Macey and the district attorney had presented the signed agreement, which included the plea agreement and Greco's part to cooperate and provide corroborating information involving their investigation. The agreement had been signed by the US attorney from the Southern District and Judge Solomos. Silverman was there and gave his approval for Greco to agree to the deal with his signature. He would have to withdraw as a trustee to the funds for the next twenty-four months, but that was part of the trade.

LaCola looked nervously over Greco's shoulder. "Gentlemen, we have nothing to hide and are happy to cooperate. Mr. Vincent is providing your agent ... ah ... what is his name?"

"Marco Richards." Answered Connie Samples.

LaCola continued. "Yes, I think he has all the reports. I do not know how helpful it will be, but we fired Mr. Bloom and Mr. DiNapoli, and we have made considerable effort to improve our operating effectiveness."

Greco could hardly hold the pen; he was shaking and had a look of despair. He questioned his next move but could not turn away from it. He knew he would be the sacrificial lamb and would need to take one for the union. It was about protecting the family.

Silverman stood to his left and said, "It is all good, Nick. Vincent is over there giving them the reports for the annuity. We should be good. You are doing a very brave thing for your family. It is all good, and I think we have made a good deal."

The cooperation agreement was sixteen typewritten pages, all double spaced, and there were eight copies. He was used to signing thousands of checks and document over the years, but this would be the most important document he would ever sign. His hand shook as he took the pen and signed his name on each of the copies. The signature was different on each copy, since he shook throughout the entire ordeal. He wondered which family Silverman was referring to.

Chris went over to Goldin and asked if he could have a private word with him. They went up to the seventh floor, and Chris walked toward the HVAC equipment room. Goldin followed. As they walked in, Chris turned the light on.

Goldin spoke first. "I want you to know something important. You need to understand that my future is connected to your future. Let me say it another way: we are connected at the hip and are Siamese twins."

"Paul, what are you trying to tell me?"

Goldin's facial expression became more serious. "Chris, I have gone out on a limb for you. I have vouched for you, and what I am about to tell you is important. If you betray the union, you betray me, and then I can no longer protect you. Both of us will be displaced. Actually, let me be more direct: both of us will be lost—maybe forever. It's that simple; you and I are on the same team, permanently. We are in the same boat, and if the boat sinks, we both go down with it. We have no life preservers on this voyage, which has already sailed. Do you understand? We are out to sea. There needs to be mutual trust in our relationship. This FBI guy, Colonel Macey, has years of experience and will try to trip you up. He is like a sly fox, since he has been chasing lots of rabbits over the years. Stay away from him, and do not lead him to anything. We have been through a lot, and you have seen and learned a lot about the union."

"Paul, I am going to catch the train back to Albany in a couple of hours and need to give you something."

Chris placed his briefcase on the tool bench. He opened it and removed the green and red folders which he had removed from the accounting area on the seventh floor. "I have to return something to you. These folders are the key to the operation, and I now know how it was accomplished. I must congratulate you on how you put it all together. I know the seventh-floor secrets and the role your auditors play." Chris smiled, sure of himself as he faced Goldin.

"The red folder is used for the underpayments, and the green folder has the reports with the overpayments. Neat and clean way to keep track for your auditors as they reconcile the deals made not with the shop stewards, but with your contractors. And yes, our new job-sensitive rate file makes it easy for your auditors to easily adjust the rates according to the deals the union has made with the contractors. Some pay more and some pay less, and it is a perfect way to launder the money before it gets into the computer. Ingenious to allow the rates to change by job. That is the way it has to work. So what if you use it to skim a few million dollars from the pension fund every year? The members still get the benefit credit and lose nothing. The reports are entered into the computer and everything is in balance, so you end up with a laundry that produces a product that is neat and clean. So, Paul, I want you to know that I trust you with the knowledge that I know how it works—and I think that by giving this back to you, you may be able to finally trust me."

Goldin was stunned and looked puzzled. He shook his head slowly from side to side. "Chris, but how … but how did … but how … did you …," he stuttered.

Chris continued. "Paul, I think we can finally trust one another. The important question is not how I found out, but why would I share this with you? Yes, I have evidence, but why would I tell you all this? Why would anyone give it up? Well, it just came to me that the only way I could earn your trust was to give you something I did not have to give you. I decided cash in my insurance policy. Give you something that I did not have to give, and that was the only way to prove to you that you can finally trust me. I think we can both agree that trust is a mutual thing. Must go both ways."

The accountant was still shaking his head in disbelief. He then looked down at the folders in his hands. "Chris, thank you." He stopped for a moment and then looked up at Chris. "Yes, we are good, and I feel relieved. I am looking forward to some golf at your club and many dinners at Café Italia."

Goldin took the colored folders and the reports and handed them back to Chris. "Here. I trust that they are safe with you."

Chris could only smile as he leaned forward to Goldin and whispered in his ear, "Paul, I have all the pieces of the puzzle. I see the picture. I want you to know that no one will ever put them together. I think both of us finally understand the true meaning of trust."

Goldin moved his right index finger up to his face under his right eye as he gently placed his finger against the skin below it. He then pulled down his finger, exposing the white of his eye as he looked into Chris's eyes. A broad grin lit up his face as he said, "We see one another eye to eye. Is that how it is done?"

Chris nodded and returned the old Sicilian sign of agreement.

CHAPTER FORTY

THE FINAL FAREWELL

T WAS THREE DAYS BEFORE the new year, and LaCola had decided to have a going-away party for Greco, celebrating the success of the new software installation. The new computer was now running perfectly. LaCola decided to have a celebration luncheon for the entire staff, as well as the union trustees. Chris thought that everything at the union was centered around food, just like with his family as he grew up 150 miles to the north. They had several platters of Italian lunch meats and dozens of Italian rolls along with bowls of salads and olives, and of course there were hotel pans of rigatoni, sausage, and meatballs. They had ordered everything from Da Umberto's, and the desserts were delivered from Ferrara's on Grand Street in Little Italy. There were several boxes of Italian pastries and several dozen cannoli. They even had wine and liquor, since this was a holiday celebration. The entire staff would be drinking, since they all had been given the afternoon off.

It was a small reward for all the extra effort the staff had provided. The implementation had taken nine months, and it had been an intense experience for everyone. Denise and Frank were there, but Williams had decided not to attend because he had tired of the city and wanted to spend time with his son, who was a high-school wrestler. Chris had provided 150 baseball caps with his company logo on the back. The front had a message signifying the success of the project: "I Survived the CAPS Conversion."

Goldin walked over to Chris to congratulate him. "Chris, thank you. We are all very pleased. We got through the conversion, and your team was outstanding. Ernesto is very pleased, and I spoke to Sonny yesterday and expressed my satisfaction. We are all relieved that the government is finally off our ass and have enough information that should keep them satisfied for some time. I have something for you. Happy New Year. I have learned that Agent Marco Richards plans to resign from the FBI and has talked to you about a job. I guess he likes the computer more than being an agent. One more or less FBI agent is not going to make any difference."

Goldin handed Chris an envelope. "This has the payment we agreed to for the source code, and we will keep the software on the maintenance program for the next three years. You should be very pleased. I think we are also caught up with your invoices and the software licensing fees."

Chris responded, "Yes, we have some clients in the Midwest, and Marco is a good fit for our company. I do not think he was happy with all this cloak-and-dagger stuff and did not like New York City. He is a Cubs fan. I need another superstar like Pete Williams, and he has already accepted the position as vice president of government information systems. They wanted to send him back to his old job as an analyst, but he would be working in Washington. We get to stick Williams back in development, away from our clients. I have promised Williams and Richards a small piece of the business. We are going after all the class-one railroads, and they have been just wonderful to work with."

"Really?"

"Yes, Union Pacific, Illinois Central. The Acheson Topeka and Santa Fe, and I almost forgot, the C&O Railroad in Virginia. They all pay Medicare claims, and we are the only software company that has fully integrated the Medicare coding policies within the covers of our claims system."

"That's good to hear. We will certainly be in touch. The bricklayers are looking for a new system, and I mentioned your name."

"Well, we are changing directions and now working with managed-care organizations, so I am not sure we will be able to handle another union conversion like we just went through. We need a few months away from the city. Maybe in June. Marco also has a connection with Medicare and wants to use our audit system to audit Medicare claims. We would receive 10 percent of the money we recover for Medicare."

"Well, I will be up in the spring, and let's talk about it over a round of golf and then dinner at Café Italia."

"Sounds good; come up anytime. Thanks, Paul. I am glad it is working out for everyone."

Greco walked over and reached his right hand out to Chris. "Thank you for all that you have done. It was a pleasure to work with you, and we expect to see you at the next trustees' meeting to congratulate you. And by the way, Frank is a real asset for us, so we expect to continue to make good progress as we get the system stabilized. Frank is working out just fine, and I hope you are not upset with him for taking the job with the union. I guess we did steal something, Frank, but they cannot convict us for that one." He laughed.

Chris extended his hand and shook Greco's. It was not sweaty, and he thought, "This guy Greco is not so bad after all. Maybe I misjudged him. I think I could actually get to like him."

Chris went over to say his goodbyes to LaCola and left early to catch the 4:15 train back to Albany.

Greco finally gave up on the party just after three and asked LaCola's driver to chauffeur him home to Staten Island. That evening, he watched some game shows on TV and then found a movie on a DVD to watch: *The Godfather*, his favorite. At around ten, he began to doze off and did not see it through to the end. He went into the bedroom and put on his pajamas. His wife had already gone to bed but was not asleep. She had been watching *Jeopardy*. He would often suffer migraine headaches and would take a few aspirin to numb the pain. He went into the bathroom and took three pills. He came out, switched the television to the off position, and lay down next to his wife. He turned over and stretched his head toward his wife, Marie, to give her a good-night kiss on the cheek.

"Good night, Mama. I love you."

He laid his head on the pillow and never woke up. When they performed the autopsy, they discovered that he had enough poison in his system to kill three horses. They would never figure out how the poison got into his aspirin bottle.

CHAPTER FORTY-ONE

UNSPOKEN LESSONS

CHRIS FELT SAFE FOR THE first time in months. He was grinning and was anxious for the train to arrive back in Albany. He had a golf game tomorrow and was confident that he would play well. The roar of the diesel engines and the rhythmic clatter of the train wheels against the track separations were soothing. Chris rested his head against the seat back and loosened his tie. He was comfortable and wide awake as he peered out the window to get one last look at the river, since he was done with New York City. He took a long, slow breath of fresh air and relaxed as he breathed out a long sigh of relief. He knew that it would be quite some time before he would need to make another business trip to New York City. His business was done with the union, and he was relieved with how everything had worked out. Chris thought about what his father had said: "Work with your brains and not your hands." He could not get it out of his mind—but it did not matter. He did not want to forget them.

He now saw it more clearly: the labor leaders envisioned themselves as leading a worthy and righteous organization that made life better for their members. The criminal acts that were performed were for the good of the members. This is the way it was done, and they believed that their ways were necessary for the good of the family. The alliances with the criminal element were perfectly fine because the rewards for their members far outweighed the risks and far exceeded what they had to give. Everybody had to sacrifice their unifying principles to achieve what they thought were worthy goals. There was always good and bad in every decision, and when the results were weighed, they always tipped to the good side of the scale. The game would continue just as it always had, despite the FBI and the Labor Department. The bad parts needed to be overlooked because they believed that the results outweighed the means. When you added up the final score, it was always in favor of those who held the power.

The groundbreaking in Albany was just the beginning of a project that would put many tradesmen to work for many years. Much dirt had been moved, and the concrete plant would soon be completed. The project would employ thousands of workers over the next several years and become a positive chapter in American history. The project would assure the continued growth of the New York economy to create countless jobs that would nourish the descendants of the immigrants who flooded American shores in the past: the Italians, the Irish, the Polish, the Asians, and others from Asia and Eastern Europe. Even those who came over on the slave ships from Africa. The immigrants came to fulfill the promises that were made for a better life than the one they had endured in the old country. It would be better for their children and their children's children. New York City would eventually get a new mayor, and as far as Chris was concerned, the union problems would be passed on to a new administration. The country would also get a new president.

He now fully understood the meaning of the colored folders and the process they used to launder millions using the seventh-floor accounting office and the elaborate kickback schemes that the contractors and union had been using to manipulate the reported hours. This cleansing was accomplished before any of the data was entered into the system, and it was accomplished without stealing benefits from their members. More important; Chris had learned how to earn long-lasting mutual trust. It was a huge money-laundering scheme cooked up by Goldin to push back payment to those contractors who were involved in the bid-rigging schemes and was far more sophisticated than the methods used by "The Concrete Club."

When Chris thought about it, he smiled. How clever it was to simply manipulate the rates submitted by the contractors in their monthly reports. They got to keep hundreds of thousands of dollars when they lowered the benefit rates by two or three dollars per hour according to the rigged bids. It was clever and ingenious, since Goldin's auditors kept track of the kickbacks by manipulating the benefit rates using the colored folders. The rates for those who won the illegal contracts paid more through higher rates.

Goldin was happy that there was nothing in the computer that could harm the union since his New York consultants had cleaned up the data records on Bloom's software. Bloom's source code would never be found.

Chris thought about his father and what he had learned from him. The most important things in life were to try and learn those things not taught in the classroom. His grandfather had died in a coal-mining accident, and when Chris's father was only five years old, he was sent to the county orphanage. It was there that he received his only formal education from the age of five to eight. He would never again see the inside of a school classroom.

Chris's father may not have been educated, but he certainly had wisdom. He did not travel to shores afar, but he was worldly. He never had a plan but knew where he wanted to go. He may never have thought about his purpose, but he knew who he was and what he wanted to become. Chris often thought about how one goes about acquiring wisdom. Then he thought about his father, who faced many adversities. He faced them head-on, and through those experiences, he acquired wisdom. He was not certain how it worked for others, but for Chris's family, he knew that his dad persevered, even when the odds were against him. He did not win all the battles he fought, but through attitude and strong will, he faced those battles head-on and won the important ones.

His father understood that he needed to be responsible for the well-being of his family. He was kind and gentle, but he never backed down from a fight and always had a purpose. When he lost his job, he discovered ways to create income. He overcame adversity because he believed in himself and believed he could succeed. There were occasions when he became wiser even when he did not win, and he shared those lessons with his children. One would never know what the unexpected would bring or the lessons learned from those experiences. But he was always prepared. Chris was proud of his Italian heritage and thankful for the many unspoken lessons that were passed down from his father.

Chris thought about the situation he had gotten into and how he was able to find himself. He thought back and recalled both his past accomplishments as well as his failures. He also thought about what he would be expected to accomplish going forward—his dreams and his future aspirations. He came to realize that his present standing in life, with respect to who he was and what he had become, was not determined by the amount of money he had in the bank. It was all about how he had acquired the money. It was how you earned a million that made you a millionaire.

Where people end up is the result of many small decisions and only a few big ones. He knew that he could not change the past, but nevertheless, he realized that he was human and subject to the weaknesses of mind and body, and he had made and would continue to make mistakes. He also realized that he was capable of making bad decisions. It was now clear to him; he stayed the course that he had charted and had followed through with those beliefs formed long ago. You cannot change even the decisions one made yesterday. You own the decisions you make. Good or bad, you are stuck with them. He understood that many detours would be taken along life's journey, but one must make their way back to the original path chosen many years earlier.

It is normal for human beings to often wonder about the what ifs and the possibilities of the different outcomes and wonder how things would be different if we had only made other choices or chosen a different path. But that is not the way life works. Chris was a car collector and would often wonder about the cars that he had once owned and should not have sold and the cars that he could have purchased but did not. But one eventually realizes that life's journey, and the choices made along the way, do indeed result in different destinations. He knew he could get a few more miles in his journey, since he had a few more gallons of gasoline in his tank. Chris had an inner drive and felt that he could accomplish much more. He had a to-do list and imagined his speedometer as it would continue to roll forward.

Chris knew one thing for sure. He would accomplish much more in both business and in his personal life. There was an inner need to keep pushing because there had always been two words implanted in the back of his mind by his father's example: *be responsible.* They were the most important words in his vocabulary. Those were the words that turned the key to his ignition switch that started his engine. It was a tiny spark that started an unstoppable wildfire. He always had an inner need to be responsible to his family, his employees, his friends, and the people who he had met. All those people he had met or would ever meet—he would leave something of himself with them. Everyone's life is influenced by the people they meet. But he now realized that it worked in both directions, and he would take something away from those who he had met. The relationships that people develop as they interact with others, influence each other.

Chris was an Italian-American, and his values were the result of a collection of his family's history and the experiences growing up in an Italian-American immigrant family living in America. His makeup was not just derived from a culture, but rather from a shared awareness and sensibility of his family's experiences and their beliefs, which were ingrained in their Italian roots. He had an inner satisfaction in knowing that he was descended from a culture and a family that shaped his core values and that he had learned lessons in life that could not be learned in school. He was the embodiment of the sustaining ideals and beliefs of an Italian-American family. These unifying principles had grown and descended with each generation into a colorful tapestry possessing an enduring strength that cemented their values and bonded the family together into a common set of core values and inner goodness.

He now realized that if someone gave him a million dollars, that would not make him a millionaire. One had to earn it, and the process of earning it was what made a person a millionaire. It was not what a person had that determined their worth; it was what a person had become.

He also concluded that he needed to be responsible to himself. He would set an example and always try to be the best he could be, and the circumstances and other people around him influenced the choices he made. Their choices would play a role and influence his choices, and the decisions made would lead him to a different destination. Greco had made the ultimate sacrifice, which allowed Chris to break free from the union without requiring him to violate his own personal honor code. Greco's choice altered the course of not just the Greco family, but of many other families.

His good friend Bob never went to college and was proud to let people know that he went to work right out of high school. He was delivering papers at a young age, and his family was as poor as church mice. He became the largest music retailer in the country, with sales of over $1.2 billion annually. He was worth hundreds of million dollars and was truly a self-accomplished multimillionaire. Bob helped many and changed their lives for the better. There was a time when Chris's computer business needed capital and his credit line was overextended. Bob was quick to take out his checkbook and write a $50,000 check. He loaned Chris money not based on Chris's business, but based on who Chris was.

Bob had passed away a few years back but remained an inspiration to Chris. Bob influenced many lives, including Chris's. It was not just the money Bob shared; it was what Bob was and what he had accomplished. He was an inspiration to many people and changed many lives for the better. It was what Bob was and his work ethic that Chris most admired. Chris fondly recalled those Saturday mornings at 7:00 a.m., when Bob would call Chris at his office just to check to learn if he was working.

Chris knew that while he would have the time and financial means to acquire more and do more, the body would tire and may not cooperate. But there were many things that he knew were still possible, so he promised himself to never allow a day to go by without accomplishing something worthwhile. Things like helping others, watching a good movie, playing a round of golf with his buddies, reading a good book, cooking a meal for his family, traveling, and spending more to discover what he was capable of. Maybe even taking the time to write a novel about his life's experience. Even more time to put his troubled marriage back together and take his two young sons to a Yankees game.

Chris had acquired those Unspoken lessons from his father, and he thought he should pass them on to his two boys. He also thought that he may have the time to teach his sons the true meaning of trust and how a person earns it.

He thought about Frank and wished him well in his new job. The union had violated the contractual agreement to not hire his employees but did finally purchase the source code at a more than fair price and on Chris's terms. Frank had a good understanding of the software and was a good programmer, and Chris thought that things would work out for both the union and Frank. The system was up and running, and everyone contributed to the success of the new software. Going forward, the union would no longer depend on Chris, Pete Williams, Denise, or the rest of the ACS professionals, but the union would have the source code and Frank to maintain it. Chris was finally free from the union and on his way home.

He finally realized that perhaps he was not as good as others thought he was. But he now knew that he was not as bad as he thought he had become.

He patted his right suit-jacket pocket and felt the envelope. He pulled the envelope out and stared at the check inside that had been signed by Ernesto LaCola for the purchase of the source code. He placed the check with the 1 followed by 6 zeros into the envelope back in his pocket and looked inside his jacket to make certain it was in his pocket. He once again patted his right breast and heard the crumple of the envelope to make certain that it was still close to his heart. He then rested his head against the back of his seat.

It was a long way home when he thought back to the where it all began. Regardless of the road chosen, they would all, lead to the same destination. He did not know this in the beginning but now saw that the little choices that one makes at each fork in the road with little or no thought to the outcome would ultimately matter and lead to the final destination. Sometimes, it did not matter which road he took. Sometimes the path would be chosen by fate alone.

He sat on the left side of the train car with the river to his left. It was sunny, and the setting-sun rays slid through the trees from across the river; many rays flickered as they bounced off the rolling surface of the water. West Point would soon come into view. Although he had never set a foot on the hallowed grounds of The Point, he was familiar with their honor code concerning honesty and betrayal. He had often thought about that code the last several months and was grateful he would not have to abide by it. Betrayal was defined in a different way. The cadet must be loyal to the code. Any lie or cheating must be reported. He was thankful for the way things turned out in New York and that he did not have to follow the honor code that the cadets were required to serve. He was more thankful for the untaught lessons that he learned from his father.

He once again thought about the future and the possibilities of accomplishing more, as he stared at the river wondering which way the water was flowing. No one could know for certain the direction or where the water would finally end up. But then he finally understood: it really did not have a choice, nor did it matter.

The End

EPILOGUE

January 2, 1993: Rudy Giuliani announced that he would be running for the office of mayor in New York City.

January 5, 1993: A burial service and mass was held to celebrate the life of Nicola Anthony Greco at Saint Clare's Catholic Church on Nelson Avenue, the largest and one of the oldest catholic parishes in the Diocese of New York, with over seven thousand member families. Rudy Giuliani was among the 2,500 who attended the service.

January 15, 1993: The Department of Labor appointed a special attorney to serve as the temporary fund administrator for Local 4 until union elections could be held in July. He was a government appointed trustee authorized by a consent decree signed by the Department of Labor and Local 4. He was tasked with the responsibility of overseeing the election process and serving as an employee trustee on the funds until the next election. That evening, Ernesto LaCola and Sal Barone had a celebration dinner with the new appointee at Sistina on Second Avenue.

January 16, 1993: The New York district attorney was preparing his papers for the grand jury regarding the charges against Nicola Anthony Greco Junior when they discovered that they only had three kilos of cocaine in the evidence locker—one kilo short of what was shown on the police report. Angelo Solomos, the Greek judge from the Bronx, had no choice but to dismiss all charges against young Greco for lack of evidence.

January 18, 1993: Nicola Anthony Greco Junior announced that he would run for the position of fund administrator previously held by his father.

January 20, 1993: William Jefferson Clinton was sworn in as the forty-second president of the United States in front of the US Capitol. Ernesto LaCola attended the ceremony, as labor unions across America were celebrating the event.

February 11, 1993: Bill Clinton nominated Janet Reno for the position of US attorney general, to replace William Barr. She was confirmed the following month and was the first woman to serve in the role. She was confirmed by the Senate the following month. Reno would serve in that position from March 12, 1993, until January 20, 2001.

March 3, 1993: The NYPD was still investigating the murder of Charles Crowley. They had no leads or suspects and concluded that he had been a victim of a robbery.

March 15, 1993: The Hudson River Life Science and Technology Center purchased over 11,500 row houses in Albany to make way for new access roads for the new center. The seller was CK Consulting holdings, a corporation registered in the state of Delaware.

March 20,1993: The Barone Concrete Company completed their first delivery of six thousand yards of concrete from their new plant located at The Port of Albany. The delivery was accomplished with eighteen new cement trucks owned by the Barone Companies.

March 23, 1993: The new software at Local 4 ran flawlessly for the first four months since they had gone live. The union had not suffered any computer crashes. Frank Bevens loved his new job but no longer spent Sundays with his daughter. They were no longer on speaking terms.

April 1, 1993: Chester Raymond Macey was appointed as an assistant director for the Los Angeles County Regional Office. He gave up smoking on that same day.

May 13, 1993: Chris and Marco scored their first big success with their new Medicare compliance audit programs, which identified Medicare overbilling in the amount of $26 million. They earned 10 percent of the savings, which amounted to $2.6 million. The company celebrated their success with dinner at Café Italia.

June 21, 1993: Chris, Paul Goldin, and Sonny Russo played a round of golf at Wolfert's Roost Country Club after the Local 290 Trustees' meeting. At dinner that evening, Goldin offered Chris the New York Bricklayers' account. Chris declined. Earlier that day, Chris won forty dollars each from Goldin and Sonny at the country club. That evening, they were treated to dinner at Café Italia by Paul Goldin.

July 6, 1993: In a landslide victory, Nicola Anthony Greco Junior won the position of fund administrator, International Brotherhood of Laborers, Local 4. The pension trust fund had a balance of just over $525 million.

July 15, 1993: It was in the middle of a heavy rainstorm when the tightly bound corpse bobbed to the surface along the Jersey shore near the southern end of the Narrows. The highly mutilated and decomposed body had finally broken free from the wires that held it to the chair that had been inserted into concrete-filled buckets. There were no fingers on the body, and the teeth had been removed. The autopsy revealed that there were six bullet wounds, two in each knee and two in the chest. The bullet fragments that were found in the heart were the fatal two shots, and the examiner noted in his autopsy report that someone had fired a full six-bullet clip from a nine-millimeter pistol. The body was too decomposed to identify. They did however find a one-hundred-dollar gaming chip lodged in the throat of the corpse. It was from the Trump Casino in Atlantic City.

The body was found near the spot when 473 years earlier, an Italian named Giovanni da Verrazano, sailing under a French flag, had first passed through the Narrows as he sailed north into the upper portion of New York Harbor.

January 3, 1994: Rudy Giuliani was sworn in as the new mayor of New York City. There were nine murders on that day.

CPSIA information can be obtained
at www.ICGtesting.com
Printed in the USA
JSHW010039020623
42339JS00008B/232

9 781665 710893